LAST BRIDGE TO MEMPHIS

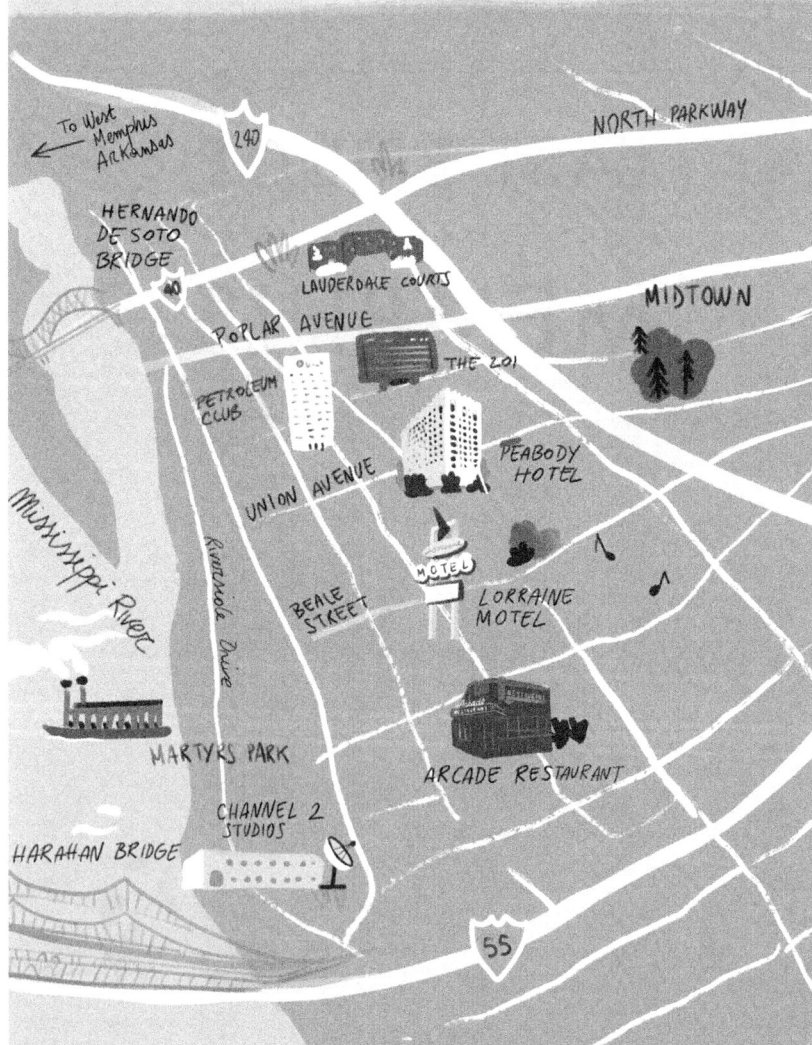

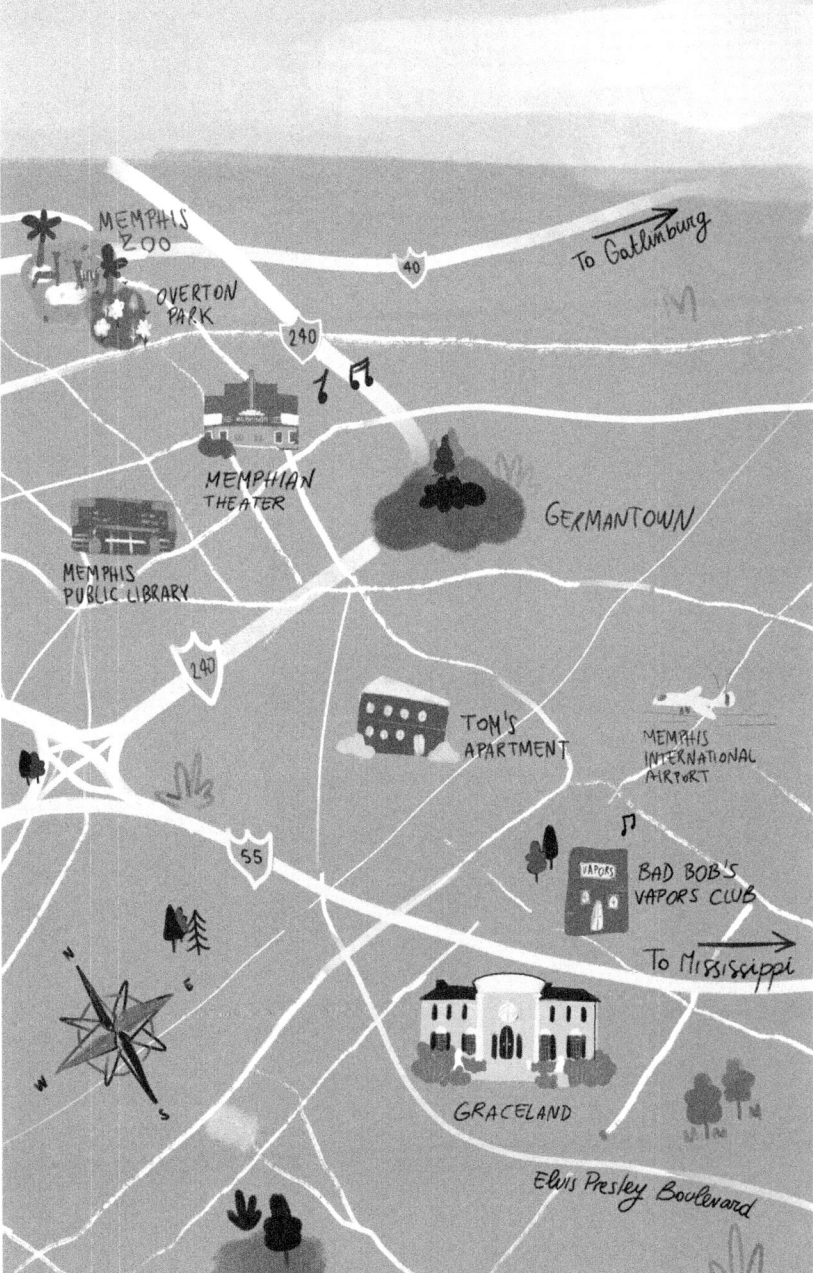

LAST BRIDGE TO MEMPHIS

A NOVEL

JIM CONDELLES

This book is a work of fiction. References to historical figures, places, and events are the products of the author's imagination or are depicted fictionally. In all other respects, any resemblance to persons living or dead is entirely coincidental.

Copyright © 2025 by Jim Condelles

All rights reserved. No portion of this book may be reproduced in any form without written permission from the publisher or author, except as permitted by U.S. copyright law.

Visit the author's website at jimcondelles.com

First Edition 2025
MoodyBlue Press

Library of Congress Control Number: 2024920518

ISBN 979-8-9916588-2-9
ISBN (paperback): 979-8-9916588-0-5
ISBN (ebook): 979-8-9916588-1-2

Book design by Kelly Carter
Memphis map by Noemi De Feo
Author photo by Fred Troilo

To Mom and Dad.
For always believing.

If in the twilight of memory we should meet once more, we shall speak again together and you shall sing to me a deeper song.

— *Kahlil Gibran*

MY HEARTACHES BEGIN

When I was four, I killed my twin.
  Everyone said so.

It wasn't murder. Not like with a gun or a knife. But my brother is dead just the same.

You never forget something like that.

Except, I recalled none of it. Not one lousy memory of the single worst night of my life. Unless you count the visions.

A living, breathing, guilty conscience of a nightmare, those visions shadowed me for decades. Spiking my brain on the playground, on the soccer field. Stabbing my dreams, waking me screaming into the darkness. Mother, bless her heart, spared few words of comfort, only an admonition to stop disturbing everyone's sleep.

When I departed for college, leaving the scene of my crime behind, I pursued journalism. Maybe if I got a job in news, I could lose myself in other people's misery, bury mine. But those soul-sucking visions stalked me from TV station to TV station, town to godawful town, trailing in my wake like a satanic U-Haul.

A freakin' sob story is what it is.

And if that's all there was to it, a damn tragedy, too. Mind you, it's still a tragedy, but that isn't all there is to the story. Because of Elvis.

I was just twenty-nine and in the midst of my stint as a reporter in Memphis, Tennessee when we crossed paths. This was ten years after Presley had the heart attack that nearly did him in. Long after he'd hung up his music career and started tagging along with the cops. The newspapers pronounced him pretty much done. Chewed up, spit out, stepped on. Drifting, doin' squat. But once he welcomed you into his world, you didn't give a hoot about all that. He had a magnetic effect. He got under your skin. He stuck on you.

"Everyone's entitled to one stupid-ass move, son," he used to say. It made a lot of sense, especially since I'd made more than one stupid-ass move myself.

Mostly, *he* made sense. Like the time he observed, "Are you sure your balls are screwed on right, Thomas? I could swear them balls ain't screwed on right."

He wasn't wrong. But when Elvis did what he did—after he committed his own altruistic stupid-ass move—I screwed my balls on right. I let go of all the stupid in my life.

Yep, I *let go*. It's what they all professed I should have done to begin with.

Which brings us back to the freakin' tragic childhood sob story.

How many times since I became twinless at four had the folks drummed their noxious refrain into my head? *If you would have just let go.* If only I'd let go of his goddamn hand, my brother would still be here and maybe I wouldn't. Wouldn't be who I was.

Not a murderer. But … a killer.

And here I stood, a quarter century later, about to do it again.

PART 1

FLAMING STAR

• 1 9 8 7 •

# 1

NEVER CAUGHT A RABBIT

The place sat perched on a well-trafficked corner of Poplar Avenue, one of the main drags through the Midtown section of Memphis. I slid out the driver's side door and surveyed the building. It must have been someone's grand Victorian home a hundred years ago. No longer grand, it had weathered some desperate battles, maybe an entire war. Either age or a cruise missile had brought down the porch roof, pitching it so low it dragged a second-floor awning with it.

Valerie stood on the sidewalk, laying a tremulous hand on her belly, her vacant green eyes staring out into a hazy gray sky of nothingness. This was the point of no return.

Scurrying around the car, I barely caught her before she staggered into the crumbling jaws of the pavement. Each footfall a potential landmine. A brick road to hell.

In a front parlor passing for a waiting room, women sat hunched in plastic chairs, hands in their laps. They broke from staring at their shoes, turning a dead glance as we entered. Maybe panic was too strong a word to describe my state. Exposed, definitely. Terrified of being seen, recognized. Later, the word would be *shame*, focused as I was on my own discomfort. *Hey idiot, your girlfriend is going through this, not you.*

I reached into my pocket, removed a bundle of twenties, handed it across the counter. A frosted partition slid open. The receptionist said we were late, but took the cash.

Alone in the Honda, I waited for it to be over, her words echoing in my ears, competing with the whoosh of trucks and buses blurring past on the boulevard. "That's what you're worried about?" Her reproach whistled through clenched teeth. "How it might *look*?"

In the waiting room, Valerie had caught me lowering my head, trying to make myself invisible, convinced at any moment someone would see my face. Would know me. From the *news*. So when they took her back to the procedure room, I left.

Still waiting. But outside, in the car.

Slumped behind the wheel, my thoughts diffused, like the fog of late July humidity overtaking the windshield. The act taking place inside that building, the one I'd laid down money for, it was a mortal sin. Not my first. Or my last. And my vanity? Not mortal, but deadly just the same.

Deadly. That was a laugh. I'd already been there, *nearly* done that. Nearly died—a long time ago. It didn't make me exceptional. Didn't absolve me of my sins. Didn't make me any less of a self-absorbed—

Well, fill in the blank. Everyone else eventually would.

Given time, given more slouching, more slipping deeper into the frayed nylon of the driver's seat, I might see my way to repentance. But not now. Not today. My dispensation had arrived, borne on the shrill cry of police sirens.

The sirens materialized into Memphis PD squad cars, three of them, lights spinning in violent circles, ripping past my field of vision, so close in tandem their bumpers nearly touched. The Honda rocked with the rushing force of a jet stream. Another police cruiser roared past, then yet another in succession. Jet stream on high octane.

Something's up.

I squinted through the side window, peering at the old house through the haze. It would be a while, for sure. She wasn't here for a pedicure. It took time.

Something big.

Curiosity may be fatal to a feline but it was a journalist's life blood. Every strand of my DNA pulsed in one direction: Go!

And yet. *Don't*, my mind implored. *Don't do it.*

The sirens receded into the distance. But they, together with the complementary voices in my head, were pleading, insistent. *Police don't go supersonic on a routine call. Check it out.*

No. I swallowed hard. *Don't.*

My eyes fell to the laminated card in the storage bin below the dash. My Channel 2 press pass. The face on the photo ID stared back, a head of unruly brown hair, cocked in arrogant self-confidence.

What would *he* do?

The keys danced in my fingers. I separated the one for the ignition and slid it home. The Accord's engine turned over with Japanese precision and, foot to the floor, I steered into traffic.

Their taillights sharpened into focus, the cops tapping the brakes. They cornered a side street, Archer Boulevard, cutting hard, fenders shooting sparks, knocking a *News 2* billboard from a bus bench. It was straight out of the *Dukes of Hazzard*, squad cars sliding and skidding every which way. Another block beyond and a sharp flex to the left, my foot jumped from gas pedal to brake, crushing it to the floor.

With a whiplash into the headrest, I swerved to a stop, mid-block on Underwood Avenue. Cops jumped out, hands on guns, crouching behind tree trunks. I grabbed a notepad and joined them.

Police, neighbors, kids. Chaos. A front door hung open. On the ground lay a shoe, a nightstick, shards of wood. A chastened dog, a Rottweiler, shrank against a fence, tail tucked, statue stiff. Accusing fingers jabbed at him, tongues wagging: *If wasn't for that damned mutt,* they said. *A nuisance is what it is. Barking, howling, crying all the time.*

Edging closer, I squeezed between onlookers. The chatter sharpened: "I just knew that motherfucker had a gun up in there!" I spun toward the voice. My elbow connected. The man turned, glaring. We exchanged looks and the stranger's demeanor softened. He smiled, nodded. *A viewer.*

A patrolman lay on his back, half on the lawn, half on the sidewalk, a fellow officer applying pressure to his chest. Another cop dropped to his knees, sobbing. If this was a storm, we were in the eye.

In the next instant, the storm roared back with a shattering burst of plywood, limbs, and torsos exploding from the house, a frantic running battle between two cops and a large man, sizeable around, though not particularly tall. The man's hands were cuffed behind him. He was shirtless, bleeding from the head and hobbled in one leg.

Two more officers joined the scrum. Together, like lumberjacks felling a tree, they struck the big man high and low with handled wooden clubs. Spit and blood atomized into the languid air. Animal cries from the suspect, if that's what he was, punctuated each landed blow.

Cops pounced all at once now, six on one, a wolf pack on a carcass. Pepper spray. Kicks, punches. Batons, flashlights. No police tape, no barrier of any kind divided spectator from gladiator. We were close enough to taste the acrid sweat, flinch from the pinprick splatter. Close enough to intervene. But no one did.

A final blow, a baton strike behind his knees, sent the big man crashing.

At curbside, firefighters leaped from an ambulance, turning a furious focus to the fallen officer, taking vitals, packing gauze into the wound, loading him into the vehicle. Their efforts ignited a new round of rage as patrolmen pounded fists onto the hoods of their squads.

Amidst the turmoil, another cop strutted into the frame, a soaring, musclebound figure, his white shirt in contrast to the dark blues of patrol officers. A supervisor. He stepped astride the handcuffed man on the ground. Wielding his baton, he thrust it between the suspect's shoulder blades, holding it there. The man lifted his head, his bloodied mouth gurgling in protest.

Although his back was to the crowd, the officer's voice rang clear. "Look at you now, you fat, sorry, miserable sonofabitch."

The line of onlookers parted as a second orange and white Memphis Fire Department EMS vehicle lurched to the curb. A medic hopped out, running toward the injured suspect.

The officer in white held out a hand to block him. "Back off fireman, we got this covered."

"Excuse me?"

"We're good here."

"Screw you," the medic said. "You've done your job, now let me do mine."

The police supervisor pivoted out of the way, but remained hovering over the medic as he got to work. The cop turned his head to survey the scene, his focus—and mine—shifting to an unmarked patrol car across the street.

I froze.

It may have been mid-summer and nearly a hundred degrees out, the sweat oozing from my every pore, but I could feel the chill bumps rising on my bare skin. From within that patrol car a passenger tossed a leisured gaze in my direction, locking his eyes. *A look of recognition.*

The car door opened. Not your typical cop, this guy was older, rounder, his features shrouded in oversized gold-rimmed sunglasses. He stepped out.

Wait, isn't that—? It was tip of the tongue. No, deeper. *Back* of the tongue, the very connective tissue of it. The edge of consciousness.

I know that face.

And then, gone, my view blocked by a breadbox of a van rolling to a stop on the street. Emblazoned on the side of the truck, garish red and blue letters shouted: NEWS 2 MEMPHIS. Perfect. And whoever they'd dispatched from the station would have questions.

If they see me.

With no explanation for my presence here, I sure as shit wasn't sticking around long enough to manufacture one. I had to get back to that place. Back to Valerie.

Patrolmen began corralling bystanders behind yellow tape, crowding people shoulder to shoulder in a solid mass. I assessed my options. To get around all these bodies I'd have to breach the police line. Once to my car, I figured I could put it in reverse and back it down the block. Clear of the emergency vehicles, I'd zigzag up Underwood to Poplar and—

"Hey, Tom, what the heck!" The driver of the news van hopped out, shouting my name, making a beeline for me.

Hell had arrived. There'd be no escape.

2

RECONSIDER BABY

He did a double take. It must have seemed peculiar to see me in street clothes, alone at a crime scene. "I didn't know they sent a reporter."

Eddie Harrington, long and lean, with an open smile and a whisper of a mustache, had been a Memphis TV fixture since the days of film. One of the first black news photographers in town, he was also one of the first at the station to accept me without judgment when this kid from Illinois signed on with Channel 2 earlier in the year. If I had to be trapped by a co-worker—and trapped I was—I was glad it was Eddie.

In a stammer, I explained I was off today, happened to be driving by, saw the cop cars, checked it out. As Eddie listened, a clock ticked in my head. *I. Have. To. Go.*

"Uh, Tom?" he said. "You got some blood. There, on your face."

I swiped my cheek, a little too fast, a little too hard.

"I think you got it," Eddie said. He reached for the two-way radio in the truck. "Hey, I better tell the station you're here."

"Hold up. Before you call in, let's get some video." Ulterior motives abounded for delaying Eddie's check-in. The competing TV studios were nearby but hadn't yet arrived. If we worked fast, we'd be the only ones with video of the aftermath. But of more immediate self-interest,

I needed to get Eddie started so I could get the hell out of there.

We waded into the crowd, the photographer recording B-roll: officers conferring, measuring, talking into radios, and—an absurdity I'd witnessed at many a crime scene—medics struggling to work around the cuffs still binding the suspect's hands. Whatever the guy may have done, he was no threat to anyone now.

The dog I'd seen earlier padded his way to his master, licked his face, and lay down next to him. *There's your opening shot for the story.*

My watch said five-thirty. Three words pounded my brain. Valerie, Valerie, Valerie.

"I know you!" came a shout. "You're that news guy." He was a silver-haired gentleman, in a tan t-shirt, hands in the pockets of a pair of brown flat-front slacks. "You look younger in person," he said. The man laid a hand on my arm. "Y'all gonna put this on your station? Ain't nothin' new. Come out here any night, cops always be bustin' somebody up. Just ain't usually a white fella." Typically, I'd ask a bystander like him what he'd witnessed, put him on camera. But I wasn't here for that. I wasn't here, *period*.

On the lawn, the paramedic turned his back to fetch something from his kit. The tall cop, who hadn't left his side, saw an opening. He crouched low, setting a knee on the suspect's chest. He appeared to say some words, then stood, tugged his uniform, and strode off to his vehicle.

I flagged down Eddie. "Did you get that? Just now with the guy on the ground?"

"I think so. Do you wanna grab some sound?" The photographer nodded at the silver-haired witness. I let out a resigned breath, took the microphone, and wheeled to face the man, the clock in my head still ticking.

"Sir, what did you see?"

"Didn't see nothin'." He eyed the cops swarming the scene. "Nothing I'm gonna put on that camera."

When I motioned to Eddie to stop recording, the witness leaned in with a conspiratorial bent to his head. "A white guy got the shit kicked out of him by them cops. That's what I seen."

Well, there's a sound bite. If only we were rolling. "How did it start?" I asked.

"Over a damn dog."

"A dog." I jotted *dog* in my notepad.

"Cops beat his ass over it," the witness said. "Whooped 'em through the front door. And then he shot 'em."

"He shot the cops?"

"Yeah, after they bust in. And they shot back. Pop, pop, pop, pop, pop. Musta been thirty shots. The guy's damn lucky, I'll tell you what."

"How's that?"

"If he'd a been black, I reckon they'd be callin' for a hearse about now."

The microwave mast telescoped from the roof of the live truck. Eddie stood by the side door, a hand on a controller, watching that the dish at the end of the mast didn't snag a tree or power line on the way up. The rectangular dish enabled us to beam a TV signal to the tower, miles away at the station.

Eddie reached for the two-way as the voice of the assignment editor barked through the speaker: "I thought Cirone was off today."

Waiting to key the mic in response, Eddie turned to me. "They want a six o'clock live shot. Can you do that?"

A confounding question. *I don't have time to do a live shot.* "Eddie, listen, I gotta head down the street for like five min—"

At the far end of the block the live trucks of the other two TV stations rolled up. It was as close as they could get. Police had the street barricaded. Squad cars, fire ambulances, and tactical units not only surrounded our Channel 2 van, they hemmed in my car. Even if I *could* ditch Eddie and his live shot, I was trapped.

"Tom, they need an answer. They're saying they *need* you to do it."

Say no, and they'd have my job. But what was the alternative? If I stuck around, did the live shot ... guaranteed Valerie would walk out of that clinic, find me gone, and never want to see my face again. It was probably happening right now. I was a rat in a no-escape maze, every path leading to a punishing electric shock. J-School did *not* prepare me for this.

It was almost a quarter to six.

"I'm not supposed to be here," I said. "I'm not dressed for it." I don't know who I was trying to convince. In the maze experiment, eventually the rats give up trying to escape. Learned helplessness, they call it.

Just before the top of the hour, a police spokesman gave a brief statement. One cop shot and critically injured, the suspect and the cop transported to Baptist Memorial Hospital.

Eddie lent me an earpiece. I pushed the sweat-matted hair from my face and stood by to go on the air.

Doing a live shot is playing a part. You know your lines and deliver them. But this was no movie soundstage. Out here on the mean streets a reporter narrows his eyes to the camera lens, the news equivalent of blinders. The earpiece allows the producer to cue you, while also rendering you deaf on one side. In other words, you're a standing duck. *Is a nutcase gonna run up and sucker punch me? Is some yahoo about to jump behind me screaming, 'fuck'?*

Live TV. A combat zone.

The anchorman read the intro from the desk in the News 2 studio: "A police-involved shooting in Midtown at this hour. Our Tom Cirone is live at the scene with details, Tom?"

> "The incident started outside the house behind me. According to neighbors, the owner began arguing with Memphis police

responding to a disturbance call. The homeowner retreated inside. At some point shots were fired. One officer was hit. The suspect also appears to have been injured in the altercation. Witnesses say the whole thing may have been precipitated by a barking dog. Reporting from Midtown, Tom Cirone, News 2."

Eddie signaled we were clear, off the air. I yanked out the earpiece and felt the frown lines rippling across my forehead. A half-assed live shot. I didn't report all I knew, all I'd witnessed. But what had I seen, really? And what about that cop lording over the suspect? And the man in the unmarked car? *What am I doing here on my day off anyway?*

It was well past six. *Valerie.*

As the photographer went about rolling cables and securing gear, I scratched out two paragraphs of notes in longhand, ripped the page from my notebook and tossed it on the dash of the news van. A producer could type it up for the ten o'clock update.

Eddie stopped me as I turned to leave. "Crazy how you happened to be here."

"I'll see you Monday," I said, and kept going.

The street had opened up, the show was over. Even that old dog seemed to sense it. He'd been pacing the sidewalk near my car since the ambulance took his owner away. He crossed in front of me, hesitating, sniffing. I bent at the knees, scratched the dog's ears. He held still a moment, and head down, padded away, disappearing into the gaping doorway of the house.

Key in the ignition, engine still running, I bounded from the curb, jumped the missing step, jerked the doors to the building. Locked. The waiting room, dark. Everyone gone. *Valerie,* gone. Collapsing to my knees, I dropped my face into my hands, choking on sweat and carbon monoxide.

At first, I didn't see it. Didn't hear the stirring from within the blue-purple Wisteria hugging the old house. The thing was the size of a half-starved squirrel and it was mewing and dragging its emaciated backbones across my Reeboks.

"Where's your mommy, little one?" I pulled back the vines expecting to see a litter of kittens. No sign of nest nor mom. An outcast.

I can relate, my friend.

He was an odd sort, in white and black fur, a circle of white for a face, a crescent of black crowning his head, extending like sideburns. *Catburns, perhaps.*

For a second I smiled, my first of the day. Until the blast of an air horn shattered it. On the boulevard, a cement truck thundered past, rocking my Honda as those squad cars had done. The sound propelled the kitten off the ground, all fours splaying in unison. This was no place for a stray. I couldn't leave him here. He'd end up under the wheel of a car. Just like my—

The kitten followed me to the Honda, straining on his hind legs against the door frame. I scooped him up and set him on the floor boards in the back.

I was gonna need some cat food. And a litter box.

Running again. Up the stairwell, two steps at a time. Valerie's place near the university, where some of the interns took apartments for the summer. I tapped the knocker. Once. Twice. Took a breath. Harder now. Once. Twice.

Nothing.

The kitten. I sprinted back to the car, returned cradling the tiny bundle. Held him up in front of the peep hole. "Look what I found, Val! Can you let me explain?"

On the other side of the door, the deadbolt slotted shut with a fury. Followed by the clang of a chain latch engaging.

The polished brick of my cordless phone weighed down my hand as I dialed. A pointless exercise, I did it anyway. Somewhere after fourteen I lost count of the rings.

Stupid. So stupid. SO STUPID!

I slammed the phone into its base. Picked it up. Slammed it again. My fists flew in a vicious one-two, hammering the laminate of the kitchen counter. Eyeing me, the kitten skittered to a corner, curling into a ball.

Next to the phone, a framed 4x6, a snapshot from two months ago. Valerie and me snuggling on a picnic blanket at the Sunset Symphony. Our first night together.

I laid the frame face down on the counter.

The ten o'clock news said Memphis police officer Carter Howard was in critical condition with a bullet lodged against his spine. They identified the suspect as Carl Walker, forty-six years old, expected to be charged with attempted murder, assault, and resisting arrest.

Why did they massacre the guy? And why did he shoot the cop? I couldn't figure it. But the conditions of the cop and the suspect, their motivations, the pending charges, none of it mattered. Today, the finger of justice would point only to me. Today, I'd committed my own crimes.

3

BLUE SUEDE NEWS

Deep in the bowels of the WMDW-TV Channel 2 studios, I inhabited a quarter of a pod of desks, shared with another reporter and a pair of producers. An arrangement so intimate you could smell yesterday's lunch and today's deodorant.

My desk had a unique vantage point within this journalistic jungle—although desk was too big a word for it. Call a newsroom workspace a desk and you might as well call a toaster a barbecue grill. It was a chair and a typewriter buried beneath scripts, papers, and videotapes. The unique part came in my proximity to power. Across the aisle to my right stood the glass-walled domain of Lee Cravens, the news director, my boss, and the guy who more or less ran the operation.

On the day back in early May when I first met Valerie Layne, I'd just ripped a script from my IBM Selectric as Lee's booming voice erupted from his office. Peals of laughter followed, the boss's meeting with the gaggle of fresh-faced summer interns wrapping up. Valerie had stood out like a tall, dark exclamation point, crowned as she was with a luminous shade of deep red hair.

She emerged, I rose, and we found ourselves nose-to-nose.

"I'm Valerie." She offered her hand. "You know … like the song." Her green eyes flashed, then she looked away, her face flushing.

"Anyways, my folks watch you all the time on the news."

She was maybe twenty-one. And although I wasn't yet thirty, with the "my folks" crack, I was Jurassic, my chances with her about gone extinct. But the odds fell in my favor when the news director asked me to coach the interns on their broadcast writing. The assignment carried a bonus: getting close enough to Valerie to work up the nerve to ask her out.

On our first date we met at Captain Bilbos downtown on the riverfront. When the food came Valerie did something that still got me no matter how many times I'd seen it. Before lifting her fork, she lowered her head, dimmed her eyes, and thanked the Lord. But with the piety came an intensity I found attractive, a determination that defied whatever stereotypes I may have held about Southern women. It made me want to help her get there—even if "there" was the same godforsaken career I had chosen. Over seafood casserole she told me she'd just graduated from a small Christian college and grew up in Jackson, Tennessee, a town about ninety minutes from Memphis, church and family near and dear.

"But don't be scared by all that," she said.

"As long as you're not scared that I'm Catholic and from Chicago."

By Memorial Day we'd spent the night together. Come July we were in big trouble.

After the police incident in Midtown, my weekend consisted of filling the cat bowl and setting up a corner of the apartment for the little guy. That, and dialing. Dialing and listening. After a dozen calls and dozens more rings, I understood Valerie was never going to pick up. I told myself I'd see her at work.

Monday morning, the interns huddled in the break room, not a redhead in sight. In the news director's office, Lee pressed the phone to his ear. He nodded, looked out from behind the sea of plate glass and eyeballed me. He set down the receiver. Waved me in.

"Tom, you know who that was on the phone just now?"
I shook my head.
"That was the intern, Valerie. She ain't coming in today."
"Okay."
"She ain't coming in tomorrow, neither."
"Uh …" I could feel the bottoms of my feet starting to sweat.
"Didn't wanna tell me why, exactly, but she's movin' back to Jackson is what she said." Lee had been leaning back in his chair. Now he allowed it to spring him forward until he was inches from my face. "Happen to know anything 'bout this?"
I shook my head. Swallowed.
"I'll bet you don't. Get outta my office."

Minutes later, a sharp holler knocked me out of a bewildered trance. "Tom, you comin'?"

Susan Quinn hovered to my right. "Comin' or not?" she repeated. "Or did you Krazy Glue your ass to that chair?"

As executive producer, Susan ran the morning meeting. The big-boned, big-mouthed mama hen of the newsroom, she seemed to enjoy forcing the staff to endure this daily obligation—a ludicrous round robin—each of us expected us pitch a story idea. Sometimes you just made shit up. You'd mention you heard something on the radio, say, self-wiping toilet paper, how about we do a story on that? Everybody would laugh and then they'd move on to the next victim.

Going around the room, it was only a matter of time until she turned to me with a casual, "So, what was up with your live shot Friday? Your suit at the cleaners?" But she didn't. No one questioned why I was in Midtown on my day off or why I happened to be at the scene of a shooting *as* it was unfolding.

When Susan finally called on me, I suggested the obvious, a follow-up story. Over the weekend, officer Howard's condition had worsened. But the suspect, Carl Walker, had been transferred to a jail cell. Through some miracle, or incredibly poor aim, despite a wild flurry of police bullets, he'd barely been grazed.

The executive producer studied the rundown, a sheet of paper with the rough plan for the night's newscast. "Okay, here's what we're gonna do," Susan said. "Janelle, find out what MPD is saying today." Typically, they threw me on the hard news, but Janelle Foster had better contacts at the cop shop. Putting Janelle on the beat had been a shrewd move. In the local news ratings wars, having a young black woman cover the police helped Channel 2 stand out in a key demographic. "Tom," Susan continued, "you and Eddie head back to the neighborhood for reaction. I want a live shot for six." She lifted her chin. "And maybe wear a tie this time."

Already my shirt hung like wet wallpaper, matching my mood to a T. As Eddie and I went door-to-door we found neighbors in agreement on two things. The early August heat. And the dog. In that order.

That's how it was with Henrietta Sutton, an elderly woman who answered our knock in a house dress and slippers. "Hotter'n hell and half of Mississippi ain't it?" she said. "I don't know how you fellas stand it."

"Could you tell us what you saw Friday night, ma'am?" I asked.

With her eyes fixed on the camera lens, she told us she'd been outside pruning flowers that day when the first patrolman arrived. "He starts in with, 'You can't be letting your dog be disturbin' the peace.' So then, Carl asks if he's under arrest and—"

I held up my hand. "If you could, ma'am please, look this way," I indicated myself. When she glanced again at the lens I said, "As if we're having a conversation. Try to forget the camera's there." She obliged and I asked her to continue.

"When the officer says, 'No, you're not under arrest,' well, Carl turns back towards the house. And that's when the officer sticks out his foot."

"Wait, the patrolman did what?"

"He done stuck his shoe in the door to keep him from closin' it. Now Carl's a big man. He's pushin' from the other side, and the policeman can't get it all the way open. Carl's breathin' heavy. Shouting. Sayin' this was his house and they had no right."

Mrs. Sutton's gaze drifted past me to the house across the street, where yellow tape still marked off the front porch. "I ain't never had much use for that white boy. And that animal of his did run around yippin' and yowlin' day and night. But I don't see why them patrolmen had to break down his door and do like they done." She put a hand to her cheek. "They drug him out and beat him senseless."

"Did you see anything else?" I asked.

"That policeman went around back of the house."

"A cop went around back?"

"Yeah. Gets out of a black car, goes out back a piece, and comes around again after it's over. Big cop in a white uniform, struttin' around like he owns the place, standing his self over top of Carl. Gave me a funny feelin'."

"How so?"

"That big cop. Seen him around here before."

Eddie snapped the camera from its tripod and I handed him the mic. Mrs. Sutton tapped me on the shoulder. "Honey," she asked, "when is this interview gonna be in the paper?"

Among her many dictatorial roles as executive producer, Susan reviewed reporters' story scripts. I stood at her desk, meek and mute, a school kid waiting for his essay to be marked up. She slashed red lines of ink across the part about the officer's foot in the door. As she moved her hand down the page, a bright red "X" appeared through Mrs. Sutton's sound bite, the part where she said the cops beat Carl Walker senseless.

"Susan, that's the meat of the story," I said. "She's an eyewitness."

"*You* say it's meat." Without looking up she pushed the typewritten script back across the desk. "Bring me some sizzle next time."

Except for the death rattle of window air conditioners battling the heat and losing, the block stood quiet. The neighbors remained inside, but I could feel their eyes peeking behind drawn shades. A standing duck once again, I wanted to get this live shot done and call it a day.

The Walker case led the six, but I was not the top story. The newscast launched with a voice-over "chyron," electronic words on the screen, the nuts and bolts of "what we know so far about the investigation into the police-involved shooting in Midtown." Anchorman Lin Harper's stentorian delivery reminded me of a down-home Ted Baxter, an affectation intended, I supposed, to mask his native West Tennessee twang. Into the camera he droned that reporter Janelle Foster had just spoken with MPD Major Gene Tipton.

Eddie had arranged a small TV in front of me, tuned to our broadcast. I watched, waiting for my cue, feeling my jaw come unglued as the sound bite of Major Tipton rolled on the screen and into my earpiece:

> "*When approached about a dog complaint, Mr. Walker refused to comply with a lawful order. He retreated into the house, firing a single shot from a .22 rifle, critically wounding Officer Carroll. Upon dropping his weapon, Mr. Walker continued to resist. Under difficult circumstances, MPD officers demonstrated extreme professionalism and restraint in ultimately subduing the suspect and taking him safely into custody without further incident.*"

Measured and definitive words. And complete crap. True, it appeared Walker fired on police. But where was the part about officers busting through his front door? *Subdued?* What I saw was a defenseless man beaten to within an inch of his life. Did police show *restraint*? Was that what they called it?

I got the "stand by" and the anchorman tossed to me. "News 2's Tom Cirone has been following this story and is live with neighborhood reaction tonight. Tom?"

From behind his camera, Eddie thrust an index finger in my direction.

You're on.

I knew exactly what I planned to say. I didn't need to read from notes as most reporters did, bobbing their head up and down every few words like a dippy bird toy. If you couldn't hold a couple of thoughts in your brain and spit them out you didn't belong in this business. But suddenly, I wasn't so certain what my thoughts were telling me.

This senseless incident on this ridiculous block had blown up my relationship with Valerie. What was a pathetic career in television worth compared to the hurt I'd caused? Besides, I didn't care for that police statement at the top of the news. Didn't care for it at all. *I was there.* I saw what I saw. This may have been the land of cotton, but I couldn't just look away, look away.

I delivered my intro to the camera, and then listened back to the taped story as it played on the air. A few minutes ago, I'd been focused on getting done and getting home. That wasn't going to cut it anymore.

I lowered my mic hand. "Eddie, I don't think I can—"

"Stand by," Eddie shouted. "Ten seconds back."

Live reporting is a walking, talking minefield. You get a minute and a half of broadcast time, maybe two on a slow news day. They toss you an open microphone. Then they shout "go" in your ear and you're on. Free to deliver whatever words you choose, in whatever order they happen to pass from your glib lips. And they let you do it. Crazy they trust you to do it. Trust that you don't slander anyone. Trust you don't deliver yourself or the station into a shitstorm. I was about to stress test that trust to its limit.

The video package ended. My face popped up on the monitor. I turned to Eddie's camera.

> "Back live in Midtown, and one note before I toss it to the studio. At the top of the newscast, we aired a Memphis police statement saying Carl Walker precipitated this incident. That he resisted arrest. But witness statements contradict that version. Some neighbors telling me they thought Walker did nothing to provoke a confrontation. In fact, they say police broke down his door."

I took a deep breath, considering how far off-script to go, and then went there.

> "By all accounts this was a troubling, disturbing event to witness. Indeed, I was one of those witnesses. Now, mine is just one observation, but I saw no resistance on the part of Mr. Walker. The suspect appeared handcuffed when pulled out of the house. Cuffed and helpless on the ground when police struck him. And the question is ... regardless of what Carl Walker allegedly did ... does that justify police breaking into his house and then, in the words of one witness, beating him senseless?"

In my ear, the producer cut in, his voice sharp with annoyance. "Wrap it up."

> "So, Lin, until we get further details, it's going to be difficult to draw conclusions around exactly what happened here ... and why. Back to you."

I ripped out my earpiece, looking up as Eddie clicked the camera from its tripod mount. He shook his head, muttering, "Mmm, mmm, mmm. A bit personal there, Tom?"

"Yeah, I guess I got a little ... intense."

"Don't get me wrong," he said. "It was well put and all. But there's an old saying. 'Don't be plowin' too close to the cotton.'"

The radio in the truck squawked. "Eddie, put Cirone on. Now." It was the news director. I'd never known Lee to pick up the two-way.

I steadied myself, keyed the mic. "This is Tom."

"Tom, Jesus Christ, are you out of your mind?" As loud and clear as Lee's voice transmitted through the radio, I was certain his bellowing could be overheard by every perked-up ear back in the newsroom. "I just got off the line with Major Tipton. He wanted to know why my reporter was going off on the department live on the air. And I had no goddamned answer."

"Lee, if you're asking me what I was thinking," I said, cupping my hand around the microphone, "I was thinking that sticking Tipton's statement at top of the newscast was a mistake. If someone had checked with me first …"

"Checked with—? Tom, you don't get to decide what we run in the show. Let's get that straight. And you don't go off speculatin' just because you don't like what you hear." The mic remained open, capturing the rumble of his exhaled breath. "You and me, son, we're gonna have us a nice little chit-chat about this in the morning."

A good reporter knew not to express his opinions on the air. "Report the story, don't *be* the story." It was a cardinal rule. Breaking it, a sin of journalism.

Maybe that was the problem. What did I know of sin? When I was eight, I made my first confession. I told the priest I'd shrieked in anger at my mother, shouting that she hated me and loved my older brother best, the one I *didn't* kill. The Father, shrouded in gloom behind a gilded screen, said, "I absolve you from your sins." And that was it. Magic. Forgiven.

I have greatly sinned, in what I have done and in what I have failed to do.

The prayer of penitence drummed into me as a child aptly described a compound sin. I'd done Valerie wrong. I'd failed my profession.

That night, the mournful whine of aircraft engines glided through my bedroom window. Federal Express freighters, throttling down, the vanguard of their approach to Memphis International Airport. One after another, a never-ending flight of jet-propelled geese in formation. Six months ago, I'd considered Memphis just a stopover town, as it was for those cargo planes. Almost from the day I got here I started sending out resumes, searching for the next job, the next big thing. Then a sweet girl with deep red hair and intense green eyes walked into the newsroom and for the first time I stopped searching.

After midnight, I dialed Valerie again, not bothering to count the rings. I drifted off to sleep, imagining a million packages on magic carpets, floating into the backs of shimmering airplanes, bound for faraway realms, and dreaming I could fly away with them.

4

MEMPHIS, TENNESSEE

The Channel 2 building inhabited prime waterfront property on the south side, high up on a ridge known as the Chickasaw Bluffs. From here, you could make out the famous M-shape of the Hernando de Soto Bridge spanning the river downtown. But much closer to the station, a relative stone's throw, three other parallel bridges dominated the view. A half mile by car—or walking distance if you cut through an ancient chain link fence—this trio of bygone, cantilevered structures clawed their rusted fingers into the muddy banks of the Mississippi.

The southernmost, the Memphis-Arkansas Bridge, or what some folks called the "old bridge," carried I-55 across the river. The nearest, the Harahan, supported a pair of east-west freight lines. Its industrial-apocalypse trusses loomed over the station like a fallen Martian tripod from *The War of the Worlds*.

Its bridges defined Memphis, every bit as much as the river they spanned. Down the Mississippi streamed the cotton, the blues, the fragrance of barbecue. And across that river flowed many a dreamer hell-bent on big plans in the big city. No doubt those same bridges carried many away, broken.

And I was next.

I was sure of it the moment I returned to the newsroom in the morning and Lee rapped his knuckles on the glass wall of his office.

"You got a piss-poor attitude, son," he declared, not waiting for me to sit down. "And you're damned rough around the edges."

Were my edges rough? Definitely. After all, I *had* been involuntarily "separated" from my first, third and fourth television stations. Seven miserable years and five cities. TV market to TV market. *Attitude* to blame, no doubt.

"You probably think you're smarter than us," Lee was saying. "Hell, maybe you are. Using words like 'precipitated' on the air. Let's leave that stuff to the weatherman. Precipitated. Jesus."

Lee Cravens ran a major newsroom in a big metropolitan city, but he was, in every respect, a good ol' boy. A good ol' boy and he looked the part. Probably a linebacker in high school, he remained menacingly large, thick around the waist, with short cropped sandy hair and a ruddy complexion, especially when angry. And he was angry right now. To him I was an alien, a novelty hire, a token from the deep North, who happened to be a strong reporter and adept at the bread and butter of TV news, live shots.

"Just because you got yourself a fancy Emmy Award in your last gig up there in Milwaukee, and we stuck your face on a billboard when we hired ya ... that don't' make you the shit. You follow me?"

My eyes drifted, taking in the world outside the window where a manicured lawn flowed to the bluff at the river's edge.

Lee waved a hand in my face. "Are you payin' attention, Tom?"

I nodded.

"Son, I ain't asking much of ya. Just stick to the damned script. That means don't be rockin' the boat when it don't need to be rocked. Keep your opinions off the air, or we'll take *you* off the air." He smacked his palm on the desk. "Now, get the fuck outta my office."

He followed me out the door. He wasn't through. "And clean yourself up for chrissakes. That suit a yours looks like it's been rollin' around in a box of goddang kitty litter!"

News 2 Memphis. A godless bubble. A snow globe without the

snow, a fish tank swimming with idiots and assholes. In that regard, no different from any other newsroom. To work there was to be boiled each day in a simmering pot of babble peppered with profanity. To the outside world, a newsman was a star. Inside, you were excrement. They wiped your face in it every chance they got.

The suspect in the police shooting was a teacher at Memphis Catholic High School. A call to the school produced a terse "no comment." According to a story in the *Commercial Appeal*, the morning newspaper, Carl Walker lived alone, although his mother had shared the house in Midtown for many years before she moved to Frayser, a neighborhood on the north side of town. Scanning the phone book, I found her.

The assignment desk paired me with our chief photographer, or "photog" in the vernacular, a sharp-nosed, square-jawed guy named Dilly Ditton. Since my first day at Channel 2 he'd had his tail in a knot around me. He loved giving me crap. What we used to call "busting chops" back in the neighborhood. He was especially skilled at it.

He started in on me as soon as I got in the truck. "No intern ride alongs today, huh?"

"No, I guess not."

"So, how *is* your little friend Valerie?"

"What's that supposed to mean?"

"Nuthin,'" Dilly said. "I just heard she'd been sick last week. Throwin' up in the ladies' room and stuff." He put a Styrofoam cup to his mouth and squirted dark juice into it. "What I heard, is all."

Mrs. Walker met us on the front porch. She was a large woman, similar in stature to her son, not tall, but sturdy. We didn't ask to come inside the house and she didn't offer. Dilly set the camera on a tripod, I grabbed the mic, and before either of us was ready, she began talking.

"Carl is a good man, a good teacher. He's a good boy. A good Catholic boy. He watched your reports on the news, by the way. Said you tell it like it is."

"Ma'am." I looked at Dilly, he gave me a thumbs up. He was rolling. "Police say your son opened fire on police. Why would he do that?"

"He didn't deserve none of it," she said. "Somebody's got to pay for what they done."

"Have you been able to talk with him?"

"Carl said he was arguin' with that n—" She stopped, cleared her throat. "That neighbor that called the police. I put it all down to him. None of this happens if he shuts his damn mouth."

"Mrs. Walker, does Carl admit to shooting that officer?"

"There's more going on than y'all know," she said, turning away. "Now if you'll excuse me, *Days of Our Lives* is fixin' to come on." Mrs. Walker pulled open the screen door and disappeared into the house.

On the drive back to the station, Dilly went on about Walker getting narc'd by his neighbor and pounded by those cops and how "that's what you get for livin' in a dark neighborhood." I supposed he figured it was safe talking that way around me. I figured it was best to let him keep on thinking so.

5

MYSTERY TRAIN

The next morning, I arrived at work with an aggravating deodorant slogan ringing in my brain. *Never let 'em see you sweat.* Probably dreamed up by some Madison Avenue ad jockey who hadn't enjoyed the pleasure of an August day in Memphis. Dry idea, my perspiring ass. Nine in the morning and you're already drowning in your own stink. Oh yeah. They definitely saw you sweat.

At the back door of the TV station, I spared a glance at the Mississippi River swirling past the bluff, steeling myself for another day in the news jungle. Then, pouring myself into the building, I lingered a moment in the mail room—just long enough out of the sun for my body mass to revert back to a solid.

My eyes, slowly irising in the dim vestibule, alighted on a package poking from my mail slot. A padded brown envelope. From the feel of it, something small and solid tucked inside. No stamp, no sender, no return address. Only this, in shaky, almost childlike block lettering:

TO: TOM CIRONE, NEWSMAN WITH A PLAN, CHANNEL 2

For all I knew it was a stick of dynamite. Maybe part of me hoped it was. I'd already blown up everything else in my life. Why not the station?

Cradling the package like a Waterford crystal, I tiptoed into the newsroom, lowering the envelope to my desk. I picked up the phone.

She answered on the first ring, her greeting dripping with honeysuckle nectar. The same every time. And it got me. Every time. "Hey good lookin'. What's cookin'?"

Probably our receptionist used the line on all the fellas. And so what? From the day I interviewed for the reporting job, Candace Kane had taken a liking to the new guy and I guess I had a little crush on her, too. She exuded Southern sex appeal—that indefinable feminine kryptonite that makes such suckers out of northern boys. Her puppy dog brown eyes and impossibly precious name were just the icing on it.

"Candy, hey. I got this plain envelope in the mail. No postage. Do you know how it got here?" I flipped over the package. Maybe I'd missed something. *Like a detonator.*

"To tell ya the truth, it kinda gave me the heebie jeebies," she said. "I found it propped up outside the lobby doors at seven-thirty. Something wrong, Tom?"

"No. But if it's a bomb, you'll know it when I rip it open."

"Very funny."

I could hear another call ringing on Candy's switchboard and I turned back to the package. Slid a finger along the flap. Nothing went boom. *Better luck next time.*

Tilting the envelope produced a black audio cassette tape. Black and blank. No label. No note, no hint of what might be on it, who sent it, or why.

Wait, something. Scribbled on the A-side of the tape, three faint letters in black marker: TCB. An acronym. Maybe it stood for something long ago. It tickled a memory, but I couldn't tease it out.

Up on the assignment desk they were having a good laugh about the latest Elvis sighting. Something about him hanging with the Memphis cops again, and then a quip: "Hang on tight to your jelly donuts, officers!" Followed by a drawling holler across the newsroom directed at yours truly.

"Hey, Tom! When you're done fondling your girlfriend's mixtape, how about getting out there and doing your job?" Ben "Bubba" Reece was our assignment editor, the guy who listened to the scanners, sifted through news releases, and generally harassed reporters out the door. He favored wire-rimmed glasses and plaid bow ties. He parted his black hair down the middle and sported freckles across his nose. In other words, he resembled no "Bubba" I'd ever known, and maybe that was the point.

"Where exactly am I going?" I shouted back.

"Downtown. MPD just called a news conference," Bubba said. "Ride with Janelle. She's waiting for y'all in the garage. Now, get off your butt and let's roll, *Rambo*."

And there it was.

Rambo. Endearing at first, not so much nowadays. One of our co-anchors coined the "Rambo" nonsense the week I started at the station. My last name, Cirone, sounded like "Stallone." Sylvester Stallone starred in the *Rambo* movies, so naturally, I became Rambo.

It never quite clicked. I considered myself more Italian Stallion than crazed killing machine. But ultimately, the name took on a meaning all its own.

I dropped the cassette tape back in the envelope. I'd play the damn thing tonight.

In the station garage, I hopped in the news van with Janelle and Dilly for the short drive downtown to the towering edifice of authority known as the "201," the Shelby County Criminal Justice Center at 201 Poplar. We crammed into a tight, airless conference room, news photogs jockeying for space on the floor with the other TV, radio, and print folks.

Major Tipton stepped to the podium, head down, hands shaking, as he read from a prepared statement. "At five-thirty this morning, Officer Carter Howard, a decorated veteran of this department, succumbed to his injuries incurred as a result of the shooting on Underwood Avenue. Charges against the suspect, Carl Walker, will be upgraded to second degree murder."

The room exploded. Two reporters bolted for the door to fight for the single pay phone in the hallway. Janelle and I remained; our deadline was later. Major Tipton opened it to questions.

"Can you confirm the cause of death?" one reporter asked.

"We're charging Walker with murder, Don. What do *you* think?"

I raised a hand. I raised a finger. Two hands. Two fingers. Reporters next to me, behind me, in front of me got called, some asked follow-up questions. There was a theater, a dance to press conferences. Part news gathering, part show business. I was all about one for the money, not two for the show, but as I watched Tipton ping-ponging among reporters, I realized at this rate I was never going to cash in.

"Major Tipton." I rose from my chair. "Witnesses say Officer Howard stuck his foot in the door, and with the other officers, essentially broke into the Walker house."

A reporter to my left shouted, "Sit down!"

I tried again. "Might this justify a self-defense argument?"

Someone muttered, "Who *is* this clown?"

The police major cleared his throat, his focus fixed on the top of the podium. "A member of the Memphis Police Department is dead. Doing his job and gunned down in cold blood. I'm not going to dignify your questions."

The presser was over. I turned to see Janelle rolling her head.

"What?" I said.

"Isn't it obvious?"

"No, it's not."

Janelle snapped her notebook shut. "Look. I worked hard to earn a level of trust with the police. Not the easiest thing when you're the black girl reporter on the good ol' boy beat. Maybe you can get away with all that speak truth to power bullshit. But I can't. Not in this town."

That anonymous envelope I'd found in my mail slot—return address unknown—glared at me from the top of the desk. Alas, no stick of dynamite, only a plain cassette tape. As I stood to leave for the night, I swiped the envelope and headed out.

Five minutes south on I-55, I popped the cassette into the tape deck and hit PLAY.

At first, nothing. Hiss, white noise. Probably somebody's idea of a joke. My finger hovered over the EJECT button, tapping it, ready to push.

A guitar downbeat emerged from the car's speakers, followed by a string of fast-picked notes, repeating. After a moment, singing. A man's voice and a faint echo ringing behind it, the way those old songs from the fifties did. If they'd recorded those songs in a tile shower, that is. The lyrics told of a train, a long black train with sixteen coaches. The words, the melody, they evoked a curious melancholy. And something else. The tune bizarrely called to mind the man I'd locked eyes with the other day, the older cop in the big sunglasses staring back at me from across the police scene.

The singing ended and the strumming faded. I took a hand from the steering wheel, ready to hit STOP. But there was more. A throat clearing. A cough. A baritone voice, muddy at first, sharper as it drew closer to the microphone. More halting and more deliberate than the singing, but the same person.

"A wise man once said, uh … I can sing you the song, Jack, but I can't give you the ear to hear it." The hiss on the tape rose, fell. "Maybe *you* don't wanna hear this, and maybe I can understand why you're doin' what you're doin'. What is a man, if not himself, and all that. But keep in mind, son, if you done poke a gator in the eye, it ain't gonna just lay there and take it."

That was all of it.

I rewound the tape and played it again. This didn't feel like a joke. Someone had gone to the trouble of recording it—backwoods homilies and all—and delivering it to the station. Was it a threat? A warning? After repeated playings the song remained unfamiliar. *But that voice.*

The boss summoned me again in the morning. My proximity to his office had its downsides. I was point-blank range.

"Janelle told me about what happened at the police presser," Lee started.

"And what was that?"

"You're on the wrong track." He folded his hands, studied me. "You're twisting things as if the police are the bad guys. That dog won't hunt."

"Oh, it's hunting," I said. "Isn't it my job to keep asking questions?"

"Your job is what I tell you it is."

"Is that right?"

"Tom, don't be an asshole." He reached for the file cabinet and pulled the top handle. "I've got a drawer full of resume tapes. Plenty of talent out there. Every one of them people would *love* to have your job."

In a twisted way, these lectures always reminded me of the old *Mary Tyler Moore Show*. That time when Lou Grant tells Mary Richards that if she doesn't like the job he's doing, she's fired. And if *he* doesn't like the job *she's* doing ... she's fired. In the newsroom, an ever-present sword of Damocles hung over your head. From the moment you arrived in the morning until the end of your shift you lived under the threat of that sword. They called it "at-will" employment. Meaning, for any reason or no reason at all they can and "will" show you the door.

Lee sighed, his jaw muscles relaxed. "Look, we thought you were a great hire. Hell, we felt lucky to land somebody such as yourself. Big market talent, ethnic flavor, the Yankee thing."

Okay, I tended toward olive skin. I had the dark brown hair and five o'clock shadow—which I smothered with TV makeup. Hell, some folks said I looked like a young Al Pacino, only taller. On my worst days, maybe, I *could* be more *Scarface* than *Rambo*. So, sure, I'd accept "ethnic." But *Yankee*? No one had slung that epithet at me since I'd worked in Alabama years ago. A photog at my station had informed me that Yankees were like hemorrhoids, a pain in the butt when they come down and a relief when they go back up.

Suddenly I wanted to go back up. Up and out. A TV career was measured by how high on the market ladder you climb. New York was the ultimate, Los Angeles, number two, Chicago three, and so on. At the bottom were hick towns you wouldn't even figure did newscasts, in remote regions of Montana or North Dakota. In between was a vast wasteland. You worked your way up, preferably quickly, so you didn't get stuck for life reporting on pork belly futures in Terre Haute, Indiana—or for that matter, sweating your ass off in Memphis, Tennessee.

Lee slammed shut the drawer of resumes. "So. We squared away on the Walker story, now? I do hope we can put this all behind us, Tom."

At six-thirty I crossed the newsroom to the sports office, a warren of pennants, banners, programs, and stacked videotapes tossed among three workstations. Our sports director was a wiry, raven-haired Cajun boy named Bobby Bugg. He'd grown up in the late fifties, been around Memphis a number of years, and often talked about the pivotal role the town had played in the development of the blues, R&B, rock 'n' roll, and all that. If anyone, he'd know what song was on that cassette tape.

In 1987, your search engine was word of mouth. Or a helpful librarian (more on that later). If you wanted to hear a song, or learn its name, you needed to buy the CD or vinyl, or happen upon it on the radio. You could also ask a knowledgeable friend. When I caught up with Bobby, I recited what I remembered of the first few lines until he put up his hand.

"That's a golden oldie," he said. "A cat named Junior Parker recorded it, Sun Studios and Sam Phillips, you know. But the first time I ever heard it, someone else was singin' it. My aunt took me up to Shreveport to the Louisiana Hayride. I couldn't have been more than nine or ten. One of the performers that Saturday night was a young pup with a funny name. Elvis. He sang your song that day. *Mystery Train*."

The *voice* on the tape. That oddly familiar face in the squad car. They belonged to the same man! *Tip of the tongue. No, deeper.* The realization crawled its way out of my mouth in a croak. "Presley."

"The one and only." Bobby backhanded my shoulder. "Mr. C., you okay? Why you askin' about that song anyways? Heard it on the radio or something?"

"Yeah." I turned for the newsroom. "No. Not exactly."

6

ACT TWO WAS WHERE WE MET

A pink sheet of WHILE YOU WERE OUT memo paper awaited me on Monday. A certain law professor at Memphis State University needed to speak with me. *Urgent.*

His name was Innis Honeycutt. Told me he was representing Carl Walker. He'd seen my reporting on the case and had something to show me. "Bring a cameraman," he said.

We met on the front steps of the Walker house on Underwood. With his plaid bow tie and his courteous demeanor, Honeycutt struck me as more professor than trial lawyer. Maybe civil litigator. None of it shouted "criminal defense attorney."

The door had been returned to its hinges, but inside, wood splinters still littered the floor, blood stained the hardwoods, piles of newspapers lined the hallway. Bullet holes riddled the far wall. The place was a bonanza for B-roll.

"Carl watches your station, you know," Honeycutt said. "He mentioned *you* in particular."

"Yes. Mrs. Walker said the same thing."

The lawyer frowned. "*Mrs.* Walker?"

"Carl's mother."

"Of course," he said, his facial muscles relaxing. "Well, let me get to the point. I had a couple of third-year students do a forensic walk-through. They discovered something the police apparently overlooked. This bookshelf over here near the front door."

I followed Honeycutt across the room. "See this one book here?" He pulled out a tattered hardbound copy of *As I Lay Dying*. "Now, keep in mind, according to police, Walker fired just once. A bullet they say did *not* exit Officer Howard's body."

As Eddie rolled video, Honeycutt stepped back out of frame, holding out the book. "Take a close look. There. Can you get your camera in? See that?"

I leaned in behind Eddie, studying a round hole in the spine of the Faulkner book. The back of the bookshelf where it had rested was splintered, a projectile embedded in the wood. As I spun around to face the rear of the house, the point the attorney was trying to make became as clear as that bullet's trajectory.

"Mr. Honeycutt, has anything been moved?"

"Not a thing."

"Do you mind if we put a mic on you?"

At the time of the shooting, Honeycutt pointed out, the bookshelf would have been in *front* of Walker and *behind* the police officers. He emphasized that the official report had Walker firing only one shot, hitting Howard and remaining lodged in the officer's spine. But this was evidence of a *second* shot. Walker could not have fired both. My interview broke the news that night.

> Honeycutt: *"Based on Carl's position and where police stood their ground, the bullet through that book cannot have been fired by any of the officers at the front of the house. If we assume for a moment it was Carl's shot which lodged itself in the bookshelf, then who fired the fatal shot?"*

Every story on the Walker case got close scrutiny from the executive producer and news director. They debated the "who fired the fatal shot" sound bite. Lee's hand had hovered over the line with a red marker. I said, "Would you rather the attorney say it in the bite, or me say it on camera?" The news director pulled back his hand. The sound bite stayed.

Two days after my report aired, the mystery train pulled into the station.

Candy Kane usually closed the switchboard and locked the lobby doors at five on the dot. So it caught my attention when extension 200, the front desk phone, rang at my desk at five after.

"Tom?" Her voice tremored. "I have uh ... a gentleman here. In the lobby."

"Okay. It's a little late in the day. He's asking for me?"

"He says his name is ... Danny Fisher?"

"Am I supposed to know who that is?"

Her voice hushed, as if cupping a hand over her mouth. "Tom?"

"Yes, Candy."

"Don't think I'm crazy or nothin' but—" There was a long pause. "Gosh darn it, but it's ... I mean, I think it's actually ... it's ..."

"It's what?"

"Tom, just come up front already."

I sure wasn't aware of any Danny Fisher, but okay, I'd play along. Candy was sweet. It was cute how she wore her hair in a ponytail most days. Even her name was precious. But I'd heard she was seeing someone at the station, a chisel-faced, muscle-bound character who happened to be one of our videotape editors. No sense in tussling with that.

Through the break room, past the coffee machine, I headed down the long, narrow hallway with the skylights and through the doors into the public lobby of Channel 2.

I noticed the sunglasses first.

They covered half his face, gold frames with amber lenses in oblong shapes dipping halfway down his cheeks like deep-sea goggles. He made himself at home with an arm draped across the top cushions of the long, low visitors' couch and stared through the windows at the river. His knee bounced up and down in time to some internal metronome.

Candy nodded in his direction and I approached, putting out my hand. He didn't take it.

"Hello Mr. Cirone." He stood, sizing me up.

A strange feeling overcame me, not déjà vu exactly, but a close cousin. The man was a touch under six feet, about my height. Generous sprays of silver shot through his thinning sandy brown hair. His eyes, what I could see of them through the glasses, seemed pinched, puffy, as if he'd just woken. A halo of Brut surrounded him.

He pointed to the double doors. "Let's talk outside. Public places make my ass itch."

A mustached man in dark slacks and a black sports coat joined us as we left the building. Rangy but menacing, he locked his eyes on me as the three of us walked several paces, coming to a stop amidst the cluster of satellite dishes arrayed in front of the main entrance.

The man in the sunglasses faced me, hands on his hips. "Here's the deal. If we're gonna do this ... this thing ... then you don't officially know me."

"Well, I don't."

"Good. Now, anytime you may hear from me again, and I'm not saying you will, but if you do, it's gonna be Danny. Danny Fisher."

"Danny Fisher," I repeated.

"Call it an alias, a code name, or whatever."

"Okay. Why are we here, uh, Danny? I mean, why are *you* here?"

"Because I don't like to see no injustice. Never have. If I can right a wrong, I'll do it."

"That's very noble."

"You mocking me, son?"

"I'm not mocking you," I said. "But this is all just a little bizarre."

As I studied the man's face in the glare of the afternoon sun I understood Candy's fluster. At first I hadn't discerned any markers of the famous image. No thick, black, trucker-style sideburns. Hair no longer styled in the iconic quiff. For sure, he was *not* wearing a sequined jumpsuit. Just a middle-aged guy in a button-down shirt and slacks. But as he spoke, his lip curled to one side. And dangling from a chain around his neck, a gold pendant in the shape of a lightning bolt.

"Son, I watch the news," the man who called himself Danny said. "I got three TVs up in the house. You're always the big story at six. You got yourself a reputation."

"Okay."

"No, no," he said. "You're pretty hot stuff ain'tcha? I wouldn't be here talking with you if that weren't true. You're a shit-starter. I know the type."

"I'm flattered. I guess?"

"Well, listen, Mr. Ted Koppel, junior, there's something y'all need to know, you and your news station."

"Yes."

"The man missed."

"He missed?"

"And now *you're* in the dang crosshairs," he said. "With your broadcasts about the shooting and the bullet and all."

"You mean the Walker case?"

"Do you have wax in your ears, man?" He looked at his bodyguard, if that was what he was. "Does this kid have wax in his ears or what?"

"Wax in his ears, boss."

"Listen," Danny said, "I ain't gonna be your special friend here. It's strictly *impersonal*, I just don't want to see somebody get hurt."

"Somebody?"

"You, son."

I shook my head. The guy talked in riddles.

"Look, I done said too much, already." Danny gestured to the man in the black jacket and they both began to move. "But take my advice," he said over his shoulder. "Be real careful whose shoes you're steppin' on."

The men retreated to the parking lot, entering a beauty of a black sedan. The car sported four round headlights, a pair of pointed front fins, and two chrome pipes running the length of each side. Not the Batmobile, but maybe its stunt double.

Somehow it fit. He was no Bruce Wayne, but the man called Danny did come off like a low-rent caped crusader.

7

MEMORIES

Thursday night after work the male members of the newsroom assembled at *Earnestine and Hazel's*, a dilapidated South Memphis dive bar. Some called it a juke joint. The sign over the door said "sundry store" but it hadn't been that in ages. Folks claimed the upstairs used to be a brothel. For all I knew, it still was.

We gathered here together to join in unholy ceremony, better known as a bachelor party. Fellow reporter Lukas Boone was due to be married Saturday.

Lukas and I went back a few years. We'd worked together before, in Alabama, and I considered him a friend. The tricky part was, I'd worked with his fiancée, too. Dixie Maxwell had produced the ten o'clock news at our station in Mobile. Lukas had the day shift, I was nightside. So, I saw more of Dixie than Lukas did. Often, after the news, Dixie and I stuck around. Sometimes over a drink at Big Jack's, a local joint. Okay, maybe we'd kissed once or twice. But then I left for Milwaukee and Lukas landed a job in Memphis. I hadn't seen Dixie since. Now the two were getting hitched.

Bobby Bugg staked out a corner table, a pitcher in front of him. The sportscaster waved me over, filled my mug, clinked it. "Hey, brother. Here's to matrimony."

"What am I supposed to say to *that*?"

"What's on your mind? Not weddings, obviously."

"If you really want to know, I've been thinking about *that* guy."

Bobby's eyes followed my finger to a poster on a far wall, a young man in slicked-back hair, a pink jacket and black slacks, his legs spread, a guitar slung around his neck.

"Is this about that dang *Mystery Train* song?"

"Have you ever seen him around?"

"Elvis?" Bobby gestured to the table at my back. "He's right behind you."

I whipped my head. The table was empty. When I turned around, Bobby was full-out laughing. "Man, you are wired tonight. What's goin' on?"

I shrugged.

"If you're asking if the dude gets out much, the answer is no," he said. "Not anymore. But he always stayed close to Graceland, even during the good times."

"What does he do with himself?"

Voices swelled, a jukebox blasted Wang Chung. I leaned closer as Bobby said, "He likes to ride along with the police sometimes."

The weatherman, Timothy Burnside, and Ronnie Patton, another of our reporters, arrived. Bobby gave a slight nod as they came through the door. "You know the story, right?" Bobby went on. "It was ten years ago now. It about killed his career."

I did know the story. Some of it, anyway. In the summer of 1977, I was focused on college classwork, but I remembered reading something about him collapsing in his bathroom. Heart attack, they said. According to Bobby, Elvis Presley nearly died that day. They rushed him to Baptist Hospital, revived him in the ambulance. Then came reports of drugs and guns and a bunch of other wild rumors. The lurid revelations were such a shock to the collective system, even his most rabid fans felt betrayed. His entourage, the Memphis Mafia, went their separate ways, the next concert tour got canceled, and there never was another one.

Raucous laughter burst from two tables over. Bobby and I grabbed our beers and joined in. The groom-to-be was in the middle of a story that had folks in stitches. As we got closer, I realized the joke was on me and my turbulent tenure at Channel 9 in Mobile.

"This one time, Friday came along and nobody got their checks," Lukas was saying. "We had a meeting about it, some payroll screwup, but Tom was outraged. I mean none of us made a lot, and a paycheck's a paycheck, so—. Oh, hi, Tom, just telling one of your famous stories."

"Infamous," I said.

"So, Tom went ahead and stood up like Norma Rae or something. 'This is outrageous,' he goes. 'We can't be expected to work without pay!'"

"I did *not* say that."

"He goes, 'As journalists, if we'd heard of a company making people work without pay, we'd be investigating it for the news!' Then he declares, 'This is why people join unions!'"

No one cared about my denials, any more than they had when they'd fired me on the spot that day. So I didn't bother. But Lukas wasn't finished.

"Now, in Alabama, mention unions, you might as well call Jesus a black man." Lukas caught himself and turned to Ronnie. "No offense, man."

"Oh, offense *definitely* taken," Ronnie said.

"You ended up waiting tables for a while, didn't you, Tom?" Lukas had a wide grin now. I grinned back, slitting my eyes.

"Hey," he said, "remember that stalker chick? Guys, Tom was seeing this girl from Prichard, out by the university. Turned out to be nuttier than a squirrel turd. I forget, Tom, did you actually, you know, *do it* with her?"

"Great memories," I said. "Whose bachelor party is this, anyway?"

"When Tom finally dumped the crazy bitch," Lukas went on, "she was having none of it." Across the table Trace Kunkel, Candy's bench-pressing boyfriend, appeared to be hanging on Lukas's every word. "So this wacko chick went around town writing nasty stuff about him in lipstick. Women's room walls at Waffle House and Applebee's, right, Tom? Saying he had AIDS and some shit. Not the kind of publicity you want when you're on TV."

Knowing all the crap I crammed into my short time in Mobile, Lukas's trip down *my* memory lane could have gone on for a while yet. But a commotion overtook the bar and cut short the tell-all. A police officer had strutted through the front doors. A lady cop. She aimed straight for Lukas and started reading him his rights.

Lukas was a good Christian boy. This was going to be interesting. The officer removed her hat, spilling a mane of chestnut hair to her waist. She shoved Lukas back in his chair, straddled him, and unbuttoned her top button. A pair of handcuffs appeared.

That did it for Lukas. Somehow he squeezed his husky frame out from beneath the woman. Hyperventilating, he hoisted the chair in front of him, swinging it lion tamer style. The lady cop stood back and surveyed the room, saying, "Okay boys, who's the real stud here?"

Trace jabbed me in the ribs. "How about you Tom? You like fucking the cops." Trace had arranged for the stripper. And he had it in for me tonight.

I ignored the comment and stepped to the bar. A moment later, Timothy threw himself into the chair, the "police woman" in his lap, burying the weatherman's face in her high-pressure zone. When it was over, I returned to slap Lukas on the back, said my goodbyes, and stepped out onto South Main.

Across the street, its neon marquee doused, an unassuming blonde brick building housed the *Arcade Restaurant*. A fifties-style diner long past its heyday, at this time of night the *Arcade* anchored an eerily quiescent corner of Memphis. To my right, Central Station, an antiquated rail depot, towered in faded glory over the block. Turning for my car, I became conscious of footsteps crossing the intersection.

"The boss wants to see you." In the green glow of the traffic light,

I recognized the big man stepping onto the curb, the mustached bodyguard from my encounter with Danny Fisher at the TV station. "*Arcade*. Now," he said, resting a hand on my shoulder.

"It's past one," I said.

"He's waiting."

A single pale lightbulb illuminated a row of stools at the counter. Several rows of seating in washed-out blues and yellows sat empty in the shadows. From within this gloom, a voice called out.

"Here he is!" Danny waved from a back booth on the far left, near the rear exit. "Welcome to Tom's Diner."

"Not *my* diner," I said, feeling my way toward him.

"Like the song, son. Suzanne Vega." He shook his head.

"I know *Luka*. They play that one a lot on the radio."

"Nah, *Tom's Diner*. It's on the album. I'll bet it's gonna be a hit one day, too." He motioned for me to sit opposite him.

I slid warily into the worn vinyl cushions of the bench seat. "How is this place even open? Isn't this a breakfast and lunch joint?"

"Let's just say I know the owner. Besides, ain't been much business 'round this neighborhood lately."

"Some might call it a ghost town," I said, and then quipped, "Are *you* a ghost?"

He studied me through those amber-tinted shades, his lip curling in a half-smirk. "I'm thinking maybe 'Tom' doesn't suit you, anyways. You're more of a *Thomas*, aren't you?"

Photos lined the walls. Movie posters. Album covers. I found myself wanting to hold one or two of them up to my host's face. An *un*-reality check.

"My mother calls me Thomas," I said.

"Your mama's a good woman." He pulled off his glasses and considered me, as I did him. Ancient acne scars pocked his face. He had his hair combed back, a generous amount of it gray and spilling past his collar. He looked to be in his fifties, roughly my father's age. Still had those ice blue eyes that used to make the girls swoon. But the fire behind them now smoldered rather than flamed. Mostly, he struck me as a big country boy.

"Thomas it is, then. That's more your style. Like Thomas Aquinas. A real philosopher. And a wiseass." He smacked his palm on the table.

I flinched.

"You seem jumpy, Thomas. Are you jumpy?"

"I've met celebrities before, but ... how did your guy know where to find me?"

"Hell, I ain't no celebrity. I'm just a punchline, man. Dontcha read the papers?" And there went his lip again, one side rising slightly higher than the other. "*You're* the famous guy on the news. I seen your face on them billboards around town."

He can't be serious.

My eyes veered to a frame on the wall, a young Elvis Presley in a flowery red shirt, a lei around his neck, the cover of a soundtrack album called *Blue Hawaii*.

"I see you starin' at that picture there. Ain't no ghost, but that sucker's *long* gone."

"Danny," I said. "This is—"

"Got kids, Thomas?"

The question stopped me cold. Not because it was so left field. But because it conjured Valerie, her slender waist, her ever-so-tiny bump. My voice caught in my throat. "No. I don't."

"I got a daughter. Folks comin' out of the woodwork these days saying they're my love child or some shit. But there's just the one. A grown woman now. Nineteen. About the only thing worth livin' for."

My hand went to my temple. Way too early for a hangover.

"Are you sure you're all right, son? Let's fetch you somethin' to drink." Danny leaned out of the booth and hollered. "Travis, we need a couple of cokes. What kind for you, Thomas?"

"What kind of what?"

"Coke."

"Yes, that's fine," I said.

A smile cracked Danny's face. "And who's on first, right?"

He twisted in the direction of his bodyguard, who'd been pacing behind the counter. "Lizard, bring the usual belly wash for our young friend here." Danny fidgeted with the place setting, unraveling the silverware from the napkin. "That's Travis Lister. I call him Lizard, trust him with my life." He slid out the butter knife. "Just don't mess with him. He'll cut ya to pieces!" He lunged across the table, thrusting the knife at my neck, and I recoiled again, my knees slamming the underside of the table.

"You *are* jumpy, son."

When Travis returned with two bottles of Pepsi, I had to laugh, remembering that in these parts a Coke is not a Pepsi, but a Pepsi *may* be a coke, and a coke might also be a Dr. Pepper.

"I watch your news station," Danny said. "But tell me something, why do y'all run the same damn stories at ten that you ran already at six? It's never nothin' new."

Before I could answer, he said, "What kinda name is Cirone anyway? Eye-talian?"

"Italian, yes."

Danny sipped his cola and grimaced, pounding his chest as if coaxing out a reluctant burp. He set down the bottle and reached into his jacket, pulling out a large leather wallet.

"You know, years ago I got myself deputized. Sworn in." He unfolded the wallet onto the table, revealing a half dozen police badges stacked in rows. One stood out: RESERVE CAPTAIN, MEMPHIS POLICE. He glided a soft hand across the surface of each medallion, caressing them, a look of almost childlike fascination in his eyes. "I got friends at city and county," he said. "I carry a gun, understand. Two guns. A third in my boot. I'm a karate grand master. I may be getting on, but I know how to defend myself, you follow?"

"Actually, I don't."

"Ever heard of *The Prophet*?"

"It's an old book, right?"

"It's *the* book, man. It taught me a very important lesson. It says a man may have the ability to sing a song, but he can't give nobody the goddamn ear to hear it."

I jerked upright. The singer. The ear. It was the aphorism from the cassette. "So that *was* you," I said. "The tape."

Danny leaned back, swirling his Pepsi, exciting the carbonated liquid in the bottle. "Sure, I sent you that cassette. You seem to be a guy in need of some divine guidance."

"Yeah, but, 'newsman with a plan.' Seriously?"

"Well, you do, don't you? Got one, I mean?"

"In my line of work, plans mean shit," I said. "You go where the wind takes you. In my case the wind blew me way off course. Uh, no offense."

"Memphis'll sneak up on ya, son. Give it a chance." Danny tilted his bottle toward the far wall. "I see you're still studyin' them pictures up there. You know who I am."

"Yes. I know who you are."

"Then you know I don't need to be stickin' my neck out for some dang TV reporter."

"So why are you bothering?"

"Well, you might say, I'm a very bothering fella." He began folding up his wallet of badges. "Them police that beat on that white boy over in Midtown ... dontcha get why they mighta been pissed?"

"Five or six cops whaling on the guy. Nearly killed him."

"Anything else catch your eye?"

"An unmarked squad car on the street," I said. "Maybe a very familiar someone looking my way."

Narrowing his eyes, he shoved the wallet back into his jacket. "Shit, son. You gotta try harder than that." He waved to Travis. "Lizard, go ahead and bring the chariot around." Danny pushed back from the table. "Good night, Thomas."

You may wonder why wasn't I more intimidated, more awestruck after a sit-down with the King of Rock 'n' Roll. Dumbstruck maybe, but not awestruck. Mostly, I couldn't understand why he kept seeking me out. Besides, old celebrities didn't faze me. I'd interviewed them. Shook their hands. George Wallace, a shell of his former fiery self, in his last throws as governor of Alabama. Ronald Reagan during the '84 presidential campaign. Bob Hope, Jesse Jackson, Marlo Thomas, tons of folk.

Once you've done this a while you realize that up close, they're just people. And Danny? Maybe he was right about not being a celebrity any longer. I mean, if it had been Peter Gabriel, or Whitney Houston, or say, De Niro or Streep, sure, those were famous names. That's why I went right on calling him "Danny." Elvis was the name of someone who existed in the past, on vinyl records, and in blurry videos and black and white newsreels. Whatever he may have been back in the day, you'd need to preface it with the word "former."

Two in the morning. Back at work in six hours. And yet, instead of steering for home, I turned the car south on Main and headed for the TV station.

It was just a few steps from the rear door of the studios to the deserted editing bays. At the end of the darkened hallway stood a wire-framed storage rack, a shelf for each news photog.

How had Danny put it? *Anything else catch your eye?* The woman across the street from Walker, Henrietta Sutton, she'd mentioned something. The tape from her interview was in the stack of Eddie's raw shooting tapes. I pulled it out, popped it into an edit deck, hit PLAY. Two minutes into the interview, I turned up the audio.

"What else did you see?"

"That policeman went around back of the house."

"A cop went around back?"

"Yeah. Gets out of a black car, goes out back a piece, then comes around again after it's over. Big cop in a white uniform, struttin' around like he owns the place, standing his self over top of Carl."

On Eddie's shelf he'd stacked maybe twenty-five boxes of Beta tapes, labeled and dated. I silently praised his organization. The tape was there, the initial footage from the scene. On it Eddie captured a shot of a tall cop, a supervisor. Just as Mrs. Sutton had recounted, the tape showed him bent over Walker. It was only about ten seconds of video.

I played the segment again. Froze it. The editing console allowed you to advance the tape frame by frame. I clicked it back, forward, back. The cop never faced the camera, but as I jostled the image, the more it appeared Walker, through bloodied lips, was saying something in answer to the officer. Why hadn't I reviewed this tape before? Then I remembered. I hadn't returned to the station that night.

In the hallway, the outer door squealed. I'd hoped to have a little while longer before the morning crew showed up. It wasn't that I was doing anything wrong exactly, but someone might get the wrong idea. I ejected the tape and clicked off the monitor just as he poked in his head.

"Lordy, it's Tommy Cirone, ace reporter." Dusty Ford had a way of pronouncing my name with an exaggerated drawl, *SIGH-rone*, rather than *SIR-rone*. "What dragged you out at this ungodly hour?"

An institution for a generation of Memphis TV viewers, Dusty hosted an early-bird program called *Mornin' Critters*. A round, genial man in outsized oval glasses, he'd sit at a nailed-and-glued-together plywood relic of a set that probably dated to the era of *Howdy Doody*. In a tie and white shirt-sleeves, he commented on the news and interviewed guests. It was the station's highest-rated local broadcast.

Dusty regarded me with a mix of paternal concern and professional disappointment. "Now, Tom, say it ain't so. You're not fixin' to ditch our fair station so soon?"

He assumed I was here making resume tapes, to send out to greener pastures. A TV career was a never-ending cycle of applications and rejections. Like Sisyphus, you rolled that boulder up the hill again and again only to have it roll back. You hoped one day the boulder would stick. Any other time I might have indeed been here rolling that boulder. But not tonight.

"Wait," he said, eyeing the TV monitor. "It's about that story you been followin', ain't it?"

I nodded. Told him the boss wanted me to stop doing what I was trained to do, getting the story, whether it makes waves or not. I said I guessed we didn't want any waves.

Dusty grinned. He probably thought I sounded naïve, and maybe I did. "Let me tell you a little something about your boss, Lee Cravens." He sank into a chair. "'Round these parts there's but three colors. White, black, and redneck. Lee may wear a jacket and tie, but under that tie, well ... let's just say his kind don't take to your kind. Ain't right or wrong, just how it is."

I swiveled in my chair, fiddling with the edit controls. Dusty stood to leave, chuckling at my discomfort. "I got a pot of coffee brewin' in the newsroom. Help yourself."

The rest of the morning crew would be here soon. I thanked him but said I should be going. In my notebook I wrote, *Who's the supervisor in the video*? I stroked double-underlines beneath the question, packed up, rounded the corner and reached for the back door. It flew open, body slamming me into the wall.

Trace Kunkel, looking as surprised as I was, shouldered past me and into an edit bay.

"You're here late," he said. "And you shoulda did that stripper. I know you wanted it."

8

LITTLE SISTER

It was like a day in the newsroom, only better dressed. Most of the station gang showed for the wedding reception, the dearly beloved and the not-so-dearly. Timothy Burnside fell into the latter category. He tended to spoil whatever goodwill his chiseled features generated—when he opened his mouth. Timothy was a "talker." He could strike up a conversation with anyone, especially if the topic was himself. Or as Susan put it: "That weatherman spouts ten words a second, with gusts to fifty."

At the appointed hour, to the accompaniment of *Walking on Sunshine*, Dixie and Lukas strutted into the room. The bride, her hair done up in loose blonde curls, was the image of the "Lady in White" from *The Natural*. Dixie made you want to knock a homer into the stadium clock. Maybe I would have. Once. In the receiving line, she asked for a kiss. "Right here. On the cheek." As I obliged, leaning in, Dixie whispered in my ear, "Save a dance for me, Tom."

I didn't want to save a dance for Dixie. Sure, she'd been a friend, probably the best I'd had in this business. A good listener. Maybe too good. She'd let me cry on her shoulder many a night and I'd spilled an extra-large load of dirty laundry. But she was more like a sister, now. Or maybe we were cousins. Kissing cousins.

Hanging over the dance floor there was enough Aqua Net to

furnish both Mötley Crüe *and* Van Halen. I spied Candy Kane angled against the wall, her hair out of the ponytail, her long, delicate figure filling out an emerald silk dress. "You're not alone, are you?" I said.

"Well, no, but—"

"But what?"

"But I wouldn't mind bein' asked." She turned her eyes to the floor.

Despite all the flirting—if that's what it was—in the station lobby, and over the intercom, we'd never stood cheek to cheek. Candy felt fragile in my arms, wispy, as if she might break if I squeezed too hard. As we swayed to the music it dawned on me that weddings made it acceptable to do with co-workers what you wouldn't dare do in the newsroom. She laid her head on my shoulder, her dirty blonde hair cascading down my back. I felt weightless. Almost involuntarily my arms encircled her, pulling her in.

"Hey!" A caustic single syllable. A sharp poke in the back.

"Trace." Candy gasped. She dropped her hands to her sides. Trace Kunkel, who'd "accidentally" slammed the back door into me early Friday morning, cast us alternating glares. He clenched his fists, the biceps swelling under the sleeves of his suit.

"She's all yours, Trace," I said, stepping backwards.

I made it all of two strides off the dance floor. An arm locked into mine and whipped me around. "You owe me, Tommy-boy," Dixie said, shoving me back into the fog of hairspray.

Dancing with the bride. A ballet fraught with delicacy and propriety. The dress, the young woman in it, virginal, taboo. How close do you stand? Where do you place your hands?

"You look beautiful," I said.

She smiled, laid her wrists on my shoulders, and started to sway. The song was by Anita Baker, a ballad about being in someone's arms, caught up in the rapture of them. It was as if Dixie had planned it.

"And *you* are very handsome," she said. One hand snaked down my tie, lingering at the tip.

I took her hand away and held it. "I sometimes wonder if this will ever be me," I said. "You know, getting married."

"Oh, I know you will." Dixie's lips glanced my cheek. Her arm found its way inside my jacket, around my waist. "Tom?"

"Yes?"

"It should have *been* you."

I stopped dancing. "Don't say that."

"I mean it," she said. "Here. Today."

"Dixie, I—" Whatever deflecting comment I had in mind got lost in the next instant as another couple loomed to our left, spiraling into us like a conjoined dervish. The blow staggered me off balance and wrenched Dixie away.

One half of the offending dance partnership was familiar: my colleague Janelle Foster. Her date was a beast of a man, towering a good six inches over her. Fair-haired, dripping with privilege, he resembled one of those arrogant young suitors in *Gone With the Wind*.

He stood back, feet spread. "Hey, I know you," he sneered. "Aren't you the piece of shit doing that reporting about Carl Walker?"

I glanced at Dixie, winked, and said, "Well ... depends on who's the piece of shit asking."

And then I found myself flat on the floor looking up at Dixie's garter.

Janelle had a hand on her date's elbow, pleading with him to move off. Dixie helped me up, brushed off my pants. The music stopped, every eye in the ballroom on the sideshow.

"What is your problem, dude?" I shouted.

"My problem?" The guy swatted away Janelle's hand. "Ever been called out on a run that could *end you*, hotshot? I didn't think so. But you get in front of your camera, with your little electronic dick in your hand, and you second-guess what we do ... when we're out there protecting *your* ass."

He shoved a fist into my chest. I shoved back.

From out of nowhere the groom jumped between us. Ronnie Patton and Bubba Reece appeared on either side and for a second I wasn't sure whether they were there to break things up or to get a better view of the action.

Ronnie spoke first. "Tom, don't do it, he's a cop."

"Okay, so he's a cop," I snapped. "I don't give a shit who he is."

Dixie spun on the groom. "Lukas, I am not going to allow them to ruin my wedding. Make this stop." Ronnie latched onto my arm, Lukas laid a firm hand on the cop's shoulder. Janelle positioned herself directly in front of her date, her pleading eyes searching his.

"If I were you, newsboy, I'd watch my back," the guy shouted over Janelle's shoulder. He grabbed a fistful of her dress and dragged her out of the hall.

Ronnie turned to me, his eyes on my forehead. "You might want to clean that up."

I fingered clump of blood-matted hair. The guy had smashed me with an open palm. "Wait," I said. "Janelle's dating a cop?"

"And how about a drink?" Ronnie pushed me toward the ballroom doors.

Dixie blew me a kiss, took a deep breath, and walked to the DJ's table. She spiraled her arm in the air, hollering, "Can we get this party started again?"

Timothy leaned against the bar, nursing a half glass of wine. "Hey, Tom," he called over. "I heard what happened out there. Talk about the night they drove old Dixie down, huh?"

I told the weatherman it wasn't very funny and got in line for a drink. To my left, wafting L'Oreal and Obsession, stood a slim, but shapely young woman sporting a wide-brimmed hat. Southern belle all the way. Had probably been a debutante, or a Miss West

Tennessee. Her dress was sheer, almost see-through, with a delicate flower pattern, offsetting her straight black hair and severe dark eyebrows. Timothy had his eye on her—and on me.

The debutante turned in my direction. Took a step back. Gestured with her drink. "Does it hurt?"

"Nah. You should see the other guy."

"I did. Big jerk." She held out her free arm at a right angle, as you might do at a business meeting. "Ashley Weaver. How do you do?"

How do you do. Corny, charming, *and* disarming. "I'm Tom."

"Bride or groom?"

"Neither." I realized the second I said it how unfunny it sounded. "You mean whose side? I'm a friend of both."

"Hmm." She took a deep drink. "Dixie never mentioned you." Pulling a napkin from the bar, she dipped it in her glass and dabbed my forehead, first burning, then numbing my facial insult. "Are you with anybody, Tom, friend-of-both?"

Before I could answer, Timothy detached himself from the bar and squeezed between us. "So, Tom," the weatherman said. "No date tonight? I thought maybe … Valerie?"

No, Timothy, but thanks for asking.

"Who's Valerie?" Ashley said.

"Oh, that's Tom's young intern *friend*."

Hurricane Timothy had struck. This was no careless whisper. He knew exactly what he was doing.

Down the hall, the music swelled. Nodding to Ashley, I said, "What do you think?" In reply she held out her hand, fingertips down, like a belle at the ball. Except this belle had downed too many Vodka tonics. She took a stumbling step toward the ballroom. When I suggested she set down her glass, she said no, she could dance with a drink in her hand.

We made our way to the floor, where I steadied her hips with my hands, managing a shaky two-step. "How do you know Dixie?" I asked.

"We went to high school here in Memphis." Ashley told me she studied nursing in college and worked at St. Francis, a hospital on the east side of town. I wondered how she balanced an obvious affinity for partying with such a demanding job. She directed me off the dance floor and back to the bar. "And you and Dixie are ...?"

"We used to work together. In Mobile."

"Oh? What did you do down there?"

This was a switch, she didn't know me from TV. "I was a reporter," I said. "At the station. With Dixie. And Lukas, actually."

"Well, well." She dragged a hand across my scalp. "You do have the hair for it."

At the end of the night Ashley asked if I wanted to get together sometime and I said, fine. But I wasn't sure I meant it. The weatherman's mention of Valerie reminded me I only recently stopped dialing her phone, and only because the number had been disconnected. I'd begun mailing cards and letters to her home in Jackson. The message always the same: *I'm sorry.*

In truth, I had no interest in starting anything with anyone, even a debutant who could pull off a floppy sun hat at a wedding.

9

DON'T BE CRUEL

They passed around an article from the *Commercial Appeal* in the morning news meeting. The newspaper interviewed attorney Innis Honeycutt about the "magic bullet" found in Carl Walker's house. The story had one detail I didn't have. The state crime lab had agreed to look into the evidence. I typically didn't give much credence to what the newspaper wrote, but this story was *validation*. Obviously, if it was in the paper, it was golden. Television news lived with a perpetual inferiority complex. Stories we broke couldn't be truly legit until the print guys wrote it up. Susan set down the paper and asked if there was a follow up we could do.

"The whole thing boils down to, when a cop asks you to stop, you stop," Bubba said. "He says jump, you jump. End of story."

I said, "Even if the cop is breaking the law?"

"Especially."

Lee jumped in. "What *is* the law on this?"

"Might be a good sidebar story." Susan turned to me. "Rambo, why don't you check it out? Take Dilly with you."

"Sidebar," I muttered. It was exactly how it sounded, a story hanging off the side of the main story. A throwaway piece.

"What's that, Tom?" Lee pounced, and I knew I'd made a tactical error.

"Nothing. I'm heading out."

"No, no, please explain. Is it *beneath* you?"

With everyone's attention on me now, I was trapped. "No, it's cool. Thank you. Love it. It's great." I slunk away to go find my photographer.

Instead, I found the interns, crammed into an edit bay, reviewing the tapes they'd put together over the summer. Resume tapes that may or may not land them an entry-level job. This was their last week at the station. As the heavy days of August doglegged into September the interns had come to me less and less for writing advice. Judging by their sideways glances, to them I must have fallen somewhere between Jack the Ripper and Ted Bundy. They practically shrank whenever I approached.

There was no avoiding their voices or their glares as I crossed in the hallway looking for Dilly. One of them had just said, "How's Val doing?" The question was addressed to an intern I knew as Taylor, a college friend of Valerie's. Taylor flicked her eyes in my direction, projecting her answer. "She's okay, I guess ... *considering*." She turned her head full to the door, her eyes shuttering to slits, as did every eye in that edit bay. Yes, I was definitely a serial killer.

I swallowed and poked my head in. "Say, uh, guys ..."

All eyes snapped wide, their pupils now question marks.

"If you talk to her. Valerie, I mean. Could you, uh, tell her that I'm ... that I'm ..."

"That you're sorry for being a royal jerk?"

"Yes. Could you tell her? You know. For everything."

They exchanged glances. One of the interns snorted, and they all turned back to the video screens.

Carl Walker's attorney hunched behind his desk, his jacket off, his sleeves rolled up, fanning himself with a sheet of paper. As Dilly clicked his camera into the tripod, Honeycutt set down the paper and slid it to me.

"A plea offer," he said. "My client is declining it. We see no benefit to Carl entering a guilty plea. Their case against him has as many holes as his unfortunate living room wall."

"What's your defense strategy, then?"

Honeycutt glanced at the camera, and then returned his gaze to me. "There was a notable case involving Memphis police back in the seventies. Not a perfect comparison, but it gives us some guidance. A young man named Edward Garner, shot and killed by an MPD officer. Only fifteen. And unarmed. But the police said he was running from a burglary. The city argued deadly force was justified to prevent a suspect from escaping."

"As Walker was allegedly doing, retreating into his house?"

"In a general sense," Honeycutt said. "But, in the Garner case, the boy's family challenged that argument at the U.S. Supreme Court. Finally, just a couple of years ago, in 1985, the justices ruled in their favor. They said deadly force is *not* justified unless an officer has reason to believe someone poses a threat of serious injury. They ruled that using such force against a fleeing suspect may constitute a violation of the Fourth Amendment."

"Could you argue something similar in the Walker case?"

"Perhaps."

"And *after* the gunshots? What about the beat down?"

"Once a person is restrained," he said, "it's hard to fight back. That's why it's one of the first things police try to do. It's all about control. In this case, the officers claim Walker put up a fight. But we know he was handcuffed. These two things cannot both be true."

"But it's the official police version that matters in court," I countered.

"Yep. There were a dozen or more officers at the scene," Honeycutt said. "And none of them saw anything amiss? Silence and complicity. That's what we call the blue wall."

Carl Walker lay on the ground, the tall cop in white, his back to the camera, straddling him. I'd pulled out the videotape again, cued it to those ten fleeting seconds. If I rotated the dial frame by frame, I could hold it on the exact moment a slice of the officer's profile came into view. I punched PAUSE to freeze it, picked up the phone, and dialed Janelle's extension.

Her face tightened as she entered the edit bay, fixed on the fluttering still-frame on the monitor. She tossed back a long string of black hair. "Tom, I have a script to finish. What do you need?"

"Janelle, I didn't know you were dating a cop."

"Is that why you called me in here?"

"This guy." I pointed at the screen. "Do you know him?"

"It's from the back. Could be anybody."

"Yeah, but you're tight with these folks. Look closely."

She grabbed the controller, jogged the image a frame forward and reverse. "Like I said, could be anybody."

I liked Janelle. She was a tough, smart reporter on an unforgiving beat. But being evasive wasn't her strong suit. Not that she owed me the intimate details of her personal life, but I did deserve a straight answer. "Look, please help me out here. Your date at the wedding wanted to rip my head off over this case."

"Who I'm seeing is my concern, not yours. I gotta get back." She turned and walked out.

As I reached across the edit console for the eject button, the wall extension rang. I wheeled the chair into the hallway and grabbed the phone. The general manager's secretary said I was required upstairs in Ransom Bishop's office. Ransom was Lee's boss. Lee may have been in charge of news, but Ransom ran the entire station—ratings, sales, and making profits for the corporate owners. I'd met the GM before, but I'd never been to that part of the building. Being called up to the big boss man's office late in the afternoon … suffice it to say, it wasn't going to be good news.

Ransom met my eyes as I entered. Lee was in the room, too, but looked away. When I sat down I realized a third person was with us, someone I recognized as the station's personnel director.

"Tom, do you know why you're here?" Ransom's unruly white eyebrows popped, rising in sharp counterpoint to a luxuriant and well-combed head of wavy black hair.

I shook my head.

"Here's the deal," he said. "As a federally-licensed broadcaster, we have standards to uphold. Moral standards."

"Okay."

"When those standards aren't met, well …" Ransom swept his arm to include the other two men. "We're concerned about how you've conducted yourself."

"Could you be more specific?" I had an urge to press a hand against my ribs, still the drumming inside. What had I done *now*?

"You want specifics, Tom?" Lee cut in. "I'll give you specifics. For one, we looked the other way when you dated an intern." I flinched and the men exchanged knowing looks. "Yes, don't act surprised," he said. "You did a piss-poor job hidin' it."

My voice cracked. "How is this relevant to—?"

"Hold your horses. I'm explaining it to you. You are *on* the news. Hell, you're a strong player. We've been considering you for an anchor spot. You've made a name for yourself, for better or worse." Lee cast a side glance at Ransom. "But here's the pickle. That night back in July you *just happened* to be at the Walker crime scene? What exactly was it you were doing down in the ghetto on your day off?"

I took a deep breath. "I was driving by. Saw cops racing to the scene. I followed."

"Huh. You wasn't in the area on *other* business?"

"If I was, that business is my business."

"Is it now?" Lee's eyes flashed, ready for the kill. "Well, the next thing ya know, Valerie Layne's up and left. These internships ain't easy to come by. So, when that little girl quit a month early, right after that, uh, business of yours? Right after both y'all happen to take the same Friday off? Mmm, mmm, mmm. We Southerners may look dumb to you, Tom, but we ain't *that* stupid."

I stared at the floor, biting the inside of my cheek.

Lee took his time with it now. "People talk. Young girls talk. Young interns. Hear tell about a certain clinic a few blocks away in that same Midtown neighborhood." He paused, relishing the moment. "Turns out you ain't so high-classed as you think you are. Jesus, do we need to say it *out loud*?"

The personnel director, who hadn't said a word, snickered. The four of us sat facing each other until it became almost unbearable.

"Tom, we'll keep this between us," Ransom said, finally. "We like you. And we surely don't want all this stuff about you and that girl and what y'all did, well, to stain your career at Channel 2."

It was as elegant a threat as you'd ever hear.

10

ONE NIGHT OF SIN

When I returned to the newsroom from the GM's office, the police scanners were still squawking, typewriters still clicking, voices still shouting. But it was just so much white noise. The last thing I needed was for station management to pound me over the head with the jack-hammering disgrace already living inside my skull. But there it pounded.

An excited conversation animated the assignment desk. Something about Vapors nightclub and a thing Saturday night. Dilly waved a fax promoting an "Elvis Tribute Show." He said they were trying to get up a group to go. Anxious for a distraction after the ass-chewing upstairs, I said I was in.

I don't know why I thought it was a good idea to invite the woman I'd met at Lukas's wedding. Beers with the gang from the station would not have been her idea of a date. But Ashley agreed to tag along.

Bad Bob's Vapors, a low-ceilinged, piss-scented, hole of a dive, squatted on a gray acre of concrete just west of the airport. During the day you wouldn't give the building two glances. But late at night—and it was known for its very late hours—it was destination number one for cheap beers and cheaper entertainment.

With each sip, the sting of the veiled threats and condescension from the bosses faded, the foreboding bubbling away like the foaming brew in my cup. Hell-bent on having a good time, and sufficiently lubricated, I asked around the table if anyone had ever heard Lee Cravens' "size don't matter" speech. "Yeah, that's how he talked me into taking the job," I said. "He goes, 'Son, TV market size don't matter. Don't matter anymore than does—"

Ashley elbowed me in the ribs, cutting me off before I made more of a fool of myself.

"All kidding aside, Rambo," our co-anchor, Kimberly Kilmer, jumped in, "Size *does* matter to these guys. I interviewed with a news director this one time, and you know what he told *me*? He says, 'Honey, you're only gonna get so far in this business with them little chestnuts.' Yeah, I told him what he could do with his nuts."

Kimberly was on the young side for a prime anchor in a large market, twenty-six, maybe twenty-seven. On the air she poofed up her brunette mane in a riot of hairspray and dangled herself with gaudy jewelry that played havoc with the studio cameras. The viewers ate it up. She was a Memphis native and that counted for a lot. As did the fact she joined us for beers. Kimberly was one of the guys.

"The men who run this business are pigs, Tom. Always have been." Kimberly looked me square in the eye, my chagrin rising with her every word. "I've known it since my first job in radio, reading headlines off the wire. The DJ crew made it clear as day when they told me the only reason I was hired was so's they'd have a pretty piece of ass to look at every morning."

A blinding swoop of sequined polyester assaulted the stage, saving me from further embarrassment. The show was underway. The performer flexed his cape, motioned to the band, and plunged into a passable *Heartbreak Hotel*. Thus launched a bewildering sequence of pretenders, one in a tiger print jumpsuit, another in a Star Wars stormtrooper uniform, and one done up as a woman, who billed themselves as the Drag King.

"This is freakin' sad," Ronnie said.

Dilly shifted in his seat. "What do you mean?"

"The whole Elvis thing. It's pathetic."

"Right." Dilly squared up in his chair; these were fightin' words. "And your dude 'Wacko Jacko' is the second coming, I suppose?"

"First of all, Michael Jackson is not my dude, but if you're comparing—"

"He needs to decide what color he is, first."

Ronnie kicked back, his chair dragging the floor. At the screech of it, the singer on stage stopped cold, in the middle of *Burning Love*.

"Guys, calm down." I set an arm on Ronnie's shoulder. The last thing we needed was a bar fight. You could just see the write-up in the *Commercial Appeal* media column.

"Let's all agree," Bobby said, ever the musicologist, "without Presley there'd probably be no Michael Jackson. Or David Bowie. Or Madonna for that matter."

Presley. Danny. Whatever he wanted me to call him. It all rushed back. The Walker case, the mortifying session in the GM's office that afternoon. The beer buzz fizzled, the sour mood returned. I got up to take a leak.

Coming out tonight had been a mistake. In the men's room I made up my mind to go back to the table, gather Ashley, and head home. I was going to be no good for her or anyone else tonight.

My hands still wet from the sink, I pulled open the restroom door, not looking, not thinking how the men's and women's rooms stood close, side by side. A sudden bump—in hockey they would have called it a hip check—knocked me back, knocked me nearly back through the men's room door. This was no accident. This was a deliberate tackle.

She was stunning. An *older woman*, maybe thirty-five. Her champagne blonde hair, parted down the middle, swelled in thick feathered waves past her shoulders. Crisp, hip-hugging Sassons accentuated a pair of impossibly long legs.

Our eyes met.

"Hey, you." She poked me in the ribs, a needle-sharp fingernail digging a pinprick into my shirt. "You're drippin'. Let me help you with that." She took my wet hands, lifted them to her chest and zig-zagged them palm down, across the curves of her body. "There," she said. "Ain't that better?"

This was not the first come-on I'd had in a bar. It happened, especially following a few beers, or Jello shots, or both. But no one had ever dried my hands on their breasts. As I slipped free, I saw the gold band on her finger. The large diamond. *Married*.

"You're that guy from TV." She looked me down, then up. "You're even better lookin' in person, Tom Cirone." Her routine struck me dumb, as she leaned back on her heels, tucking in her lower lip and drilling her eyes into me. "My girlfriends and I been watching you over there at your table," she said. "You're the big man on campus, ain'tcha?" She let herself fall forward, sandwiching into me before she righted herself. Reflexively, I looked down.

"Oh." Her eyes followed mine. "Do you like these?" She fanned her hands across her chest.

"Do I *what*?" I finally found my voice.

"I said, do you like ... mah ... boobies?"

How many rounds had I had now, three—or was it four? *Where's the camera? Is someone filming this?* "Well, yes," I said. "Yes, they're very nice."

She repeated my words, "Yes, they're very nice," attempting, but failing, to replicate my flat, midwestern accent. "Tommy, I'm insulted."

"Okay," I said. This woman was playing with me. I could play, too. "They're *phenomenal*."

She smiled, a guileless smile that produced the tiniest of lines from the corners of her eyes and a crinkle on the bridge of her nose. "So, how 'bout you buy me a drink."

"Could be you've had a few already?"

"Now, that ain't very polite." She swayed on her heels again. I braced myself to catch her. Or was that part of the game?

"I'd be glad to get you a drink, but—" I gestured to my table.

"Uh-huh." She pivoted her head toward Ashley. "You with that pretty little thang?"

"That's right."

"Well, I tell you what. Once you get done with all that over there ..." She swirled a finger in circles. "... why don't you come on out to my house? I'll be headin' straight home. But I won't be headin' to bed. Not right away." She flipped back her hair, relishing the shock on my face.

I could feel my temperature rising. Rhetorically and physically, she was out of my league. *Barroom queen in Memphis*, indeed. "I'm flattered. I mean, you're very attractive, definitely very—" I inhaled deep, a musky wisp of patchouli injecting direct to my brain.

"Listen, gorgeous," she said. "My husband's gone. I mean *real gone*. He don't care what I do, if that's what you're frettin' about." She took out a slip of paper, jotted something down, and took my hand, closing it around the paper. "You *do* like my boobies, don't you?"

She sauntered off, joining a table of three or four other women. One of them smacked her arm. There were giggles all around. I got the impression they'd put her up to it. I tucked away the wad of paper.

When I got back to the table, Timothy practically flew out of his chair. "What was *that* all about, tiger man?"

"Just a viewer," I said.

"Uh huh. Some view." He stretched his body so far backwards he nearly toppled over. "She's hot. You should go for it."

I downed the dregs of my beer. Ashley shot me a look that said *let's go*. By the time we stood, my admirer and her friends had already left.

Ashley lived on the east side, in a part of Memphis called Audubon Park. We were nearly to her exit when she asked it.

"That woman in the bar tonight. Was she hitting on you?"

"C'mon Ashley, seriously."

When we got to her apartment, she invited me up. A no-brainer. She looked beautiful tonight, even if she *had* spent the entire evening downing mixed drinks. She'd been a good sport. I had to respect her ability to tolerate the Elvis show, the entire Vapors vibe, probably holding her nose the whole time. Still, I hesitated. My head was elsewhere. I walked her to the door, leaned in.

Ashley curled her lips. "You're just going to kiss me once, and that's it?"

"Okay, I'll kiss you twice." I moved in again but she pulled her mouth tight. Turning the key, she entered the apartment.

"Listen, it's late," I said. "Next time, okay?"

She shut the door without saying goodnight.

Back in the car I pulled the piece of paper from my pocket, flattened it on my leg, flipped on the overhead light. I squinted at the name. Absorbed it. *Meredith*. Underneath, in handsome cursive, a Germantown address. Nice suburb. I unfolded a map, slid my finger across until it landed on the street. Not knowing what I was doing, not thinking at all, I pressed down on the gas, steering the Honda toward the onramp for I-240, the way home to my place. But it also led—if you kept going—to Germantown.

It started to drizzle. I clicked on the wipers, popped in a Bruce Hornsby cassette, and told myself I could still turn off at my exit, everything was fine. *What's the worst that could happen*? Hubby bursts in, shoots you in the head? *But on the other hand* ...

Call it stupidity, call it circumstance, for weeks I'd failed the test of self-control. Fighting myself and losing. Fighting. Losing. Tonight, the fight was out of me. I *wanted* to lose myself. Tonight, I wanted to lose control.

The car continued on, past my exit.

A solitary post light marked the house. I coasted to a stop, cut the headlights, peered out the passenger window. Stroking several fingers through my hair, I stepped out of the car.

What if it's some sort of trap? I faltered at the front step. But then she opened the door. A black lace robe was all she had on, and it was barely on. Even in the dusky haze of the entryway I could see there was nothing underneath.

"Meredith, I presume?" I made a show of reading the name off the scrap of paper, mustering what voice control I could, calming my nerves as I did before a live shot. It belied the skip in my heartbeat, the blood pulsing in my neck, through my chest, through my everywhere.

She reached for my hand and in one fluid motion pulled me in, shut the door, turned the lock. She shuddered her shoulders and the robe fell to the floor. I was not mistaken about what was underneath. And it *was* phenomenal.

From that moment, all restraint abandoned me, as did my shirt, my pants. Her fingernails raked my hair, dug channels into my scalp. Droplets of perspiration snaked from my neck, across the curves and valleys of my back, chills boomeranging up and down my spine. She cradled my head in her hands, her baby blue eyes boring into mine, unyielding, unblinking.

She crushed her trembling lips against mine. Again and again, a spark, then a flame, the lips feeding the fire. She was an arsonist and I was her crime. Pushing off from the wall, Meredith reached for my hand and led me upstairs, in the dim glow of a solitary hallway lamp.

Flinging me to the bed, she took the lead. My head sank down, down, down into the mattress, my senses aroused with the musk of her sweat, the brush of her hair, the electricity of her fingertips. My mind flashed with the incongruous thought of our clothes in a co-mingled pile in the entryway. And then I could no longer think.

Neither of us had uttered a single word, not a syllable since I'd crossed the threshold. Only the tapping of the rain broke the quiet. That, and my fractured breath, rising and falling in time with the undulating rhythm of the golden goddess above me. If a climax can be put into words, and if those words were a prayer, I prayed them that night.

Older women. Oh. My. God.

An ecstatic cry, raging and feral, shattered the silence. Her eyelids flew open, snapped shut, flew open again. The full weight of her body collapsed onto me, into me. Her lips glanced my cheek, her breath caressing my ear as she sighed, "Lord have mercy, child, it's been a long time."

11

A MESS OF BLUES

Meredith. Her name fluttered and flapped on the front porch of my mind like a sensuous flag in the wind. I played the night back. We did it more than once. She'd wanted me to stay, but I thought better of that. Just before dawn, I drove home.

Making love like this was an escape. A surrender to emotions I struggled to express outside the bedroom. But it came with a catch. The women in my life equated intimacy under the sheets with passion of the heart. For me, those weren't always one and the same. That spelled trouble. But if it was wrong, I didn't care. Not this time. No apologies. Not to myself, not to anyone.

Susan assailed me Monday morning as I rounded the corner to my desk. "Don't sit down, we need you out the door!"

I staggered to a stop. "A little detail would be helpful."

"Press conference. Janelle's got the skinny. Charges against two MPD officers. She's already downtown. Now go!"

Maybe it was my empty stomach talking, but glowing in the morning light, the towering brown monolith of the 201 reminded me of a triple stack of French toast. Under the building's shadow, an array of microphones assailing him, the prosecutor laid out the indictment.

On the night of July thirtieth, Officer Carter Howard responded to the Walker house, followed by Sergeant Buckley Poole and Officer Floyd Landis. The three struck Carl Walker with nightsticks through the opening in his front door. As they burst in, Mr. Walker retrieved a rifle and fired one time. Despite Walker surrendering to officers in the house, the men continued to inflict blows as they brought the suspect out.

"Today we are charging Sergeant Poole and Officer Landis with reckless endangerment and failure to intervene," the prosecutor read from a statement. "As painful as this incident has been to our department and our community, the actions of these officers were unlawful and have to be viewed outside the scope of the tragic shooting."

At six, I wrapped up my story, tossing it back to the anchor desk with an aside that these new charges against the officers threw the case against Walker into question. I didn't want to believe that simply stating the obvious on the air could incite the wrath of our audience, but over the next several days the station switchboard erupted. Although Candy tried to screen the calls, a flurry of angry viewers rang through to my desk.

"Why are you defending a murdering piece of filth?" one caller raged. When I tried to respond, the phone went dead.

The line lit again. "How many times you been shot at in the line of duty, asshole?" Click.

That week saw rumors of an organized boycott of Channel 2, talk of protests outside the station. I began to question my role in stoking this. How could I suppose what somebody would or would not do in a life-or-death situation? But viewer phone calls were one thing. A newsroom turning on you, that was something else altogether.

"You must be loving it, Tom," Bubba quipped in the afternoon meeting. "You got the prosecutor to charge those cops."

"You're joking," I said. "They're not doing it because of a few stories on the news. And if anybody cares, I think you're gonna be surprised how this all turns out."

"Okay, Nostradumbass," Dilly said. "Enlighten us."

"For one thing, they're focusing on the wrong guys. What about the other shooter?"

Lee waved a dismissive hand. "Aw, hell, Tom. Quit pissin' and callin' it rain. Who said anything about another shooter?"

"The ballistics might—"

"There you go crusadin' again," Lee said. "Have you ever stopped to think why no one else in town is pushing these cockamamie theories?"

"Actually, I have."

Janelle, who'd sat silently following the debate, leaned forward. "Maybe Tom, it's because there's nothing to it."

"Or maybe," I blurted, "it's because every reporter in this town is in bed with the cops." The moment it came out of my mouth I knew it was a mistake. "Janelle, I'm sorry. I didn't mean—"

"If you ask me," Ronnie Patton cut in, "It's all about ego. The officer's ego and Walker's ego. Neither willing to back down. Now the city's gonna pay the price."

"You mean a lawsuit?" Susan said.

"Millions for a cop's ego."

"Rambo, would *you* get a cut?" Dilly crossed his arms and looked around the room.

Janelle locked me with a simmering glare. The others, with their smarmy sarcasm, their smug faces turned in my direction ... you might say it all hit my last nerve. "Okay, you know what?" I jumped to my feet, flinging my reporter's notebook to the conference table. "Fuck y'all."

Dilly rose, taking an aggressive step toward me, but Sheila Meeks, the ten o'clock producer, stood too, wedging herself between us. "Tom, it sure tickles me when you try to talk Southern," she said. "You're never gonna get it right, but points for effort."

I had to hand it to Sheila. She'd mustered exactly the right words.

A true pioneer as a black woman producing a large market newscast in the South, she was a smart, tough journalist. Plus, she hadn't lost her sense of humor, or humanity. "Now sit all y'all's asses down, people," she said, "and let's get back to the rundown."

The one person not in that meeting, the person who rarely made an appearance in any news meeting, was the main anchor, Lin Harper. The guy spent his hours in a glass office at the far end of the newsroom, feet on the desk, clipping his fingernails. He seemed content to mosey over to the assignment desk at five-thirty, peruse his copy, straighten the pages, and make sure he had as many, if not more, stories to read as Kimberly. Then he'd retreat to the makeup mirror.

But even in absentia, Lin was a topic of discussion thanks to extensive quotes the "dean of Memphis TV" had given to the *Commercial Appeal*. The article, about the state of local media in the Memphis market, featured our anchorman's thoughts on the so-called lack of aggressive news coverage here. "There isn't a whole lot to investigate," the paper quoted Lin. "It's not a wave-making town. It's not a rock-the-boat kind of town. Never has been."

Lin had this catch phrase he used, opening the broadcast the same way for years. *"Hello and welcome to all of you at home. Here now the news."* It was like an Ink Spots song. Same intro, every time, night after night after night. He always had a tan, the leathery kind. He was not an especially attractive man. His sneer reminded me of the Grinch. The Grinch who stole the newscast.

That afternoon I rapped on the door to Lin's office. I could smell the ribs even before he waved me in. A platter from Leonard's Pit Barbecue lay before him. On the wall behind his chair hung a large framed photograph of an aquatic bird soaring over a lake.

"Took that at a thousand yards," he said. "Long lens, three hundred millimeter."

"You're into photography?"

"A hobby. I like to shoot stuff. Sometimes I take the camera, sometimes the rifle. Sometimes both. Photo or trophy, you never know which you'll bring home. But you didn't come by to admire my pictures."

"I saw the piece in the paper today," I said. "Are you happy with how it came out?"

"I presume you aren't?"

"If you're asking me, not really."

"Go on," he said.

"Well, I was hired to do exactly what you're saying we *don't* want to do. I thought we *wanted* to make waves."

"What are you, Tom, twenty-nine, thirty?"

"Uh huh."

"Yeah, I remember those days. Rattle cages. Rock the boat. But you know what happens when you make waves? The boat starts swaying. The people in it, maybe they get seasick. Some fall out and drown. And then the boat capsizes. No boat, no people, and everybody's dead."

"I'm not looking to kill anybody," I said, "but I do wanna piss some people off, if that's what needs to happen."

Lin picked up a rib and bit into it, watching me sideways as he chewed. "I've got a grown son. From my first marriage. He's confused, same as you."

"I'm not confused."

"Aren't you?"

"Look, Lin, you can mock me if you want, but I think our job is to dig up what the bad guys out there are trying to bury."

"Out *there*?" He sucked the barbecue sauce from his fingers, popping each one with a chef's kiss. "You know what the people out there want? They want to come home from their crap jobs, set their asses down, crack open a beer, and watch *Dallas* or *Cheers*. Maybe *Cosby*, although I don't get the appeal of that one. And when the news comes on, you know what they wanna know? Is it gonna rain tomorrow. That's it. They don't want to hear the Soviets are fixin' to nuke us or that Reagan's gone senile. And they sure as hell don't want some high and mighty reporter from up north stirring up a bunch of shit."

"Lin, I guess there's nothing more to say."

"What do they call you in the newsroom? *Rambo*, or something? Well, Rambo, you ain't all that. I've been at this station twenty-some years. That's a dang career, my friend. When you have that, then you come on back and tell me what I can and cannot say in the goddamn newspaper."

My fists clenched. I wanted to grab that Leonard's barbecue and shove it down his throat one rib bone at a time. "I'll let you get back to your dinner." I got up to leave.

"Look kiddo, I didn't get this office by pissin' on folks. This thing you got goin' with the Walker case? You *are* pissing people off. Hell, you're pissing me off, too. So, a word to the wise. Cool it. You'll live longer."

"Thanks for that advice," I said. "I hope you won't mind if I don't take it."

He smiled. It was the smile of a mob boss. "Door's always open," he said, reaching for another rib. "Oh, and shut it on your way out, will ya?"

12

THE WONDER OF HER

Eddie shouldered the camera and we high-stepped through overgrown weeds to the backyard of the Walker house, half grass, half pavement, demarcated by a chain link fence. The idea was to shoot B-roll for an extended feature for the hyped-up weeks in October and November known as "sweeps"—the season when the news ratings services collected the TV viewing stats that station management would crow about or bitch about later.

Defense attorney Innis Honeycutt had suggested someone could have fired a shot from behind Carl Walker. What if we walked around the rear of the house to see for ourselves? It was technically trespassing, but a journalist did a lot of that.

Two cement steps led to the back entrance. Holding open the screen door with one hand, cupping my eyes with the other, I peered through the glass. A narrow kitchen. A Formica table to one side, big enough for four chairs. I could see clear past it, to the front of the house—to the bookshelf. The one Honeycutt had pointed out, with the bullet lodged in it.

"Get a shot through the door, Eddie," I said. "Maybe start wide, then zoom in."

He'd barely started recording, when, with a rustling of gravel underfoot, a silver-haired woman approached from the adjoining property, chasing behind a toddler. She came up to the back fence and set a hand on her hip.

"Y'all reporting on that stuff went down?"

"Yes, ma'am," I said. Eddie lowered his camera and joined me at the fence.

"What all you been putting on the TV," she said, "they's talkin' like it was all started over some mangy mutt."

"Wasn't it?"

"Dogs been loose around here before," she said. "Cops don't need that for an excuse. They'll hassle you for breathin'."

She stopped, seeing Eddie had brought the camera back to his shoulder. "Don't you be stickin' that thing in my face." She looked down at the young boy. "Malcolm, we're gonna be on television."

"What's your name, ma'am?" I asked.

"Francine Boyer. They call me Franny."

She ran a hand through her hair and tugged on her shirt. "Wish my son was home to see this," she said. "He's always been interested in TV. Loves to putter around with VCRs and whatnot. This here's his boy. I watch him during the day."

"So, Franny ..." I extended the microphone across the fence. "You say it wasn't about the dog?"

"Carl had got up somebody's nose, is how I see it."

"What makes you say that?"

She hefted the boy into her arms, with a grunt. "I think I said enough."

I motioned for Eddie to return to shooting B-roll. I pulled out my notebook. "Franny, you say Carl Walker had it coming?"

"I wouldn't put it quite as you say." She looked past my shoulder. "But ain't you find it peculiar, all this stuff in the news, and not a peep outta *her*?" She nodded toward the house.

"Her?"

"She probably behind *all* of it."

"Mrs. Walker?" In the notebook I jotted, *Walker's mother*.

"Not the mama. The wife. Ask her about what *she* done to bring this on. Her and that cop used to come a callin'. White fella. He was here that day."

I scratched out *mother* and wrote, *wife?* Also, *white cop.*

"Ma'am, did you see anything from back here?"

"Nobody ask me, but that cop done broke bad. That's all I got to say."

The switchboard lit up again that first week of October. But it wasn't another round of verbal abuse. These new calls were genial, if no less persistent. Candy said she didn't know what to make of it.

"Who's the new lady friend, Tom?" she asked me. "Why all the mystery?"

The callers' ruses were imaginative, if transparent. A "councilwoman from Covington" had "a vitally important civic matter to discuss with that good-lookin' guy on the news, Tom somethin' or other." Another needed Mr. Cirone to come on down to Olive Branch right away and settle a bet "about whether he's as tall as he looks on the TV."

So, I took the call from the councilwoman. And the lady from Olive Branch. One and the same, they had a single request: to see me again.

"Is that so wrong?" Meredith asked.

"It's not wrong exactly," I said. "Well, maybe it *is* wrong."

If circumstances had been different, if she wasn't married, I might have admitted I couldn't stop obsessing about her these past weeks. Instead, I said, "What are you doing tonight?"

We took in the eight o'clock movie, *Dirty Dancing*. Held hands, necked, shared a bucket of popcorn. She giggled. I blushed. We got takeout from Dixie Queen, brought it back to my place. My place being a one-bedroom unit in a vinyl-sided complex in southeast Memphis. A luxury apartment by no means, but the best I could manage on a measly reporter's salary.

I'd barely opened the door when Meredith squealed. "Wait, who *is* this adorable little fella?" No longer scrawny nor squirrelly, the kitten pounced onto Meredith's powder blue Chuck Taylors the second she stepped inside. She swept up the kitten in her hands and brought him to her face. "What's his name?"

Name. *I'd never given him a name.* "I didn't ... I haven't ..."

"Jeez, Tommy, how long have you had him? A baby's gotta have a name." She extended the kitten in front of her, studying his features. "He looks a little like ... well what a hoot. It's Elvis! I mean, if Elvis was a little kitty. Don't you see it? Crooked lip, black sideburns?"

Catburns, I'd called them when I first found him. "Elvis it is, then," I said.

Meredith lifted the kitten over her head, peeking behind the tail. "Uh, time out. Maybe not. I hate to break it to ya, but I do believe Mr. Elvis is a she."

"Well, that won't do." I scratched the back of my head. "How about ... um ... now what's his wife, or, ex-wife's name again?"

"You mean, Priscilla?"

"Yeah, that's it!"

"Priscilla. I love it!" Meredith ran the kitten's whiskers against her cheek. "Miss Priss. We can raise her together. Our beautiful daughter."

"You are *crazy*."

"No crazier than someone who has a pet and never names 'em."

Miss Priss leaped from Meredith's hands, onto a side table. The kitten zoomed into a small display arranged there, crashing down a stack of cubes.

"Hey, what's this all about?" Meredith said, picking up one of the objects, its four sides bearing a garish number, its top cut through with a cylindrical hole.

"That's my mic flag collection. Petty larceny from places I've worked." I took the cube from her hand, set it back in its place. "These are the logo holders they put on the microphones for the news. A parting gift, to myself. When I leave a station."

"And will you be taking one from Channel 2 soon?"

"Meredith."

"What? It's a normal question," she said.

"Look, I doubt I'm going anywhere. But some days I do just want to get the hell out."

"Why?"

"It's complicated." I ran my hands across the smooth surfaces of the cubes, each one a totem infused with stinging memories. There was a Channel 9, a Channel 11, and a Channel 28. I lifted the one for Channel 4, from my first job, a station in upstate New York where the talent level, mine and everyone else's, was barely above college TV.

Meredith examined the mic flags, held them one by one, trying to understand the world of broadcast news and its vagabond lifestyle. "Can you be persuaded to stay here in Memphis?"

"You're married," I said.

"For the moment."

"What's that supposed to mean?"

"It means I'm mad about you."

"Wow. Okay." I set down the Channel 4 mic flag and gestured to the small sofa, an overstuffed tan Broyhill, the single piece of adult furniture in the apartment.

"Tom," she said, settling in next to me, "I know this is messed up and ... and ... I don't blame you if you think I'm a terrible adulterin' person."

Tears puddled her eyes. Her head fell to my shoulder and her body shook. I ran my hands through her hair, kissed the top of her head.

"Listen, we've seen each other exactly twice," I said. "The first time was, well, mind-blowing." That made her giggle through the sobs. "And going to the movies with you tonight was astonishingly normal. But—"

"But I'm married," she said. "I get it."

"And all the more reason to tap the brakes a little here." It might have been the most grown-up thought I'd ever spoken out loud.

The clothes would stay on tonight.

Meredith collected her things from the front seat, pausing before getting out of the car. "Tom, I need you to know something. The girl that came on to you that way at Vapors, it ain't who I am."

"You mean, 'boobies' and all that?"

"God's honest truth. I never used the word before in my life."

Mah lahf. Warm melodic notes of magnolia. Her voice exuded it. When we met, I was too buzzed to hear it, too infatuated to see it. Tonight, it was all I *could* hear, *could* see. She was southern as sweet tea. Downhome as biscuits and gravy, chicken pot pie, and red velvet cake.

Meredith leaned across the seat and planted a good-night kiss, soft bales of cotton against my lips. I'd fantasized about our first torrid night together. Fantasized every day since. But I now had something equally compelling to obsess over. The wonder of her, of *us* together. I'd known her barely a few weeks, but already she tugged at my heart.

Through the windshield I caught the glow of a lamp in the front room of her house, a shadow moving behind the curtains. Meredith followed my eyes. "I must have left the hall light on," she said, too quickly.

"Are you okay going in?"

"I'm fine."

She was fine. I wasn't. So, there it was already. A fantasy crashing to the ground. Jealousy, confusion, whatever you wanted to call it. And I had no right to feel any of it.

13

EDGE OF REALITY

Just after eleven, I rolled out of Meredith's Germantown neighborhood, my head flooded with the futility of whatever I thought I had with her and the delusional notion of ever putting down roots in Memphis.

Bypassing the road home, I drove west toward the city. In the trunk of the car were several blank video cassettes. I had a mind to return to the station and convert them into resume tapes. Here less than a year, and I'd already overstayed my welcome at Channel 2. I'd blown it with Valerie. That much was already established. I could never forgive myself for that day and she'd never forgive me, either. Now Meredith. Yet another path to perdition.

The downtown exit was nearly upon me when I realized the headlights in the rear-view mirror hadn't left my tail for miles. Two glistening, scanning eyes, changing lanes when I changed lanes, slowing when I slowed. Rather than continue on to a deserted TV station, I proceeded north on Riverside Drive, steering toward a neighborhood where I knew there'd be people around at this hour.

Beale Street.

At one time a bustling nexus of music and culture, the street was a shadow of its old self, a few clubs clinging to life amid blocks of crumbling facades—which would have collapsed in a pile of bricks had they not been held in precarious stasis by iron scaffolding.

A blue light flashed from the car behind me. *A cop!* At Second and Beale I pulled the Honda to the curb and looked to my left as the vehicle approached, its tires crackling over the pavement like Rice Krispies. A black sedan, its iridescent finish reflecting the glow of the street's neon, rolled to a stop parallel to my car. Its window descended into the frame. Danny Fisher leaned across the front seats.

"Hello, Thomas. Whaddya know?"

I lowered my window and surveyed Danny's ride. Its seats were upholstered in red and black leather. A console between them sported a thick-handled revolver, an intricate piece inlaid with gold and silver. Mounted in the floor, a car phone, and you didn't see that every day. Affixed to the dash, a police scanner, red lights flickering and squawking with radio traffic.

"What *is* this car?" I said.

"This here is a Stutz Blackhawk, son. Dontcha know nothin'? Lock up that Tokyo-mobile of yours and get in."

From somewhere a harmonica howled, and a mean, *"How many more years ..."* As the pulsating blues ping-ponged the four corners of the intersection, the bass notes punched through the thick night air, music made visible in the juddering windowpanes lining the clubs. A gaggle of pub-crawlers exploded in laughter across the street, but no one looked our way.

"Were you tailing me?" I said.

"Well, let's just say the car I was followin' happened to have *you* in it." Danny reached across the dashboard and clicked off the police light. "Now get on in. I ain't gonna bite your ass."

"I thought you were a cop."

"And you wasn't wrong." He rolled forward and pulled in front of me.

I locked my car and stepped into the Stutz. "Where's Travis?"

"Lizard? He's workin' his day job tonight."

᠅

He bit his lip as he drove, his limbs in perpetual motion, his fingers rapping a drumbeat on the wheel. He shifted his shoulders, pedaled his leg, giving the impression of someone late for an appointment—or desperately holding it in.

"Your date dump ya?" he said.

"Not exactly."

"What's her name, then?"

The lights of Beale danced off the hood of the car, a kaleidoscope of greens, reds, and blues not unlike the psychedelic trip through the monolith in *2001*.

"Meredith," I whispered.

"Speak up, Thomas, what did you say?"

"Her name is Meredith."

"Meredith. Sexy name. Is it serious?"

"Well, to be honest ..." This was turning into an interview. I hated being interviewed. "How come this sudden interest in my love life?"

"I'm just sayin', maybe you oughta try thinkin' above your waist."

"Excuse me?"

"You know, Thomas, folks assume I musta banged like a thousand girls in my day. Truth be told, not even close."

"Wow, I would've thought—"

"*You* need to try using your head." Danny tapped a finger against my skull. "The one up here, not down there. There's more to life, you know. A woman is so much more than that. Don't you make the same mistakes I did." He lowered his hand back to the wheel. "Blonde?"

"What?"

"She's blonde, ain't she?" The Stutz steered onto Fourth Street. "And married?"

"Why do you ask?"

"Is she?"

"As a matter of fact, yes," I said. "That's the problem."

"Problem. A good word, Thomas Aquinas. You seem to like problems. Are you looking for trouble?"

"No. Things just ... happened."

"You mean, y'all ate supper before you said grace."

"Well, when you put it that way ..." I took a hard swallow.

"Like I always say, everyone's entitled to one stupid-ass move, son." He cast an eye into the rear-view and flicked the turn signal at the next corner.

Danny drove on through the ill-lit streets of south Memphis in distracted concentration, his hands focused on the mechanics of the car, but his eyes staring off, again and again, into the night sky. When he slowed at a traffic light, I swiveled to face him.

"Ever heard of the blue wall?"

He pulled to a stop, inspecting himself in the mirror. "Blue wall? That's what they used to call the mess of cops standin' between me and those crazy girls bent on tearin' me up. Man, all I had to do was burp and they'd scream."

"No, I mean—"

"You got them police on your mind."

I nodded. "You drive around a lot. But not always alone."

"Where you goin' with this?" he said.

"You were there. At the Walker place. You were the guy in that unmarked car."

Danny turned onto Linden, west toward the river. He was navigating a large circuit. In a few blocks it would bring us back to Beale and my car.

"Thomas, I got a lot of time on my hands. Sometimes I fly out to the coast. See my kid. Mostly, I'm here in town, so I ride along with the PD. Nights, mostly. Keeps me from sleepwalkin' around the house, anyways."

"They have pills for that," I said, and instantly regretted it. I knew better than to make a crack about drugs. I uttered a simple, "Sorry."

"Pills'll kill you. Smart kid such as yourself oughta know that."

For several minutes he drove without speaking. I was sure I'd insulted him. Finally, he put a fist to his mouth, cleared his throat. "I tried to get a meetin' with President Reagan this one time. Wanted to tell him about my DEA drug enforcement credentials. His people listened real polite, with all sorts of, 'Mr. Presley we sure thank you for reaching out,' and this and that. And then you know what they said? They just said, 'no.'"

I suppressed a laugh as we rounded the turn to Front Street.

Danny side-eyed me. "Yeah, I was at Central Precinct that afternoon in July. Call for backup comes in. This lieutenant, he hears the street address and takes a special interest in it. Asks me to come along. The boy's a bit of a rooster. I suppose he thought it was a chance to show off."

"I saw you there," I said. "You witnessed it."

"And you. Hard to miss. Let's just say your white ass was conspicuous in that crowd."

"This lieutenant, what did he do at the scene?"

"Well, he went around back. Took his rifle with him," Danny said.

"And ...?

"And, what?"

Turning in my seat again to face Danny, I said, "I think maybe you know more than you're saying."

"You calling me a liar?"

"No, I just—"

His foot crushed the brake pedal. The sudden stop flung me into the dash. I looked up to a palm in my face and the click of an automatic mechanism, unlocking the doors.

"Get out. Get your ass the fuck outta my car!"

"Danny—"

He reached for his revolver and cocked it. I pulled on the door handle and tumbled hard into the gutter, my head connecting with the curb.

14

I FORGOT TO REMEMBER TO FORGET

Snow falling. Wipers wiping. Twins up front with Mom. A rush of air, a sharp cry. We're gone. He's gone.

The rattle and rumble of trash trucks in the alley behind Beale jolted me back to consciousness. Still dark, but the purple glow in the eastern sky said it was near morning.

Not my first time laid flat in the street. That would have been twenty-five years ago, in Chicago, as the story was told, when my twin brother and I somersaulted to the frozen asphalt of the Dan Ryan Expressway.

From that day on, even as a kid, the idea of predestiny took hold in me. No changing the past. No changing the future. No shifting the blame, either. I was the one who survived. Okay. Maybe I would again. So, I took risks. With my life, my career, my relationships. When the outcome's already been written, what did it matter?

For years, I'd been all too willing to put the past behind me, were it not for those execrable flashes of violence. Head to the pavement. Guaranteed to bring it all rushing back.

Timothy cornered me in the edit bays that afternoon. He said there'd be live music at the Peabody Hotel tonight, as good a time as any to kick off "sweeps" with the team. My head still pounded from its overnight appointment with the street. I was in the middle of finishing a script, Dilly was waiting to edit the story. It was crunch time.

"What do you think, Tom? You in? You can bring that girl you stole from me."

"Dude, I'm on deadline. Can I get back to my desk, please?"

The weather guys always had time on their hands. What did Timothy do all day, anyway? The job basically involved ripping the forecast from the weather wire, scribbling on some maps, and ad-libbing in front of a green screen for two or three minutes. But Lin Harper had been right. It was all anybody tuned in to see.

The weatherman himself was nothing if not tenacious. Timothy would keep talking to you after you'd insisted you had to go. He'd keep talking to your back after you'd said goodbye and left the room. He was doing it now.

"Okay, okay," I said over my shoulder. "I'll see you tonight."

The hotel anchored a full city block downtown at Second and Union. Its mammoth neon sign announced *The Peabody* for miles in every direction. The summer parties on the rooftop beneath that sign were legendary, with glorious sunset views of the skyline, the Mississippi River, and the flatlands of Arkansas beyond. The roof was also where the ducks slept.

That night, the famous Peabody ducks were tucked in bed, their day shift swimming in the lobby fountain long over. The hotel liked to say the Mississippi Delta began there. It certainly was a fact a lot of liquid flowed in the opulent lobby bar.

I invited Ashley to join us after she got off work at the hospital. Most of the crew would come direct from the station after the ten o'clock news. I'd already taken my first sip when our sportscaster walked in. He summoned the bartender and ordered a Miller. I waited for him to lift his drink before I broached the subject.

"Bobby, do you remember that intern last summer? The one with the red hair? We were seeing each other. Kept it kinda quiet."

"Positive about that?" he said, arching an eyebrow.

"Did the whole damn station know?"

"Man, it's a little frickin' hard to hide that shit in a newsroom, and y'all didn't try very hard either."

I gulped a mouthful of beer. "Lee and Ransom confronted me about it the other day."

"Hell, she's not even at the station anymore."

"That's just it," I said. "Valerie left because ... well, I did a bad thing. And they wanted me to know that *they* know."

"So you slept with an intern. I'm not sayin' you showed great judgment there, but it happens. Learn from it. And move on."

We sat with that for a long moment. I wanted to tell him more, finally unburden myself. But the opportunity vanished. Timothy had arrived, and behind him, the rest of the gang. A few minutes later, Ashley walked in, still in scrubs. She bypassed our table and went straight for the bar, joining us with drink in hand.

As the house band tuned up, Kimberly launched into a story about her co-anchor, the time Lin had to read a story about this new rock group he called, "In Excess." When Kimberly corrected him on the air, spelling it out, saying it was actually *I-N-X-S*, he'd gone red in the face.

Everyone at the table laughed so hard, no one noticed the synthesizer and saxophone kicking in and the first slide guitar notes echoing from the amp. At the staccato burst of drums and the start of the vocals we all looked up from our beers.

"Is that who I think it is?" Kimberly squinted, trying to place the voice and the face. The singer's hair was wavy, blondish, brushed back and extending below the collar. A long, red coat covered a plain black t-shirt.

"That's freakin' Steve Winwood!" Bobby shouted.

The song was *Freedom Overspill*, a recent hit, with its punchy brass notes and urgent lyrics, words of wounded pride, staying up late, and pouring out one's guts—all of which spoke to me tonight.

"This is unbelievable!" I shouted over the music. But according to Bobby, it happened in Memphis all the time. Musicians came here to reclaim their mojo, find their soul.

Winwood leaned into the microphone. "I want to do another one for you," he said in a reedy English accent. "You may remember it. We're about to put it out again in a remix single." He began fingering the massive synthesizer. The thing was tiered, with four stacked rows of keys. He'd gotten only a few bars into the lyrics when I lost my breath.

Why did it have to be this one?

He sang of a girl who'd touched him deeply, like jazz on a sweltering day, only to blow away on the wind. The record had been all over the radio a few years back.

Valerie. You know, like the song.

Valerie was gone, Winwood sang. Valerie was *gone*. I dragged the back of my hand across my eyes. The room started to spin.

Ashley tugged my sleeve. "Tom? Are you all right?" She looked at me sideways and returned to her drink.

Winwood beseeched Valerie now, begged her. Please, please, call on him. As the drums pounded, Winwood finished with a cry, a declaration: He was the same boy he used to be. The music stopped, the set was over. Winwood moved to the bar.

The song may have ended, but it played on in my ears. It was a scene tailor-made for a tactless comment and Timothy did not disappoint. "'Valerie,'" he said, his voice booming across the table. "Great song, Tom. Go figure."

Ashley wanted me to follow her home and I had no objections. I didn't want to be alone tonight and she wouldn't need to settle for two pecks on the lips this time.

At her apartment she brought out a bottle, some of the wine spilling over my hand as she poured. She teetered forward and kissed me. Her hair drifted across my face. I ran my hands down Ashley's back, pulled her close, and then let my chin slide to her shoulder.

"Tom? Don't you want to?"

"I think so. I mean, yeah." I closed my eyes, saw Meredith *standing, bare-skinned, robe crumbled at her feet*. "Of course," I said.

Ashley refilled her glass and led me to the bedroom. She turned down the lights, then crossing her arms, she pulled off her top from the bottom up. Her scrub pants dropped to the floor. She lay herself flat on the mattress, arms at her sides, unmoving.

I stood, flummoxed, at the side of the bed. "Ashley, have you *done* this before?"

"Don't be insulting."

"You're drunk."

"I am *not*." She slapped a condom in my hand. "Now get over here and stick it in me already." She slithered farther down, waiting.

As I joined Ashley, the *Valerie* song rang in my ears. Meredith's face floated in my mind's eye. And that's the vision I chased. Meredith. The tips of her fingers, the taste of her lips. It was the only way I could complete the exercise.

15

SUSPICION

Eddie bounded into the newsroom at five-thirty, huffing as if he'd just run a marathon.

"Tom, I can't find it."

"You can't find the shots? Check the timecode."

"No, the tape itself," he said. "The original tape from the scene."

"It's missing?"

"Been doing this a long while, man. Never misplaced a tape or a reel of film."

Eddie had spent the afternoon editing our "sweeps" piece on the Walker case. I'd asked him to fold in a new development to the story. In mid-October, one of the accused Memphis officers, patrolman Landis, had copped to a guilty plea. It meant a reduced charge and a light sentence.

But to do the story justice we needed the missing video, the original tape of that bloody incident on Underwood Avenue. It was essential. Irreplaceable. I rolled my chair, stood, then cleared my throat and prepared to make an ass of myself.

"Everybody! Listen up!"

On a typical day in the minutes leading up to six o'clock, the newsroom was a raucous hive with the crazy-meter dialed up to eleven. But a well-placed outburst could slice through the din, the squeals and squawks of the police scanners, the whine of the dot matrix printer.

"There is a Beta tape missing from editing!" I shouted. "A very important shooting tape from Eddie's camera." A dozen blank faces stared back.

"Tom, can this wait?" Bubba said from behind stacks of scripts collated for the anchors. "We're getting ready for the show."

Show. Everyone insisted on calling what we did a show. We weren't putting on a show. This wasn't the Ringling Fucking Brothers Circus. It was like calling the *Commercial Appeal* a comic book. They put out a newspaper and we produced a newscast. That's what it was, and that's what I called it.

"No, dammit, it can't wait," I hollered back. "It's the only video we have of the crime scene. Maybe y'all think this is a funny prank. But it's not, and I want it the hell back in Eddie's cubby."

Eddie squeezed my shoulder, his voice muted. "Tom, I'll keep looking. I didn't say someone took it. Just that it's gone."

I closed my eyes, exhaled. I'd last seen the tape several weeks ago, when I asked Janelle to identify a freeze frame of that cop at the scene. A minute later I'd been summoned to the general manager's office to get chewed out, flagellated, and shamed. Had I left the tape in the machine? I couldn't remember.

Chastened, I addressed the newsroom again. "Guys, sorry. It's an important tape. If you see it, let me or Eddie know."

Bubba started slow clapping. "Rambo is *back*!"

"Yeah, he never left," I muttered.

It had been weeks since I'd glimpsed those shadows behind the curtains at Meredith's house. Weeks since I allowed myself to think of her as anything other than someone else's wife. But now I stood at her doorstep, with a well-founded trepidation.

Meredith had invited me for dinner, assured me it was safe, and

I wanted to believe her. This time, at least, I saw no evidence of her ex lurking around the house. Still, I couldn't help looking over my shoulder as I tiptoed inside. She settled us together on the sofa and got around to the one thing she'd been preoccupied with since our last date.

"Those dang microphone thingies."

"The mic flags in my apartment?" I laughed.

"And how you're always fixin' to hit the road."

"Sometimes these TV jobs don't work out."

Her face darkened. "Well, I don't know what's so funny about it. And I don't know what you're running from, neither. But maybe it's time to stop."

Grabbing my shirt by the collar, she pulled me toward her. Before it was done, I knew the first night we'd had was no one-hit-wonder.

Her hair tumbled across her eyes, the morning rays highlighting her waves in streaks of gold. *Still asleep*. I slid back the covers, pulled on my boxers, and stepped to the cold floor. My first time here had been brief, impulsive. This was neither of those. But another man lived or had lived here. I was in *his* house, waking up with *his* wife.

A rolltop desk filled a corner of the bedroom. FOR SALE flyers lay atop it in a neat pile. Seems Meredith was a realtor. I stepped closer to investigate. Next to the flyers, a renewal form for a Tennessee driver's license. A name stood out on both: *Meredith A. Ryder*. I scanned the state document. The date of birth, *August 3, 1954*. A Leo, and not so much of an older woman after all. Thirty-three. The question of age hadn't come up in conversation. Neither had an occupation, a last name, a zodiac sign. I pushed the papers back in place. Meredith was stirring.

"Tommy?" Her voice, slurry with sleep, called across the room. Her hand patted the nightstand, reaching for a pair of tortoise shell eyeglasses. She looked adorable in them. I hadn't realized she wore contacts.

"Good morning, beautiful," I said.

A flat, round plastic container rested near her eyeglass case. I walked over to it. "I was just noticing these. Are you ... I mean, are you taking ...?"

"Them pretty little pills? Never had much call for it before. They're nearly expired, but yes. Something tells me I'm gonna need more." She kissed her finger and put it to my lips. "Let me ask the same of you, lover boy. Have you been safe?"

I nodded. But had I? It always felt like Russian roulette. With Valerie I'd gone without a condom one time. That's all it took. One shot. One bullet in the chamber.

Meredith fixed fried chicken for supper. The way her daddy used to cook it, she said, with real buttermilk and peanut oil. Her mother lived out in Somerville, east of Memphis, she told me, but her father had passed away a few years back.

"Daddy didn't have much use for Yankees, bless his heart," she said. "But he surely would've made an exception for you."

We ate in silence. I enjoyed watching her. It didn't matter if she was talking or laughing or chewing gum. She may have sold houses for a living, but Meredith already occupied real estate in my head. Something about her unlocked me. Between her brash, country airs, and my Yankee ways, we understood each other. A perfect match. If not for one thing.

I set down my fork. "Meredith, this house. Me being here. I mean, what about ...?"

"Hubby?" She reached for a napkin. She had an adorable habit of covering her mouth while she chewed.

"Yes. Does he still live here?" The furnishings, what I'd seen of them, were a collection of tasteful, if austere, early American. The style touches here and there, exclusively feminine. "Where's his stuff?"

"All put up. Boxed up," she said. "What he didn't already haul away when he slunk on out." Her eyes flicked toward the front door. Was Meredith expecting him to bust in at any moment?

"But you're still married."

"In name only."

"And kids?"

"No kids," she said. "Not even close."

"Go on."

"You don't need to hear none of this. It's ain't pretty."

I reached for her hand. "I just think you deserve better."

"And if things were ..." Her eyes met mine. "In a heartbeat, Tommy. If things were different, I'd be with *you* in a heartbeat."

The naked honesty of it rocked me. To express such feelings without hesitation. What did this woman see in me? What did she feel in her beating heart that I couldn't feel in my own?

Meredith pushed her plate away, sighed. "If you want to know, the whole thing with him was a farce. I liked his folks well enough, and marrying into that was exciting in a way. But it was all for show."

"For show? You mean he's—"

"No, he's not ... Jesus, no. He's just ..." Her face flushed. "He's a nice-lookin' fella, well-off family, good job, all that crap."

"Then what?" It was too easy for me to slip into *60 Minutes* mode. She felt cornered, I could see it in her eyes.

"What I'm trying to tell you is, he's not into me. He goes for girls of a ..." She paused, considering her words. "Different complexion, I guess you'd say."

"He left you for someone. A black woman."

"Don't get me wrong, I got nothing against blacks and whites datin'. Except he was supposed to be *married* to me. First, it was some school teacher. Now I hear he's shacked up with a girl he knows from work."

At the mention of work, my curiosity got the best of me. "Where's work? If you don't mind me asking."

Meredith reached across the table. "Did you want more biscuits?"

"Thanks," I plucked one out of the bowl. "So, where did you say he works?"

"Uh, the city." She rose from the table. "I'm gonna reheat this mac and cheese. It's gone stone cold."

"The city," I said. "I know folks downtown. Do you think I know him?"

"No, Tommy, you don't. And can we drop it now, mister reporter?"

When we'd finished dinner, Meredith excused herself, and I carried the dishes into the kitchen. A small hallway connected the kitchen and dining room. As I passed through a second time, something caught my eye. The edge of a long, black zip-up case set atop a row of built-in shelves near the ceiling. I had a feeling whatever was in it didn't belong to Meredith.

"Whatcha lookin' at?"

I spun around. A nightgown had replaced the sweater and jeans. It flowed behind her like a red silk train.

"You, of course," I said. "You look delicious."

"Well, come upstairs, tiger, and have a bite."

We only made it halfway to the landing before an electronic ringing echoed through the house. The cordless phone. Meredith said she had her answering machine off, and the phone would just keep ringing if she didn't grab it. She told me to go on up.

I sat on the bed, fidgeting with my top button when Meredith appeared in the doorway holding the phone. She had the look of someone puzzling over an impossible riddle. "It's for you ... *Thomas*."

"Me?" It made no sense.

She gave me a long look, holding her hand over the receiver. "Who did you give this number to?"

"No one."

She raised the phone in my direction, and yanked it back, with a questioning turn of her head. I took the handset, hesitating, my eyes fixed on Meredith's.

He didn't bother with a greeting. After my hello, he hollered, "Can you believe this shit?"

"Danny? What the—?"

"A bald starship captain? Thomas, the guy has a French name, a British accent and he's bald. Don't tell me by the twenty-fourth century they haven't cured baldness!"

"Danny, are you really calling here to talk about the new *Star Trek* show?"

There was a pause and I could hear him breathing on the other end. "The dude is onto you," he said.

"What dude?"

"Questionin' neighbors. Interviewin' lawyers. You've stirred the pot bigtime. I had a hunch the other night. I know so now."

"Wait, this isn't even my phone. How did you get this—?"

"Son, you need to stop flapping your lip and listen."

I shut up and listened, as Meredith glared, arms crossed, at the other end of the bed. I'd have to explain to her that Danny was a source on a news story. At least that was no lie. But how he got her number? No idea. Clearly, this wasn't going to be an apology for kicking me out of his car. Or, maybe the call *was* the apology.

"You go and take a close look at that guy I told you about," he said. "You prove what he done, and you might could have yourself a story. And maybe rid yourself of a couple of problems."

"Danny, I *have* looked."

"Thomas, my grandma, ol' Dodger, rest her soul, she had a sayin'. Never made much sense to me at the time. She'd say, 'A guilty fox hunts its own hole.'"

"Can I ask—"

"Listen, I'm goin' away. Won't be back for a spell. If things don't go so good … well, I might not be back at all." There followed a long wheeze and a cough. "I done stuck my neck out telling you this much. Now, you go and do what you have to do."

The line clicked.

Meredith threw back her hair and swiped the phone from my hand. "Now, who in the Christ is Danny, and why is he calling *my* house and askin' for y'all?"

16

GONE, GONE, GONE

In the last week of the TV ratings period, they finally aired the "investigation" into the Carl Walker case. Wasn't much of an investigation, and since Eddie's tape hadn't materialized, we had little video to support it with. As I watched the story that night I had a sobering thought. Maybe the missing tape wasn't a prank.

She was dating a cop, sure, but still, I doubted Janelle could have anything to do with it, even when she swung around to my desk after the "sweeps" story aired. Even after she told me she needed to share something with me and asked if we could find some time to talk about it tomorrow. That worked for me. She and I were set to co-anchor together, filling in for Lin and Kimberly over Thanksgiving.

Only problem, Janelle didn't show up Thanksgiving Day. Or the day after.

So I rode the anchor desk solo, joining the crew for the obligatory turkey and fixins plates provided by the station—spending much of the time thinking about Meredith. What was she doing while I was eating microwaved food at my desk in the newsroom?

I didn't have to wonder for long.

Saturday afternoon I answered a knock at my apartment door and there was Meredith, sporting a tan leather jacket, sunglasses on her head, and a string of keys in her hand.

"Tommy, I got a wild hair." That was the entire pitch.

Parked at the bottom of the stairs, a blue and white Ford Bronco, its front end dominated by a wide chrome grill. The vehicle suited her. Smart, sexy, unpredictable.

"What do you say?" She tossed the keychain.

"What's this?" I fumbled the catch, the keys slipping through my fingers.

"You drive," she said.

"Seriously?"

"I like my man to drive."

"I'm your man, now?"

"Why not?" It was as much a challenge as a question. I could think of several reasons why not, but kept them to myself. "Where are we going?" I broke out laughing, bending for the keys. "Can I get dressed first?"

In a perfect world I could tell Meredith the truth about Danny, even fill her in about the night Steve Winwood sang *Valerie* in this very spot, but this world wasn't perfect. Instead, I shut it all out of my mind as we sat with our drinks at the Peabody lobby bar. We'd turned our chairs to face the fountain, its marble lion heads spouting water from their mouths. The ducks flapped and floated in circles, no doubt anticipating their upcoming performance.

"Where *did* you come from, Tom Cirone?" Meredith tilted her head to my shoulder.

"I came from the men's room. And then you dragged my hands across your chest like a paper towel rack, remember?"

"Tommy, hush up, there's people around!" She slapped the back of my hand. "Truth be told, maybe I wasn't caring too much how I acted that night. I'd just gotten some ugly news. I was just ate up with it. Thought a few drinks might make it go away. Them girls I was with caught me spyin' you at your table. So when I pounced on ya it was partly just to scandalize 'em. And they were scandalized, all right. But it wasn't *only* that." She stuck a finger in her glass, stirred the ice. "Obviously."

"But how were you so sure I'd show up at your house like I did?"

"For starters, the way you looked at me. Your eyes about swallowed me whole. A girl just knows." Meredith nodded toward the bank of elevators off to the right. "Hey, ever been to the rooftop?"

"Is it nice up there?"

"The sunsets are to die for. Come on."

We were so wrapped around each other we'd been blind to the crowds lining a red carpet leading from the fountain. A nightly ritual was underway, the march of the ducks back to their palace on the roof. We grabbed our drinks, shouldered between the tourists, and slipped into an open elevator. The doors closed and we were alone. Alone except for five mallards and one wide-eyed gentleman in a bright red blazer. *The Duckmaster.*

I fell against the wall of the elevator, clutching the railing. "It's a flock of ducks!"

"Actually, not a flock," the red-blazered man said. "And you're not supposed to be in here." The indicator began to rise through a dozen floors on its way to the top. "But since y'all are," he said, "there are many names for a group of ducks. A 'flock' is ducks in flight. But in the water, in the fountain, for instance, you'd call them a *raft* of ducks."

"So what do you call ducks in an elevator?" Meredith fell out laughing. The Duckmaster smiled, but I didn't think he found it very funny.

"I'd call it, watch where you step," I blurted, and Meredith bent over again, tears pouring from her eyes. We were still in stitches when the doors opened at the Skyway level, the Peabody rooftop. I swept my arm in an "after you" motion and the ducks skittered ahead of us to bed.

The skyscrapers had begun to glow; a cool breeze from the west caressed our cheeks. It was a good thing we'd brought our drinks because the rooftop bar was closed. We lingered along the wrought iron railing, watching the river dance in the twilight.

Meredith nudged me with an elbow. "Hey, tell me about your first."

"My first what?"

"Your first time. I'll bet you were a stud at fifteen and sneaked some lucky girl into your bedroom."

"Meredith, jeez!" I took a sip, swirled it in my mouth. "Okay. I was nineteen, not fifteen. Living in a college dorm in Ithaca, New York." I squeezed her arm. "You sure you want to hear this?"

"Yes, I want to know all about *my man*."

"There you go again." I said. Her lips parted, the last of the sun kissing her teeth in lavender, and I continued. "There was this fire alarm around midnight. Out on the street this one girl comes up, grabs me. An upperclassman. But a tiny thing, long stringy blonde hair."

Meredith nodded. "Get to the juicy part."

"Okay, the juicy part. She looks me in the eye and declares, 'I want your virtue.'"

"Your virtue?"

"She wanted to steal my innocence."

"And did she?"

"Yes. *And* my virtue."

"Silly man. Nobody took your virtue. It's still right here." She poked a finger over my heart. "You're a good one."

"I *have* been told otherwise." I smiled. No point in telling her that any decency I may have once had was blown out that car door with my twin brother.

"I know you're joking, but I've seen the other kind," she said. "Tell me more."

"Are you sure?" I said, glancing at my watch. "It's getting dark out."

"I get the picture, Tommy. You've been around the block."

"Knocked on a few doors, maybe." I gazed out over the river, grinning wider now. "Then you took me around the world."

"Okay, Casanova, you've got a real way with words. And with women, apparently."

She leaned in to kiss me just as the Duckmaster emerged from the duck roost. "You do know the rooftop bar is closed until spring," he shouted. "Maybe y'all should get a room?"

"Aww, go fuck a duck," Meredith giggled under her breath. Draping an arm around me, her fingers fluttered, twirling the hair at my collar. For a minute we stayed that way, regarding the purple sky, the skyline lights like fireflies skimming the Mississippi.

"Hey Tommy?" she said, turning to face me. "The duck guy."

"Yeah?"

"Let's take his advice …"

"Okay."

"… and do it."

"Do what?"

"Get a room."

The desk clerk took a dim view of the luggage-less couple before him. "Mr. Duck Man said we should get a room," Meredith sputtered, before I could say a word. "So, we're getting one."

In the elevator, we fell into each other, like Kathleen Turner and William Hurt, our body heat rising with the floor numbers. Unlike the movie, we weren't plotting to blow up the husband. Tonight, the only explosions would take place between the sheets.

It took two tremoring hands to steady the room key, slide it in the lock. The handle turned, we stumbled across the threshold, and collapsed to the carpet in a pile of limbs and lips. With the back of my shoe I swept the door, shutting it behind us with a click.

We were gone, gone, gone.

17

A FOOL SUCH AS I

When Meredith dropped me off at the apartment Sunday afternoon two messages awaited. My hand moved to the answering machine, anticipation and dread imbued in a single hovering index finger. Whoever invented these devices had found a way to package anxiety in the blink of a tiny red light.

> MESSAGE 1: "*Tom, sorry to call you at home. It's Janelle Foster. I didn't mean to blow you off last week. Can we try this again?*"

The timestamp said it was sent Saturday, yesterday.

> MESSAGE 2: "*Tom, Janelle again. Can we talk today? Come by my place. I'll be here.*"

This second message was sent an hour ago.

The address Janelle provided pointed me to a downtown high-rise, a prime location, each apartment with a balcony overlooking the river. The moment I rounded the corner to Front Street I saw the patrol car. The marked MPD Crown Vic idled at the curb, opposite the entrance, an officer in the front seat, window down, arm out. He stepped from the car as I reached for the button to Janelle's unit.

"Sir!" he shouted. "I advise you not to go up there."

"Is that an order, officer?"

"It's a warning."

I took my hand from the buzzer.

He was young, younger than me, his black hair cropped in military style. I figured him for a rookie. "I know who you are," he said, crossing the street now. "If I were you, I'd stay out of it."

"Sorry, but I was invited." I stepped back as a tenant pushed through the door. I held it for them, and slipped into the lobby.

When the elevator opened on her floor, Janelle's cries echoed up and down the corridor. I pushed against the door to her unit. It swung open. "Hello? It's Tom. You okay?"

I took a stride into the apartment, stopping dead at the opening to the kitchen. A man held Janelle pressed against the counter, doubled over. His hand closed on her throat. Janelle's eyes bulged. Purple welts spotted her neck.

"Hey!" Even from behind I could tell the guy was a cop. "Get off her!"

The assailant released Janelle. As he turned, his hand dropped to his utility belt. "What the fuck?" he said, unsnapping the clasp over his sidearm. "You're like a bad penny."

With the pounding of hard shoes on linoleum, the young officer from downstairs burst into the apartment, shoving past me. He held both hands in front of him. "Bone, let's beat it," he said.

As Janelle retreated behind the kitchen table, the guy called Bone wheeled on me. "Cute. You bangin' her, too?" The voice, the hulking stature, the Anglo-Saxon chiseling. It was the jerk who'd flattened me to the dance floor at Dixie's wedding. He elbowed his partner out of the way and bent his face to mine.

I stood my ground. I wasn't going to be blindsided this time. "Maybe you should listen to your partner here. Beat it. Unless you want this all over the news tonight."

His face hung suspended above my head for a second, his pungent breath drawing water from my eyes. Then he barreled past me, his partner following him out.

Janelle rushed to turn the lock, putting her back to the door. Dark tentacles creeped across her face, her arms. Some of the bruises looked fresh, others, days old. I said she needed to report this to the police. Her answer, an incredulous, "Are you kidding?"

She pulled out a chair and gestured for me to sit.

"Tom, you asked if I knew the cop in the video. At the Carl Walker scene. I blew you off."

"Yeah, you did."

"That was him, just now. Lieutenant Bone Harper. We've been seeing each other the past year."

"I can see why you'd want to cover for a boyfriend, but—"

"He's Bone *Harper*. Lin Harper's son."

The awkwardness at the wedding, in the newsroom, at the cop shop. Even Lin's hostility. In an instant it crystallized. Janelle wanted to keep it on the down low. I got that. But so did our anchorman. His progeny was a Memphis police officer.

"Tom, there's something more," she said. "That videotape. When you stood up at your desk, shouting it was missing? I about lost my lunch." She swallowed and looked away. "Gosh, this sucks."

"What?"

"A few weeks back, in the newsroom, Lin noticed Lee go upstairs to the GM's office. When you went, too, Lin asked me to grab whatever you were working on in the edit bay. The terrible part is, I would've. But when I went to find it, the tape was already gone."

"And what does this have to do with your—"

"Bone's got a temper. I think you've already figured that out. And when he raises a hand to me ... well, I'm not making excuses. He's a good cop, but something's tearing him up."

"A good cop? Jesus, look at those bruises. You didn't get those all today. That's why you missed anchoring over Thanksgiving, isn't it? Janelle, you have to tell someone about this."

"It's not that simple." She turned her gaze to the window, tracking a freight train lumbering along the river bluff.

Janelle had assuaged her guilt by telling me about the tape. That, I understood. But she was holding something back. "All right," I said. "What am I not getting?"

"Tom, you're an excellent reporter. And a nice guy. I know I haven't been the kindest to you, and I'm sorry." She got up and unlocked the door. "But I'm okay now. Go home."

Two weeks later, Janelle pressed domestic assault charges against her boyfriend. The *Commercial Appeal* reported that when he failed to show for his shift at Central Precinct, a warrant had gone out for the arrest of Memphis Police Lieutenant Jonathan B. "Bone" Harper, son of the noted Channel 2 anchorman.

"Have they thought to ask Lin where he's at?" I raised the question to anybody in the newsroom who'd listen. "Maybe the guy's hiding out at Daddy's house." Judging from the looks I got, I might as well have suggested the Confederacy should have packed it in after Vicksburg. But I wasn't the only one thinking along these lines.

Lee waved me into his office that afternoon. "We're going to have to cover this story," he said, brushing his hand across his buzzcut, "and do it with some delicacy, given it involves one of our own."

"*Two* of our own."

"Okay, spill it."

I took a deep breath and sat down. "Janelle asked me over to her apartment a couple of Sundays ago. Said she wanted to share something with me."

Lee squeezed shut his eyes. "You witnessed the assault."

"Yep."

"Jesus Christ."

"And I realize now everybody's been covering for her *and* for our anchorman. Seems his son, Bone, is a cop who's been dating our police beat reporter. Apparently I'm the only fool in the city of Memphis who didn't know."

"Tom, enough." Lee went back to rubbing the top of his head. "One of the reasons I wanted to talk to you, before you dropped this new heap of steaming donkey dung on me, was to let you know you did a fine job anchoring over Thanksgiving. Ransom thought so, too. The viewers *like* you. You add an element of ..." He struggled to find the words, had to twist himself into knots to summon a compliment. "An element of grit," he finally coughed out. "Now someone else might call it hardheadedness, stupidity, even." He flared his teeth, more grimace than grin, but I figured this was his clumsy way of saying the station needed me.

"Thank you. I think."

"That said," Lee went on, "we may be askin' you to step up sooner rather than later. I'm fixin' to chat with Lin this afternoon about the whole situation."

"I'll be sure to wear my flak jacket."

Lee's eyebrow popped. "Don't be a smartass."

At two-thirty, the news director invited Lin Harper to join him in his office. I had just returned from the break room, popping my can of Tab, when the first cannon volley erupted.

"Uh oh, kids," Bubba quipped, coining a golden phrase that afternoon, "Lin's done lost his vertical hold." The newsroom froze, all eyes fixed on the show behind the glass.

"This is absolute horseshit, Lee!"

The two stood nose to nose. Lee dropped a fist to his desk, the concussion nearly knocking the name plate off the door. "It's called conflict of interest. And if you'd ever made the slightest effort to do right by that son of yours, we wouldn't be havin' this here conversation."

"You're out of line!"

"It is what it is," Lee said.

"It's bull crap is what it is."

You could see the spit fly, and I thanked God for the glass barrier. Someone started a running bet over who'd throw the first punch.

"I'm the only thing holding this station together and you're telling me you're gonna turn it over to that goddamn brat pack out there?"

"Lin, calm the hell down."

"Go fuck yourself! Don't tell me to calm down."

As we stared, mesmerized, jaws comically hanging open, an object flew. I flinched, as you would in a 3D movie. The TV remote bounced off the glass and crashed to the floor. I'd had a news director throw a remote at me, too. It was their weapon of choice.

"Lin, we go way back. Hell, we're practically family." Lee bent to retrieve his clicker, and for the first time, saw he had an audience in the newsroom. "So I'm gonna look past this here 'conversation' and you're gonna go do your goddamn job."

The door opened and suddenly typewriters, scanners, printers, desk chairs, all became objects of intense focus, anything other than catching Lin's dead-eyed wrath as he stalked across the newsroom. The anchorman passed within inches of me, electrifying the hairs on the back of my neck.

When Lin had retreated to his office, Susan leaned across our pod of desks, saying, "If looks could kill, Tom."

The anchorman simmered behind his door until news time. But during the B block of the six o'clock he boiled over. His script pages had gotten mixed up. On-air he appeared to stumble, losing his place in the story. What we didn't see—but what T-Bone, the floor director, told us later—was that during the commercials, Lin treated the studio crew to a full-on tantrum.

"Who's the moron that ripped the scripts?" he'd screamed,

focusing his fury on the teleprompter operator. In the lexicon of the newsroom, "ripping" scripts didn't mean tearing them to pieces, it meant separating the five-part carbon sheets into ordered piles for the anchors and crew. When no one confessed to having performed the task, Lin sent his copy airborne.

"Someone explain this. Now!" His eyes looked ready to launch from their sockets. "Goddammit!" He slapped his palms on the anchor desk, unhooked his microphone and stomped out.

With Lin AWOL, the technical director had switched to a single anchor transition for the weather segment, and Kimberly threw it to Timothy. The forecast called for falling temperatures. But Timothy, being Timothy, couldn't resist dropping a quip that would be lost on the viewers. "Cool tonight, Kimberly, but a little hot here in the studio."

After the newscast, we learned an engineer in master control had kept recording the camera feed during Lin's frenzied commercial break. The mics were cut, but Lin's pantomime, gesticulation, and careful lip-reading were more than enough to tell the story. Some genius in the edit suite had the idea of looping the video and mixing it with the song, *Maniac*, from *Flashdance*. It was the must-see blooper reel over the holidays.

18

NOT ALL RIGHT, MAMA

Invites had gone out for the station Christmas party weeks ago. I mulled over asking Ashley. Considered inviting Meredith. *What were the rules on bringing a married woman to a company party?* Now the event was only days away and I'd procrastinated myself out of a date.

I was nearly out the door on Monday evening when my extension rang, Meredith at the other end of the line with an invitation of her own.

At six, Timothy had forecast a wave of severe thunderstorms. For once, he was right. Lightning bursts lit the rear-view mirror on the drive to Germantown. I toggled the radio between AM 560 and 600, both stations advising motorists to stay home unless you absolutely needed to be somewhere. Check. I needed to see Meredith.

She opened the door and I didn't care about forecasts, advisories, or anything else. Her lips were wet with Merlot and suddenly so were mine. I'd missed her and told her so. I launched straight into news of the Christmas party and surprised myself with the words out of my mouth. Would she be my date?

Meredith's face collapsed, dragging my smile with it.

"Look, if you can't for whatever reason—"

"Tom, it's really sweet of you." She fussed with the hem of her shirt sleeve.

"So, then?"

"Who all will be there? Would it even be appropriate? You know, me being—?"

I said the entire station was invited, including the staff, reporters, anchors, and their spouses or dates. When she said she figured I'd be taking someone else, I told her, of course, I could, but I was asking *her*. I said I didn't care about her being married, as long as her husband wasn't there. I thought that last part was pretty funny. She didn't.

We took sips, set down our glasses, picked them up again. Breaking the heavy silence, I said, "Look, I'm sure you're right."

"You're angry with me."

"More like, frustrated. Some days it seems I'm living inside a movie where they've all read the script, and I'm the only one ad-libbing. They know how the story ends and I'm groping for my lines."

"Tommy, nobody knows how the story ends. That's part of life."

"No, dammit, you're not getting it." I swallowed the rest of my wine. "What about us? What even is this?"

Meredith's eyes began to fill. I'd gone too far.

During dinner, the lights flickered, bathing us in brief darkness before clicking on again. Meredith brought out candles. I talked shop. Had she seen the news about Janelle Foster and the Memphis cop? They had a warrant out for him. Some guy named Bone Harper. Turned out I was the only one in the dang newsroom who didn't know he was the anchorman's son—that is, until I walked in on him trying to strangle Janelle. How insane was that?

Meredith stared at the floor. She didn't appear to be tracking with the story. When I acted out Lin's on-camera meltdown, her eyes strayed to a spot past my shoulder.

"Are you okay?"

"I'm fine," she shrugged. "Let's clean up these dishes."

My inclination was to keep drilling, try to solve whatever was troubling her. But if I'd learned one thing about women, it was they wanted you to listen, not fix the world.

Meredith joined me on the sofa just as a house-rattling clap of thunder exploded. The lights blinked again, outdoor furniture banged in the wind. "If we're gonna be blacked out," she said, "we might as well get cozy."

Her fingers worked the buttons on my shirt, the buckle on my belt. I lay back, swallowed by the cushions. I began to float. I could do this all night, if I could stand it.

We swapped positions, Meredith's body sinking into the sofa. Buried as I was, my senses submerged, I didn't notice at first. But as I came up for air, there it was. A shadow, a movement, a rapid fire of muffled clicks. *Outside.*

Lightning cracked, casting a monochrome flash of something or someone crossing in front of the window. A chair screeched across the patio.

We were not alone!

Meredith followed my eyes to the sliding glass door. "Tommy, what's wrong?" She curled her fingers around my ears. "Get your sweet self back down there."

"Wait," I said. "Hold on a sec." I reached for my boxers. Panic coursed through my veins, prickling my naked skin. I wanted to shake the growing nausea, assure myself it was only the wind. I sat up, pulling on my shirt. "Is somebody screwing around?"

"Well, yeah," she purred.

"No, God. I mean … I saw something. Outside just now." I stepped to the glass door, exposed and ludicrous in my shorts and open shirt.

"The only thing I been seein' is stars," Meredith said. "I was fixin' to pass out." She joined me at the window, frowning. "What's going on?"

I put a finger to my lips and pushed open the slider. A swirl of dried leaves rushed in. I'd expected a blast of chill air, but an unnatural warmth overtook the room. The sky presented a featureless canopy of clouds, with a pale greenish cast. I'd never seen anything like it. Or maybe I had. Once.

We both heard it now, a splash, branches snapping, and a heavy thud. Someone tripping, scrambling. A vehicle starting. I rounded the side of the house in my bare feet just as the blur of red taillights retreated into the driving rain.

Meredith had remained at the patio door, a comforter draped around her shoulders. I ushered her inside and pulled shut the door. "They knocked over a chair," I said. "Ran off and into a car. What were they doing?" I gave her a hard stare.

"Don't look at me that way. I don't know what's going on any more than you do."

She sounded sincere and maybe she was. But something inside me twisted. I wanted to rethink the entire affair. I wanted to shake up the puzzle in my mind and re-assemble it from tonight back to the beginning.

"I think they had a camera." Balancing on one leg, I slid the other into my jeans. "Meredith, did anyone know I'd be here?"

"You mean, who all did I tell that we'd be makin' love tonight? Oh, only the whole town. Yeah, I wrote it up in *Memphis Magazine*." She shrunk back, shaking her head. "What the hell, Tom, seriously, with all your damn questions?"

"This is how people get blackmailed," I said. "If that's what this is, I'm so screwed."

"I don't know who's screwin' who here, but I'm pretty sure we been screwin' each other. And up until a minute ago, I was likin' it." She fell back to the sofa and pulled the blanket tighter.

"I didn't mean it to come out that way. It's just … this feels like a setup."

"Well, I don't appreciate the tone," she said. "If you're accusin' me of somethin', be a man and come out and say it."

"Listen, somebody *was* out there. Your husband maybe? Or someone he hired?"

The zipper on my jeans caught. I struggled to bring it home, the adrenaline that had me chasing around the house a moment ago, dissolved. Gone, too was the warmth in Meredith's eyes. She fixed them on the patio window as I grabbed my jacket and turned to leave.

"Please, tell me you have no idea what's going on," I said.

"Tom, you're bein' crazy right now."

"That's not a no." I slammed the door behind me.

19

SWING DOWN CHARIOT

The rain fell in heavy daggers, and if anything, the air had grown warmer. The tops of trees flirted with the ground, groaning against the wind, a gust blowing against the car door as I jumped in, just ahead of it slamming.

From the front seat of the Honda an incessant beeping competed with the wind and thunder outside, my pager buzzing and flashing the number of the assignment desk. I wasn't about to turn around and use Meredith's phone. I'd return the call when I got home.

Walking in the door just before ten, I found the answering machine casting its red blinking beacon against the dark ceiling. Five messages. The first, from the station. I played it and hit STOP, picking up the phone. Sheila, the night producer, told me there'd been a massive tornado and it was all hands on deck in the newsroom. I said I could be there in thirty minutes.

The illuminated number "4" flashed on the machine. I hit PLAY. A message from Meredith. I hit skip. Again, Meredith. Skip. All four from her. She'd been crying, wanted to talk. I didn't have time for this. I found Miss Priss huddled under the couch and carried her to her cat bed. I refilled her water, poured out some food, grabbed an overcoat and boots, and left.

~

It was almost eleven when I got to the newsroom, but it may well have been midday. Bubba Reece, in perpetual motion behind the assignment desk, tuned police scanners with one hand, talked into a phone with the other. On the monitor above the desk, Timothy, live on the air, ran through the latest storm track.

Bubba waved me over. "Don't take your coat off," he said. "We've got a confirmed tornado across the river in West Memphis. Eddie's getting the truck ready. We'll want you for the morning show. Go!"

Crossing the Mississippi is a passage between realms, the yawning river dividing east from west. Tonight, it was something more biblical, a bridge from purgatory to hell. First landmark in this apocalyptic landscape: the Mid-Continent truck stop, what was left of it. Here, at the confluence of the two great perpendicular interstates—I-40 and I-55 after they cross separate bridges from Tennessee into Arkansas—cars and trucks lay about, jackknifed, flipped, scattered across four lanes of highway.

We paused for B-roll, then lumbered on, making a circuit of West Memphis. Here the shell of a convenience store, its front façade intact, but two sides gone; there a Motel 6, flattened. A town zippered open, its insides looking out, an x-ray vision of rooms without walls, a tableau of bedsheets in trees, books in the street, toys in the gutter.

Amidst the remains of an apartment complex, dazed tenants milled about, kicking through debris, salvaging what they could. On a concrete step, a pajama-clad woman sat swaying, sobbing. It took me a moment to process what she held in her hands, a small child, arms hanging limp, tiny fingertips brushing the pavement as the woman rocked. The sight of it stopped me cold, pulled me back, ages back. To another child, another time.

Blood on the bumper. Face in the snow.

I teetered in my seat, half-whispering, half-muttering. "Eddie, should we? I mean—" I cleared my throat and began again. "We should get some shots of this, no?"

"Should we. Good question," he said. "I don't want to, but I will."

It was what we did. Pointing cameras at people during the worst moments of their lives. A few hours ago, folks here had been watching TV, laughing around the dinner table, maybe having sex. *As I was just doing.* I scanned the debris field, a shattering panorama of despair, the remains of humanity, stuffed animals, family photos, busted furniture. Ground zero.

Years ago, as an intern at a station in Syracuse, I shadowed a news crew covering a house fire. It was an old Gothic, the city had hundreds of them. I'd creeped behind the cameraman, the fire's intense heat pushing against me like a solid mass. My eyes lowered to the threshold of the house. A charred heap of rags blocked the doorway. As my focus sharpened, the rags became a person, or what had been one. A pair of blacked-out sockets stared from the distorted clump of viscera. I froze, locked in, unable to move until the photographer jolted me out of a zombie trance, shaking my shoulder, saying, "Hey, kid, you okay?"

My first body. First as a journalist, anyway.

They don't place a priority on sensitivity, no extra credit for empathy, when they hire the next pretty face for the news. In the dark early morning hours in the godforsaken city of West Memphis, Arkansas, those were the qualities I dredged from within. Without them I'd be no more than a stenographer of tragedy.

Eddie mounted the Betacam on his shoulder, I accepted the wireless mic from his hand, and we approached the grieving mother.

"Ma'am?" I said. She continued rocking the lifeless baby. I could see now it was a little girl. "Can you tell us what happened?"

"My sweet pea is gone." She pushed back the girl's dark braided hair, revealing a swollen circle of dried blood. "We was readin' a story. She couldn't sleep. All the thunder and the wind. And then there's a sound like a roaring beast, like the Almighty himself reachin' down and grabbing our buildin'—" She dropped her head and pulled the child to her chest. "I had her, I *had* her. Why couldn't I hold on? Why'd I let go? Why, Jesus, why?"

I set a hand on the woman's shoulder. "It's not your fault," I told her. I wanted to believe it. Even if I didn't believe it of myself.

She cast a mournful eye to the dark clouds overhead and asked me to pray with her.

So, I did.

The temperature had plunged in the hours since midnight. We warmed ourselves inside the truck, as Eddie got to work on the edit station. Out the window, the moon projected a greenish-yellow glow behind the clouds.

"Eddie, you see that?"

"That's some bad juju," he said. "Never saw nothing like it."

"I did, a long time ago. I think it's all right."

"Say what?"

"I know. It sounds weird," I said. "I was a kid, back in Chicago. Thunderstorms scared the crap out of my big brother. One night my mom heard him crying. She pulled back his covers and said she wanted to show us both something. When she opened the window shades—"

A hollow knocking sounded through the truck, someone hammering on the side panel. "Y'all want to talk with the mayor?" the man called out. "He's available right now."

"To be continued," I said, and we jumped out.

A small gaggle of reporters surrounded the West Memphis mayor. I carried Eddie's tripod, his "sticks," and set them up. He flipped on his light, I leaned in with the mic.

"We've confirmed five fatalities," the mayor said. "Many others, we fear, are injured. Searches are underway, building by building, block by block."

"Mayor," I asked, "did the city have any warning about the storm?"

"None," he said.

The first hint of daylight had just made itself known over the flat eastern horizon when the two-way radio squawked, the newsroom asking, could we go live at six-thirty?

Eddie peeked over his camera. "Ten seconds. Standby."

The morning anchor tossed to me and I launched into my intro. The dead, the injured, the estimated property damage. "Cold facts don't do justice to what photographer Eddie Harrington and I witnessed overnight." That was the cue for the control room to roll my taped package.

> "Among the victims, an elderly man crushed to death in a boarding home, a woman found in a field, a one-year-old killed when the tornado tore through her apartment. And then there were the walking wounded. The lucky ones ..."

In my ear, the producer told me I had a minute to "stretch," meaning talk longer than planned. As possessed as I was with the magnitude of the carnage, I had no trouble filling that minute.

"The sun is just coming up," I said into the lens when they returned to me live. I walked slowly to my right, Eddie tracking me with the camera. "You can see what is now revealing itself to the people of West Memphis this morning."

I stopped, bent to a knee, picked up a fist-sized chunk of concrete, tossed it aside. "What do you say to a young mother, clutching her daughter's lifeless body? That's what last night was about. No amount of cradling will bring that little girl back, but there she was, rocking that child, rocking, rocking." Eddie's face took on a curious mix of smile and frown as he spied me over the viewfinder.

"I've been up twenty-four hours," I continued. "I'm probably not making sense. But I have to believe one thing. There *is* a higher power. He gives ..." My voice caught and I broke eye contact with the camera. "... and he takes."

Standing again, I walked toward Eddie as he backed up, keeping pace. "A little while ago, before sunup, the clouds started to break. There was an otherworldly tint to the sky. It gave the moon a, well ... it looked green. It brought back an old memory, of when I was a boy. One night during a frightening thunderstorm my mom said to look for the green moon after the rain. 'It means everything's all right,' she said."

I gazed skyward, and then reconnected with the camera. "Moms tell lots of stories, you know. And I never saw that kind of moon again. Until last night. And so, I have to trust it's gonna be all right. And my wish is that today, this week, over the holidays, if you love someone, tell them. If you care for someone, show it. There's no guarantee for tomorrow. For the survivors here this morning, all that's left is the hope that one day soon ... it'll be all right again. Live from West Memphis, Tom Cirone, News 2."

Yanking the earpiece out, I dropped to my knees. Eddie set down the camera, putting a hand on my shoulder. "That was damn fine, Tom. Damn fine. I never knew you had them feelings in ya."

Neither did I.

Eddie stepped away and I allowed the tears to come. There was no playbook for this.

20

DIRTY, DIRTY FEELING

As of Wednesday, a warrant remained out for Lin Harper's son, still evading custody. If it weren't for the tornado, that story would have topped the news across the region.

At the far end of the newsroom Lin sequestered himself in his office. He'd been banned from reading any police-related stories on the news, the upshot of his shouting match in Lee's office. *Not much for you to do these days, is there, Mr. Harper?* And it served him right, having raised a no-good son to be a no-good cop. *Karma's a sumbitch, ain't it, Lin?*

I tilted back my chair, feeling smug, maybe a little self-satisfied, my hands cupped behind my head. But I met resistance, something thick, unyielding. The linebacker torso of Lee Cravens. He'd been looming over my shoulder, watching me watching Lin. The chair sprang forward, my kneecaps hammering into the desk.

"Are we a little jittery?" he asked.

"Should I be?"

"Come see me."

On the carpet in Lee's office, my eye caught something, a small piece of plastic the size of a thumbnail. I bent to pick it up.

"I see you found the remains of my clicker," he said.

When I set the broken piece on the desk, I noticed the manila envelope.

"Shut the door, Tom. Sit down." Lee pushed the envelope at me with the tips of his fingers. "Someone slipped this under my door. Go ahead. Open it."

Out slid four black and white glossies, poorly exposed, terrible photography, but artistic expression was not the goal here. There was nothing to do but stare, slack-jawed, at the images, placing one beneath the other until I'd viewed them all.

Lee ripped the photos from my hands and slapped me across the face with them. "Are you an imbecil?"

I looked back into the newsroom. Several heads returned my gaze through the glass. I'd be looking too if I was on the other side, and I wished very much to be on that other side.

"Do you know who that is?" Lee tossed the photos to the desk.

The images were from Monday night, taken, as I'd feared, through the patio window. You could make out Meredith's profile and the side of my face. There was fog on the lens, it was dark, but you could see exactly what we were doing.

You *do* know who this is, Tom," Lee repeated.

"Yes."

"Do you, son? Because surely nobody could be *that* ignorant." He pointed a thick finger at the face of the woman kneeling between my thighs. "That fine gal doin' you right there? That's Meredith Harper."

"Meredith Harper." It came from my throat but it was someone else's voice.

"Lin Harper's daughter-in-law, dumbass." For that matter, Lee was speaking in tongues. "*Wife* of police Lieutenant Bone Harper. Get it now, moron?"

My chest seized up. *This is what a heart attack feels like.*

The evasions, misdirections. Meredith's confounding behavior the other night. Would it have been too much to tell me she was related by marriage to the guy who happened to anchor our news?

Lee's mouth continued moving. "Tom, you have learned *exactly* nothing."

The guy at the wedding. I'd been sleeping with his wife! That's why he decked me. Wait, no. I hadn't met Meredith yet. But the other day, at Janelle's apartment, what was it Harper had said? *You bangin' her, too?* I swallowed hard.

"Tom, are you listening to me?"

"I'm listening, but I don't—"

"Holy Moses, I can explain it to you, but I can't *understand* it for you." Lee spun his chair to the window. "Here's how it is." He swiveled back. "First you impregnate a young intern, then you take her to get rid of it. You call the police liars live on the air. On top of all that, you decide you're gonna screw the wife of a cop who also happens to be the daughter-in-law of our main anchor! Oh, and you just happen to show up at Janelle's apartment when said cop is allegedly committing assault. Did I miss anything?"

"You captured it beautifully."

"Tom, I want you to finish up what you're workin' on and get the hell out of here. You're done for the day." He slid the photos into the envelope and closed the flap. "Jesus, you're a mess. You make a drunken racoon look presentable. Have you even slept?"

"But what is this, Lee? What's the point of this?"

"The point is, you're an embarrassment."

"But it's not like the *Commercial Appeal's* gonna print those photos on the front page."

"I don't give a rat's ass if they do or they don't or if they get posted on every goddamn telephone pole in Memphis for the dogs to piss on. It's all the same. It brings disrepute to you and besmirches our television station."

Finally, his words began to sink in. "Are you firing me?"

"Christ, no, I'm not firing your sorry ass." His tone softened. "You did a fine job on the West Memphis coverage. Nobody's forgotten that. You're an important part of this team. But if it comes out you're intimately tied into this whole Harper shitstorm, you can forget about all the credibility we've built, *you've* built, over this past year."

I sucked in a dry breath. "What about the Christmas party?"

"The *what?*"

"It's tomorrow night."

"Shit, son. You're not thinking of bringing—" Spit flew from Lee's mouth. He dragged a sleeve across it. "I mean, you're not stupid enough to—"

"Of course not." No need to admit I'd asked Meredith to the party and she declined.

"Okay." He dismissed me with a wave of his hand.

"Wait. What happens with these?" I reached for the envelope, but he snatched them back across the desk.

"Nothing. Them photos stay right here." He dropped the envelope into a drawer and shut it. "Now go home."

I'd stepped halfway out the door when Lee called back. "And Tom?"

"Yes?"

"Keep it in your damn pants."

I could tell by the way Susan tucked her chin as I gathered my things that she'd heard that last exchange and probably more. I knew she wanted to ask, but I wasn't sticking around.

Maybe Lee was right. Maybe I *had* learned nothing. But what was the other thing he said? *This was slipped under my door.* Not dropped off in the lobby. Not sent by mail. Who'd be looking to bring me down? Who'd be in a position to slip something under the news director's door? I scanned the newsroom until I landed on that other glass office. *Long lens photographer, my ass.*

As I got up to leave, Susan jumped from her seat, a hand on my arm. "Tom?"

Here we go.

"I wanted to tell you, great job out there on the tornado story. And if it makes you feel any better," She lowered her voice to a whisper and cupped a hand to the side of her mouth. "I like sex, too."

21

SURRENDER

The *Petroleum Club* sprawled across the entire top floor of the NBC Building downtown—National Bank of Commerce, not the television network. On most evenings, you'd find the elite of white establishment Memphis here, dining on porterhouse steak and pork ribs, making deals and telling tales. Tonight, the club was reserved for Channel 2, with artificial Christmas trees anchoring the four corners of the ballroom, and a small stage with a podium set against the windows. The annual WMDW-TV Christmas dinner was one of the few perks the station gave to its employees and it was a disaster from the get-go.

Last minute, I'd invited Ashley. She came ready to party, in full-on sequins, a sparkling, short-skirted, tight-fitting rainbow that crinkled like cellophane when she walked.

At the bar I ordered a white for Ashley, a red for me. We found Timothy and Bobby there, engaged in a debate about Indiana college hoops. Timothy killed me with the Indiana stuff. He made his nondescript home state out to be some kind of paradise on earth. He considered John Mellencamp the crown prince of rock, and *Cherry Bomb* the greatest song ever recorded. Timothy stopped mid-sentence, his ogling eyes scanning my date.

"What?" Ashley said, smoothing out her hip-hugging sequins.

Timothy smirked. "Just surprised to see you. I mean, *here*."

"Does anyone know what he's talking about?" Ashley turned to me with a shaky laugh.

I said, "Timothy, how much have you had to drink already?"

He looked past me and continued to address Ashley. "I just wasn't expecting you with Tom tonight."

"Good to see you, too, weatherman," I said. "We'll catch up later." I put my arm around Ashley's waist to guide her toward the ballroom but her feet stayed glued to the floor.

She said, "Wait. I want to know what he means exactly."

"Hey man," I said to Timothy, "don't you have a tornado forecast you can go screw up or something?"

"Funny you should mention that, Tom." His eyes remained on my date. "Because I heard you had quite a stormy night yourself. Or should I say, steamy?" Surprisingly on point for a guy who missed so many forecasts, and it dredged up the image Lee had placed in my mind: photos posted, dogs pissing, on every telephone pole in Memphis. *How many people knew about that night?*

I tugged Ashley's arm and moved us into the main room. Against the wall, near the doors, leaned a large man in uniform. Security. An off-duty cop.

At a front table stood Lin Harper, a cocktail glass in one hand. With his other, he directed a finger at Ransom Bishop. A bottle of Jack Daniels sat between them. Lin drove his fist into the table and the Jack jumped. The room was noisy, few people noticed, but it looked ugly and I wanted no part of it. I reached again for Ashley.

"Will you stop dragging me around?" She wrenched her arm away. "I'm not a damn puppy dog." As she whirled to face me, her elbow knocked my drink hand. The wine glass tipped, sending an angry splotch of red blooming into the white cotton fibers of my shirt.

I steadied the glass, extending it at arm's length. "Jesus, what are you doing?"

"Gosh, sorry." Ashley reached for a cocktail napkin, but I held up my hand.

"It'll only make it worse," I said. "Awesome. Just awesome." If I'd been shot point blank, it couldn't have looked more perfect. Branded. Like a scarlet letter.

"I said I was sorry." She took a gulp of wine. "Where's *your* apology?" Around us, people headed to their seats. "And why is your weather guy always making weird comments?"

"Ashley, let's just sit down."

We took our places at our assigned table. Janelle had already settled herself there, as had one of our advertising salesmen and his wife. Dilly rounded out our group. Two tables over sat Kimberly Kilmer and her date. I'd heard she was seeing the first baseman for the Memphis Chicks. He looked very much the part of the young jock with the trophy girlfriend.

Lin broke off the conversation with Ransom and found his way to Kimberly's table. A handsome blonde woman I presumed was his wife took the seat to Lin's right. She'd also taken possession of the bottle of Jack and helped herself to a couple of fingers.

Once everyone had their salads, the general manager walked to the podium and tapped the microphone. "Let's raise a glass to 1987, a fantastic year!" Ransom unfolded a sheet of paper. "What I have here is a page from the November Nielsen ratings. I am proud to tell you all tonight, Channel 2 is back!"

Polite applause and some clinking of glasses. But one person remained impassive. While his wife threw back her whiskey, Lin stared off, his gaze fixed on the chandelier in the center of the ballroom.

"Our six o'clock numbers are up," Ransom continued. "A thirteen rating and twenty-two share. We're only a few points behind Channel 6 at ten as well. So keep on doing what you're doing and here's to grabbing that top spot in 1988!"

The GM inhaled his drink, crunching a sliver of ice. "One more thing and I'll let y'all get to your dinners. I know we've been getting ready for Christmas. But this past week we had an awful tragedy.

It brought out the best in all of you, staying on the air, doing your jobs." He scanned the room until he caught my eye. "Tom, your work out there in West Memphis was some of the finest I've seen."

"Oh, Jesus Christ!" Forks dropped, heads snapped in the direction of Lin's table. The anchorman's face had gone purple. His wife laid a hand on his arm, telling him, I imagined, that he was embarrassing her in front of all these good people. "No, goddamn it," Lin shouted, ripping his arm away. "I am not gonna sit here and pretend this is all just—"

Lin flinched, whipped his head. The ballroom doors shot open with a splintering kick, and a massive, sandy-haired man surveyed the room. He wore a brown wool coat, black pants, and a look of homicide on his face.

For the first time I could put the name and the assailant together.

The security man at the door held out an arm. "Now Bone, you ain't supposed to be here." Bone Harper shrugged off the guard's hand and staked out a direct line to my table. The guard trailed him, shouting, "Lieutenant Harper, you need to turn yourself in."

"Why? So this bitch can celebrate while I get locked up?"

At first I thought Harper was calling out Janelle. But as he said the words, his eyes lasered on me. They were blue and cold, orbs of glacial ice. He reached my chair, jerked it around, and with a meaty hand, pile-drivered my throat. I crashed backwards against the table, fighting for air. Water glasses toppled, silverware dug trenches into my back.

"You stay the fuck away from my wife, maggot!" Spit flew from Harper's blistering lips. He reared back, balling his other hand.

I had only one defense. Words. "Seems that's more your department," I croaked.

Bullseye.

He released my throat and pivoted to Janelle, but a half dozen men had pounced from their tables, a human shield surrounding her. In the back of the room, the security guy shouted into the house phone. Ashley, still in her chair, glared at me, her mouth a gaping pit.

Lin approached, almost on tiptoes, angling his way between people and tables. He grabbed his son with both arms. "That's enough, Bone. Get on back to the h—"

Harper wrenched free from his father's grasp. "Sorry Daddy, but I'm about done with all y'all." He swept his hand behind his coat.

Someone shouted, "Watch out, the boy's got a gun!"

Several men surged forward. The room fell silent, and there was a moment of confusion, *what to do next?* The only sound was the discordant clink of fork on plate, one of the guests, a spouse, blithely spearing his salad.

The ballroom doors punched open again. Ransom seemed to be in a rolling negotiation with several uniformed police officers. The general manager lost the argument, whatever it was, as the cops pushed past him.

"You know what has to happen now, Lieutenant," said the first officer to approach. "Are you carrying, sir?"

Harper looked at me before glancing at his hip. "My service weapon."

The officer reached behind Harper's coat, his hand emerging with a sidearm. "Do you have any other weapons on your person?" Harper shook his head.

The arresting officer flipped the handgun over. "Christ, the safety was off," he said. "Were you planning on discharging this?" The officer switched back the safety and slipped the gun in a jacket pocket. "We gotta put the cuffs on ya now. Please turn around." It was genteel and respectful and exactly how you'd expect one cop to treat another. "Jonathan B. Harper, we're placing you under arrest for suspicion of assault, domestic battery, and evading a warrant."

Watching Harper frog-walked out of the ballroom struck me with a dizzying moment of empathy. I couldn't argue with the guy's rage. I *was* sleeping with his wife.

As officers loaded him into the elevator, Harper erupted in a last blood-boiling cry. I imagined the foul epithet echoing its way all twenty-nine stories down, crashing against the marbled walls of the ground floor lobby.

"Motherfucker!!"

It was the exclamation on the night and clear to everyone in the room just who the *motherfucker* was.

Ashley's eyes drilled into me. "You *are*, aren't you?"

"I am what?"

"Go to hell, asshole. You've been screwin' that psycho's wife? You're disgusting."

I must have been a sight, shot-through-the-heart wine stain on my shirt, flaming throat from Harper's hammer grip, a rash of embarrassment bubbling up my cheeks. People eventually returned to their dinners, moving food around their plates, but they feasted on us. I could almost taste the gossipy cadences.

"You've never been into me!" Ashley jabbed the air with her finger. "Not for one second! What a joke." She walked off, her dress spinning glitter like a disco ball.

And then there was one, my former seatmates having suffered a sudden, simultaneous, debilitating thirst that could only be quenched at the bar on the opposite end of the ballroom. I had the table to myself.

"You okay, buddy?"

And then there were two. Kimberly had sneaked up behind me, setting a hand on my back.

"Sure, doing just fine after a tabletop tracheotomy." I stabbed a fork into my chicken. "Yeah, and my date dumped me in front of two hundred colleagues. So, chances are I won't have a job by the end of the night. And oh, by the way, I have a red wine stigmata on my shirt. But thanks for asking."

"Totally get it, dude." she said. "It's like Bon Jovi." Kimberly struck an air guitar pose. "Shot ... through the heart ..."

I knew what she was trying to do, but it wasn't working.

"Listen, Tom," she said, "you're an okay guy. I mean you're pretty hard on yourself. But sensitive too, beneath the Rambo bullshit."

"You're the one who gave me that ridiculous name!"

"Well, maybe it's time for a new one. Like, uh ... Holden Caulfield."

Impressive. Points for knowing *Catcher in the Rye*, even if the comparison didn't exactly fit. I pulled out a chair and Kimberly took it.

"So, obviously you're acquainted with Johnnie B. Bad."

"Say what?"

"Jonathan Boniface Harper," she said. "The second."

"That's his actual name?"

"He goes by 'Bone,' as you've already figured out." She cast a thumb toward the doors at the back of the room. "But what's all this about you and his missus?"

"He thinks I'm ... you know."

"And are you?"

"I'd rather not talk about it."

"Well, sleeping around like that. You're playing with fire."

I pushed the chicken to the side of the plate. "Tell me something I don't know."

"You wouldn't guess it, but the guy's a real blue blood," she said. "His namesake, Lin's father, came from old South money."

"Pride of Memphis society, right?"

"Except, Bone wanted nothing to do with it." Kimberly lowered her voice, glancing back at her table. "Not since his mother died. Lin remarried, and let's say, his focus was not on raising a grieving young boy. I wouldn't go so far as to call the new wife, 'Mommy Dearest,' but Bone's stepmom over there could give Joan Crawford a run for her money."

"How do you know all this?" I asked.

"Oh, you learn a thing or two about a thing or two sitting next to Lin Harper the Great every night. I tell you what, though, I don't know where that boy got his good looks, but it wasn't from papa."

Maybe I'd underestimated our young anchorwoman. She'd just made me smile on a joyless night. "So, what are you saying? Johnny 'B' chose to be a cop just to piss off his old man?"

"Bone could have gone to Vanderbilt. Turned it down out of spite and went to Memphis State."

"Prodigal son," I said. "I know the feeling. Except, in my case, I left home and never came back. When I was little, I fell out of a moving car. *We* fell out of a car, my twin brother and me. Only one of us walked away. But I never considered myself lucky. Not after—" I shoved the dinner plate to the center of the table. "Anyway, I blame myself. My family certainly does. I've been running from it ever since."

"How does that make you feel?"

"Wow," I said. "Come for the rubber chicken, stay for the psychoanalysis."

"Anytime you need to talk." Kimberly pushed out her chair. "I should get back." She patted me on the wine stain. "Hang in there, Holden."

22

EASY COME, EASY GO

A haze of cigarette smoke hovered near the ballroom ceiling, the icing on the nauseating olfactory confection of barbecue spices, aftershave, and cologne. Hugging the walls, I felt my way to the elevator lobby and fresher air. For me, it was party over.

I fell onto a bench, listening to the cranking of pulleys and gears churning in the mechanical penthouse, watching guests come and go, one elevator car on its way down, one rising from the ground floor.

The doors dinged. Opened. It took a moment for my brain to catch up with my eyes.

Glamorous. I'd never seen her done up like this. Black heels and a shimmering red gown, her lips a matching shade of ruby. She held a patent leather handbag and she'd styled her hair in blonde waves, feathered across her shoulders. With her sparking blue eyes and her dress the color of holly berries, Meredith decked the halls like a Christmas angel.

She spotted me instantly. "Still need a date, handsome?"

"Meredith. Jesus. Why are you here?"

"You invited me, didn't ya?"

It was a droll comeback. Had this been any other occasion I would have loved her for it. But this was not the time for cute. "Do you have any idea what's going on? They have pictures of us. Exactly what I was afraid of that night. I'm probably gonna lose my job."

"Holy Lord, Tommy."

"You lied. You lied about everything. Your prick of a husband, your husband *the cop*. I work with your freakin' father-in-law, for chrissakes!"

She stomped a heel on the floor. "I know, I know, I know."

Meredith had balls for showing up tonight, I gave her that. But if she thought all would be forgiven and forgotten, she was mistaken. Of course she'd demurred when I'd asked her to be my date. She couldn't show up to the party with the leader of the newsroom brat pack. Lin Harper would blow another of his many gaskets. And yet, here she was.

"I'm sorry I kept it all from you, okay?" Meredith conjured a sad smile and placed a hand on mine. "Can't you understand why?" Her mascara, which had been crisp, racy even, when she stepped from the elevator a minute ago, streaked and bubbled below her eyes.

"Your husband got arrested tonight," I told her.

"Yes. I saw. They were puttin' him in a car downstairs."

"So you've been lurking a while," I said. "Or did you come here *with* him?"

"God, no, of course not. Is that what you think of me?"

"Meredith, I don't know what to think. Who to trust. Not you, not the people I work with. Not even myself. This ... whatever this was with us ... it was a freakin' mistake."

She took a step and lay her head against me, her shoulders quaking. I pushed her away. "You can't do this. This is my station party. People are looking. You need to go."

I leaned across her to push the down button on the elevator. Meredith ran a finger under her nose and looked past me into the ballroom. "She looks nice."

"Who?"

"Your date. You were with her the night we met. She's very pretty."

"She's not you." The words hung in the air, suspended between us like a guilty confession.

Our eyes locked. And then Meredith staggered, her mouth dropping. "Wait, what happened? You look—"

"No, I wasn't shot, if that's what you're thinking. Just some careless person and red wine."

"Well, I'm glad you're all right. Them tornados. All this with Bone. And at the house the other night …" Her voice trailed off. The elevator doors opened. Meredith backed onto it. "Merry Christmas, Tommy."

A part of me wanted to leap into that elevator with her, out into the crisp December air, where the night would be just beginning. A part of me, a deep place inside of me, stirred. Already missing us, missing what we had. Maybe I only missed what I *thought* we had.

The elevator closed, and I stood for a moment transfixed as the floor numbers descended. Finally, turning toward the men's room, I nearly collided with Ashley. She'd been standing at my heels, arms locked across her chest.

"How long have you been there?" I stammered.

"Long enough. But then again, I'm just 'some careless person.'"

"Oh, jeez."

"But really, who's the careless one? How many girls you got going, anyways? Besides stupid me, that is?"

"It's not—"

"I was your second choice for tonight, wasn't I?"

"What do you want me to say?"

"Say nothing. You're super skilled at that."

Timothy emerged from the ballroom, pulling on his coat. "I'm heading out, Tom. See you Monday." He made for the elevator, and then seemed to consider something, like Columbo, the TV character, turning to leave, only to stop and say, "*Just one more thing.*"

"Ashley, you need a ride?" Timothy asked.

"As a matter of fact, yes," she said. "Would you mind carrying me home?"

"Carry you? Well—" Timothy's face expanded into a pearly-white grin.

"Not like that, dummy," Ashley slapped him on the shoulder. "I mean, drive me."

Timothy made a show of bending an arm at the elbow and Ashley slipped her hand in the opening. That was when I realized the weatherman had a lot more cunning than I gave him credit for.

As far as I could tell, no one squatted in the stalls. No crumbled piles of slacks and belts paired with disembodied legs. A moment to myself. Let it pour out. Let me piss away this godawful night. I had a good stream going when the sound of hard-soled shoes echoed against the tiles.

Eight urinals lined the wall. I stood unzipped, at the farthest from the door, staring at the wall. I wasn't up for eye contact or small talk, not tonight and not in the john. The shoes clicked to a stop in the stall to my left, with the sound of a belt unfastening, and a familiar voice.

"There y'are. Been looking for ya." Lee's voice reverberated along the porcelain row. It stopped my stream. My first thought was, *Couldn't you give me some space here?* Then: *Oh, please, not now, not at the Christmas party.*

"I thought maybe you'd cut your losses and left," Lee said.

"I just needed some air. Not that it's any ocean breeze in here."

"Ha-ha, good one, Tom."

Standing mano a mano at the urinal, you just want to get it done. And by all means *do not look down*. But that wasn't the worst of it. Lee had laughed. And he was *smiling*.

He turned back to his business, and from the sound of it, Lee had done plenty of business tonight. "We need to talk," he said.

"Can I zip up first?"

He laughed louder, but then placed a serious hand on my shoulder, studying the bruising on my throat from Harper's death grip. "Son, that looks nasty." He was right. In the mirror I was the picture of a bear attack victim.

Lee led me out the door. "C'mon, let's go chew the rag some."

We came to a small meeting room off the lobby and I saw we weren't going to be alone. The general manager waited there, perched on the edge of a corner table.

"I'll cut right to it," Ransom said. "Lin's goin' on leave. This thing with his son, it's just too hot. We want you to take the anchor chair on an interim basis." Ransom leaned forward in anticipation. "You'll start right after New Year's."

Suddenly I was Bob Cratchit after Scrooge told him his salary was about to be raised. I didn't know whether to jump for joy or call for a straightjacket.

"Tom?" Lee snapped his fingers in my face. "Still with us?"

"I'm here," I said. "Just stunned." Stunned was an understatement. A minute ago left for dead, now I was live at six and ten.

"It's a messy situation, but we'll get through it," Ransom said. "I know it's sudden. Set with it a bit." He pushed off from the table. "And get yourself a clean shirt, boy. You look like you went to war with a dang ketchup bottle and the ketchup won."

Yes, so they tell me.

I watched Ransom leave, and kept on staring at the empty doorway.

"Something troubling you?" Lee said.

"Tonight ... when Lin grabbed his son during the dinner ... I swear he said something about getting back. Back to the house maybe. He was hiding him there, wasn't he?"

Lee patted me three times on the shoulder, as a dad might with a child. "Don't you worry none about that. Lin ain't comin' back till this is all sorted out."

I started to open my mouth but Lee kept on going.

"That said, don't be thinking all's hunky dory for ya just because Lin's in the shitter. Puttin' you on the anchor desk, that's Ransom's doing. Wouldn'ta been my first choice." He ushered me out the door, eyeing my scarlet letter. "Good Lord, you're a bloody mess."

"It's wine, not blood."

"Not yet, anyways."

"What's that supposed to mean?"

"In case you didn't notice," Lee said, "that boy had murder in his eyes tonight. I do believe he's capable of it. You wanna go ahead and keep on screwin' around? You'll find out."

At the end of the week, I dropped off Miss Priss with a cat-friendly neighbor, and the prodigal son flew "home." Back to Chicago. Back to the old house. And the old questions. There were always questions.

I'd barely stepped through the door when Mom started in with the evergreen, "How's work?" I considered answering with, "Would you prefer the good news first, or the 'I got caught on film with my pants down' news?" Instead, I said it was all fine, told them I'd be starting as main anchor at the beginning of the year, a pretty good pay raise, definitely a step up.

"Well, it may not last, Thomas." Mom had never been what you might call a big booster of my career. "You've thought things were going fine before. Milwaukee, Mobile, Springfield, and that other one I can't ever remember."

"Utica, Mom." I couldn't believe my mother was itemizing my failed TV markets.

"Your father and I just wish you had a fallback," she said. "Maybe something in computers, like your brother."

My older brother the computer whiz. "Nah, Mom, I think I'll stick with this for a while."

"Okay," Dad said. "You know we want the best for you."

"Married with kids," Mom added.

"Yep, yep, yep, working on that for sure," I smiled my best news anchor smile. "So, ravioli tonight?"

I booked my return flight for New Year's Eve. The last day of the year had to be the most depressing of all and I had no interest in being around family or anybody else on this particular one. But before I left, I summoned the nerve to revisit some auld lang syne.

My mother had wiped the kitchen countertops for the third time that morning when I put a hand on her arm. "Mom, I talked about the green moon on the air the other day."

"The what, now?" She moved to the sink, dishtowel at the ready.

"Remember when we were kids, during a storm at night? How you'd come in and say, look for the green moon and all that?"

"Oh, that old fable? You boys were young, I had to tell you something."

"You mean you made it up?"

"What do you think, Thomas?"

What I thought was, my mother had just taken a sledge hammer to my childhood. "Well, I've been wondering about something else," I said. "About the time, you know. The car. On the Dan Ryan Expressway."

She froze, her towel hovering over the faucet handle. "Now, why on earth would you want to dredge that up?"

"I don't know. Sometimes I get these flashbacks, these fragments of—"

"And …?" She snapped the dish towel down and turned a stone face to me.

"That's the thing," I said. "Did it happen the way everyone said? Did I really—"

"Thomas, we told you *all* about it many times. You two were sitting up front with me. Then you started fiddling with the car door. It flew open. And you both …" She picked up the towel again. "You *know* all this. What's done is done." She stood rock-still, at one with the granite countertop, staring at her reflection in the faucet. "Go get your bag. You're gonna miss your flight."

23

ARE YOU LONESOME TONIGHT

Dick Clark on the TV, half past eleven. They'd dropped the big apple thirty minutes ago in New York, but the whole thing was being replayed for the sake of us hicks in the Central time zone. I dumped my luggage in the bedroom, filled Miss Priss' bowl, and then got a few snacks from the fridge and plopped down in front of the tube.

With two minutes left until midnight, I was in a battle with my falling eyelids. The eyelids were about to declare victory when the cordless phone jumped to life. I let it ring to the machine.

"*Tommy, it's me. Pick up. Pick up the phone.*"

My eyes fell shut again, but the machine was still talking.

"*Goddammit, if you're there ... Just. Pick. Up.*"

I picked up. "Jesus," I said, "you gotta be kidding me. Meredith, what are you doing?"

"Isn't it obvious? I miss you."

They were the words I so wanted to hear and yet they stung like a broken promise. "I'm watching the countdown," I said.

"Same. And in case you're wondering, I'm by my lonesome. In the house. All alone on New Year's. Ain't that pitiful? Why are we alone tonight, Tommy?" She paused. "Oh. Unless you're *not* alone."

"Nope," I said. "No one's here but me and the Doritos."

I could hear her chuckle on the other end. "You just made me smile out loud, mister."

"Look, what do you—"

"What do I want? *You*, stupid," she said. "Don't you get it? Everything we have, the connection between us. How you look at me. How you ... touch me. That's *real*."

"If you're asking whether I miss you, too, okay, yes, I do. But what exactly do you want me to say?"

"Say you love me."

60 seconds to go. In Times Square, the big apple descended.

"Meredith, you do realize your husband wants me dead. He broke out of hiding, got himself arrested, just so he could strangle me in front of the whole station!"

"Can I come over? Let me come over, Tommy." There was a weariness in her voice, cracking how it does when you haven't slept, when your head's running on an infinite loop. I couldn't imagine what she was going through as the wife, even estranged wife, of the man in the news right now. But putting that aside, everything she said was true. With her I'd felt—*allowed myself to feel*—a level of passion and vulnerability unlike any I'd ever known. But this woman needed more than I could give her.

"I don't think you heard me," I said. "I want to *live* to make it through 1988. And maybe keep my job. I am *not* going back to some small market reporting gig. And I sure as hell am not going into computers and moving back home with Mommy and Daddy!"

"Tommy, I have no idea what all you're talking about but—"

On the TV, Dick Clark stood at Forty-fourth and Broadway, ticking away the final seconds of the year. "And here we go ... five ... four ... three ... two ... one ... *leap* ... and ..."

A giant "1988" flashed on the screen. The announcer said an extra leap second had to be dropped in at the exact moment between 1987 and 1988. Something about making up for the irregular rotation of the earth.

"We're in '88!" Dick Clark shouted the words and that made it official. The broadcast cut to shots of couples kissing, strangers hugging, people breaking out in song.

"Tommy?" Meredith's voice, fragile, distant, through the phone line.

"Yes?"

"Happy New Year."

"Happy New Year, Meredith. Good night." I set down the receiver, grabbed a chip, and turned up the TV.

Where would I be a year from now, when the big apple dropped again, when 1988 turned to 1989? I thought about that extra second Dick Clark was talking about. I clamped my eyes tight and tried to hold back the earth's rotation with my mind. Tried to freeze the clock between old year and new—and just for a moment, will all my dreams to leap into that second of time—suspended between yesterday and tomorrow, between the pitted road behind me and the uncertain path ahead.

PART 2

CHANGE OF HABIT

• 1988 •

24

IF I CAN DREAM

Imagine walking into a theater in the middle of a movie. That was arriving for work in the afternoon. You enter a newsroom that's already in full hustle mode, anxious to catch up on what you missed. This was my shift now. Two to ten-thirty. Tonight would be my first newscast as the official unofficial, indefinite fill-in main anchor until Lin Harper returned, or died, or went to jail, and they found a replacement for him, which wasn't me.

If I had any notion of getting a big head, the *Commercial Appeal* was there to disabuse me of that. I was following a legend. The paper as much as said so in its media column.

> **HARPER OUT AT CHANNEL 2**
>
> Lin Harper is TV royalty, a fixture to Mid-South audiences for decades. But his fate is uncertain, removed from the anchor desk in late December in the wake of domestic assault charges against his son.
>
> Memphis Police Lieutenant Jonathan B. Harper was arrested December 18 at the Petroleum Club. Lt. Harper, who is married, was taken into custody while trying to contact the alleged victim, his former live-in girlfriend, Channel 2 reporter

> Janelle Foster. Channel 2 news director Lee Cravens declined comment on any connection between the arrest and Lin Harper's removal from the air.
>
> Replacing Harper is newcomer Tom Cirone, who joined WMDW-TV early last year. Cirone has made a name for himself, covering crimes and natural disasters, but has been criticized for, at times, inserting himself into his stories.

Inserting himself. There was a phrase. It summed it up perfectly, the bad and the ugly, in two succinct words.

Leading the six o'clock rundown, an update on the Bone Harper case. Lieutenant Harper had been released on bond. I hadn't spoken to Meredith since the stroke of midnight. The thought that Harper might try to move back in with her made me want to hurl.

Settling in the studio, I adjusted my chair, straightened my scripts. On television, everything looked shiny and sharp. But like most everything else on TV, the news set was an illusion, a plywood house of cards, nailed, glued, and taped together like community theatre scenery. The seams of the desk were splitting, the backlit numeral "2" flickered behind me. The padded chairs reeked of years, maybe decades, of butts in the seats. There was a metaphor there, I was sure.

Kimberly entered the studio at five minutes to six, taking the chair to my left. The crew lined up the three cameras, one focused on each of the news anchors, with the center camera zoomed out to capture both anchors together, the "two-shot."

Growing up Catholic, I'd always said my prayers, but I hadn't been especially observant of late. Yet tonight, just before the red light came on, I silently moved my lips in a few verses of my own creation. Over the weekend I'd scribbled out the words for amusement, blasphemous as they may have been:

Give us this day our daily news,
And forgive us our press passes,
As we report sinners, crooks, and jackasses.
And lead us not into sensation,
But deliver us good ratings. Amen.

Closing my eyes, I *breathed*, and using a trick I'd learned from the movie, *Broadcast News*, I sat on the tail of my sports coat. It irked me that the vacuous anchorman in that film was named Tom, but I tried not to dwell on it.

The station logo faded up on the monitor, the announcer's impossibly deep voice booming from the in-studio speakers:

YOU'RE WATCHING WMDW-TV CHANNEL 2.

Thus rolled the new intro, the words gliding across the screen, my name chyroned on a weekday news open for the first time in my career. But they got it wrong, or so I thought.

NOW, LIVE FROM MEMPHIS AND THE MID-SOUTH ... TOM CIRONE ...

... KIMBERLY KILMER ...

"Kimberly, how come they put *my* name first?"

... WEATHER WITH METEOROLOGIST TIMOTHY BURNSIDE ...

"Because you're the man ... *and* the F-N-G."

... AND BOBBY BUGG SPORTS ...

"The f-in what?"

... THIS IS NEWS TWO ... AT SIX.

The studio speakers went quiet and the audio transferred to our earpieces.

"The fucking new guy!" Kimberly shouted.

The image on the screen dissolved to the two-shot, the twang of the producer's voice cutting into our ears. "Guys, the mics are hot."

Rising from neck to forehead, a tide of crimson rolled across Kimberly's face. As a matching red light glowed above the teleprompter, I swallowed hard, and began the newscast.

"Good evening, Memphis. As Kimberly was just saying, I'm Tom Cirone ... the, uh, new guy."

25

NOT A KID AT FIFTY-THREE

During a ten o'clock newscast that first week I read a story about a North Memphis house fire. A space heater had toppled over. Firefighters found five small bodies huddled in a back bedroom closet. Next story, a mother and her boyfriend arrested for locking a child in a dog cage, slowly starving the boy to death. Next, an honor student mistakenly killed in a gang shooting.

Sitting at the anchor desk, night after night, coldly delivering one tragedy stacked on top of another—it was not for the faint of heart. I wondered whether being exposed to extremes of humanity day in and day out warped your mind. Maybe the entire construct of working in television news brought out the worst in people. In me.

As soon as I got home I collapsed into bed. I wasn't cut out for this soul-sucking grind.

From far away, it roused me, growing closer, louder each second. My hand swung to the nightstand, knocking the phone receiver from its cradle, silencing the electronic assault.

A voice, manic and wide-awake, shouted, "Thomas! Are you up?"

"Who is this?" I pawed at the clock radio, tilting it to read the time.

"Do you know what today is?"

I switched on the light. "No."

"It's my goddamn birthday."

"Happy Birthday, Danny."

"It *should* be happy. Mama always said every year on this earth is a blessing. But I tell you what, right now, good-time Charlie's got the blues."

"It's two in the morning," I said.

"And I'm ready to get out of this house."

"Wait. How did you get my number?"

There was a pause on the other end. I thought I heard him laugh and then caught the sound of a hand slapping paper. "You're in the damn phone book, Jack. Right here in black and white."

Danny gave me a set of driving directions. He called it a special place, a place he went at night sometimes to "cast out the demons." He said to meet him there. *Now.*

It was just a line on the map, so why did driving from Tennessee to Mississippi always feel like a descent into oblivion? Martin Luther King, Junior may have once said Mississippi sweltered in the heat of injustice and oppression, but at the moment, it was a frozen wasteland. An early January snow storm had dumped six inches on us, virtually shutting down the region. It was nothing for a Chicago kid, but people here didn't have a clue what to do with snow, or how to drive in it. Fortunately, there was no one else on the highway at three in the morning.

I exited at Goodman Road as instructed, my tires crunching the hardpack snow. Down a crossroad about a mile farther along I spotted the Stutz Batmobile, parked beside a long, gray building. The sign out front said *Horn Lake Firing Squad, Gun Range & Barbecue.*

"You dragged me here for target shooting?" I called out, my frozen breath disappearing into the wind.

"Yep. Members only, like the jacket," he said. "And you're my guest."

"It's twenty degrees out."

"Well, let's get on inside then." Danny shouldered a duffle bag. It pulled him down on one side. He seemed slighter, more tentative in his movements since I'd seen him last. "Damn shame what happened up in West Memphis," he said, dragging a leg as he walked. "Somebody oughta do a benefit concert or something for them poor folk."

"Like *you*, maybe?"

"Shit, not me, son. Even if the Right Reverend Admiral Fucking Parker came begging. I'm outta that business."

"If you ask me, that's a shame."

"I ain't askin'."

The building comprised a long, low-ceilinged chamber with a series of parallel shooting bays. Danny disappeared into an office and all at once the banks of fluorescent lights buzzed to life. When he came back he unburdened his sack on a counter, zipping it open to reveal a small arsenal of long guns, pistols, and ammunition.

He hefted a beefy black handgun. "This little baby is a Beretta ninety-two. Seen the movie, *Lethal Weapon*?"

I nodded, yes, in fact, I had.

"Once I saw that film, I knew I had to have one." He turned the gun over, caressing it. "A friend on the force helped with the red tape."

He dropped the Beretta in my hands. It felt solid, heavy, an aptly named lethal weapon. "You know your guns," I said.

"It's a hobby, Thomas. What's yours? Sleepin' with police wives?"

Posted on every goddam telephone pole.

I fumbled the handgun, letting it fall to the counter. "Say what?"

"I said, you got a pair on ya. But, are you sure your balls are screwed on right, Thomas? I could swear them balls ain't screwed on right." He waved a hand in the direction of a red lever on the wall. "Now, c'mon, let's go kill some targets. Flip that thing over there, will ya?"

A motor started and the back wall of the bay folded like a garage door into the ceiling. A blast of frigid air filled the room. Snow covered the lighted range beyond, terminating in a series of berms and hills.

A step-button on the floor activated a pulley mechanism and sent out a target. It reflected the light of the full moon as it floated to the far end of the range. Danny handed me a set of hearing protectors and popped open a pack of gold rifle cartridges.

"These are three-oh-eight Winchesters. You want something dead at extreme range, that's the ammo for you." He motioned to a needle-nosed ash black rifle. "And this right here is a custom-built Colt AR-10. It's a damn killing machine. It can rip the ass off a possum at five hundred yards."

"Impressive." I said, not knowing whether it was or not.

He loaded the magazine, chambered the first round, then raised the rifle, aiming for the distant target. "That's about ... two hundred yards." He winced, clenching his gut, as he positioned the butt of the weapon into his shoulder. He put his eye to the scope. "Of course in this kind of weather, you wanna adjust your aim some, what they call Kentucky windage. Then all you need to do is set your feet, exhale and ... squeeze, squeeze, squeeze."

The rifle exploded with stunning force, but his body barely shifted. The intensity of the gunshot shook my chest cavity. I could only imagine what it would do to exposed eardrums. I thanked God for the earmuffs.

Danny relaxed, pointing the rifle to the floor. He stepped on the button and the target came swinging back. It was one of those old-time ones, a 1930s gangster, black wavy hair, one eye closed, pointing a revolver. A single hole penetrated a spot along the bad guy's jaw.

Taking out a pair of gold-trimmed reading glasses, Danny studied his handiwork. "May he rest in pieces," he chuckled. "Been doin' this a long time. The Army gave me a marksman's medal. I made sharpshooter."

"I can see that," I said. "Do you hunt?"

"Well, I asked this doctor once, 'Doc,' I said, 'what's the quickest way to drop a man cold?' You know what he told me? The Doc goes, 'Shoot for just under the neck. Below the ear. Put a bullet there. It's instant.'" He smacked the hole in the target for emphasis.

"When I said hunting, I didn't mean murdering someone."

"You know, Saint Thomas, if it came down to it, I think I could do it. If there was no other choice. You never know. Maybe I'm fixin' to right now." He grabbed the Beretta from the counter and before I could flinch he leveled it at my nose and squeezed the trigger.

"Bang!"

The word burst from his lips and he fell over howling—a full-throated roar—which startled me almost as much as the click of the trigger. As mortified as I was, I joined in. The breath from our combined laughter cascaded into the range.

Still smiling, Danny drew back the slide on the handgun. He held the weapon out in front of him. "I never chamber the first round, see?" He set down the Beretta and sent another target into the night air. "Your turn."

Danny pressed my hands onto the rifle, shoving the stock into the side of my chest. When I put my eye to the telescopic sight, it was a revelation, its magnification delivering the distant target in exquisite detail.

"Inhale, exhale, hold," he instructed. "Spread your feet. Now squeeze." The rifle came alive, slingshotting my body backwards. After recovering from the shock, I was anxious to see how I'd done.

"Not bad," Danny said, examining the bullet hole piercing the lower torso of the target. "Mixed nuts, anyone?"

"Lucky shot. But there is one guy I wouldn't mind nailing that way for real."

"Not you, Saint Thomas. You're just a mild-mannered reporter."

"Am I?"

"I will give you this. You stood up to that cowboy cop, foolish as it was."

"How much do you know about that?"

"Son, I got a suggestion. When things go wrong, try not to go with 'em." Danny flipped the switch to close the bay door and packed up his weapons.

A minute later we were outside again, at the cars.

"Hey," I called out, "have a happy birthday!

"Fifty-three and headin' south." He groaned and slid into the driver's seat, clutching his abdomen. "Hell, I'm so ancient, my nose hairs got nose hairs."

26

WHAT'D I SAY

The other shoe dropped in the Walker case later in the month when Sergeant Buckley Poole joined his colleague in taking a plea. Guilty on a single count of misdemeanor reckless endangerment. I knew what it meant. The city and its police department were closing the books on this embarrassing sideshow, clearing the way for prosecuting Carl Walker for the death of Officer Howard.

Only, I wasn't ready to turn the page. I found Eddie in an edit bay and asked for his help.

"That depends." Eddie said. "Is it Tom the reporter askin', or Tom the big man with the butt in the anchor chair?"

Eddie had a point. Since my elevation to main anchor, the whole vibe around me had shifted. No longer the pariah. Rambo, no more. I'd gone from newsroom pond scum to exalted jay bird singing a nightly serenade. Mind you, I'd done nothing to deserve it, other than the fact of my ass being in the big chair.

I scratched my chin. "I think it's *not* the guy with the butt asking. It's the other one."

Together we fetched all the tape we had on the Walker story. I wanted to sift through it frame by frame. Eddie inserted the first Beta cassette into the machine and hit PLAY. Up came a series of disjointed clips, scenes we'd edited into stories so far, five or ten seconds each. But the video sequence I was hoping to see wasn't there, the police supervisor standing over Walker. Since we'd never used that shot on the news, and since the original tape was still missing, we didn't have it now.

Next, the stuff we shot from the back of the Walker house. Eddie felt we were trespassing that day, but as I stared at the monitor, I realized sometimes crime does pay.

"Roll that back. Play it again," I said.

Eddie twisted the dial to the left and the electronically-displayed minutes and seconds scrolled in reverse like a video time machine. He hit PLAY, and a moment later hit PAUSE, his eyes blinking at the screen. The freeze frame depicted the point of view of a person standing on the back porch, looking through the rear door into the house.

I said, "Tell me what you see."

"If someone was down low enough on these steps ..." He pressed a finger against the TV screen. "... those cops in the front of the house wouldn't have known they were in the crossfire."

His words slammed me back in my seat. "Wait, Eddie, what was that?"

"I sure don't know. What'd I say?"

"You said 'crossfire.'"

"Yeah. Seen it before. If there's people pointing their weapons and standing at both the front and back doors at the same time—" He swiveled to face me. "Hell, they don't call it a shotgun house for nothin'."

I leaped to my feet and pounded the thin plaster wall of the edit bay. "Holy crap!"

"Tom, what?"

"You incredible photojournalist. You brilliant, brilliant man!" Eddie pushed his feet against the floor, rolling away, not sure what to make of me. I ejected the Beta cassette, passing it carefully into the photographer's hands. "Eddie, don't let this tape out of your sight!"

Candy buzzed my desk phone just before five. I had a visitor. Even before I pushed through the lobby doors, I heard the familiar giggle. Meredith had on a black wool coat with a fur fringe, her hair tied back, and barely a touch of makeup. She leaned across the circular front desk and the two of them were in stitches. They stopped cold and turned, guilty smiles on their faces.

"You two know each other?" I said.

"We might've been previously acquainted ..." Candy suppressed another laugh. "You got a good one here, Tom."

I raised an eyebrow and addressed Meredith. "What brings you here this afternoon, *Mrs. Harper*?"

She reached for my arm, thought better of it, withdrew. "You're doin' great on the news. I didn't know they were puttin' you on the anchor desk."

"Yeah, well, with the other guy, your father-in-law, aiding and abetting a felon and all. *Alleged* felon." I walked her to the long couch by the windows. "I kinda got the job by default. Is that why you're here? To talk about my career?"

"I didn't want to do it over the phone."

"Do what?"

"Tell you." Meredith took a long breath. "I'm filin' for divorce." She lifted her left hand, waving her fingers. The diamond was gone, replaced by a pale ring of skin.

"So, no more Meredith Harper?" Using her married name repeatedly was cruel, I knew it. Seeing her, I felt cruel. "What does Meredith *Ryder* have to say about it?"

"Where'd you come up with *that*?"

"I might have seen it somewhere." I slumped back into the couch, my hands slipping into my pockets.

"It's my maiden name," she said. "I'm changin' it back.

"And hubby's just fine with all this?"

"It's not up to him."

I raised my voice. "Isn't it?"

Candy lifted her head from the reception desk, caught my eye, looked away.

"I know you want me to say some words," I said, more softly now. "Make everything all right. And if I never said the words out loud to you, well, it's because—"

"Because why?"

"You want to know why?"

"Yes."

"I'll tell you why." This was the tricky part. The part where words always failed me. The part about feelings. My eyes dropped to the floor. "I don't know why."

Meredith folded her hands in her lap. "Tommy, there's something else I gotta tell ya."

"I'm listening."

"I found a gun in the house. A big one."

27

SEPARATE WAYS

When Meredith described a black zipper duffel tucked up on a top shelf in the hall, I knew exactly what she meant. I'd seen it. I sent her home with a couple of pieces of advice. One, leave the gun where it was. Two, change all the locks.

Next day, I tried to put her and her husband out of my mind but instead found myself back at the scene of the crime, the *Petroleum Club*, the last place I wanted to visit again after the Christmas party.

The assignment desk sent me to cover a celebration of the recent induction of the inaugural class of the *Rock and Roll Hall of Fame*. According to the news release, this would be the first Memphis gathering of the homegrown recording artists since the event. I wondered, would Danny be there? Would he acknowledge me?

One of the guests intercepted us the moment we entered the ballroom, a man in his sixties with shock of thick red hair, bangs dangling over his forehead, a full beard and mustache. He extended a meat hook of a hand. "Sam Phillips. Glad you boys could make it tonight."

We shook. "This is Dilly. I'm Tom."

"Oh, I know who y'all are. You're doin' a damn fine job on the news."

It was off-the-wall crazy, this legendary music producer, founder of

Sun Records, discoverer of Elvis, watching *me* on the news. But then again, Danny said he watched our news, too. I thanked him for the compliment and asked Phillips if he had a moment for an interview.

He started off talking about the night they'd been inducted into the Hall of Fame. "We finally talked Elvis into goin'. Then ya had Ray Charles, Chuck Berry, the Everly Brothers, Little Richard, so many greats—" He trailed off as another familiar face entered the frame. "Speak of the devil, Jerry Lee, you stinkin' sonofabitch, how the hell are you?"

I wanted to pinch myself. Sam Phillips *and* Jerry Lee Lewis together in the same room! Our sports anchor and music maven Bobby Bugg would trade all the crawfish in Louisiana to be in my place right now. For the next few minutes, the two bantered back and forth as if Dilly and I weren't there. Something about the contentious legal battle between Elvis Presley and his former manager. Phillips called it a bad break-up. "We ain't givin' up on him, that's for damn sure," he said. "He's still got a lotta livin' to do."

Lewis peered across the ballroom. "Is the man comin' tonight?"

"No, he ain't gonna make it."

"Damn," Lewis said. "The boy's gotta snap the hell out of it. Remember that *Live Aid* thing a few years back, when they offered Presley a prime spot? Woulda been the comeback to kick all comebacks to hell. Everybody asked him, begged him practically. Jagger, Tom Petty, Madonna, hell even Bob Dylan. Goddamn Beach Boys reached out. He said no to all of 'em. What was his reason, Sam?"

"He just wasn't ready," Phillips said.

"Hell. Wasn't ready. Even before all that shit went down with him in '77 he was hidin' himself inside Graceland. Never even went to the damn Grammys to collect his hardware. It's been ten years or more, for cryin' out loud. Just a friggin' shame."

Jerry Lee Lewis headed for the bar and Phillips turned back to the camera.

"You know what the *real* shame of it is?" he said. "They're putting the goddamn *Rock and Roll Hall of Fame* in Cleveland! Shit, rock 'n' roll was invented *here*. In Memphis, Tennessee. So, now, they want to build some kind of pyramid, down by the river, like some kinda damned booby prize. Is that supposed to make up for it? This ain't fuckin' Egypt!"

Phillips could read the look on my face. As gut-honest as his diatribe was, given his Moses-come-down-from-the-mountaintop fire and brimstone, he knew none of it was going to make it on the air tonight.

At ten, right before weather, we ran the story. None of the off-color comments about the Hall of Fame nor the ain't-it-a-shame about Presley made the cut. We came out of the video and I mentioned proceeds from the event would go to Saint Jude Children's Research Hospital. Unfortunately, one honoree was missed tonight, I said. The one, in fact, who started the whole rock 'n' roll thing.

As the camera pulled out to a three-shot, Timothy cocked his head and slid his chair forward. "You mean Elvis left the building?" He eyeballed the camera, snickering.

"No, Timothy," I said. "He couldn't make it tonight."

"Did anyone even notice?"

Stuck in the middle, my co-anchor cleared her throat and forced a smile. "So, Timothy, a warm-up for the weekend?"

"Wait, Kimberly," I pivoted to face the weatherman. "As a matter of fact, yes, people noticed. I for one would have loved to interview him tonight. Who wouldn't want that opportunity? Now, why don't you stick to what you know and go click your little clicker and point to your pretty maps?"

Whatever may have compelled me to rise so publicly to Danny's defense, my rejoinder to the weatherman earned me a sharp reprimand from the boss. The next afternoon I was happy to flee the newsroom—and Lee's wrath—for an hour, even though I expected it to be a bit of a wild goose chase.

The campus covered several acres in Midtown, not far from Overton Park. We pulled the van into a loading zone across from the limestone-columned entryway. Engraved in block letters, it announced, "Catholic High School."

The receptionist in the main office cast a wary look on Eddie and me she as delivered the perfunctory, "May I help you?" Before I could answer, her eyes widened and she said, "You're from the news."

"Yes, Channel 2. We've been covering the Walker case."

"Carl's a good man, a good teacher. We're real broken up over it," she said. "But y'all can't be here."

"We're trying to tell his story," I said. "Talk to folks who worked with him."

"Unfortunately, all personnel matters are confidential." The woman sneaked a glance at the door to the inner office. "You'll have to take that up with the diocese."

"Maybe you could put us in touch with his wife?"

"Like I say, I can't give information about any of our teachers, not Carl nor Diana."

"Diana?"

"Mrs. Walker," she said. "And now honey, I'm gonna have to ask y'all to leave."

"Thank you ma'am." We backed out of the office.

Climbing into the passenger side of the truck, I marveled at how people often divulged things to reporters without realizing it. "Eddie did you catch that? 'Personnel matters.'"

"I didn't get what she meant."

"She said, '*any* of our teachers,' and mentioned Carl *and* his wife."

28

3764 HIGHWAY 51 SOUTH

March roared in with a brutal wake-up call, and not the kind that rips you out of bed at two in the morning with Danny on the other end of the line. I'd known for a while that I shared virtually the same birth date with the famous pop singer, Andy Gibb. He'd turned thirty at the beginning of the month and I was set to join him in hitting the big 3-0 a few days later.

I walked into the newsroom on my birthday as the wire machine banged out the terrible bulletin:

ANDY GIBB, BROTHER OF THE BEE GEES, DIES IN ENGLAND AT AGE 30

Inflammation of the heart, they said, and drugs may have played a role. Can't say I was in the mood for cake and candles that night.

After the late news, instead of heading home, I pointed my car south on Interstate 55, exiting on the outskirts of the Whitehaven neighborhood, all told, a journey of eight miles. Impulsive. A wild hair, as Meredith might say. But this was where my instincts delivered me.

It seemed an odd location for an iconic mansion. Sure, the house was set well back, on a wooded hillside, but the neighborhood had gone to pot. The property faced a garish commercial strip and bordered fast food joints, car dealers, mobile home lots, roach motels. A long time ago they'd rechristened this stretch of road from Memphis all the way to the Mississippi state line, "Elvis Presley Boulevard."

Someone once described Graceland as an antebellum funeral parlor. Seeing it now, late at night, in lonely isolation, the two-story columns called to mind a grand mausoleum, the cold light of the street lamps casting its stonework in a ghostly pallor.

I hadn't given any thought to what I'd do once I got there. You didn't just walk up and ring the doorbell. For one thing, there were the gates, adorned with metallic mirror-image figures of a guitar player. They'd once guarded, I supposed, against the crush of adoring fans who'd swarmed here. Interlaced across the gates, musical notes dotted the meshwork like the pages of a song book. A fieldstone wall extended the length of the frontage. Graffiti marred a section of it. Someone had tried to scrub it off, but you could still read it:

THE KING IS DEAD. LONG LIVE PRINCE.

The wall was not especially tall, nor very secure. Anyone could hop over the thing. I ran my palm along the jagged stones, wondering what would happen if I tried.

"Can I help you?"

I jumped back a step, startled. The voice had come from nowhere and very near. "Yes, actually," I said, speaking into the air. "This is a little weird, but I'm an acquaintance of, uh, the man inside."

A figure stepped out of a small guardhouse, Lizard, the security guy. "Oh, it's you. From the TV," he said. "Did the boss send for you?"

"Well ..."

Lizard held up his hand. "Listen, buddy, he's doing poorly tonight. No visitors."

"Okay, but if you could just tell him I was here?"

"Uh huh. Now get on home. This neighborhood ain't safe."

"It's Travis, right?"

"Last I checked."

"Travis, isn't this all a little bizarre?"

"How you figure?"

"All this." I gestured at the guardhouse and the gate, spreading my arms wider to include the grounds, the mansion. "Does he live alone?"

"No, he don't live alone."

"Are you the whole security force?"

"Kid, what do you want?"

"I just—"

With a crunching of feet on gravel, a figure descended the drive. "Hey, what are you two conspirin' about?" Danny half-jogged toward us, arms swinging at his sides, propelled by gravity more than muscle. "Go on and let the boy in."

"Boss, shouldn't you be resting?"

"Open the goddamn gates."

Travis pushed a button. A mechanism began to work and the giant gates swept inward.

"That's all right, Lizard. We're gonna walk and talk a bit." Danny wore a pair of white workout pants, double black lines running down the legs, and a thin nylon windbreaker—too thin, I thought, for the chill air tonight. Travis had said Danny was doing poorly and I could see that now. He bobbed his head, he sucked rapid, shallow breaths. His knees gave out every few paces, not a limp exactly, more of a studder step. A labored walk down a lonely street.

"I feel like I only just saw your ass on the news a few minutes ago," Danny said. "Too bad about that Gibb fella, huh?"

I nodded and Danny set a hand on my shoulder, leading me up the drive. "Wanderin' yourself down here. This time of night. That's a daring feat, even for *Rambo*."

"How do you know—?"

"It's a good one. John Rambo's a complicated guy. I wish *I'd* given you the name." We stopped halfway to the house. "I got cameras everywhere, you know. I could see you peepin' and hidin' out there. Thinking about jumping the wall, weren't you?"

"To be honest, I'm here because ... because it's my birthday."

His lip curled, exposing a row of flawless teeth. "I see. And you want to shoot something ... or someone?" He smiled wider, an electric smile, contagious.

I smiled back. "Not exactly."

He squinted past the towering oaks, at the traffic on the boulevard below. "You know, when I went into rehab, the city council wanted to change the street back to plain old Highway 51. I guess I was just one big embarrassment to them politicians."

"It didn't happen though."

"Nah, they didn't have the balls to do it."

Through the trees you could just discern the glow of golden arches, the outlines of a strip mall, vacant storefronts, empty lots. I wasn't sure why, but the sight of it hurt my heart.

"By the way," Danny said, "what you done a while back on the news. About me bein' a no-show and all. How you put that weatherman in his place. That was somethin'. What I mighta once called TCB. Takin' care of business."

"Yeah, my mouth tends to get ahead of my brain," I said. "That's Rambo for ya." I waved a hand toward the street. "I see you've got a McDonald's down there. One time they told me to go cover this story, Cabbage Patch mini dolls in the new Happy Meals. Remember that frenzy? That same night in the news there was a multiple shooting, a fire, a fatal crash. Those were real stories. But nope. Parents rioting, getting into fist fights trying to snag some plastic toys. That's what they wanted me to cover. I swore up and down in the newsroom. I would *not* do the Cabbage Patch story. But in the end they made me do it."

Danny rocked his head. "Ever heard the song *Old MacDonald*?"

"Sure."

"They made me sing it in a movie. Made me sing this crazy-ass kids song."

"That's nuts."

"I stormed out of that recording studio hoppin' mad. I think I mighta cussed every name in the book that day. But I had to do it. And then come time to film the scene on the soundstage, and here I am sitting on the back of a fake truck, a glorified country bumpkin in a white sport coat, lip-syncing to a bunch of dang farm animals."

"I feel stupid now," I said.

"Don't make no difference how far you've come, son, sooner or later you're gonna get spread-eagled. Happens to the best of us." He started to move again, managed two or three paces, then folded to his knees. "Thomas, how do you do it?"

"Do what?"

"Get the juice to do the news every night."

"I never thought of it that way."

"You mentioned pills one time," he said. "Fact is, I was sick, man. So I took them drugs to deaden the pain, and not all of it was physical. But that shit damn near killed me. And after the world found out about it, well, it might as well have killed me. Nobody cared when I finally quit the stuff. The damage was done." Danny set his hands on his hips and arched his back, his face to the night sky. "But back when those doctors first started writing me all them scripts, it was 'cause I needed 'em to perform. To get me going on stage. And to calm me down after."

"I'm not doing two shows a night like you did," I said. "Well, I'm doing two newscasts, but not performing on stage in front of thousands."

"Don't sell yourself short. Your thousands may be lollygaggin' on the couch throwing down Chee-toes instead of panties, but they're still out there. You just keep doing your thing, so's they'll come back the next night."

"How did *you* keep them coming?"

"No encores. Not one, in all my shows. I don't believe in it. Just get off the stage and keep 'em wanting more. That's the way to live. And that's the way to die. There ain't no encores in life. No damned second chances, neither. This here is *it*, boy."

Danny rubbed his hands together and directed his gaze at the pale lights illuminating his namesake thoroughfare below. "Hey, this cold air's bitin' my ass. Wanna come up to the house?"

I staggered, turning an open-mouthed face to the Colonial-style mansion at the end of the drive. *Join the man inside Graceland?* All I could manage was a wordless nod and a questioning finger point toward the front door.

In the next instant, Danny dropped my arm with a wicked chop. It stung. He had a mean karate strike. "Aww, fuck no. I ain't lettin' you up there, Thomas." He doubled over, his laughing breath crystallizing in the air between us. "Nobody's allowed up there no more except family, Lizard, and maybe the few so-called friends I got left. The place ain't a dang museum, son!"

Travis had been shadowing us a few steps back. Now he put out an insistent hand. Danny straightened, groaned. A bone cracked. *Getting old sucks.*

"Okay, okay, Lizard. I'm goin' back on in. Show the man out." Danny took a halting step. "Hold on. I almost forgot." He pulled something from his jacket, thin and black, silver-edged. He held it out in an open palm.

"This here's an Italian switchblade. Rizzuto Estileto Milano," he said, enunciating each syllable. He depressed a gold button on the handle. A blade whipped out, with a slight, but solid, click. I jumped back at the size of the knife and the quickness of the mechanism.

"See, it says it right on it. Milano." He dropped the knife into my hand. "Take it. You might need it. It's a dangerous fucking world out there."

The thing felt heavy. Heavy and illegal. The blade alone must have been four inches long.

"How do you close it?" I juggled the knife until Danny pressed a crossbar at the hilt, folding it back inside its handle. "Thanks," I said. "I mean, I don't know what to say."

"You don't need to say nothin', Thomas."

"Boss, you best get inside," Travis urged. "You know what them doctors told you."

Danny nodded and wobbled away. He looked frail, vulnerable, despite his large frame. Something compelled me to call after him, a memory, a bit of trivia I'd read in a magazine once.

"Don't!"

He stopped, without turning around. "Don't what?"

"*Don't.*" I said. "Your hit song. Number one on the charts in 1958. The week I was born. Just wanted you to know."

"Happy birthday. Now, go home, Rambo." He flapped an arm over his head and continued alone into the house.

At the gates, as Lizard closed them behind me, I loitered, lacing my fingers through the songbook mesh. "Travis, what's wrong with him?"

He cast a glance back at the house before answering. "Stomach trouble. He's had it for decades. Flew outta town for some procedure last fall to try to clear things up. Something to do with the colon and all that plumbing down there."

"Sounds awful," I said.

"It is. He calls it his G.I. blues."

29

LET'S PLAY HOUSE

The *Commercial Appeal* ran a feature in the paper through the 1980s called *Elvis Has Left The Building*. Seeing the King around town had become such a rarity, the newspaper took to publishing surreptitious pictures of him out and about. It seemed a light-hearted gag on the part of the editors, but it ceased being a joke on April Fool's Day, when I turned up in the latest column.

The picture showed a pair of grainy figures. A telephoto shot. A third person, his back to the camera, stood between the other men, dark helmet hair, medium build, wearing a suitcoat. I knew the shape of my own head. The facial features of the other two, despite the soft focus and the black and white reproduction in the paper, were clear. The caption read:

SPOTTED AT GRACELAND MONDAY NIGHT

```
53-year-old Elvis Presley and two companions
are out for a late stroll on the grounds in
Whitehaven, in this photo by a Commercial Appeal
photographer. Mr. Presley appears outfitted in
a running suit, speaking with a member of his
staff and an unidentified individual. We'd like
to publish your sightings. If you have an item
suitable for Elvis Has Left the Building, please
```

```
send it to the Commercial Appeal, 495 Union
Avenue, Memphis. Photos cannot be returned, but
if published, we will pay you $25.
```

The newspaper sat on the six o'clock producer's desk, folded open, the photo visible in the bottom right corner. Of course I'd already seen it, stared at it, obsessed over it, when I scooped my copy of the paper from the doorstep this morning. Now it lined Miss Priss' litter box.

No one shouting expletives, no typewriters clacking. Just the occasional squawk of the police scanners. This was the Zen of the newsroom after eleven—when everyone had gone home for the night. Finally alone with my thoughts, I dialed the phone.

"Tommy…?" The sound of my name meandered through the line, two syllables on a lazy river. "This is a surprise," Meredith whispered. "I guess I thought I'd never hear from you again."

"I went by Catholic High the other day," I said.

"Okay."

"Then I remembered you telling me something about a teacher."

"You mean with Bone," she said, her voice dropping.

"Yes."

"Jesus, you woke me up for that?"

"What about it, Meredith? The teacher and your husband?"

"Tom, I'll tell you what I know. But not like this. Not on the dang phone."

"I can be there in about thirty."

"I'll put on some coffee."

She answered the door in an untucked men's shirt and sweats, her bed hair pushed to one side. As we sat at the kitchen table, a dim overhead light dangling between us, Meredith told me she'd been doing what I'd wanted, hanging back, leaving me alone these past weeks. I said I didn't know what I wanted, but what I did know was that the station still had those photos of us and I suspected her in-laws were behind it.

Her face darkened. This wasn't the social visit she might have hoped for. "You want to keep dragging my tail through this stuff and I'm trying to put it the hell behind me," she said, stirring her coffee with an angry clang of spoon against cup. "You asked me about some teacher. Yes, Bone shacked up with her. We fought about it. I lost. What of it?"

"Was her name Diana? Maybe Diana *Walker*?"

She returned a blank stare. "Jesus. It was years back with him and that teacher."

"But it might explain why your husband has a hard-on about Carl Walker."

"Just drink your coffee." She was done with being questioned and I'd been too loose with my language. She watched me sip. Waited for me to finish. "You wanna take a look at that thing I found?"

"The gun?"

"It's still up there." She pointed to a shelf in the hall, the same place I'd seen it the last time I was here. "Can you reach it?" she asked. "I needed a footstool to get it."

Fully extending my arm, I could just grasp the strap. I yanked, and the bag toppled over the edge, crashing to the floor. We stood, transfixed.

"Holy crap. What if it was loaded?"

"Footstool next time," she said. We laughed, and for a second I forgot myself, mesmerized by her lips, the crease of her smile. She sensed it, my guard down. She took a step, and with two hands around my collar pulled me in and kissed me.

"What was that for?" I said.

"There has to be a reason now?"

"Well …" I looked at the shrouded weapon on the floor. "Let's open this up."

Unzipped, the duffle bag revealed the truncated, but lethal, barrel of a sawed-off shotgun. It wasn't the type crafted using a circular saw in a garage somewhere. It looked purpose-built, the kind used by special forces or SWAT teams.

"Meredith, are there guns stashed all over the house?"

"What? No. I don't know. Maybe it's been there all the while and I never—"

I put a finger to her lips and spun my head. Living in apartments I'd become sensitized to the sounds of strangers in close proximity, car doors slamming, music playing, footsteps on stairs. *Footsteps ...*

"Tommy, what—"

"Shhh. Hold on. I hear something."

"Is this an April Fool's prank?"

"Not unless you're pulling it. And besides ..." I glanced at my watch. Past midnight. "It's April second."

Now Meredith heard it. Shoes on the walkway. Keys jangling on a chain. "Tommy, zip the bag. Put it up."

I hefted the thing as high as I could stretch, inching it with the tips of my fingers.

"Put it up! Put it up!"

The steps stopped, a key clicked in the lock.

We had nowhere to hide, not in the kitchen, and for sure not here in the hall, where we stood exposed. Meredith switched off the lights, her hands flapping, beckoning me to a storage closet beneath the stairs, closing us in just as the bolt engaged at the front door.

"You never changed the damn locks?" I sputtered.

Now it was Meredith's turn to hold a finger to *my* lips. Someone was in the house. Heavy steps, conducting a room-to-room search. *As a cop would.*

A flashlight cast about, its swinging rays visible through the gap at the bottom of the door. Meredith slipped her finger away. We stood inches apart, face to face, not breathing, not moving. I felt a hand on my chest, then another. She began slowly, quietly, unbuttoning my shirt. My arm slipped around her waist. I parted my lips and pulled her to me. She trembled and there we held, a Rodin *Kiss* frozen in marble.

In the hall, a heavy object slid across a shelf. A zipper peeled back. *He found what he was after.* My hands searched Meredith's face in the dark, my fingers brushing her eyebrows, looping her hair behind her ears. I laid my head against her shoulder, whispering, "Breathe." She exhaled, the coffee still pungent on her breath. The zipper again, the scrape of the bag off the hardwoods. Steps growing closer, stopping. *Thinking.*

I imagined Harper, his mouth gaping, huffing like a bull in heat, contemplating the closet door. He was probably debating whether to fling it open and shoot his wife dead right there, together with that asshole from the news. Two for one. A single blast ought to do it. It occurred to me I couldn't have made an easier mark of myself if I'd tried. My Honda was parked in the street, smack in front of the house.

The footsteps receded. The front door opened. Shut. Silence.

Meredith erupted in laughter, exquisite, explosive, and so unrestrained I worried our intruder would hear it from outside. I took her face in my hands and brought our lips close once more. We were magnets of opposite polarity, pulling, pulling ...

She pushed off, shoving me against the wall. "Tommy, stop." Clearly, there'd be no making out under the stairs like teens hiding from parents. Meredith reached for the closet door. "We're not going there again until you tell me."

"Tell you—?" My fingers went to my lips. Hot to the touch.

"Quit playin' games. You can't keep hiding your feelings in a dang closet. Just tell me already."

I stepped past her, into the hallway. "Can you switch on a light?"

She handed me the stepstool. I stood atop it. No surprise, the gun was gone.

"Now what?" Meredith asked.

"Now nothing. No, something. Change your locks, for chrissakes."

"It won't matter what I do," she said. "He could break in anytime he wanted."

"And has he?"

"Why are you always interrogating me?"

"Meredith, this is ridiculous." The night had spiraled so far afield, I'd almost forgotten why I came. "Listen, about that teacher Harper was seeing ..."

"You are making me batshit crazy with these stupid questions." She lifted the stepstool, slammed it to the floor. "What about *my* question?"

I knew what she wanted, but I couldn't reciprocate. "Right now I just want to live," I said. "Maybe later we can talk about feelings."

"If that's how it is, then you oughta leave." She hurled my jacket.

My swift exit called to mind the Southern saying about the door. It did nearly hit me where the good Lord split me.

30

HEARTBREAK MOTEL

Fifteen minutes later, I pounded the steps to my apartment, still smarting from the literal and figurative door slam at Meredith's house. So maybe I did a little slamming of my own, flinging the apartment door shut with such violence it rattled the dishes in the kitchen cabinets and sent Miss Priss scattering to the safety of the bedroom.

The sight of Priss, her hazel eyes flashing down the hall in terror, instantly lowered my temperature and pushed the close call with Harper to the back of my mind. I set down my jacket and headed after my frazzled cat.

"Priss? Where did you get to?"

Her melodic purr, that soft rumbling deep within her throat, gave her away. She'd fled to the comfort of her favorite nighttime hideout, a stinky old blanket laid atop my dresser.

"There you are, baby."

She watched me approach, her eyes softening in the cool half-darkness of the bedroom. I felt for the light switch, flipped it on, then reached over to stroke the scruff of her neck. Priss jerked away, baring her fangs, raising up on her hind legs. Her ears twisted round and she fixed her eyes in the direction of the window opposite.

"C'mon, Priss." I tried again. "I'm sorry. Will you accept—"

The drywall behind us exploded, bursting outward in a spray of paint chips and powder. A millisecond later the bedroom window shattered into a crystalline spiderweb, radiating outward from a ring of pulverized glass.

I snatched Priss with two hands and hit the deck, rolling to a stop against the bed. There I held until I'd convinced myself it was safe for either of us to move. I craned my neck in search of the offending projectile. I was not disappointed. Embedded in the wall, the blunt end of a bullet, its trajectory within a whisker of Miss Priss' perch.

Jumping to my feet, I swiped the light switch to darken the room. The floor crunched underfoot with scattered shards of glass as I dropped back down, crawling to the window. Nothing to see, save for a pair of taillights receding onto Mendenhall Road.

The responding MPD officers said it was likely an "errant bullet." Happens all the time in Memphis, they said. They conducted a perfunctory search of the brush below my window, the street and grounds beyond. Took some photos, asked some questions, gingerly removed the bullet from my now-violated bedroom wall. Told me they'd be in touch. But I knew they wouldn't.

At first, it puzzled me that Harper—and I had no doubt it was him—knew exactly where I lived. But then I realized a cop could easily run a search on a license plate. Hell, it was even simpler than that. As Danny had pointed out, all my info was out there for anyone to find. *In the damn phone book.*

After the cops left, I swept up the glass, then scrounged the apartment for an old U-Haul box. As Priss cocked her head at me and pawed at the tape dispenser, I affixed a square of corrugated cardboard over the window and cranked up the heat.

After the warning potshot, if that's what it was, I took to carrying Danny's switchblade every day. It became a part of my wardrobe, like a wristwatch. A very sharp wristwatch.

The knife rested deep in my back pocket when I left the station a couple of nights later, crossing the gloom of the parking lot. I stopped midway. Someone lurked in the shadows next to my car. I pulled out the switchblade and fingered the release. Then I saw the Stutz. And Danny. The passenger door flew open.

"Are we going somewhere?" I slipped the knife back into my pocket.

"Just get in, son."

I obliged, hunching into the cramped jump seat. Danny behind the wheel, Travis rode shotgun. We turned onto Riverside Drive, cruising north in silence until we reached a neighborhood just above downtown. As we rolled slowly past a public housing project called Lauderdale Courts, Danny finally spoke.

"This is where I grew up, Thomas." He gestured to a drab, three-story brick building. "Apartment three twenty-eight. Wasn't much, but Mama kept it clean. See them front steps? I used to sit out there and pick guitar."

I found myself wanting to tell him I'd grown up in similar circumstances, in the projects on Chicago's southside. But this night wasn't about me.

He steered the car farther north, pointed out his old high school building, an old record store or two, then turned back the way we came. "Ya know what the folks livin' in the Delta used to say about Memphis? They'd call it, 'Them lights up the river.' It was a magical place. A place you aspired to. Make your dreams come true here."

A seasonable chill filled the night air, but sweat beaded around Danny's eyes. Something about the street lights slanting into the car brought out more of his gray than I'd noticed before. "Years ago I used to have my own dream," he said. "A nightmare, really, that one day I'd be totally on my own, just me, no manager, no fans at the gates. Alone, and no future. That dream surely came true, didn't it?"

"Boss," Travis said, "I don't think—"

Danny held up his hand, silencing his bodyguard. I knew not to say anything, either. Danny had his way of getting around to things eventually.

A few minutes later, south of downtown, the Stutz pulled onto a bleak, narrow section of Mulberry Street, a street in name only, barely an alleyway. Travis stayed behind, leaning against the car, watching Danny and me walk off in the direction of an abandoned motel imprisoned behind chain link.

Sprawled along the sidewalk lay a small campsite, little more than a tarp draped over a rig of industrial piping. Someone stirred from within and tossed back the flap. She was a slight woman, in her thirties, sporting short-cropped black hair and square-framed glasses. She took a long, careful look at Danny. She didn't seem surprised in the least to see him.

"I know who you are," the woman said.

"Yes, ma'am." Danny averted his eyes.

"I thought you was dead."

"Oh, no, ma'am. Some say that. Hell, some wish that."

She put a hand to her glasses, raising them. "Well, you still got your looks." Danny glanced down, shuffling his feet as the woman went on. "What y'all doin' walking these mean streets, anyways, disturbing my sleep?"

"It's twenty years ago tonight," Danny said, "and I wanted Thomas here to see the place where it happened."

As I studied the woman, I realized I knew who she was, just as she knew Danny. She was the last resident of the infamous Lorraine Motel. We'd covered it for the news. She refused to leave, until a posse of Shelby County deputies dragged her out.

"Twenty years since they shot him down you mean," she said. "And not a thing's changed."

"Yes ma'am. I mean, no ma'am."

"You," she said, turning to me. "I seen you around, newsman. You were here when they evicted me, weren't you?"

"I was, yes."

"Stormed the place and tossed me into the gutter. They put this here rickety fence around it, but that won't stop me from showin' you, if y'all want."

She led us through an opening, through tall weeds and across a gauntlet of jackhammered concrete. We climbed a flight of exposed metal stairs, finally stopping at the landing.

"There it is, Room 306," she said.

Plexiglass surrounded the balcony. A wreath adorned with white and red flowers hung from the railing. The room itself was locked, its powder blue door flanked by windows, one with curtains drawn, the other framing a simple plaque etched with a star and a cross. In the amber glow of the streetlights I could just make it out:

MARTIN LUTHER KING, JR.
JAN 15, 1929 – APR 4, 1968

The woman pulled out a flashlight, directing the light to the concrete floor, illuminating faded stains at our feet that may or may not have been the dotted remnants of blood.

"They wanna put a civil rights museum here," she said. "A civil wrong is what it is. Put that money toward jobs and helpin' people. Turn the Lorraine into a shelter for the homeless. That's what Doctor King would want."

"'The time is always right to do right,'" Danny muttered, training his eyes on the windows of a vacant building just across the way.

"Do right?" The woman swung the flashlight's beam at Danny's face. "Mister guitar man, what you need to do is take off your cryin' pants already, and get yourself out there again, doin' what God intended for you to do."

Danny lowered his head and we lingered an awkward moment before the woman led us back to the street and disappeared into her tent.

It was a one block walk back to the car, but Danny made the most of it. As I followed a half step behind, he peered into the ghostly gloom of South Memphis, singing a low melody from a very old song. Fragments of lyrics drifted from Danny's lips, a tale of strange fruit swinging from poplar trees.

He stopped, casting a hand toward the sky. "Mama used to say if I sang during a full moon, my brother Jesse would hear me. He was my twin, you know."

At the word, "twin," I lost my bearings, my feet stumbling onto the backs of Danny's shoes.

"You okay, son? You about gave me a flat tire."

"Yeah. No. It's just that you mentioned your twin brother. I'm a ... I mean, I was a—"

Danny turned to face to me. "You study numerology, Thomas?"

I shrugged.

"See, everybody's got a number." He held up five fingers on one hand, three on the other. "Mine's eight. I came into this world on the eighth, Jesse departed this world on the eighth. I'll probably die on the eighth. Now, the Chinese, they seem to feel eight is very lucky. Not for me. For me, eight is a damned lonely number."

"I don't know what my number is," I said. "But if I had to guess, I'd say it's minus-one."

Danny shook his head, started to say something, then turned back to the sky. He drew an arc across the heavens with his arm. "You see that?"

"The moon?"

"And the stars all around. Didja ever just let your mind drift up there and hang in space with 'em? I mean, just be up there, man. Just floatin'." Danny squeezed his eyes shut, creases expanding to his temples. "Don't think of nothin' else, just them stars and planets."

"Okay."

"You know, Thomas, sometimes if I concentrate real hard I can make 'em move."

He started walking again and I followed. "Do you do this a lot?"

"Only for the last 50 years."

The Stutz stopped short, flinging me forward into Travis' seatback. We'd returned to the TV station parking lot.

Danny spun in his seat. "Thomas, I didn't come by your work tonight just to give you a midnight tour of Memphis. I was out at East Precinct earlier. They was showin' a movie. I think you know the film. It came from your cameraman."

Eddie's tape. *Of course.* Enshrined at the cop shop as a twisted form of bulletin board material.

"They were playin' it in the break room," Danny said. "Your friend Bone Harper, he's there too, although he ain't supposed to be. All watchin' that scene at the Walker place, the poor sucker half-dead on the ground. Wasn't much to it, just a few seconds of video. But man, them cops at the precinct were whoopin' and hollerin' like they was ringside at a Jerry Lawler match."

31

Y'ALL SHOOK UP

You might call the next few months a dead run. Going exactly nowhere, doing exactly nothing. Truth be told it wasn't only the weatherman who had time on his hands. News anchors didn't have much to do either, particularly between newscasts. It was a dangerous interval, alone with your thoughts, just you and the cacophony of the nightside newsroom.

Eddie showed me how to access the roof once, through a hidden stairwell just off the sales office on the second floor. It became my go-to evening hideaway. If you could call sitting among the asbestos cladding of a TV station roof a hideaway—exposed as it was, open to the air, the river to the west—the rusted bridges menacingly closer from up high. But here I sat, a latter-day Mark Twain in his pilot house surveying the Mississippi.

On the horizon, the sun had begun its languid descent. At this angle, this time of year, it was a Martian heat ray. It could bore a hole into your brain. Down Riverside Drive music pulsed in muted fits, patriotic music, *God Save the Queen* followed by the *Star-Spangled Banner*. It was the start of the Sunset Symphony, the big finale of the "Memphis in May" festival. From my perch I could make out the bandstand, albeit from a distance, the stage lights just coming on.

"It's a lot better from down below, you know." Kimberly stood in the stairwell hatch, squinting, a pair of sunglasses in her hand. "Whaddya say? We can cut through Tom Lee Park. It's only about a ten minute walk."

We reached the southern end of the crowd just as James Hyter took the stage. No point in pushing any farther to the river. It was a solid wall of folding chairs, picnic blankets, and booze.

"What's the deal with this guy anyway?" I said, a little out of breath from the brisk hike to the downtown riverfront.

"Jim Hyter?"

"Yeah, and this *Old Man River* stuff."

"If you'd grown up here, you'd get it." Kimberly said. "The Mississippi just calls us back to our roots."

Roots. Cotton and slavery roots. And here was James Hyter, an elderly black man with his trademark gray-tinged mustache and thick-rimmed glasses, with his otherworldly baritone bass voice, honoring a number from *Showboat* of all things. A song about life under the yoke of the white boss man.

Bend your knees and bow your head,
And pull that rope until ... you're ... dead.

I could relate to their misery—toting that barge, lifting that bale. This year had been a miserable slog, butting my head against everything and everyone. The last warm feeling I'd had was huddling in a dark closet with Meredith. I'd brooded about that furtive kiss for weeks. I was brooding about it now. And my co-anchor could read me like an open songbook.

"Girl trouble, Tom?"

"What?"

"And let me guess. Does it start with 'wife' and end with 'of Bone Harper?'"

"You're well-informed," I said.

"The sex is hot, right?"

"Jesus Christ, Kimberly."

"Don't be such a prude. Hell, just about anyone at the station with a vagina has eyes for you." She slipped an arm in mine, tugged on it. "But a word to the wise. That one you're foolin' with ... she's no good for you."

"For your information, I'm not 'fooling' with anyone at the moment."

Behind us the audience erupted in roar worthy of a football stadium, if football crowds also sobbed, cried, and sang in unison. Hyter had them in his hands now. He'd reached the overwrought crescendo.

Ol' man river, that ol' man river ...

"I don't know Miss Meredith all that well," Kimberly shouted, dialing up her voice over the rumble around us. "But, like father, like son, they say, right? And maybe like daughter-in-law, if you know what I mean. Don't kid yourself. That girl's a Harper. Plus, she's someone else's wife. Why would you want to mess with that?"

He just keeps rollin', he keeps on rollin' a-long!

The closing notes triggered a stampede to the parking lot, hordes of wine-, sweat-, and tears-soaked bodies cresting toward us. From within this human tidal wave someone called out. "Look y'all, it's lover boy!" They shoved one of their number out of the pack, the woman recoiling off my chest, eyes wide. She turned to Kimberly. A knowing look exchanged between them.

Kimberly smacked me on the back, a little too hard. "I'll leave you to it, Holden. See you at ten."

We stood alone, face to face. Meredith and me. People flowed past us, around us. We were a sand bar in the Mississippi, an island in the stream.

"Why are you here?" I said.

"Uh, the concert?"

"Right. But *here*."

Meredith's nose crinkled. "It's the way out, dummy."

We blinked at one another in mute fascination. God knows it could have gone on until the crowd deserted the riverbank and the lights went out. Were it not for a burst of twisted blasphemy tossed in our direction.

"Jesus H Presley on a stick!"

It spat from my one-time holiday party date, homing in on us, dragging a folding chair—and Timothy—behind her. "Hell, Tom," Ashley hollered, "you still sniffin' 'round this raggedy old housewife?"

A woman in Meredith's group shouted, "Hey now!" and her circle of friends lunged forward. Meredith waved them off. "It's all right. Can't you see she's skunk drunk?" She leaned into Ashley's face. "Little girl, why you bein' so ugly?"

"You's the ugly one. *Bitch.*" The words splattered from Ashley's mouth, on the breath of Zinfandel. "You *and* your cheatin' bitch of a boytoy." She whipped her arm back, the one with the chair, sweeping it in a wide arc. No doubt the wine was in play, but if Ashley was targeting Meredith, her aim was off by a country mile. The chair landed with a dead crack, flat against my pelvis.

Time froze. Timothy's mouth hung to the ground, for once speechless. Only Meredith remained in motion. She blew a strand of hair from her face, reared back, and as coolly as punching a selection on a vending machine, sunk her knuckles into the other woman's jaw.

Ashley collapsed in a tangle of bangs and mud, and Meredith stepped over her, straddling the prone figure like Ali over Liston.

"Timothy, do something!" Ashley swiped an arm across her swelling face. "Defend me, you moron."

"This is *your* fight," the weatherman said. "I'm not getting involved."

"Not getting—?" Ashley struggled to stand but refused Meredith's hand-up. "Now I know why they call you Tiny Tim, you little dick."

"Ashley, c'mon." Timothy reached for her arm but she swatted him away, too. He bent to pick up the chair instead. "Let's get you home."

I clamped a hand on Timothy's shoulder. "Hey man, ignore what she said. You're everything she needs. And good luck with all that."

"And good luck with *that*," he answered, nodding at Meredith, and walking off.

The women with Meredith had been high-fiving all around but she wasn't partaking in it.

"Your knuckles are gonna be sore tomorrow," I offered. "Why'd you do it?"

"You damn well *know* why." Meredith spun, and stalked away to join her friends.

The crowd cleared. I turned back for the TV station. Stopped. Several paces in front of me, just visible through the bobbing heads and torsos, a striking couple strode toward the parking lot. All smiles and hugs, and with a hand firmly clamped onto the backside of her shorts, Bone Harper strode arm-in-arm with Janelle Foster.

Son of a bitch.

32

TEDDY BEAR

A few days later I found myself playing catch up—and make up—at the Memphis Zoo. One way to deal with the surplus of time a news anchor enjoys is to go out and cover a feature story once in a while. This one involved a giant Panda named Xiu Hua. Pronounced, as Bubba informed me on my way out the door, "Shoo-wah. Like the Van Halen song. Shoo-bee doo-wah and all that."

The panda was on loan from Mexico for the summer and she was arriving this afternoon. Eddie and I nearly missed it. The news crews from the other stations had preceded us, circling a petite brunette in white high-cut shorts and a tan safari hat. As we rolled up, she stepped toward our truck.

"God love ya, Tom. Better late than never."

Gail Nicholas managed the media for the zoo. We'd met last spring when I covered a series of car break-ins in the area. There'd been something about her pixie nose, her shoulder-length brown hair, the way it peeked out of her pith helmet. But it was her acerbic wit that brought out the beast in me. When I asked her where the lion sleeps tonight, she said I should come to her place and find out. That night I found out. Three weeks later I met Valerie and the wild safari came to an abrupt end.

She shoved a press release through my open window.

"Sorry, Gail," I said, contrite on several levels. "We ran into traffic. But I didn't want to blow an opportunity to see the panda."

"Really." Gail lowered her voice to a growl. "Between you and me, Tom, I wouldn't use the words 'blow' and 'opportunity' around me ever again."

Gail turned to the group, in full voice now. "Xiu Hua is arriving at the back gate on North Parkway. It's the shortest route to her new home in the former gorilla exhibit. If you'll follow my vehicle I'll lead y'all over there."

"Listen, Gail ..."

"Oh, don't worry. I'm over it. I'd just be happy to know you're making good use of the gift I gave you. Is that thing still valid?"

"The zoo pass?" I said. "I think so."

"Bless your little heart. Still time to sucker some other young and foolish thing. Maybe you could get lucky again behind the primate house."

We circled out of Overton Park, via McLean Boulevard to the northern perimeter of the zoo. Ahead, a forklift reached into the back of a Federal Express truck, unloading a large bamboo-laden cage. Workmen pulled open a pair of double-wide gates in the fence. Another vehicle waited inside, ready to receive the precious cargo. Eddie hopped out and started rolling video.

The Memphis Zoo was famous, or so it was said, as the former home of one of the legendary MGM lions. And frankly, parts of the zoo looked as if they hadn't been repaired since the golden age of cinema. When not admitting giant pandas, the loading gates were presumably locked. But I noticed a man-sized, or perhaps gorilla-sized, rip in the fencing.

In my notebook I wrote, *Panda housed in former gorilla exhibit. Fence damaged along N. Parkway. Zoo needs repairs. Future story.*

"I sure hope they have the animals locked up at night," I said to Eddie, "or else they'll be wandering all over Midtown."

"Or, put another way, free zoo admission for neighborhood kids," he quipped.

"What's this about free admission?" Gail stepped beside me, tilting her head.

"Just telling Eddie about the season pass." I smiled. "Listen, Gail—"

"Here we go," she said. "Is this the part where a year later, Tom gets down on his knees begging forgiveness for dumping me?" She kicked a small stone, sending it spinning toward the fence.

"This is the part where Tom says he was a total jerk, yes," I said. "But I always thought you were—" Just then Xiu Hua caught my eye, nosing up to the bars of the cage, chewing a stalk of bamboo, charming me like the larger-than-life teddy bear she was. "So adorable," I said.

"Thank you, Tom," Gail tipped her hat. "In that case, I forgive you."

"I was referring to—"

From the truck, the two-way squawked. Eddie set down his gear and went to grab the radio, leaving me alone with Gail. She still looked smart in that pith helmet. I was about to say so when Eddie came running back, breathless, grabbing his sticks and camera.

"Tom, I think we have enough here. We gotta go."

"What's up?"

"They just dismissed the case against Bone Harper."

33

TCB

Lee waved me into his office. Janelle was already seated, her arms folded, her gaze firmly fixed on the window and the relentless river streaming and swirling just beyond the bluff.

"You heard?" Lee asked.

"I heard. But I don't get it."

"Insufficient evidence."

I looked down at Janelle. "You dropped the charges?"

"That's right," she said, without turning around.

"You two are back together. I saw you at the Sunset Symphony."

"Tom, I know you mean well," Janelle said, "but if I went ahead and testified it was just gonna blow back on me."

"What if *I* go to the prosecutor?"

"No." Lee stood.

"No, what?"

"Think long and hard about this." Lee cast a glance at Janelle. "Look, ain't nobody arguing Bone Harper's a saint. He roughed up our gal, that's a fact. Lin helped his son evade an arrest warrant. We ain't gonna forget that."

"This isn't about you, Tom." Janelle said, finally rotating in her seat to face me. "I'm just not willing to be dragged through a trial."

"But being dragged through your apartment is okay?" I muttered.

"That's unfair."

"Is it?" I stormed back to my desk, telling myself not to take it personally. It wasn't my problem any more.

Or so I thought.

At the end of July, on the anniversary of the incident on Underwood Avenue, Carl Walker's attorney let loose with a ten-million-dollar lawsuit against the city of Memphis and yet-to-be-named MPD officers. Innis Honeycutt took to the steps of the Justice Center, calling the death of Officer Howard a tragedy that could have been avoided had police not escalated a routine dog call into violent chaos.

Then he dropped a bombshell.

In light of the convictions of two cops in the case—Honeycutt called them mitigating guilty pleas—prosecutors had agreed to reduce the felony charges against Walker. The attorney took no questions, did an about face, and headed back up the steps.

Eddie finished packing up the truck. I handed him the sticks and mic, the wheels of tonight's story already spinning in my head.

"Are you ready, Tom?" Honeycutt stood an inch from my face. He must have circled back from the courthouse to evade the other reporters.

"Ready for what?"

"For your interview with Carl," he said. "I've secured a supervised release. I can have him here at six. With one stipulation. We don't have the ballistics yet, so no questions about second bullets."

When I presented the offer to Lee in the newsroom he swelled up like a toad in heat. "You wanna give live air time to a damned cop killer?" But he couldn't deny the news—and ratings—value of an exclusive interview. That tempered the moral outrage. We agreed I'd report from the field and Kimberly could handle the rest of the newscast solo.

Eddie left the station ahead of me to set up the live shot. I'd committed to recording a promo in the studio for the marketing guys that afternoon. It was cutting it close. I got downtown in my own car at five forty-five.

Carl and his lawyer cut it closer still. A minute before air, they came jog-walking from the parking structure across the street. I'd barely greeted the big man when I got the standby. My pulse rate surged. This was a "get" if there ever was one, the envy of the competition.

"Mr. Walker," I began, "you're free after a year behind bars. But you still have a criminal trial pending, and now a civil suit. What's going through your mind tonight?"

"My thoughts are the same as they were then. If I didn't stop this assault by them police officers that broke into my home, I'd be dead today."

"Take us back. What started it?"

"I suppose it was Shep. My dog. He likes to run around in the yard. Ain't no crime in that. Then Officer Howard shows. Says something about leash laws. Said if he had to come back one more time he'd shoot the dog himself."

"What happened next?"

"I turn to go inside, but the officer sticks his foot in the door." Carl pulled out a balled-up yellowed handkerchief, dragging it across his forehead. Despite the effort, streaks of sweat remained in the grooves of his worry lines. "Then the guy reaches 'round the door with his nightstick and starts swinging."

"And at some point Sergeant Poole arrived?"

"Between them two, they must have hit me fifty times. And then a third officer comes up. Has a nightstick, too. Whacks me with the handle part of it. About cracked open my skull. Then the three of 'em fell in on top of each other and I crawled off into the hallway."

"What are you thinking at this point?"

"These guys are fixin' to kill me, that's what I'm thinking. If you were bein' beaten to death in your own doorway you'd do anything to stop it."

"And you grabbed your rifle?"

Carl reached again for the handkerchief, mopped the top of his head. "All them guns pop off the same time. Mine, theirs. I could see Officer Howard been hit."

"Did you allow the police to cuff you?"

"I was not fightin' how they said. That's a lie. They drug me outside and started in again. Kicking and hitting me all over."

In my ear, the producer gave me the wrap signal, but I wasn't about to wrap anything up.

"This one cop gets in my face," Carl went on. "Kneels down real close. Tells me I'm lucky he didn't put a bullet in my brain."

"Wait, say that again?"

"The guy threatened to shoot me dead right there."

"Mr. Walker, we've never heard that detail before."

"Because I never told it. Except to my lawyer."

"Can you identify this officer?" Just off camera, Honeycutt slashed a frenzied hand across his neck.

"My lawyer's telling me not to say anything more about it."

"Do you believe your gunshot hit Officer Howard?"

"I thought so," he said. "That day."

"Thought so?"

Honeycutt stepped in front of the camera and tugged Carl out of frame. "Mr. Cirone, the interview's over," the lawyer snapped.

I thanked Carl and his attorney and threw it back to Kimberly in the studio. Sweat channeled the back of my shirt. I handed Eddie the mic, smiling to myself, picturing this interview fitting perfectly onto my resume reel. I could almost taste my next shiny newsroom. Maybe St. Louis, or Pittsburgh, or Chicago even.

A hand grabbed my shoulder, spinning me round, jerking me back to Memphis.

"Are you outta your flippin' mind?" Honeycutt, red in the face, released his hand. "We stipulated you would *not* go there."

"Your client went there. I didn't."

"You're being cute. It doesn't suit you."

"Look, we want the same thing," I said. "For the truth to come out."

Honeycutt scoffed. "Son, you got me all wrong. I want the city to pay for what they did. But you're kidding yourself if you imagine this is about the truth. There ain't no such thing. A journalist, of all people, ought to appreciate that." He cussed under his breath and huffed off, prodding Carl toward the parking garage.

The interview was over, but now I had more questions.

"Eddie," I said, "when you get back to the station, tell them I might be late." My eyes tracked Carl and his lawyer crossing Washington Avenue. "Say I went to grab some dinner."

"Uh huh. And what are you really up to?"

"Eddie Harrington, you're a stand-up guy. And a Rembrandt with that camera."

"I prefer Henry O. Tanner," he said. "But thank you. Now, what's the caper?"

"It's time for some TCB."

"Say what?"

Sprinting for the parking garage across the street, I shouted, "Taking care of business, Eddie! Taking care of business!"

34

HARD-HEADED WOMAN

Carl and Honeycutt mounted a stairwell, exiting on the second level of the parking structure, bee-lining to a mammoth car, silver and white, with a squarish tombstone-shaped grill—the eight-cylinder boat on wheels known as the Cadillac Fleetwood. I timed it out as I jogged back to my car. It would take a minute or two for them to roll down the ramp and stop at the pay window.

But where to? Not the house on Underwood. Honeycutt would have found Carl a new place to dwell by now. I had a hunch, and it had seemed like a sound plan a moment ago, but now it fell apart in the details. What if they were only driving to Perkins for dinner?

The Cadillac inched onto Washington, its right signal blinking. I slumped in my seat—that's how they always did it in the movies—waiting for them to pass, grateful I'd driven my own car to the live shot. They turned onto Danny Thomas Boulevard, merging with the interstate, and so did I, keeping several car lengths behind. A few minutes later, they exited at Lamar in the Cooper-Young neighborhood, not far from Midtown.

The lawyer's car pulled up a driveway on a modest street lined with ranch-style homes, pale brick fronts, red-shingled roofs. From my spot a half block down I could see Honeycutt get out of the Cadillac and Carl squeezing his frame through the passenger side. A woman stood waiting, arms crossed, at the front door.

Carl reached out to hug the woman, his milky jowls in stark contrast with her spare brown cheekbones. The woman permitted the embrace but her arms hung limp from her shoulders. Honeycutt came up behind and ushered them into the house.

Within five minutes, the door sprang open and the men emerged, returning to the car. When Honeycutt's Cadillac rounded the corner, I made tracks for the house.

A shout answered my knock. "I told y'all not to come b—" The woman froze behind the screen door, her eyes taking in the notebook in my hand. "What are *you* after?"

"I'm Tom Cirone, Channel 2."

"I know who the hell you are. Carl and that hillbilly lawyer put you up to this?"

"No ma'am. Are you Diana Walker? I went to Catholic High asking for you, but they wouldn't tell me how to contact you."

"That's one thing they done right."

"Mrs. Walker, I've been following your husband's case. I was there last summer when police arrested him."

"I know. I watch the damn news." She opened the screen door and poked her head out. "Where's your cameraman, honey?" When I told her I was alone, she raised an eyebrow and gestured for me to come inside.

"Mrs. Walker—"

"My name's Diana Braxton. Though there's some that did used to call me Missus Walker at the school."

I pulled a chair from the dinette. Diana sat opposite. A dog lay curled in a pet bed in the shadows of the next room, eyeing me, a Rottweiler who could only be Shep.

"Miss Braxton, I know I have no business asking, but what did you and Carl and the lawyer discuss just now?"

She took a long look at me, a penetrating study that started the hairs prickling at the back of my neck. She pulled out a cigarette. Her nails were long, bright red, a single one on her left middle finger tapered to a point. She worked the lighter, turning her head to the side, watching me with one eye as the smoke forced the other shut.

"You're a lot better looking in person, you know that, Tom?" She was in her late thirties, maybe forty, with glistening black hair falling to her shoulders. She had deep brown eyes that lit up when she smiled. "I'll bet the girls just love to run their pretty fingers through that head of hair of yours."

I ran a hand across my scalp, let it drop. "Some, do, yes."

"Well, good-lookin', you're right." Her smile faded. "You got no business askin'. But I'm gonna tell you, anyhow."

I flipped my notebook to a blank page. "Do you mind if I take notes?"

"You gonna put this on TV?"

"No." I closed the notebook.

She took a drag on the cigarette and twisted it out in an ashtray. "You know what that lawyer man and Carl wanted? They wanted to get our stories straight."

"You were there that day?"

"That ain't the story they were talking about," she said.

"Okay."

"It has to do with that two-timin' cop. The one with the famous daddy."

"Bone Harper," I said.

"Johnnie B. For the life of me I don't know how I ever let that perverted sonofabitch lay a hand on me."

"You had an affair with Harper?"

"He come visit with my kids at the school. 'Officer Friendly,' you know, talkin' about livin' right, avoiding drugs and such. All the while, he's spyin' my black ass across the assembly hall. Waltzes up to me like God's gift on a white horse, askin' for my number. Says he's hot for teacher. How's that for some lame shit?"

She crossed to the kitchen window, picked up a magazine and fanned herself, turning around and arching her back against the counter. "Damn, Tom, is it hot tonight or what?" Her eyes fell to the floor, rose to my face, then descended back again, but this time not all the way to the floor. Sweat gathered under my armpits. *What was I thinking, coming here?*

"Carl didn't know nothin' about our little affair," Diana said. "Not at first, even though I was living with him at the time in that Midtown shithole. Johnnie B and me was doin' it right under his nose. Then that prick cop started shackin' up with some snotty-ass reporter from your station. That's been all over the news."

"Yes."

"Can you believe he came sniffing around here after all that broke, his limp dick hanging between his legs, asking me to take him back?"

"Almost makes you feel sorry for the guy," I said.

"Hell. I kicked his ass to the curb. So, yeah, you could say this shit's been goin' on for a minute. And don't get me started on that dumb blonde of his."

"Harper's wife."

"Dumb blonde. Ain't even smart enough to know her dude's doin' black chicks on the side."

"Well—"

"How about you, Tom? *You* like black girls?" She pulled her hair back and held it, waiting for an answer. I might have said, "It depends on the girl," but I didn't get the chance. Through the open window came the sound of tires on gravel.

The Cadillac Fleetwood had returned.

Diana jumped from the counter, wild eyed. "You best get your butt outta this kitchen, newsman. Carl musta forgot his Depends or something." She directed me down the hall. "My bedroom. The door sticks. You have to shut it tight."

Twilight filtered into the room through a pair of high windows. Enough light to see that the bed was slightly curved at the foot. I didn't have to sit on it to tell it was one of those ones filled with water. On the night stand lay a copy of *Catholic Digest*. Beside it, the latest *People Magazine*. The cover story caught my eye.

Lisa Marie Presley
LOVE ME TENDER

The words below the headline said Elvis Presley's "little girl," twenty and pregnant, had gotten married. I held the magazine up to the window and flipped to the article. Something about a small ceremony at the Church of Scientology in West Hollywood. The bride's famous father walked her down the aisle. *So that's why I hadn't heard from Danny. He flew to California for the wedding.* Scientology. I wondered what he thought about *that*. The word "pregnant" also stood out. Danny was going to be a grandpa.

I stepped to the bedroom door and put my ear to it. The squeak of the screen door, footsteps scraping the threshold. "Forget something?" I heard Diana ask.

Honeycutt's voice now. "Carl wasn't sure we'd been clear on that other thing."

"So y'all wanted to come back and check, because I'm that stupid, right?"

"Di, that's not what he's sayin'."

"Carl, hush," Honeycutt said. "Here's what we need you right with, Diana. What's past is past. I don't have to remind you it's whatall got this whole mess started."

"You mean, them threats to go to internal affairs, and expose how Lieutenant Harper is a sick fuck—"

"Diana—"

"—who likes to violate black ass and whatever *else* wanders into the bedroom?"

"Diana, Jesus. Enough."

There was a long silence, and then Carl's voice. "Haven't we suffered enough over this? Haven't I suffered? Look at me, I'm practically a cripple."

"And whose fault is that?" Diana said. "You had to go and threaten him. Had to be a big man, tell him you'd have his badge over it." It occurred to me Diana was putting on a bit of a show for the unseen listener behind the bedroom door.

"I got my head bashed in and rotted in jail for a year." Walker's voice raised an octave. "I kept quiet. For you!"

"Puleeze."

"Enough!" Honeycutt shouted. "Diana. Are ... we ... clear? The civil suit against those officers, that's our shot. You want a piece of the settlement? Then let's don't muddy the waters. All this other talk, that's back pocket stuff, if need be. Our bargaining chip with the city."

"It's always about the money with you lawyers ain't it?" she said. "All right. My lips are sealed. See? Lips, all sealed up nice. Good with you, Carl, baby? You go on home to ya mama, now. I'm sure she's got a nice country ham and a fried pie all warm in the oven waiting for y'all."

The front door slammed and a moment later the car started. I still had my ear to the door when Diana pushed into the bedroom, sending me staggering backwards onto the water mattress.

"Tom, Tom, Tom. You sure got an earful," she said. "Did you get it all down in your little notebook?" She stepped to the bed, hesitated. "Now what do I get?"

Her lips fell on me before I could move. They were soft and wet, her tongue pushing through, tasting of dusty saliva and Tic Tac. I'd never liked kissing smokers. I didn't like it much now. But for a second, I allowed myself to feel it, enjoy it even. Until she went for my waistband.

They called Memphis the buckle of the Bible Belt—ironic, as folks here spent a fair amount of time dropping their pants. Tonight I wanted mine to stay tight around me. I broke the lip-lock and pushed her hands away. Diana tumbled from my lap with an acrobatic flop, the kind those NBA guys do when they're fouled.

I reached down to help her up. "Listen, Diana, if I gave you the wrong idea, I'm sorry."

She stood, flicking away my hand, then backed into the doorway, blocking my exit. "Sorry, my ass."

"And I'm sure it's a beautiful one." I took a step forward. "But I have to go."

The blow came from my right. A backhanded slap. I staggered, feeling for my face. Even in the darkened room I could see the blood. She'd sliced open my cheek with that painted stiletto fingernail.

"I won't be made to look a damn fool," she shouted, shoving me into the hallway. "Now get out. Get out my house." I pocketed my notebook and lurched to the front door. She shouted it again. "Get out my house, I said! Get out my house!"

Her hollering chased me down the block and into my car. She was still hollering as I pulled the door shut and fired up the engine as fast as it would turn over.

35

THE RECORD SHOWS

Poised on the edge of a kitchen chair, her whiskers twitching, Miss Priss waited to pounce. Waited until I'd finished the combination breakfast and lunch peculiar to my sleep and work schedule. A kitten no longer, she landed in my lap like a ten pound sack of fur and bones. She pawed my hand as I reached for the cordless phone, only springing back to the floor at the sound of the beeping keypad.

For two months Meredith and I had been playing phone tag, cursory, noncommittal messages on our respective machines. Maybe I preferred it that way. Maybe I'd let my co-anchor's admonitions about "Mrs. Harper" take root inside my head. Maybe I was relieved each time Meredith's machine answered. I had no expectation this time would be different.

This time was different. Meredith picked up.

Caught off guard, I improvised a discordant "Happy Birthday to You." I figured she'd be stunned I even knew what day it was. But I didn't count on the silence, a soul-crushing nothingness that lingered so long I thought she'd dropped the phone and walked off.

"Tommy?"

"Surprise," I said. "Shocking to hear from me, I know." We hadn't talked since the Sunset Symphony. I apologized for that. She told me I was right about her knuckles but they'd eventually healed.

I took a deep breath, and in more leap of faith than ad-lib, blurted, "I know it's last minute, but are you free tonight, birthday girl?"

A long sigh. Then, no, she had plans. The girls were taking her out. Crushed, but undaunted, I tossed a Hail Mary. "How about Saturday night?"

Sitting in the newsroom a few hours later, I was still shaking my head over the promise of my first date in months. What were the odds of a second chance with Meredith? How would I explain the scratch on my face? I'd have to pick up a birthday present, of course, and—

My extension lit, followed closely by its rude electronic scold of a ring tone. At the other end of the receiver, a wheezing rhythm of heavy breathing. And then, that voice.

"Thomas. I'm rentin' out the movie theater. There's a new film I've been wanting to see. What say you join us?"

I wasn't sure which was more astonishing, the request, or that Danny himself had called me. "Oh, and bring that gal of yours," he said. "The blonde. You *are* still seeing her?"

"As a matter of fact—"

"You *do* know where the Memphian Theater is located, son."

"Yes."

"Good. See you Saturday. Midnight."

Meredith didn't know it yet, but we were going to the movies.

The main branch of the Memphis Public Library tucked itself away on a tree-lined stretch of Peabody Avenue—about four blocks south of Catholic High School. Carl Walker's house on Underwood Avenue stood just a few blocks over. This neighborhood was becoming a habit.

The librarian's eyes followed me from the moment I entered the main reading room. On the youngish side to be in this type of job, with long brown hair worn down and a flower print shirt tied together at the waist, she was hardly what I'd expected to find behind the reference desk. "Doing research for the news?" she said, peering up at me with recognition.

"Personal interest, actually. I'm looking for recent items about Elvis Presley."

Growing up, I couldn't say I'd followed him much. Elvis had faded into the tapestry of the seventies, touring the country, catering to sold-out arenas full of screaming mid-life women and their husbands. Tonight at the movies I'd be entering into his private world. I needed a better understanding of this man and I needed it quick.

The librarian nodded with a fervor, as if I'd expressed an interest in nuclear physics. "Elvis. That's a fascinating subject. I'm a fan myself." She slid from her desk and invited me to follow. "We have hundreds of reels of microfilm in the Memphis Room." She pointed to a row of carrels. "Set yourself up in one of these and I'll be right back." She flattened a hand to her chest. "I'm Tracy, by the way."

One o'clock. Saturday afternoon. A few hours before I'd need to get ready for my date with Meredith. I settled into a pea green padded chair. A microfilm reader took up most of the space in front of me, a hulking thing the size of a dorm room fridge. The machine allowed you to read newspaper editions on spools of film without soiling your fingers with awkward pages of newsprint.

The librarian returned cradling a dozen small boxes, each with a neatly-typed label. "We have all the back issues of the *Commercial Appeal* and the *Press Scimitar*," the morning and afternoon papers, she explained. She laid the boxes on an empty chair.

"Tracy, thank you."

She remained motionless. "You know how to work the microfilm reader?"

"Yes, thank you, again," I said.

"All righty. I'm right over there if you need me."

I slid the first reel from its box, threaded it into the reader, and flipped on the screen. August 1977. President Carter announces the creation of the Department of Energy. In New York, police capture the "Son of Sam" killer. The Space Shuttle Enterprise has its first test flight. Then, the morning edition for Wednesday, August 17. Front page:

HEART ATTACK STRIKES KING OF ROCK AND ROLL
ELVIS CRITICAL AFTER COLLAPSE AT GRACELAND

```
Elvis Presley suffered an apparent heart attack
early Tuesday at Graceland. The 42-year-old King
of Rock and Roll was discovered unconscious in
his personal quarters. Paramedics rushed Presley
to Baptist Memorial Hospital where he was admitted
in critical condition. The attack was the result
of severe cardiovascular disease, according to
hospital officials. They cited contributing factors
including hypertension and chronic abdominal
conditions. Doctors declined to provide the
details of Mr. Presley's treatment but said they
were hopeful of a full recovery.
```

According to the story, his staff discovered Presley face down on the floor of his bathroom. Medics found a weak pulse and worked on him in the ambulance. Initial reports said nothing about drugs. When pressed at the hospital news conference, the only drugs doctors cited were those he was taking for high blood pressure and for a colon problem.

I advanced the microfilm through the following days as initial concern for his well-being turned to shock and outrage. Salacious details began to surface, reports of a toxic cocktail of prescription medication found in Presley's system. The terms "OD" and "drug addict" cropped up in more and more stories. In the 1970s, those labels were career death.

When he came to in his hospital room, Presley would have learned that scandalous stories dominated the news around the planet. I pictured him reaching for the television remote, seeing words like "overdose" and "overweight" flashing across the screen. If he had one of his handguns nearby he might have shot out the TV.

Reporters settled on a damning narrative: Years of drug abuse had weakened his heart, his liver, his intestines. The stories resurfaced embarrassing anecdotes from the previous few years on the road, describing a downward spiral, Presley increasingly out-of-shape and unfocused, slurring and sometimes forgetting the lyrics, often canceling performances due to "illness."

His recovery would take months, with a return to concert touring out of the question. Ultimately, his father, Vernon, persuaded Presley to admit himself into a substance abuse rehabilitation center in Minnesota. Rock stars and drug rehab were nearly synonymous by 1988, but back in '77 it was a reputation-crushing combination. One story summed it up with the headline, *Way Down: The King's Tragic Life in the Fast Lane.* In much of the public's mind, Presley became nothing more than a punchline—gossipy fodder for *Entertainment Tonight* and crude one-liners on late night television.

A vibration, and a shrill *beep-beep-beep* jerked me into the present. My pager displayed Meredith's number, appended with an additional three digits: 1-4-3.

When I returned to the reference desk with the microfilm, Tracy greeted me with an eager smile, saying she'd located back issues of *Time, Newsweek,* and *Rolling Stone.* She slid the magazines across the counter. I thanked her, fingering the pager on my hip.

"Say, Tracy, you're a librarian."

"You noticed."

"I mean, you answer a lot of questions. Are you familiar with the codes people use when they page someone?"

"Maybe. What did you get?"

I passed the device across the reference desk. As she studied it, color deepened her fair cheeks. "Well, it seems you have an admirer. The numbers one-four-three in beeper code mean someone is saying 'I love you.' They match how many letters are in each word," she said. "I-love-you. One-four-three."

As she handed it back, Tracy kept her grip on the pager for a second too long. "Is she the one who gave you *that*?" She indicated the pink slash on my face.

"God, no," I said. I tried to laugh but it came out a snort. What had I done to provoke such inelegant displays of jealousy from a librarian I'd only just met?

With a twinge of guilt, I realized the librarian had gone through the trouble of bookmarking the magazine articles with sticky notes. They depicted a latter-day Shakespearean tragedy. Between recovering from a weakened heart, detoxing from pills, and battling in court for control of his career, Presley missed the rest of the seventies. His ex-wife gained custody of their daughter, Lisa Marie. His father, Vernon, died in 1979 and his grandmother, Minnie Mae, who'd lived at Graceland, died in 1980. Aside from his Aunt Delta and Uncle Vester, the last remaining kin still at the house, he had few people left to turn to, or to trust.

Lawyers' fees mounted, as did medical bills, property taxes. There was a lien on Graceland. To raise cash, he put his house in California on the market. Hocked his airplanes, too.

An article titled, *Presley Settles With Former Manager,* told of a contentious Memphis probate case in which the judge described the profits of Colonel Tom Parker as "excessive" and "shocking." But in the end, Parker got one last payday, two million dollars to sever his management agreement, effectively ending the decades-long symbiotic relationship between Elvis and the "Colonel."

Around the same time, RCA, the record company, in an attempt to engineer a comeback, invited Presley back to the recording studio. Even though he needed the cash, he refused. In 1985, he turned down an offer to join dozens of his contemporaries in the charity recording of *We Are the World*. There was talk of a duet with Tina Turner, who was having a moment in the mid-eighties, and rumors of a collaboration with the likes of Carl Perkins and Johnny Cash. Neither materialized.

My watch said three-thirty. I needed to call it quits and head home, but I dug into a last few articles. In 1986, *Memphis Magazine* revealed Presley spent his time singing spirituals, playing piano, and when he could, visiting his daughter. Various reports mentioned sightings at the scenes of police activity. On one occasion he single-handedly broke up a car-jacking in Whitehaven. Supposedly, he retained status with the Shelby County sheriff's office and the Memphis Police. I remembered him showing me those badges.

Despite entreaties from Larry King, Barbara Walters, and Johnny Carson, Presley had granted exactly one interview over the past eleven years. On his fiftieth birthday he spoke to a reporter from the *Commercial Appeal*. One section of the piece left me so dumbfounded, I copied it into my notebook verbatim, the part where the reporter called him a music legend.

> "I ain't no legend. A legend don't let the people down. I hurt the fans, my family, myself. End of the day, all a man's got is his good name. You can't get that back. It's water under the bridge, as they say. A bridge over troubled water. All them pieces of my life, you know? Y'all in the press found the bad parts, the sad parts. And I done threw away the best parts."

The quote hit me like a gut punch. It was everything he'd been trying to tell me that night outside his old apartment at Lauderdale Courts. But I forced myself to look past the crushing despair in this self-epitaph, to look past the celebrity known as Elvis. That afternoon,

I came away with a deeper empathy—and maybe a measure of hope—for the man himself, the man I'd come to know as Danny.

It was time to go. Tracy had pulled a clipping from the *New York Times* about *Live Aid*, the concert Jerry Lee Lewis mentioned a few months back. No time to read it now. I asked the librarian if she could make a photocopy and reached into my pocket for change.

"Oh, put your money away," she said. "I'll make the copy for you. Anything else I can do?"

"Yes, one thing. Does the library have a copy of the book, *Elvis: What Happened?*" I remembered the guys passing it around the dorm at college. A tell-all, written by three of his former friends and bodyguards, it hit the bookstands a few weeks before his heart attack. Many people were convinced the book, as much as anything else, was what nearly killed him.

I fished out my library card and Tracy headed for the stacks. By the time I spooled out the last microfilm and boxed it up, the librarian had returned with the book and the photocopy.

Outside, I squinted into the August haze, and settled into the triple-digit heat of the car's interior. When I tossed the book to the passenger side, the photocopy slid out, affixed with a yellow sticky note. On it was jotted, "Tracy," a smiley face, and a phone number.

I stuck the note in the book and glanced at the article, my eyes focusing on a single sentence, just an aside in the piece, noting that in 1985, *Live Aid* organizers had offered Elvis Presley a choice of spots, either with Queen at Wembley Stadium in London or with Jagger in Philadelphia. To the disappointment of organizers, he'd turned down both.

"He just wasn't ready," I remembered Sam Phillips saying.

Would he ever be?

36

IT'S MIDNIGHT

Maybe it was the way the last rays of twilight shot golden sparks through her hair. It could have been the glossy slingback heels, the red-and-white-striped halter top, the pencil skirt hugging her curves like a Lamborghini. Whatever it was, Meredith stole the air from my lungs and sent the blood in my brain running for the hills. In other words, I nearly staggered off the front porch at the sight of her.

"Tommy, Jesus," she chuckled. "At this rate, we're not gonna make it to the appetizer. Are you okay?"

"You just look so ... beautiful."

"Well, handsome, you're not so bad-looking your—" Her expression collapsed and she put a hand to my face, running a gentle finger across my cheek.

"You want to know what that scratch is all about, I suppose?"

"Yes," she said. "It looks awful."

"What if I told you a femme fatale was to blame?"

"If that's French for 'girl cat,' then say no more."

On the drive to dinner, I pulled a slim paperback from the glovebox. "Could you fit this in your purse? I got it at the library today. I'll explain why, later."

Meredith took the book and fingered a yellow slip sticking from the edge of it—the sticky note I'd absently inserted there. "And what else did you get?" She unstuck the note and held it in front of her. "Tracy. Uh huh."

"She helped me with some research."

"Did she now?" Meredith's blue eyes shot silver bullets, and just like that the lighter-than-air balloon I'd been riding crashed to the ground.

"Look, it was the librarian. She just wrote her number down. It doesn't mean anything."

"It does if you keep it."

She rolled the note into a tiny yellow ball, lowered the window, and away it went. With the book in her lap, she opened her black handbag to shoehorn it in. For a second I caught a flash of cold steel tucked at the bottom of the purse. If her looks didn't kill me, that thing could. I kept my mouth shut and drove on.

We ate at a quiet wine bar in Midtown, and aside from the piano, quiet it was. The conversation barely strayed from the questions of red or white, steak or chicken. Undaunted, I asked the waiter to bring out a small birthday cake. I leaned across the table, planted a soft kiss on Meredith's stiff lips. Finally, I presented a gift-wrapped present, a silver necklace, with a pair of sterling heart pendants. But when she held it up to her neck, I realized there was already something there, a gold chain, and a small charm forming the letters T-L-C, with some sort of lightning bolt extending from the "L."

Meredith saw my expression fall. "Oh no, don't look like that. This little ol' thing?" She fingered the charm. "I've had this for years. My Lord, I do believe I saw a spark of jealousy on that face of yours." She smiled and set the gift back in the box. "Tommy, I love it. Two little hearts. You and me."

My mall jewelry store gesture had not only broken the ice, it thawed it to a warm sauna. We left the restaurant gliding arm in arm through the chaos that was Saturday night in Overton Square. We rounded the corner, past T.G.I. Friday's, the loudspeakers blasting that infernal Rick Astley song. The air, heavy with humidity, closed around us in a comforting embrace. So comforting, I dreaded breaking the news—and the mood—about our invitation to a late-night movie. In the end, I didn't report the news as much as walked her to it, the three blocks to Cooper and Union and the neon lights of the Memphian Theater.

She stopped, studying the marquee. "What's this?"

"Hmm, let's see." With an exaggerated announcer inflection, I deepened my voice and read from the movie poster. "A towering skyscraper, a dozen terrorists, one man stands in their way."

"*Die Hard*? You're taking me to see a dang action movie?"

"You're gonna love it. Check it out. *He's the only chance they've got ...*"

"Tom, stop. It's midnight. Why are we here?"

The theater doors stood propped open, the last stragglers leaving the late show. In the lobby, the familiar figure of Travis leaned against the concession counter, waving us in.

"See? We're invited. It's your birthday surprise." I took her hand. "Remember that guy who called for me that time at your place?"

"Okay."

"He's uh—"

Danny, surrounded by three gangly men in suit jackets, sprang through a door on the far side of the popcorn stand. They were doubled over laughing. Meredith's eyes widened and I knew I didn't have to say another word.

"Tommy," she whispered. "What's going on?"

"You made it!" Danny crossed the lobby. He held out his palm to my date. "Thomas has told me a lot about you, miss, uh ..."

She said her name, and turned to me with arched eyebrows.

"Meredith, yes, of course. I like what you got goin' on with your hair tonight," he said. "Kinda like a Heather Locklear thing." Danny lifted Meredith's hand to his lips, then released it, his eyes fixed on her neck. He looped his finger around her necklace, the gold T-L-C charm. "Where did you get this little trinket, darlin'?"

"Well ..." Meredith drew out her answer, Danny hanging on her every syllable. "Back when I was a majorette at Memphis State, Elvis Presley gave it to me." She put her hand on Danny's. "The band helped warm up the crowd at the Mid-South Coliseum. He gave one to all us girls."

"Thomas, you got a shrewd one here," Danny said. "Best treat her with tender loving care."

He led us into the theater, an arm at Meredith's waist, inviting us to sit in his row. "Don't worry, son," he said, sensing my apprehension. "I ain't after your girl. She's too old for me."

As Danny's guests filtered in behind us, there appeared to be a hierarchy, a pecking order, with no one allowed to sit forward of row twelve. That was where Danny and a couple of others settled, in the center, everyone else behind or to the sides, about twenty-five guests in a room that could hold a few hundred. I'd heard about these late-night movie sessions, Memphis Mafia and all that. They'd hire out a theater after hours to avoid the fans. I doubted there were legions of rabid fans to avoid anymore.

I intended to sit next to Danny, with Meredith beside to me, one seat over. But before I realized what was happening, he pointed Meredith to the chair to his left and told me to take the one to his right. I shrugged and sat down. This was his show.

"These people here," I asked him, "they work for you?"

"Nah. Some do. Still have a few employees, some money coming in, despite what you might read in the papers. Ain't gettin' rich. But I get by." He leaned in, speaking in a stage whisper. "I met Linda right here in this row." Linda, I knew from my research, had been his long-time girlfriend in the seventies.

"She still around?" I asked.

"Let's just say, I let a good thing die." Danny cast a look at Meredith and then turned back to face me. "Been some others, though. Recently had a nice young gal living up at the house. Not sure what she expected ... but I wasn't the one." He managed a weak laugh. "Hell, I'll never fall in love again, Thomas. I know that." He twisted his head and yelled toward the small opening in the back of the theater, where the projectionist awaited his cue. "Let's get this show on the road!"

The screen came alive with the searchlights of the Twentieth Century Fox logo and the drumroll and blaring fanfare of the famous theme. As the house lights dimmed, I knew it was the last I'd see of Meredith for the next two hours.

Die Hard isn't high art, but it's thrilling in its own fashion. Terrorists with European accents holding hostages in a Los Angeles office tower on Christmas Eve. Bruce Willis playing the part of John McClane, a New York City cop who escapes within the building and bedevils the bad guys.

The furious gun battles left Danny spellbound. His every muscle twitched in tandem with the flickering images reflecting off his face, absorbing, studying each move. As the on-screen hero fashioned an arsenal of weapons from found objects, Danny shouted, "This guy's a regular MacGyver!" Midway through the film I overheard him tell Meredith, "That Bonnie Bedelia is some looker." Watching a movie with him was to endure a running commentary.

Between the action on the screen and the method acting contorting Danny's features, I strove for a connection, a link, any insight into the man. The end of the film finally opened a small window into Danny's psyche, when the Bruce Willis character admitted he'd made a mess of his personal life. Danny moved his lips, more transfixed than he'd been at any point in the film. His eyes blinked and he raised an arm to wipe them as the movie's hero confessed he'd never told his wife he was sorry.

The lights came up, folks stood, stretched, complimenting Danny on his film choice. Like him, I found myself obsessed with the movie's protagonist. Flawed everyman hero, insecure about his relationship, cracks wise, spins bad puns. A tough guy with feelings, fighting to save his relationship. Without having to ask Danny a single question, I'd come to understand him through this fictional story on screen—and maybe gained a bit of understanding of myself as well.

Meredith made her way to my side and I braced for a scolding. I got the opposite. "Tommy, what a trip! You sure know how to romance a girl on her birthday."

"Not mad?"

"How could I be? To say I went to the movies with … well, with …"

"I know, right? *And* with Elvis Presley, too."

She chuckled. "You still make me laugh, mister. It's part of why I said yes to this date. Even though you can be a big jerk."

"Guilty as charged," I said. "And speaking of which, do you have that book?" She reached into her purse, and I got a second glance at that small but deadly weapon buried inside. I asked if she'd mind if I talked to our host for a minute. She said she'd head to the ladies' room and meet me in the lobby.

I trailed Danny as he and Travis climbed the aisle toward the back of the theater. Alone, with the crowd gone, his back hunched, he seemed to shrink. It had all been a performance. A show for me, for Meredith, for the hangers-on and other guests. No need for pretense now. The curtain had fallen.

At the top of the ramp, I said, "Danny, thank you for inviting us tonight."

"Damn, son, we still doin' that Danny Fisher crap?"

"I guess I'm used to thinking of you as Danny, now."

"Then you go right on using it, Thomas Aquinas." He stopped at the lobby doors, glancing at the book in my hands. "Whatcha got there? Ancient philosophies of the Greeks?"

"I've been doing a little reading. About *you*. Was it true? The stuff in here?"

He pulled the *Elvis: What Happened?* paperback from my hands and fanned the pages. "The guys that wrote this thing set out to shame me. Embarrass me. Mission accomplished." He smacked the book into his palm. "And there've been plenty of other hack jobs since. I can laugh about it now. Almost. But at the time, it hurt. Hurt bad. They might just as well have hung me on a cross as publish that book."

"They say it destroyed your career."

"Some say that. But I'd already near destroyed it myself. And then they began bandying about this awful word. 'Addict.' That's what y'all in the press started calling me. That was the nail in the coffin, man." His lips curled into a faint smile as he handed back the book.

I'd come here tonight with a head full of questions. As I stared back at this broken man, only one remained unanswered. "Why did you ask me here tonight?"

"I wanted to meet your lovely lady, why else?" He squinted, examining my face, reaching up to tilt my chin to one side. "Hey, that cut looks nasty."

"Trouble seems to find me," I said.

"Especially when you go lookin' for it." He set his hands on my shoulders. "This thing with the cops. Still got your nerves all in the dirt?"

"You could say that." I tried to escape his gaze but he caged me with those electric blue eyes.

"Boss." Travis motioned toward the doors. "We should git."

"One sec," Danny said. "Thomas, you wanna know the truth about Bone Harper? Go ask your pretty girlfriend." He started walking. "But I tell you what. That boy ain't right. And you sniffin' around his woman, poking around the Walker thing ... well, you're a stick up his ass. And he aims to jerk it out one way or another."

Travis led Danny into the lobby and out the back exit.

A moment later Meredith emerged from the ladies' room, her face beaming. "Such a night, huh?"

37

STUCK ON YOU

After our date at the movies, Meredith and I became inseparable, a bona fide couple. One weekend it was Kenny Loggins under the stars at Mud Island Amphitheater, the next, a lazy Sunday hiking Shelby Farms Park. Many others, we barely left the bedroom.

She said I'd changed, but I figured it was more of a letting go, my new-found emotions a rising river that finally jumped its banks late that summer.

Meredith had taken notice of a small black and white snapshot in a frame near my bedside. Two young boys on a beach blanket, sporting identical grins, gaps in their teeth in the exact same spots.

"Me and my twin brother," I said. "Oak Street Beach in Chicago." I cast a furtive glance at the picture as Meredith reached for it, a gauzy memory of those long-ago days forming in my mind. "That sweet little boy," I whispered. "He sure loved life. We both did."

"I can barely tell you two apart. Did he grow up to be a TV star, too?"

"No. He isn't—" I took the frame from her hands and set it back on the nightstand. "He doesn't *do* anything. He's ... he's ..." She saw the moisture pooling in my eyes. I didn't have to say another word.

"Oh, Tommy. I'm so sorry."

"It was a long time ago."

"And you don't have to talk about it if you don't want to."

I didn't want to talk about it. God help me, I didn't. And then I did. And then I couldn't stop talking.

In early October, one of those pink "Important Message" notes landed on my desk. A number, and a name: B. Lansky. I knew the name. In these parts they called him, "Clothier to the King."

That evening, I carried the pink slip back to editing. No need for anyone in the newsroom to hear this conversation, whatever it might concern. A phone hung on the wall. I dragged the receiver into the nearest edit bay and dialed.

Lansky picked up on the first ring, said a mutual friend asked him to get in touch. I told him I had a good idea who we were talking about and Lansky got to the point. There was a "suit of clothes" with my name on it, he said, down at the store, paid for. He noted our friend must think highly of me as he was not in the habit of giving out gifts anymore. The store was located right off the lobby in the Peabody and I was free to come on down anytime to get fitted.

The entire time on the line with Lansky, I'd been in a bizarre tug of war with the phone cord. When I rolled the chair to get a look outside the room, my co-anchor's face looked back. Kimberly stood in the hallway, the phone cord wrapped in her hands, twirling it. Just twisting it round and round. I rose, untangled the cord, and had to stretch myself past her body just to drop the phone back into its cradle on the wall.

"Eavesdropping?" I said.

"Who me?" She stepped into the edit bay, sat, and proceeded to study her fingernails. "It did sound interesting, though."

"Seems I'm getting a new suit at Lansky's," I told her. "That was Mr. Lansky himself."

"Good ol' Lansky's. My daddy used to go there when they still had the shop up on Beale. Real hipster clothes. I'm impressed."

"Kimberly, seriously. What's up?"

"Well since you're asking. I got a job offer today, Tom."

"You *what*?"

"In Florida. Morning anchor in Tampa."

"That's a big market," I said. "Are you taking it?"

"Looks that way."

"Wow. Have you—?"

I had a hundred questions, but they would have to wait. My pager was sounding. *Meredith's number.* And a 9-1-1 this time, code for call back right away. When I looked up from the beeper, Kimberly locked her eyes on me.

"Will you miss me?"

"What?"

"When I'm gone."

"Listen, can we talk after the ten?" I squirmed past her to the doorway.

"You're always in a hurry somewhere," she shouted after me. "I wonder if you're in this much of a hurry under the covers."

"Jesus! What's gotten into you?"

"And *who* have you gotten into? Back with the lovely former Mrs. Harper, I hear."

"Former?" I stopped short in the hall.

"She got the divorce she wanted, didn't she?"

Did she? I gave Kimberly a hard look. "Congrats on the job. But I gotta make a call."

Even over the phone I could tell Meredith had been crying. She was all over the map. But this much was clear: Harper came by tonight. When Meredith answered the door, he'd forced his way in.

"Are you okay?" I tightened my fist around the receiver, picturing that same hand clamped around Harper's throat. "Did he hurt you?"

She hesitated. "Yes. I'm fine. And … n-no. Not really. He was mighty pissed, though. Shoved me aside. Grabbed a big duffle bag from the attic and called me some terrible words on his way out."

I offered to come to the house but Meredith didn't want me to miss the ten. Instead, she got in the Bronco and drove to the station, arriving at nine-thirty, still shaking. Did she want to report what happened to the police? She gave me a look that said, "Are you joking?" and there was no more discussion of it. I set her up on the couch in the lobby, turned on the TV monitor over the reception desk, and went to do the news.

Thirty minutes later, I ran straight from the studio, in full makeup. I leaned in to kiss her, but Meredith scooted to one side, patting the seat next to her. She looked better, had a smile on her face as she pulled an envelope from her purse. "Open it. It's the reason Bone came over."

The envelope contained a sheet of paper folded in thirds. It was a legal document from the Chancery Court of Shelby County, in the case of Meredith A. Harper, plaintiff, vs. Jonathan B. Harper, defendant. Centered across the top third of the page it read:

FINAL DECREE OF DIVORCE

Kimberly had known.

"You should frame this thing," I said, folding the document back into the envelope. "So, it's done?" Now I was smiling, too. "Signed, sealed, delivered?"

"If you're asking me if I'm yours ... the answer is yes, yes, yes." Meredith stroked a hand against my cheek. "Tommy, sittin' in your lobby tonight, I got a wild hair. Let's get out of here."

"Sure, let's go."

"No, I mean, really get gone." She began gathering her things. "Ever been to Gatlinburg? Smoky Mountains and all that good stuff?"

"Nope. Never been. I mean, I've never been to Spain, either, but I'm up for anything."

"You're silly." She smacked my arm hard enough to sting. "I'm thinking we hit the road. Celebrate."

"You and me?"

"Yes, dumb-dumb," she laughed.

"I suppose I could take a couple days off at the end of the month, make it a long weekend."

"Good," she said. "*Now* you may kiss me."

38

PROMISED LAND

Lansky's at the Peabody splashed across a glass-walled corner of real estate off the hotel's elevator lobby, a sartorial assault of technicolor coats, jackets, shirts. Hanging from the back wall, a framed black and white of a twenty-something Elvis Presley, standing with, I presumed, a young Bernard Lansky. As I absently ran my hand across a silk sport coat, a voice boomed behind me. "There he is, the man in blue from Channel 2."

I beheld the owner, the dark head of hair he'd had in the old photo, mostly gone. He wore rounded thin-framed glasses and approached me in shirtsleeves and a pink striped tie, a tailor's measuring tape draping from his neck to his waist.

"You got some interesting stuff here." I flipped through a stack of two-toned vintage bowling shirts.

"Believe it or not, it all sells. Style is style. And people will always want that. Let's see what fits *your* style." He directed me to a rack of suits in purple, maroon, black, pin-stripes. Some had padded shoulders, others hung extra-long. I pointed to a dark navy, double-breasted.

"Nice choice, Tom. Italian cut."

I slipped on the jacket and Lansky spun me around to the mirror. He smoothed out the shoulders with the palms of his hands. "You know, we get a lot of celebrities such as yourself come in here."

"Oh, I wouldn't quite call myself a celebrity."

"Well, this town loves its stars," he said. "And like it or not, you're on their TVs every night. You're gonna be part of a long legacy. Of course, we dressed up Elvis real nice over the years."

"Does he come in anymore?"

"Sadly, no. But he's still my number one man. I ain't saying there wouldn't be a Lansky's without him, or vice versa. But together, boy, what history we made."

A few minutes later, he etched the final chalk marks on the suit and said he'd let me know when it was ready.

She arrived in the Bronco on a Thursday morning, hair up, windows down, the air around her sharp with anticipation. Almost Halloween, the trees in peak autumn mode. With Miss Priss once again in the care of my cat-loving neighbor, I bounded down the stairs with my overnight bag.

Meredith opened the hatch and flipped me the keys.

"I know." I caught them one-handed this time. "Your man's driving."

We passed Nashville around noon, all the cares in the world receding in the rear-view mirror. Meredith laid a Tennessee road map in her lap, tracing the route with one hand. The other rested on my thigh, her fingers stroking like a pendulum across the denim. In time to her beat I sang, badly. A silly love song, a travel song, of flying away to Jupiter and Mars.

Ninety minutes later, just beyond a town called Crossville, the Smoky Mountains came into view, fuzzy and dark blue on the eastern horizon. I noticed Meredith taking a hard look out the window. At the road signs.

She squeezed my leg, crushing it. "Turn off at this next one, Tommy."

"We've still got a ways to go, are you sure?"

"I want to show you something."

The turnoff led to a series of country two-lanes, my curiosity growing with each mile. "This next road." Meredith elbowed me in the ribs.

"Listen," I said, "you keep clawing and poking me I'm gonna to be black and blue before we get to Gatlinburg!"

"You can handle it, big guy." She tossed a thumb to her window. "This way."

A gravel lane cut through a field of wildflowers, terminating at a solitary farmhouse. Meredith unbuckled and folded her arms. "What do you think?"

"Pretty," I said, waiting for an explanation. The house and property encompassed several acres. A split rail fence enclosed an expanse of overgrown grass. White columns supported a porch rimmed with Victorian balusters. Dormer windows peeked out upstairs. A classic Tennessee country home.

"This was my daddy's summer ranch." Meredith stepped out of the Bronco. "I guess it's gonna be mine one day. Beautiful ain't it?"

I agreed. It was a handsome place. "I remember you saying your father passed away."

"Three years ago now. A tumor. Near killed Mama with grief."

"Must have been very hard."

"Mama and Daddy, they was very close. They wanted that for me, too. I was all they had. And of course, Daddy never approved of my marriage."

I studied the wrap-around porch, the wood-beamed ceiling adorned in the delicate pale hue of robin's eggs. Meredith called it "haint blue." She said they used to paint a lot of porch ceilings that way to ward off evil spirits.

She pushed open the door, delivering the afternoon sun in dust-driven streaks across the hardwoods. Meredith led me in, then crossed directly to a side table, lifting the cover of a stereo. An LP had been left on the turntable. As Meredith lowered the needle onto the vinyl, a familiar tune emerged from the speakers, sung in a slow and sultry cadence. A woman's voice, not the usual male singer associated with it.

"This was one of Daddy's favorites. He loved Ann-Margaret. He liked your friend Elvis, too, but he always said hers was the best version of *Heartbreak Hotel*."

Meredith beckoned me, arms outstretched, fingers curling inward. I obliged, falling into her embrace. Our cheeks pressed, we swayed to the music. This trip, this detour, this house, it all overwhelmed me with a consuming suddenness. For the first time in my life I felt I belonged somewhere.

I brushed back her hair, cupping her face in my hands, my eyes searching hers. Maybe I'd had my doubts, but in her deep blues I found none. She was a rock. The salt *and* the earth. She'd have your back no matter what. She'd take a bullet for you.

"Meredith, I ..."

"Shhh. Unnecessary."

"What's unnecessary?"

"Words are," she said. Our lips met, soft and yielding cushions, a deep, lingering kiss, a persistence of vision for the soul as spiritual as it was penetrating. It was the moment I knew. I loved this woman.

I tried again. "Meredith, I've been a jerk."

"Yes." She stopped dancing. "But I did put you in a terrible spot, not telling ya ... well ..." She reached back to the turntable and lifted the needle from the record. "Tom, you treat me like a lady. I've never had that. Remember that night at the Peabody? How you told me about your first time? My first wasn't quite so romantic."

"I wouldn't go so far as to call mine *romantic*," I said.

"Well, for me, every date was a dang wrestling match. I swear they all had eight arms, snapping my bra straps, shovin' their paws down my pants."

"Meredith, you want to sit down?"

We settled into a long sofa upholstered in red and gray chenille. She leaned her head against my arm and continued.

"There was this one guy in high school. A senior. I was just a sophomore. I went to this party with him. Drank *way* too much. I shouldn'ta been drinking at all. I left the party with that boy and he drove me down to McKellar Lake, you know, that old beach along the river on the southside of Memphis. Next thing I know he's got me on my back in the flatbed of his pickup, right there on the hard metal and he's puttin' his finger—"

"It's okay, you don't have to go on."

"It was like some godawful TV movie-of-the-week. I told him no. Screamed it. 'No!' Tried to push him off but he was crushin' me nearly about. I can still hear the echo of my heels hammerin' into the hollow sides of that damn truck bed."

"I am so sorry, Meredith." Her story was as familiar as it was nauseating. I'd heard some version of it from nearly every woman I'd dated. I may have been around the block, as Meredith put it, but I'd never forced myself on anyone.

"Well here's the punchline," she said. "Turns out Daddy's waitin' up when that boy dumps me off at the house. I'm a mess, top untucked, hair matted down. Fallin' down cryin'. Daddy comes running out in his PJs, shotgun in his hands. Slides that muzzle through the window of the truck, right up in that boy's nostrils. He says, 'I don't know what you done, but hurt my daughter again and your brains'll be decoratin' the insides of this shit heap.' That was the last I seen of that boy, but it's something I can't get out of my head." She reached across the sofa for her purse. "It's why I carry—"

"I know what you have in there," I said. "I saw it that night at the Memphian."

"Daddy gave it to me on my birthday. Helluva sweet sixteen present, huh?"

"And you keep it with you all the time?"

"Yes."

"Loaded?"

"Wouldn't be much use elsewise." She set the purse back and pivoted to face me. "Listen, don't you get the wrong idea. I'm not that stupid, scared kid any more. No one's gonna mess with me again. Understand, Tommy?"

I did. I also understood that by trusting me with a searing memory, she'd opened the door for me to return the favor.

"I want to tell *you* a story now, Meredith."

She sat up, blotting her cheeks with her sleeve. "Uh-oh."

Like a good journalist, I did not bury the lead.

"I got a girl pregnant last year."

If I was expecting a reaction, Meredith didn't deliver. She nodded as if to say, *go on*. So I unfolded the story of Valerie. How she was an intern at the station and we'd started dating. After a couple of months I thought we were getting serious. Then she missed her period, took one of those tests, and it came back blue. We'd weighed the alternatives, the potential shame, her evangelical upbringing, what it might mean for my career, and hers. We figured it'd been at least eight weeks and we were running out of time.

"We took care of it at a clinic in Midtown," I said. "But the whole time she's in there, I'm focused on myself, terrified the guy from TV is gonna be recognized at that place." Meredith stared at her feet, avoiding my eyes, as I went on to describe the nurse calling Valerie, me leaving to wait outside. "A few minutes later, three police cruisers screamed past and I was gone."

Finally looking up, Meredith said, "What do you mean, 'gone?'"

"The cops were racing to some crazy-ass emergency. I put the car in gear and followed. It turned out to be the Walker incident. By the time I'd done a live shot and rushed back to the clinic, she'd already left. And whatever happened, happened and—" My head fell into my hands. "I haven't seen or spoken with her since."

Meredith took my chin. Lifted it. "Did you ...?"

"Love her? I don't know. Maybe. I mean, I'm not sure I've ever really—"

"You mean you've never given yourself a chance to. With that girl or anyone else." She patted my thigh and stepped to the front windows. "Tom, Tom, Tom, I ain't no saint myself. I'm not gonna judge you."

"Somebody should," I said.

"What y'all did ... I was brought up to believe it's a terrible sin. You both made a mistake. And then *you* made it worse, thinking only of yourself, and leaving a girl alone in an awful way. But how does that song go? We're only human. You gotta forgive yourself. And hope she does, too."

A crack of thunder echoed across the hills. The windows rattled. Outside, heavy drops clattered like pennies on the front walk. The clouds had been building all morning but the forecast hadn't said anything about rain.

Meredith turned for the door. "We best get goin' if we're gonna make it to that hotel. These lightnin' storms can be something fierce out this way."

She locked up the house and I gave a lingering glance back, hoping it wouldn't be my last. Then we made a run for it. It was only three or four long strides to the Bronco, but the sky had opened, showering our heads. In the few seconds it took to get to the safety of the truck, we were dripping from top to bottom, the rain settling in our shoes.

39

CAN'T HELP FALLING

The Cherokee people called it Sha-Kon-O-Hey, land of the blue smoke. It was plain to see why as we entered Great Smoky Mountains National Park the next morning. A milky blue haze lingered over the hilltops, a fog said to hang over the range year-round.

Meredith insisted the only way to truly see the park was to hike the ridges. I had no objection to that, but took keen interest in the notice posted on a small shake-roofed kiosk at the Clingman's Dome trailhead:

> **BLACK BEAR ALERT**
>
> Black Bear have been encountered on this trail.
> Make noise while hiking.
> If a bear approaches, shout, wave arms, throw stones.
> If attacked, fight back aggressively!

I re-read the last line. "How exactly do you fight back against a bear?"

"The idea is, don't get yourself close enough to find out," Meredith said, "You're not scared of a cuddly ol' teddy bear, are you?"

"Maybe I am," I said. "Keep that thing handy."

She giggled and patted her purse. "This little pea-shooter

wouldn't stop a bear even for one second." *Nor would the blade in my back pocket.*

The ground still slick from last night's rain, the footing uneven, we kept our distance from the edge. A couple of hours in, the trail opened to a spot called Andrews Bald, a wide, grassy expanse where the fog had burned off. We stopped, breathless—taking in sweeping views of the Smokies, the distant trees afire with color—then pushed ahead.

We soon came upon an outcropping of boulders. Beyond, a rough gravel path circled down to a narrow ridge. Evergreen trees grew out of the sloped cliffside, the ground falling off from there in a sheer vertical.

Meredith, her hair tied back, her cheeks glowing bright pink, looked as fresh and natural as the air and hills around us. I wrapped my arms around her, kissed her forehead. Her skin was soft and, despite the flush of her face, cool to the touch.

"Well?" I said, dragging out the syllable. "What do you say we ...?" Our eyes connected. No longer mere communication between us, it was communion.

She took my hand and followed me down the gravel trail. The ground inclined at a perilous angle, but I reckoned it was worth the risk. The trees and the rock face would provide a modicum of privacy. She unzipped her hooded sweatshirt. I pulled off my jacket. The rest fell away. We lowered ourselves in unison, a ballet pair pirouetting to the ground.

Meredith kicked out her legs, locking my torso in a vise, the sudden move sending loose rock tumbling over the edge of our precarious boudoir. We both shook with laughter, unleashing another spray of pebbles.

"Tommy," she purred, "Maybe we shouldn't—"

Something stirred from above. Snapping branches, heavy steps, followed by a cascade of gravel.

"What's that?" I sprang to my knees, brushing off my forearms.

We grabbed for our shirts.

"Is it a bear?" Meredith drew her top over her head.

"No, I thought that, but—" I froze up at the sight of a silhouette hovering over us at the top of the trail. "It's a hiker. Shit. Shit. Shit."

Stripped down, with the exception of my socks, I shot Meredith a look of panic. *Here we go again.* She pulled on her top. I went for my boxers. We were exposed and half-naked, in stark view of our interloper.

As Meredith stood, I reached for my jeans, clutching her hand for balance. But that only caught her off guard. She tripped across my ankle, her feet pedaling. Too late, I realized Meredith's momentum was hauling me down with her, skittering us both toward the cliff's edge.

The jeans flew from my hands. I clawed at the ground, trying to slow myself, kicking my feet against anything I could. A large boulder stood between us and the cliff. Meredith collided with it first. I crashed behind her. The enormous rock, undermined by the overnight rain, tipped, wobbled, and vanished over the side.

Meredith jerked to a stop, her torso pinned against a tree root. But I kept going, pinwheeling around her, circling to within inches of the abyss, praying the ground would hold.

It didn't.

Wipers swinging, snow drifting. Teasing, laughing. Scolding. Mommy! The door gives. The car is gone. The world is white.

My brain concussed, rippling with a ghastly vision, yet another wisp of that buried moment pressed between the pages of my distant memory. These transitory flashes—so frequent in childhood—lately seemed to be triggered by hard falls, and why was I always crashing my head?

My head. That was the problem. I'd clocked my skull into a stone wall.

It had been a drop of only a couple of yards. Nothing broken. Above me, Meredith's feet dangled, stirring a deluge of sand and silt as she clung to the edge.

"Are you all right?" I called out, rising to my knees. "I'm trying to get to you." I reached the spot directly beneath Meredith, wondering if I could break her fall.

I was about to find out.

With a sickening crack, like a snap of bone, the root holding her ripped free and the ground fell away. Meredith shrieked, dropping feet first in a riot of rocks, subsoil, and clay. As her legs shot through my encircled arms, I clamped them shut. For a second I had her. If only I could freeze the video right there. But she kept going, crushing us both to the ground in a tangle of limbs.

We weren't done.

Our bodies recoiled off each other, bouncing balls, punctured, but still going. My teeth rattled. I bit my tongue. A fingernail split as it dug into the soil and finally held. I was safe, and flat on my back, just short of the next—potentially fatal—drop off.

My eyes cracked open as Meredith, her body a rolling pin, barreled towards me. In a frenzied scramble to her hands and knees, she grasped at anything she could.

"Tommy!" she screamed.

Meredith hit me like an eight ball to the corner pocket, my legs skimming off the ledge, followed by the rest of my half-naked torso.

40

LOVE ME TENDER

Her hand seized my wrist in a death grip and mine hers, leaving me suspended from one arm like a slab of hyper-extended beef. Below us, a sheer drop into a boulder field.

"Tommy, dammit, don't let go!" Meredith's plea from above rang in my ears and somewhere behind it, an echoing call, a mirror-cry.

Tommy! Lemme go! His last words. At least, that's what they told me. That he'd screamed for me to let go. Wasn't that the story? That I dragged him out of the car with me? All these years, that's what I believed. That I should have *let go*.

I'd be goddamned if I let go now.

Flailing my other arm, I fished above me for something, anything to grab. On the third desperate swing I locked on. Debris peppered my head, coating my tongue, the taste of fear flavoring every breath. But for the next seconds Meredith's arms were as solid and unyielding as the rock face itself, allowing me to leverage my heels into the cliff, flex my elbows, and arch my upper torso over the ridge. With a primal roar, she heaved me the rest of the way to safety, then collapsed, panting onto her back.

Partly out of relief, but also over the absurdity of it, we began to giggle. Until we heard the footfalls. The hiker!

We scrambled for what garments had descended with us. I yanked up my jeans, Meredith managed to secure her top and zip her pants just as a muddy pair of boots appeared, their pointy ends protruding over the edge as they paced the rock shelf above us.

A large man peered down, backlit by the harsh late afternoon rays. I tugged at my shirt, squinting up at the silent figure. The boots kicked out a hail of gravel and I raised my arm to shield my face. When I looked again, the silhouette was gone.

"That was weird," I said. "Was that guy trying to—?"

Meredith plucked a stone from her palm. "Let's just grab our stuff and get going."

We scrambled back up, each step a painful reminder of how close we'd come to serious injury or worse. At the top, it was all still scattered where we'd tossed it in passion minutes earlier—shoes, jackets, Meredith's purse—and also something lying nearby that wasn't there before. A small green can in the shape of a hockey puck. *Smokey Mountain Chew* it said on it. I swallowed hard, shoving down the sickening feeling we'd been followed.

"You wanna go first?" I drew shut the hotel window shades and pulled off my shoes.

"I'm afraid of what I'm gonna find," Meredith said. "Let's you go first."

Under the unforgiving blue-white glare of the bathroom light she reached around my shirt and peeled it over my head, a stinging, body-sized bandage rip. "Tommy," she gasped, "it's like you got drug by a motorcycle."

Meredith had the idea of showering together. Groom each other the way chimpanzees did. But for the next half hour, with steaming holy water purifying our battered bodies, we partook in something more primal than primate, more rite than ritual.

Her hands caressed my every laceration with a healing touch as tender as the blows had been harsh. In due course, I did the same.

My hands trembling, I glided the soap in deliberate strokes across her shoulders, along the hills and valleys of her arms, across the contours of her breasts, her back, her hips. I lathered her hair, stray bubbles alighting on her eyelashes like a twinkling constellation of stars.

When the last traces of blood, sand, soil, and stone had circled the drain, I pulled Meredith into my arms and pressed my mouth to her lips. For a moment we breathed only each other's breath, hermetically sealed in passion. Her heart raced against my chest. A drumbeat pulse pounded in my ears. All at once something inside me burst. As she held my shivering form and I hers, tears descended my cheeks and sobs spilled out like a newborn's, resonating against the tile shower walls.

It was a sacrament, a baptism. The most intimate moment of my life.

Our ablutions complete, we lay in bed, Meredith already drifting off. The storms had rolled in again, flashes of lightning puncturing the window shades. As I slid beneath the blanket, Meredith murmured, soft and muted, into her pillow. "You don't have to say you love me, Tommy. But I'm gonna say it. I love you ..."

Her voice faded, her breathing settling into a gentle, steady rhythm, leaving me alone to turn over the events of the day, the mystery of our survival, the miracle of us. Thunder rolled in crashing waves across the mountains as Meredith's chest rose and fell in hushed opposition, an ocean at ebb tide.

"Good night, you crazy, wonderful creature," I whispered, my lips to her ear. Her hair, still damp, still fresh with the smell of Pantene, cast the faintest glint of gold in my eyes. "And I really do, you know. I love you, too."

I arched myself into the curve of her back. Sleep would soon override the thunder, the lightning, and underscoring it all, the tingling pain of a thousand tiny cuts.

We spent the next afternoon browsing the shops along the Parkway, the main tourist trap in town. A small stuffed bear caught Meredith's eye. It had a sweater embroidered with "Gatlinburg is for Lovers." She decided to name him "Barely Bear," for obvious reasons. We had a good laugh over it. Still giggling, we turned to leave the store. But Meredith stopped and doubled back to the vestibule.

"Tommy, wait," she said, her face frozen on the newspaper rack. I followed her eyes to the front page of the *Knoxville News-Sentinel*.

ELVIS PRESLEY HOSPITALIZED
STRICKEN ASSISTING MEMPHIS POLICE

An old file photo accompanied a short paragraph. Something about an incident in East Memphis Saturday night. Elvis transported to Baptist Hospital. He was serving a warrant in his capacity as a reserve officer. There was one other individual identified in the piece: Patrolman Jonathan B. Harper.

Patrolman. Reinstated *and* demoted. And partnered up with Danny again.

"Meredith, what the fuck?" I whipped my head. "Elvis. And your ex."

"Don't you dare," Meredith snarled. "I'm done with that guy. But your friend needs you. So, if you want to cut the weekend short—"

"It doesn't say what condition he's in." I clutched at the newspaper but couldn't coax any more facts off the page. "What good is print media anyway? This is at least twelve hours old." I dropped the paper in the rack. "For all we know he could be dead."

We sprinted down the Parkway to the hotel, packed up, and checked out.

41

HURT

Travis, his face wan, his lips pulled tight, met us at the nurses' station at Baptist Memorial Hospital. "The boss has been asking for you," he said.

"How is he?"

"Go on and see for yourself."

Danny, in a pair of mint green pajamas, reclined on a stack of pillows, a bottle of spring water in his hand. When he saw us wavering in the doorway, he smiled and motioned for us to come in. "You ain't scared to see a sick old man, are you?"

"Just glad you're okay," I said.

"I'm not okay, Thomas. I'm hurt." He looked up at Meredith. "Hello, miss. Y'all have a nice time up in them mountains?"

"We did, but—" Meredith shot me a look. "Wait, how did you know—?"

"What do y'all take me for?" Danny said. "Of course I know. Same as I know about the divorce. Plus, that sorry-ass sonofabitch Harper can't keep his damn trap shut. He's had your asses under surveillance." He raised his eyes to Meredith again. "Uh, no offense, miss."

"None taken," Meredith said.

"And now your ex-cop, I mean, ex-husband ... he's gone and messed with the wrong guy."

"What happened?" I said, taking a seat next to the bed.

"That dog did me like something out of that *Serpico* movie." Danny shifted on the mattress, leaning in close. "T'other night he had me tag along. Just servin' out a warrant over by Audubon Park, he says. So we approach this one apartment. Harper has me knock on the door. We draw our guns. The door unlocks, opens, but it has that chain thing latched. I try to push on it, but the guy slams it shut on my gun hand. I'm stuck half in, half out. So I'm pushing on the door and the perp, now he draws *his* gun. And Harper, he just stands there. Doesn't raise a finger."

"That motherf—"

"Hold on, Thomas. What happens next is, my legs give out all of a sudden and I drop to the floor. That's what saves me. Then Harper kicks in the door and collars the guy. EMTs took me in. Said my insides seized up."

Meredith put a hand on Danny's shoulder. Danny covered hers with his but withdrew it to suppress a heaving cough. "Anyways, like I said, the cocksucker's unoriginal. Stole that weasel move straight outta *Serpico*."

I tapped Meredith's arm. "Can you excuse us for a minute? I'll be right out."

As Meredith passed into the hallway, Travis entered the room, standing watch next to the door. I turned to Danny. "Jesus, Harper tried to get you killed."

Danny fluffed a pillow and stuffed it behind him with the others. "Maybe I ain't cut out for police work. Maybe I shoulda just stuck to drivin' a truck. But don't you be worryin' about me, Saint Thomas." He nodded toward the door. "Tell me about you and Lady Godiva. You two look serious."

"We are."

"Thinkin' of making it formal?"

I started to open my mouth but he threw a hand up.

"I know a guy that runs a little store on the east side of town.

Probably sold me a million dollars' worth of rings and shit over the years."

"I don't—"

"And it's not a just little trinket we're talkin' about, right?"

"I suppose not," I said.

He whistled through his teeth. "You move fast, man. Real fast. You know what wise men say."

I shook my head.

"You know, fools rush in and all that. Or is it fools and Russians? I can't never remember."

"Seriously, I think she's the one," I said.

Danny sat upright, chuckling, swinging his legs over the side of the bed. "And just how many *ones* have there been, son?"

"Okay, maybe more than one." Now it was my turn to chuckle. "Some who obviously loved me, sure. And in the past I'd look at that and think, God, I want to feel that so badly. But I didn't. Not then. Now, I do."

"Man, you are whipped, for sure. But okay, I'll put in a good word. Have 'em take care of business for you."

I was about to thank him and say my goodbyes, but he began to heave again, holding up a finger. "Thomas," he rasped. "You didn't ask me why."

"Why what?"

"Why Harper pulled that move on me."

He was right. After six hours of frenzied driving to get here from the other side of Tennessee, I wasn't thinking straight. I hadn't bothered to ask the question.

"It's because I know what he did," Danny said. "And he knows I know. And you running around with that long tall Sally out there, you're fixin' to be his next target."

"Danny, the divorce is final."

"And you figure that means shit to this boy?"

"Look, you've been hinting around something since the first time we met," I said. "But you don't have to spell it out. I've already put it together."

"He knows that, too. Harper's desperate to cover his tracks. He's a ring around yer collar, son. *Our* collars. And it's gonna take more than *Wisk* to do the job."

"Right. So when they come back with the ballistics—"

Danny's face contorted in another phlegmatic cough, drawing Travis to his bedside. My time was up. "Ballistics, shit," Travis said, slamming a palm against the wall. "I'd like to inject some ballistics into that guy's brains right about now."

"You're a good kid, Lizard," Danny said, the words choking out between hacks. "And you're right. Thomas here can go and report some ballistics mumbo jumbo on the news. But if you wanna prove something, you gotta show people something. That's the way to convict a cop."

You gotta show people something. My broadcast news professors had drummed into us that exact thing. Television is a visual medium. *Show, don't tell.* That J-school admonition echoed in my mind as I gathered Meredith and we rode the elevator down to the hospital lobby.

"Your ex is a dangerous SOB," I said. "You had to know that from day one."

"He had flashes of anger, sure, but—"

"And all that time you were married to this creep, you stuck by him? Never saw anyone else?"

"There were a few flirtations, maybe. But as soon as they realized who my husband was, they got outta Dodge."

"Which explains why you never told *me* about him."

"Yes, because I fell in love with you, asshole." When the elevator doors dinged open, she stood still, her eyes on fire.

"Okay, okay," I said, taking her by the shoulders. "And if I'm honest with myself here, I also fell in lo—" I stared at the floor. "I mean, I—"

"Tommy, hells bells." Her face opened in a broad smile. "You can say it out loud."

"Say what out loud?"

"The other night at the hotel. You thought I was asleep, dummy. But I heard what you whispered to me. I heard every blessed word."

42

I GOT STUNG

A diamond in the rough perhaps, Danny's jewelry place definitely leaned to the rough side, sitting as it did in the middle of a squat strip mall on South Perkins. As I stood paralyzed in the entryway, a bespectacled man with a receding hairline approached from behind the counter. His button-down shirt open at the collar, he sported a gold chain, adorned with a lightning bolt pendant.

"You must be Tom. He told me to expect you, I just didn't think it'd be so soon."

My eyes darted around the store. I was doing it. *Taking the plunge.* Funny, considering a literal plunge had led me to this moment. "I'm new to this," I said, "and I don't know if I can afford the typical ... what is it? Two months' salary thing?"

"Not knowin' what you make, of course," he said, "but that's not a hard and fast rule. Let me show you a few things."

The jeweler brought out a gold band with a round three-quarter carat diamond. The overhead lights reflected in the stone, sparkling miniature rainbows into my eyes.

"You know, back when he was performing, Elvis loved to give away jewelry," he said, while I studied the diamond. "At this one concert, he took out a case of my rings and bracelets and just started tossing the stuff to the women in front. Thousands of dollars of product. Bless his heart, it didn't faze him in the least. He said all he had to do was sing five minutes the next night to pay for it."

I shook my head in amazement.

"Yep, true story," he said. "What do you think of the ring?"

"Can we go a little more—?"

"Go big or go home, eh?" He pulled another tray from under the counter, producing a ring with a large rectangular diamond. The jeweler called it emerald cut. "This one is just under a carat. Combined with the side stones, you got almost one and a half carats total with very good color and clarity."

I rotated the ring, pictured it on her finger. Try as I might to steady it, the diamond shook in my hand, rattling against the glass as I lowered it to the counter.

The jeweler smiled. "The dang thing's not radioactive." He placed the ring in one of those fuzzy flip-top boxes. "I tell you what. You think about it and I'll set this one aside. I'll give you a very good price. A favor for the big guy, okay?"

Nothing like falling off a cliff to snap a guy into reality. This past weekend was nothing if not life and death real. Returning to the newsroom Monday afternoon? Insanity.

Bubba stood poised behind the assignment desk, regulation football in hand, ready to let it fly. In the break room, Dilly roared over a joke, tobacco juice spitting from his lips. Kimberly ripped copy from her typewriter, accompanied by an exquisitely drawn out, "Fuuuck!"

The football had perfect spin, I'd give Bubba that. It crossed the thirty, the forty, midfield, but with no eligible receiver, it crash landed between the desks in my pod, splitting the divider in two. The impact blew me back, delivering a lapful of videotapes and manila folders. Everyone looked up. Then applause. Bubba took a bow. Compelled, I stood, took a bow as well.

In this environment you never grow up. Arrested development, they call it. People in a newsroom, they're all Peter Pans. But even though I did fall out of a moving car as a child, I was no Lost Boy and this was no Neverland.

Janelle and Sheila rounded the desk to help clean up after the incomplete pass. "We missed you last week," Janelle said.

"We?"

"Lukas and me. I filled in for Kimberly. She made this big announcement in front of the whole newsroom. She's taking a job in Florida. Did you know?"

I nodded.

"Anyways, I got to anchor Friday night," Janelle said. "The way I see it, it was an audition. I think it would be cool to co-anchor with you, Tom."

"Yes, but ..."

"But what?"

"I read the news about your boyfriend and Presley," I said. "He's gonna get someone killed. If he hasn't already."

"Glass houses, Tom." Janelle turned back toward her desk. "And not that it's any of your business, but he's not my boyfriend. Anymore."

A few minutes into the drive home that night I saw the swirling blue light, gaining fast in the rear-view mirror. *What now?* How could Danny be well enough to be out on his own already?

Obligingly, I clicked the turn signal, pulling to the shoulder at the Kansas Street exit, a dreary industrial no man's land of rail yards and muddy creeks. I coasted to a stop, rolled down the window, delivering a rush of cold, damp air. Pulling to my bumper, a Memphis Police cruiser. Not Danny's Stutz, after all.

A uniformed officer approached, flashlight in hand, studying the rear of my car. I pulled the door handle and set a foot out.

"Whoa, get your ass back inside the vehicle," the patrolman

ordered. I couldn't see his face. He made sure of it, directing the light at my eyes.

"What's the issue, officer?"

"You have a busted left brake light."

"I don't think so." I tapped the brake pedal. It cast a devilish red glow on the man's face. "See, it's fine," I hollered out the window.

As I watched through the side mirror, the officer took the butt of his flashlight and smashed it into the taillight housing. Shards of plastic hit the gravel, tinkling like a shattered glass ornament.

"It ain't fine now," he said.

"Wait a minute." I stepped out again. "What is this abou—"

It happened quicker than I'd imagined even from cop shows on TV. He pulled his service revolver, spread his feet, and elevated the weapon.

"I gave you an order to stay in the vehicle. Now turn around and place your hands on the roof." I could hear him holstering the gun, fingering cuffs. He shoved the small of my back and I flattened against the door, the air evacuating my lungs. Once he had my hands locked together he flipped me around to face him.

"Officer Harper," I said.

"Well, well. The jig's up, the word's out." His breath reeked, his speech slightly slurred. "I'm flattered you remember me, mister anchor dick."

"Are you intoxicated, officer?"

Harper set a hand on his utility belt. "I'll tell you what I am. I'm working this all-night delta shift when I should be home drinking beer. *You* did that to me, motherfucker."

The Milano knife burned my back pocket. If I could just inch my fingers lower, get a grip on it ... *yes, and be shot dead before I even flipped open the blade.*

Harper took a step back. "So, here you are. Fresh from y'alls little skinny-dippin' trip down the side of a mountain." He fidgeted with the strap on his holster. "Did she cry on your shoulder? Tell you the marriage sucked? She also tell you about my big fat parting gift? When I came by to get my shit? Well, she liked it. Friggin' begged for it."

I didn't believe a word of it. But Meredith did admit he was rough with her that night. "I doubt very much she liked anything about you," I said.

"How do you like this?" Harper whipped the handgun from his hip and ramrodded the muzzle between my legs. I doubled over, my cuffed hands riding up my back.

"It doesn't feel very good, to be honest," I coughed out. Contrary to conventional wisdom, the blow didn't raise my voice an octave. But the kick in the nuts did piss me off. "You know, Officer Harper, all that crap you pulled? Spy photos? Taking a potshot at my place? You almost killed my cat, asshole."

Harper ripped his revolver from my crotch, and burst into in a full-throated laugh. "Hell, yeah, I figured you for a cat person, pussy like you."

I took a deep breath, steeling my face against the searing pain below. "And having us followed to the freakin' mountains, for chrissakes? Your man got sloppy. Left his can of snuff behind."

"Them Sevier County mounties are a bunch of know-nothin' hillbillies. The guy owed me a favor, but he didn't finish the damn job. If it was me, I would've tossed you both over the edge."

"And what about Presley? You don't care *who* you hurt, do you?"

"A shame ain't it? The man's an icon." Harper drew a long phlegmatic pull from his throat, turned his head and spat. "Although, these days, he's more of an 'I can't,' dontcha think?"

"The point is, you're accomplishing nothing."

He raised the handgun, his index finger dancing in and out of the trigger guard. "I'll accomplish your nuts all over the pavement if you don't shut your pie hole."

"You're gonna shoot me? Like you did with did Carl Walker? But wait. You missed, didn't you? You're always missing. Who did you end up hitting, again?"

Harper stumbled back, lifting the gun to his temple and holding it, before pulling the revolver away and leveling it at my head. "I'm gonna spill your brains, boy. I'm fixin' to do it."

"Okay, but before you do, tell me. Why did you want Walker dead? What were you trying to—?"

If he had an answer, I never heard it. For a long time I heard nothing at all.

43

SHAKE, RATTLE AND ROLL

A *blinding light. A screech of tires. A scalp dotted with snowflakes, white bleeding into red.*

Definitely morning. I put it at just after six, the deserted exit ramp from last night now rumbling with industrial traffic. It seemed my head had caught the side of a falling piano. Or the butt of a gun. I got to my hands and knees and fumbled in the dirt for the car keys. Not there. Not in my pocket. Still in the ignition!

For all I knew I had a concussion. I needed to visit the ER. But I went into work that afternoon and straight to Lee's office. I'd told no one about the assault, not Meredith, and of course not the police. But I was going to tell the boss—more than he wanted to hear.

"Tom, what the hell," Lee said, when I stumbled into his office. "You look like a wheel down and the axle draggin'."

I ignored the insult, mostly because it was probably true. "I had a run in with Bone Harper last night," I told him. "He pulled me over. Smashed my taillight and said he stopped me because the light was out. Cuffed me, pointed his gun at me, threatened to shoot me. Then he hammered me in the temple and left me for dead."

Lee shook his head. "Jesus."

"And Mary and Joseph," I sputtered. "I'm done keeping my mouth shut. I'm going to the prosecutor." I let the boss sit with that a moment, then spilled the rest. "I'm gonna say what I know about Janelle's assault. And I'm telling them they need to look at Harper's role in the shooting at the Walker house."

"Tom, take a goddamn breath." Lee put his hands out, a *let's all just calm down* gesture. "Let me talk with Ransom upstairs, get Legal in on this, too."

"Talk all you want," I said. "But I got a knot on my head the size of the Liberty Bowl that says you're not gonna change my mind."

A rap at the office door cut off Lee's rejoinder. "What, dammit?" he shouted.

"Sorry, Lee." Susan Quinn stood in the doorway. "Lukas just called in. He's at the DA's presser downtown. They released the ballistics results. The bullet that killed Officer Howard came from another weapon, not Carl Walker's gun. They say Walker fired only one round, a single slug, and it missed the cops completely. It got lodged in a bookshelf. Tom, didn't you report something like that a while back?"

The city had to have known the truth all along. It was why they'd agreed to reduce the charges against Walker over the summer. The bullet the medical examiner removed from Officer Howard's body was a hollow point rifle round. Police issue.

Harper. Back door. Crossfire.

Barking dog, resisting arrest, homeowner kills cop—everything prosecutors had pursued was meant to cement that story. Now their case was falling apart.

In the wake of the blockbuster news, I nearly forgot my bluster about spilling the beans. Forgot all about my impetuous threat to press charges in the Janelle Foster case. And it may well have stayed forgotten. If circumstances hadn't squeezed the beans right of the can.

The day it went down I wasn't even at my desk. I sat in front of a microphone, drearily voicing copy for an anchor package, the way

I did most afternoons. Cocooned in a sound-baffled audio booth, there was no way I would have heard the phone ringing in the editing hallway.

As I made my way back to the newsroom a few minutes later, our freshly-hired desk assistant accosted me. "Did you get that message, Tom? Sounded urgent."

"No, I was—" I did a double take.

"Taylor," she said, patting her chest. "I just started a few days ago."

"You were an intern last year. I remember you."

"I wouldn't blame you if you didn't. You only had eyes for ... well." Her face flushed. "Anyways, about that call. It had something to do with a videotape. I transferred it on back to you in editing, but Trace Kunkel took the message. Said he wrote it on the wall. You know, above the phone."

A poor man's memo pad, the yellowed plaster above the wall phone contained a number of old etchings, all scratched out save one. Scribbled in number two lead, a 901 phone number and the words, "Tom, call back."

His name was Nate Boyer. He said I'd put his mom on TV once. They lived behind the Carl Walker place.

"Yes, of course," I said. "As I recall, Franny told me you have an interest in video and whatnot. Are you thinking about a career in television? I'd be happy to talk you out of it."

"Aw, hell no, that ain't what this is about." He chuckled at the other end of the phone. "I don't know how to say this, but I filmed it. The Walker thing. I've got it on video."

"Say *what*?" The hairs on the back of my neck prickled.

"Truth be told, we didn't know what to do with it. The cops never asked and we never said. Then it all died down. But seeing the report on your news the other night, about the bullet and all? Like I told that other fella when I called ... I think you need to see this."

Nate gave me his address on Fountain Place, the street running parallel to Underwood Avenue. Although I knew where the house was, I grabbed a pencil and jotted the details on the wall, next to the scribbled phone number.

Shaking as a set down the phone, I spun into Eddie's edit room, wide-eyed and salivating. "You're not gonna believe this. Those folks behind the Walker place. They videoed the shooting. They have a—"

Eddie's eyes darted to the right. I turned to face Kimberly, reclining in the other chair. She'd been concealed behind the door when I barreled in.

"Thanks Eddie, for helping me with my highlights reel," she said, syrup in her voice. "I'll leave you to it." Kimberly stood and brushed past me, her hand riding the door jamb as she exited. She lingered a moment in the hallway and disappeared into the newsroom.

"Man, we gotta head out. Like *now*," I panted, gulping air every few syllables. "They have ... a *tape*. This could finally be the ... 'show, don't tell!'"

"I sure don't know what in the hell you're talking about," Eddie said, "but give me a few minutes to finish this."

"Okay, but—"

"I'm in the middle of this dub. When it's done I'll come and get you, Tom."

A young man with a close-shaved head and a button-down shirt answered the door. I thanked Nate for calling us and asked if we could bring his tape back to the station to make a copy.

Nate pushed on the screen door and stepped past us to the porch. He squinted up and down the street. "I don't have it," he said.

I shot a glance at Eddie, then back to Nate. "Didn't you call us this afternoon?"

"Yes," Nate said, "I spoke to you. But—"

"But?"

"The man already came."

"What man?"

"That man on the station. The man used to read the news."

I staggered. "Nate, what are you—? You're saying *Lin Harper* was here?"

"Made me play the video for him. Actin' all kinda strange, sayin' some weird stuff about 'my son, my son.' Didn't think nothing of it at the time. He said he was in a hurry, asked if he could borrow it. So I popped out the tape and gave it to him. Isn't he with y'all?"

"Nate, please tell us you have another copy," Eddie said.

"Aww, hell. Hell, *hell!*" Nate slammed a hand against the screen door. "I never made the connection. His son's that cop ain't he?"

I gave Eddie a *let's go* slap on his arm, followed by a simple, "Goddammit!" and we left Nate behind, still pounding his door.

In the truck I reared back my arm and whaled at the dashboard. I battered it all the way back to Poplar Avenue. I could have strung out an accompanying cold fury of expletives clear to the station if not for the interruption of the two-way.

"Tom," the radio squawked. "Are you with Eddie?"

I ripped the mic out of its mount. "Affirmative."

Bubba's voice returned from the speaker. "How about telling someone when you head out?" There was a pause but the mic stayed hot, transmitting the background babble of the newsroom scanners. "Well, since I'm your answering service today, Rambo, Lansky's at the Peabody called. Apparently your suit is ready."

"Thanks very much for sharing that across the public radio waves, Bubba."

"Oh, and hey, while you're there," he said, "go ahead and bring me back a pair of them blue suede shoes, why dontcha?"

I imagined squeezing my hands around Lin Harper's neck—ringing it, crushing it—and the neck of whoever tipped him off about the videotape. The violent fantasy so blinded me as I stalked into the hotel lobby, I missed the sleek black sedan with blinking flashers parked in the Peabody loading zone.

Mr. Lansky held out the suit and directed me to a fitting room. I had to admit, even pissed, I looked good in it. As the proprietor packed the suit in a black garment bag, my distracted eyes drifted to the lobby bar. Ducks paddled in the fountain. Tourists snapped pictures. To the right of the fountain, at a small table, two well-dressed gentleman chatted over drinks. I recognized them both.

"What the f—" I cut myself short; the kindly shopkeeper was studying me.

He stepped around the counter to hand me the suit. "I don't know what all you've spotted out there, Tom, but let's play it cool in the pool, okay?"

"Thank you for the suit, but I gotta go."

Laughter erupted from the cocktail table. On the left sat the news director of our arch competitor, Channel 6. On the right, a forced and phony smile on his Grinch face, one Lin Harper. Sure, if I'd just stolen the last bit of evidence tying my son to a homicide I'd be laughing my ass off, too. *You dumb sonofabitch, you won't be laughing in a minute.*

The garment bag hanging off my shoulder, I bounded toward the table. Worst case, I could toss the thing over his head and grab the tape. *If he has the tape with him.* A shadow loomed to my right, a surging figure. For a crazy moment I thought it was Lansky, coming to stop me. A heavy shove, like a block at the line of scrimmage, knocked me off balance. The suit spun out of my hand, helicoptering across a table, sending drink menus flying.

A booming voice called out. "Lin Harper, this is an arrest. I'm accusin' your ass of possession of stolen property." The man who'd tackled me sported a long, black leather jacket with an upturned collar. A pair of oblong sunglasses obscured his face. Flashing a gold badge, he postured, legs spread, like a white Superfly.

The man thrust a hand into the briefcase at Lin's feet and fished around. The hand emerged with a large cassette. *The VHS tape!* "I'll take possession of this now," Danny said, looking no worse for wear after his hospital stay.

Lin rose from the table, throwing back his shoulders. "You have *got* to be shittin' me. What is it, dress-up week at Graceland?"

"This ain't no goddamn joke, Mr. Harper."

Danny's practiced cool reminded me of the suave characters in his movie roles from the sixties. But Lin had his own brand of icy calm, and with a nonchalant sweep of his arm, he pitched the cocktail table forward. The weight of it dropped Danny to his knees, sending the videotape clattering to the floor. The Channel 6 news director stayed glued to his chair, his eyes bulging. After this, I doubted he'd be hiring Lin Harper any time soon.

The confrontation shattered the staid Peabody atmosphere, sending the pre-happy-hour crowd surging toward the center fountain. Someone produced a pocket camera and clicked a photo. At the sound of a splash, the group turned en masse. The crush of onlookers had pushed a young boy into the shallow water with the ducks, propelling three of the birds thrashing and flapping out of the fountain in a flurry of feathered confusion. A perfect distraction. Lin seized the opportunity, as well as the tape and his briefcase, and shouldered his way through the crowd.

Taking labored gulps of air, Danny grabbed a chair and steadied himself. Our eyes met. "Oh, hello, Thomas. I see you picked up the suit." He scanned the lobby until he spotted Lin heading for the elevators. "You comin' or not?"

I grabbed the garment bag, and dashed through the puddle of ducks. Without thinking, I reached for one of them, scooping it in one hand, its wings whipping the sides of my face. At the elevators I slid to a halt, lofting the bird at arm's length and letting go. "Hey Lin, duck!" I shouted. The waterfowl skittered across Lin's grease-laden head, fluttering and honking as it winged its way down his back and to the floor.

Danny leaped in front of the elevators, blocking Lin's escape. Or so we thought. With a flick of a finger, Lin dismissed a feather from his shoulder and brushed past us, marching toward the side doors to South Second Street.

"I swear to Christ," Danny thundered, reaching for his sidearm, "I'm gonna put a bullet in that lousy polecat!"

"Wait, look around," I whispered. "Everyone's watching."

"Maybe you're right. Too public."

We bounded out the doors after Lin, spotting him as he jogged to the valet parking lot, an open-air courtyard just south of the hotel.

Danny shouted, "Pull your truck in behind me, I might need you!"

"Wait. What's going on? How did you—"

"Thomas, I feel the need for speed. You want to stop this damn fool or not?" He hobbled to the Stutz and lowered himself in. I sprinted the half block to the news van and pulled open the driver's side door.

"Eddie, slide over. I'm driving."

"Why?"

"I'll explain on the way." I tossed the garment bag behind the seat, as the cameraman stepped over the center console. Pulling the shoulder belt around me, I said, "You better buckle up, too." I fixed my attention on the valet lot. "What does Lin Harper drive? I should know this. What kind of car?"

"That's easy." Eddie said. "He drives his namesake. A Lincoln."

"*Lincoln* Harper?"

"Kind of a cruel trick to perpetrate, right? It's a traitorous name to give to a white boy from Tennessee."

A long beige giant of a sedan skidded out of the lot, bouncing on its chassis, the underbody scraping and sparking against the pavement. "Is that it?" I jabbed a finger at the windshield.

"Yes, yes, dammit," Eddie answered.

I yanked the shifter to DRIVE and pounded the gas pedal. "Hang on, partner," I said. "We're in for a little shake, rattle and roll."

44

GO CAT GO

The news van was no match, certainly not for the Stutz, and not even for Lin Harper's land yacht. Trying to keep pace, I cut the first turn too close onto Union Avenue. The right rear wheel popped the curb, slamming back to the street and sending loose camera gear airborne in the back of the truck.

The taillights of the Stutz pulsed as Danny accelerated and braked behind Lin, a block ahead of us. I took a hard left onto Danny Thomas Boulevard, pushing it to fifty.

"Tom, if you don't kill us first with your drivin', what in the hell are we doing?" Eddie had one hand gripping the door, the other clutching the hard plastic of the dash. "You wanna force Lin off the road, take him down and grab the video? And who in the hell is Danny?"

"That's the guy in the black car ahead of us."

"Seriously, who's in that car?"

"You wouldn't believe me if I told you," I shouted over the straining engine. "Look, he's turning down Poplar!"

Traffic lights would be a problem through the Medical District. Le Bonheur Hospital lay ahead on the right, the light at the intersection transitioning from yellow to red. Danny pumped the brakes, then raced through, crossing the center line, cutting off Lin. The Lincoln lunged forward, jumping the sidewalk. It sprang back to the pavement in front of the Stutz.

"This cat's insane, man," Eddie said. "He ran that light."

"And so are we."

"So are we, what?"

"Running the light!"

An air horn blasted to my left, the front grill of a delivery truck filling the driver's side window.

"Tom, floor it!" Eddie shouted. "Floor it!"

The truck blew through the intersection, nearly glancing our rear fender, and we sped on. "What is Lin doing?" Eddie gasped. "As if we don't know who he is and where to find him."

"I don't think he has a plan."

"Do *we*?"

"Hang on!"

The humped overpass was never designed for drag racing. We hit it at sixty-five, launching like a missile. For a TV news van it gave fresh meaning to "air time." As our wheels reconnected with the pavement, my head tapped the steering wheel, Eddie's rapped the glove box.

Yellow light ahead. I pushed the pedal to the limit.

We overtook one car after another, a straight shot now. Just ahead, a blue light strobed. Danny, God love him, had switched on his police beacon. McLean Boulevard loomed, a major intersection, the light, a hard red. Lin screeched to a stop in the left turn lane, Danny on his bumper.

"Eddie, remind me. Where does McLean lead?"

"Overton Park. The zoo."

With a gap in the cross traffic, Lin didn't bother waiting for the light to change. He gunned through the intersection, screaming north on McLean. The Stutz followed. *Of course, cops can plow through red lights any time they like.*

"Well?" I shouted. "Should I?"

"Screw it!." Eddie threw up his hands in surrender. "Run, run, Rudolph!"

The van squealed as I twisted the wheel to the left and powered through the light, slamming Eddie into the passenger door. "Tom, just so I got this, before we die in this truck, okay? Lin Harper just happened to be at the Peabody when you went to get your suit?"

"Yes."

"Why didn't you go up to the sucker when you had the chance?"

"And ask for the tape, just like that?"

"That's how I'da played it."

"And that was kind of the idea," I said, pumping the accelerator. "But then Danny came out of nowhere."

"Danny again. Who's—"

"You're about to find out."

Ahead of us, the Stutz swerved into the oncoming lane, pulling parallel to Lin, clipping his front end. The maneuver forced Lin onto a side road, Prentiss Place, a narrow lane leading to zoo parking. A dead end! Eddie and I didn't have a plan. But Danny did.

Lin's Lincoln careened past a DO NOT ENTER sign, plowing through the exit lane. In season, it would have been impossible, but on a cold November day there were no zoo visitors coming or going to block his path. The Stutz roared close behind in pursuit. Bringing up the rear, I slowed the van to a crawl in the back of the near-vacant parking lot, suddenly doubting the wisdom of this entire mad escapade.

Just short of the main zoo entrance, Lin's car shuddered to a stop, its rear end elevating with such violence I thought the body might eject from the chassis. Lin jumped out and bolted for the turnstiles, waving a card, briefcase tucked under his arm. Danny lumbered from his car and followed, several paces behind, flashing his badge.

As we lurched into a spot behind the Stutz, I patted my pocket. *Lin, you SOB, I have a zoo pass too!* "Eddie, take this," I said, handing him the pass. "Follow Lin, and uh ... that guy." Do whatever you can to push them toward the back of the zoo, where they had that panda exhibit. Remember when we covered that a few months ago?"

Eddie studied the card in his hand. "You're gonna owe me for this."

"Oh, and I need to take the van."

"Of course you do."

"I'll see you inside," I shouted, and threw the truck in gear.

Along North Parkway, just where I remembered it would be, stood the broken section of zoo fencing. No surprise, they still hadn't repaired that gap. The chain links came apart with a slight tug, and I slipped through, half expecting to be jumped by a wild animal. But although this part of the zoo had been the gorilla habitat before it housed the recent panda exhibit, now it lay vacant. After a successful run, Xiu Hua had packed up her bamboo shoots and flown home to Mexico City.

I worked my way through the underbrush, rounded the old cinder block primate building, and waited. Footsteps approached, a crunching of leaves on pavement, their cadence increasing. I had a hunch Lin would try to lose us by running to the back of the zoo. Danny had called Bone Harper unoriginal. The father was nothing if not predictable. He headed right for me.

Lin stopped, panting, as I stepped out to block his path. Danny followed, and a beat behind him, Eddie, each man bending at the knees gasping for breath. I chuckled at the sight of three out-of-shape, middle-aged guys winded by a low-speed chase through a deserted zoo.

"Tom," Eddie said, huffing between words. "Don't you be ... laughing now. I ain't no ... spring chicken."

"You did pretty good for an old rooster." I swept my arm. "Eddie, meet Danny."

"We met," Eddie said. "And his name ain't Danny. Of course, you know that."

Lin steadied his breathing, glaring at us with fire in his eyes. "If y'all are done introducing your damn selves, why don't you dumbfuck keystone cops come the hell off it."

I felt for the knife in my pocket. "The tape, Lin. Let's have it."

Lin held out a hand, palm up. "Look, let's try to be professional about this."

"But this ain't professional, neither. It's strictly personal." Danny turned to me with a crooked grin. "Did you like that, Thomas?"

"*Die Hard*, right?"

"I gotta screen that movie again." He burst out laughing. The laugh degraded to a cough, wracking his body with a wheezing, whistling rasp.

Lin's eyes narrowed, as if sensing an opening. "Just look at your washed-up, sorry-ass self," he said, his voice pouring smooth as Tennessee whiskey. "You're not a well man, Presley. I think maybe they discharged you from Baptist too soon." Like a dog locked on a bone, he tightened his clutch on the briefcase. "Let me get on my way, and we can forget this clown show ever happened and you can still go on playing cops and robbers, and even keep your toy badge."

Danny drew a forearm across his lips. "Mr. Harper, you must take me for a moron." He produced a pair of handcuffs. "It's true, I was born at night. But not *last* night." Stepping to within inches of Lin's face, he ordered, "Drop the briefcase and put out your hands."

Lin returned an arrogant smirk. "Come to think of it, forget about your recent hospital stay," he said. "You shoulda bought it long ago, right there at Graceland, up in your gilded bathroom, choking on your own vom—"

Suddenly the smirk, the arrogance were gone, and Lin lay flat on his back, blood trickling from his lip.

"You decked him!" I yelled.

"I can't help it if he shoved his face against my hand, Thomas."

A young couple with a small girl in tow sauntered down the path. There *were* patrons in the zoo today, after all. Before anyone could object, Danny strode out to greet them. "Police business folks," he said, hands outstretched. "Nothing to worry about." No recognition in the girl's eyes, but the mom and dad gaped at each other as they passed, their eyes growing wide. Several more visitors rounded the curve. One of them pointed.

"Guys, move!" I shouted. "We're drawing attention." Danny took one of Lin's arms, Eddie the other, and they frog marched him to the enclosure that had housed Xiu Hua over the summer. Lin's briefcase lay on the ground, the VHS tape beside it. If Lin had half a brain he would have destroyed it rather than dragging it around all day as if it were a damn trophy. I grabbed the tape and joined Danny and Eddie behind the gorilla house.

"I have no idea how you got wind of this tape," I said, waving the video at Lin's nose. "But now that I have it back, you ought to know I'm *'fixin'* to put it on the air."

Lin spat out a laugh. "Do that, and you'll hang for it."

"Speaking of hangin' … what should we do with you now, Linny, hmm?" Danny dug into his pants pocket, producing a well-worn silver dollar. "I'm gonna toss this here coin. Heads we throw you into a cage for tiger food. Tails, we let you slither on outta here, snake that you are."

The silver coin spun and clattered to the pavement. "Whaddya know?" Danny said. "Tails. We could still arrest ya. But I think we're gonna let you go with a warning."

Lin brushed past Danny, stooping to retrieve his briefcase. "You know, Presley, my son tells me they've got a special name for you around the precinct. 'El-Piss In His Pants' they call you. If you ever had to be a real police, you'd soil yourself, the way you did that night over by Audubon Park."

With a speed befitting one of the zoo's big cats, Danny pounced, compressing Lin's pork-fed cheeks in his paw. "Harper, as a great philosopher once said … fuck you."

Lin's head snapped back as Danny released his grip.

"Aww," Lin sneered, "now I've gone and made you angry."

"You ain't *seen* me angry, Jack," Danny said. "Now flip, flop, and fly before I change my mind and toss you in with them tigers."

It was close to sunset, the zoo parking lights already glowing. Danny padded just ahead of Eddie and me, shaking his head. "Saint Thomas, you surprised the hell out of me back there. All *Smokey and the Bandit* with that news van of yours. Showed some balls with Harper, too."

"You took care of business pretty nicely yourself."

"Did, didn't I? Guess a washed-up sorry ass can still land a palm strike." Danny clicked open the car door. "I take it you ain't reportin' that blowhard?"

"For what? Tricking a guy out of a video? They'd take the tape and put *me* behind bars." I flicked a spot of dirt from the cassette. "Hey, how did you know about this video, anyway?"

"Despite Harper's insults, I can still do the job. I got sources."

"But the only people who knew about the tape were at my sta—" I turned to my photog.

"Don't look at me," Eddie said.

"Welcome to the party, Thomas," Danny said with a wink. "Damn camcorders, man. Soon everyone's gonna have one and won't be nothing nobody does that's not on video somewheres." Danny lowered himself into the Stutz and motored away.

I fished out the news van's key ring and dropped it in Eddie's outstretched hand. He bent down and went about using the ignition key to scrape a mess of dried gunk from the sole of his shoe. The noxious pancake fell away in a single clump.

"Panda poop, no doubt," I quipped.

"And you know what I say to *that*?"

"What, Eddie?"

"Xiu Hua has left the building."

45

RETURN TO SENDER

The VHS machine warmed up with an electronic whine of wheels, spools and other mysterious moving parts. The deck, one of only two in the building, held a place of honor in a far corner of the station's master control room.

It was past eleven. The night shift had gone home. The tape, labeled *July 31, 1987*, slid into the machine with a satisfying click. But when the door to master control swung open I hit PAUSE. There shouldn't have been any traffic through here until morning.

"You didn't think I'd let you drink from the holy grail by your lonesome did you?" Eddie grinned and took the seat next to me. "After what you drug me through to get it, I gotta see what's on the damn thing."

I was happy to see him and told him so. "Pull up a chair," I said, and then I hit PLAY.

The video started out shaky, camera pointed at the floor, images of a screen door, back steps. The angle straightened as Nate Boyer focused the lens on the ruckus at his neighbor's house. In a stage whisper, he provided occasional narration. "Some kinda shit's going down at Walker's place," he began.

We were seeing Nate's point of view from the middle of his backyard in the moments before I stumbled onto the scene. He panned to the right, the side of the Walker house coming into view. Bystanders lined the sidewalk, watching, pointing. "A couple more cops just pulled up," the narration continued. "I think they're tryin' to get inside."

On the tape, shouts arose from the house, a medley of grunts and muted expletives. Eddie said it reminded him of the sounds captured by field mics in those NFL Films. What we needed was a steady view of the back door. If the shot squared up, we might be able to see clear through.

As the video progressed, a sharp crack startled Nate, and the camera jerked. "That must be when the cops broke down the door," I said. The camera panned to the left, capturing a figure coming around the side of the house. Between the tilting, the panning, and the motion in the foreground, the camera's autofocus struggled to lock. The frame blurred.

"Damn! He's losing the shot!" I shouted.

Eddie, with his years of experience behind the camera, didn't flinch. He said, "It'll snap back." He was right. The picture sharpened, as did the figure approaching from the left. *Bone Harper!* A long gun draped across his arms, he peeked into a window and bent low. He reached the back screen door, pulled it open, crouched on the lower step, and aimed his weapon.

"Crossfire," I whispered.

Nate's camera angle wasn't perfect; we couldn't see past Harper, nor into the house as Walker and the officers collided. But what he did capture was explosive: Harper lowering his head, steadying the rifle. The voices inside rising again. Panicked shouts. Gunfire. This time Nate's hand on the camera held steady.

Eddie's mouth dropped. My jaw might have mirrored his, except I'd already played out this scene in my imagination many times over. I slammed PAUSE. The image on the monitor fluttered and flapped like a caged bird.

"There's your money shot," Eddie said. *Money shot.* Leave it to the news business to appropriate a term coined by the pornographic film industry. But there was no denying it. This was the climax.

Eddie gestured for me to back up the video. "Play it again, Tom."

The sequence was clear, or as clear as it could be on consumer grade VHS: Harper's gun recoils, the sound of its blast coinciding with a fusillade inside the house. Screams of "Shots fired! Shots fired!" Harper stands, wipes his pants, bends to retrieve something from the doorway. A rifle shell. He then leaves the way he came, disappearing around the far side of the house, holding the gun vertically and flush with his body as if to conceal it.

Eddie stared at the monitor for a long minute. "Run it back from the beginning."

I rewound the tape but left it in the deck, so Eddie could make a copy. Eddie said he could also reverse the process, transferring his Betacam dub to a blank VHS tape as a backup. I suggested he hold onto the Beta and I take home the VHS dub, and we could return the original to Nate.

Eddie nodded but didn't move. "That boy was aiming to kill Carl Walker," he said.

"I think so, yes."

"He shot that other officer instead."

"Looks that way."

"That's cold, man." He reached for a blank Beta cassette. "I'm worried for ya Tom."

"Me?"

"Old Lin's gonna tell Bone we have this tape. Probably has done already."

"That makes you a target too, doesn't it?" I said.

"Maybe so. But I gotta say it again. Don't be plowin' too close."

"Too late for that, Eddie. I'm already nose deep into that cotton."

∿

A copy of the *Commercial Appeal* lay sprawled across my desk the next afternoon. In the bottom right corner of the page, a small story.

> **SIGHTED IN THE WILD**
>
> A reader reports seeing the former King of Rock 'n' Roll at the Memphis Zoo this week. Elvis was said to be brandishing a badge and claiming to make an arrest. Memphis police have no record of any arrest and no comment on whether Presley is still considered a working member of the force following his collapse at the scene of a drug investigation last month. This latest incident may have started at the Peabody Hotel, where bystanders said Presley confronted a man in the lobby bar at tea time. Have photos or stories suitable for "Elvis Has Left the Building?" Contact the Commercial Appeal. If we publish your account, we will pay you $25.

A blurry photo accompanied the article, two men and a flying cocktail table. I set the paper down and laughed out loud. "Where's *my* twenty-five bucks?"

"What's that, Tom?" Trace came up behind me, running a hand through his cropped black hair. "Oh, funny story, huh?" He tapped the paper for emphasis. "Where *do* they get this stuff?" He winked and walked off.

Trace Kunkel. He'd taken the call from Nate about the video. Maybe Trace tipped off Lin. But how did Danny know about the tape? Nothing made sense. Walking the video into the news director's office made even less sense. But that's exactly what I did.

After acknowledging that Eddie and I had been late getting back to the station yesterday, I told Lee why. "We were tracking down a videotape."

"I'm listening."

"Let me show you instead."

Lee had the only other VHS deck at the station. It was oft-used and famous in the newsroom as the "ten-second audition machine." When someone applied for an on-air job, Lee loved to say they had exactly ten seconds to impress him. He'd drop in their tape and if he liked what he saw he kept watching. If unimpressed, pop, out went the tape.

As the machine sucked the video into its housing, I said, "A neighbor shot this from behind Carl Walker's house. He came forward after seeing our story about the ballistics report."

I studied Lee's frozen features while the tape rolled. His only reaction, a slight eye twitch when Harper's gun went off. Lee hit STOP and ejected the video. It wasn't exactly a ten second pop-out, but it may well have been. The sequence didn't seem to disturb him or excite him. An odd reaction to what I considered a blockbuster of a money shot.

"Who else has seen this?"

"Just me," I said. "And Eddie. And of course the guy who shot it."

"Did Eddie make a dub of this?"

"Yes, onto Beta so we can edit it into a story."

Lee jerked the video cassette out of the machine. "I'll need that Beta."

"Okay. But it's exactly what you just saw."

"Have Eddie to bring it to me." He waved the tape in his hand. "Any other copies?"

I lowered my eyes to the floor. And lied. "N-no."

"I suppose you figure you've got the scoop of the decade here?"

"I wouldn't put it that way, but, yeah. We need to air this."

"What we *need* to do is have Mel take a look." Melvin Blye was the station attorney. Having Mel "take a look" was the kiss of death.

I told Lee there was something else he should know. That Lin Harper had stolen the tape and saw what was on it. That we chased him down and got it back.

"Uh huh. Heard about that little extracurricular." Lee set down the VHS cassette, balancing it on its edge. "Heard quite a bit, actually." With both hands, he tugged on the wide center drawer of his desk. "Hear tell you're pallin' around with Presley, now. That's nothing but trouble, son." He backhanded the video, toppling it into the open drawer. "I'll hold onto this here tape. When legal's reviewed it, then we'll talk."

A bundle of letters bound with a rubber band crowded my mailbox at the apartment that night. Each envelope in the stack bore a faded yellow strip. In block-lettered typeface they read:

NOT DELIVERABLE AS ADDRESSED
UNABLE TO FORWARD

I tossed the lot of them. I had no interest in staring at my own handwriting, my months of fruitless and unanswered missives to Valerie.

Two messages blinked on the answering machine. The first, a goodnight from Meredith. She had an early house showing and was hitting the sack. It ended with "I love you." I whispered back to the machine, "I love you, too."

The other message, a man's voice I didn't recognize, until he identified himself as Travis Lister. *Lizard*.

> "Tom, I'm calling on behalf of the boss. He's having another film showin' at the Memphian. Says it would make him very pleased if you would be there. Saturday night. Midnight."

The machine beeped, the red light went dark. I glared at the device, waiting for some context. Why couldn't these things interpret messages instead of merely regurgitating them?

46

WELCOME TO MY WORLD

In the lobby of the Memphian Theater, Travis greeted me with an open smile and an outstretched hand, for the first time no suspicion in his eyes. Several other men surrounded the popcorn counter, bulging, beefy guys in denim. They looked like cops. For that matter, so did Travis.

"Where's the big guy?" I asked.

"Oh, the boss is already sittin' down. But I wanted you to meet some of the fellas from the county sheriff's office." They held out their hands and I shook each one.

Travis said, "We got a real kick out of hearing what y'all did with that Lin Harper fella the other day. You sure you're not secretly in law enforcement?"

"Like our friend inside?" I quipped. That brought a laugh.

"Say, buddy," said one of the off-duty deputies, "for the record, we ain't *all* a-holes. A few bad apples makes the rest of us look rotten. You go ahead now and put *that* on your news."

Danny hollered from row twelve, "There he is, the rebel without a pebble!" He patted the seat next to him. "No Lady Godiva tonight, huh?" He leaned in, confidentially. "If you really are fixin' to put a ring on that finger ... well, that bonehead's gonna go postal when he finds out."

"Ya think?" I said.

"The way I see it, Harper's already half crazy. He's liable to go the full deal any day now. Especially after you broadcast the tape. You *are* gonna put that video on the air?"

I told him it was out of my hands, that "Legal" was looking at it.

"Well I hope we didn't chase down that prune-faced, lardass anchorman for nothing."

"That's for damn sure!" The voice came from the next row.

Danny turned, addressing a familiar figure settling in behind us. "Uncle Kunkel, what's shakin'?" In answer, Trace Kunkel tossed a salute.

"Son, your mouth hittin' the floor," Danny said, smacking my shoulder. "*Right*. He works with you at the station, don't he? Maybe you didn't realize Trace is an auxiliary Memphis cop. Only recently made his acquaintance, but he's already given me some good intel, if you catch me."

"I do indeed." I said it casually, but in truth I was flabbergasted. Part-time cop. And a friend of Danny's. It explained a lot. I'd misjudged Candy's brawny boyfriend, or had we misjudged each other?

"Just about everyone here tonight's law enforcement. Make you nervous, Thomas?" Danny didn't wait for a reply. "Okay, let's get this mother started. Roll 'em!"

The lights went down, the screen lit up. The Twentieth Century Fox logo, the familiar fanfare, followed by a Boeing 747 touching down in the LA smog, Bruce Willis with a death grip on his armrest.

"You're screening *Die Hard* again?" I whispered.

"You betcha. Haven't stopped thinking about it."

Once more we sat through this tale of a desperate man—estranged from his wife—and the blood fest he delivers to the terrorists. But like one of the movie's hockey puck flashbang grenades, this time a revelation struck me. Danny saw *himself* in this tale. He identified with the single-minded determination of a solitary man, who, like a comic book hero, is the only one who can save the day.

When the lights came up, the guys joined Danny in our row, leaning over the backs of the seats. Somebody handed out cups of Pepsi. Danny sipped a Gatorade. "Man," he said, "I would have jumped at a chance to do this film."

"Maybe in the part of Bruce Willis's father," Travis joked.

Everybody roared, Danny the loudest. "Laugh all you want. I coulda done serious shit. Did you know they wanted me for *A Star Is Born*? Any of you numbskulls know that? Streisand came to my dressing room in Vegas. Asked me personally."

"I didn't know that," Travis said.

"Of course by then I'd ballooned out like Mama Cass. But I coulda ditched the pounds. Colonel screwed it up. All business, that guy, never gave a damn about artistry or music. The only note he ever understood was the dollar sign."

The men guffawed in unison until Danny waved his hand. "Don't leave nothin' on the table, boys. Regret's a bitch."

"You talk like it's all behind you," I said. "You're young. Look at Sinatra. He's in his seventies, still doing concerts."

"'Chairman of the Board.'"

"Right. But you're not the chairman. They call you 'The King.'"

"Ain't never cared for that name very much. There's only one King." He thrust a finger at the ceiling. "And He's up there."

"Okay, but have you ever thought about getting back on stage?"

Danny scoffed. "Thomas, you're a goddamn dreamer."

"Actually boss," Travis said, "I have the same thought sometimes."

I slurped my Pepsi, and emboldened by Travis' assent, pressed the point further. "Why *not* get back out there? Something small to start. Local. Like Vapors, that place out by the airport. I heard Jerry Lee Lewis played there over the summer."

Danny sat for a long while. I figured he was either going to slug me or laugh in my face. But the only action came from the back of the theater, a succession of thumps and swishes as the night manager flipped the seats and swept popcorn from the floor. Over the top of his soda, I caught Trace looking at me as if I'd suggested something completely off the wall, like turning Graceland into a tourist attraction.

Finally, Danny said, "Saint Thomas, sure, I've thought about gettin' back out there. Oh, I sit at the piano around the house some. But in front of an audience? If I ever tried … shit." He pushed back a matted clump of hair, revealing the tracks of crow's feet trailing from his eyes. "I'm not a well man. I give credit to God and my faith that I'm even sitting here with y'all."

"Well, you just talked about regret," I said. "Don't you—"

"Hold on a goddamned minute!" His eyes transited the men around him. "Fellas, I want to tell y'all something." He threw back a gulp of Gatorade. "Last year, while I'm lyin' on that operating table out west, I had a visitor. Now, y'all know my mama passed when I was only twenty-three. But for these thirty years I've prayed she'd come back, just send a message, anything. So here I am, under the knife, with them surgeons trying to patch up my guts. I should be out cold, but I wake up and there she is, come down from heaven, just floatin' next to the docs. She looks me in the eye and says, 'Now, son, don't you be throwin' away them God-given talents. Get up from this table and start doing what He put you on this earth to do.'"

"It's some kinda sign, boss," Travis said, the men around him nodding in agreement.

Danny pulled a roll of pages from his jacket, smoothing them out on the seatback in front of him. "Wanna talk about signs? Sam Phillips comes out to the house t'other day. Says he'd run into this up-and-coming singer-songwriter. Then he just hands me a big envelope and wishes me well."

Travis leaned forward. "I saw that envelope lying around the house. What was in it?"

Danny held up the sheet music and I caught the writer's name, Chris Isaak. The name didn't mean anything to me, but now Mama Presley's "sign" did.

"Do it." I said.

"Do what?"

"Sing it. Perform it. Whatever that song is there."

"You're out of your freakin' mind, Thomas. Why would I do that?"

"I'll give you two reasons. Your pride. And your fans. Oh, here's a third. Your mama." That drew some chuckles, and I said, "You know what I mean. But here's my point. Last year I was at the Peabody and who walks in? Steve Winwood. He just showed up to jam with the band. The crowd went nuts. If you go out onto that stage at Vapors on a night when they have all those impersonators performing, you'll make history."

One of the county cops stirred. "The kid's got a point. It sure beats the hell outta perps pointing snub-noses at you through the door, don't it?"

Danny disappeared into his Gatorade. He picked a fingernail at the label. "You know guys, toward the end, back in the seventies, it was just one jerkwater town after another. One night in East Jesus. Next night in Bumfuck, Egypt. Singin' a bunch of somebody done somebody wrong songs. But I needed the dough. So I kept on going. Nearly killed me."

Almost in unison, the big men around us lowered their heads, studying the butter stains blotting the floor.

"Sure, I read what they were saying in the papers," Danny went on, unreeling the Gatorade label from the bottle. "Tacky, they called me. Outdated. The 'potbellied patriarch of rock 'n' roll.' Hilarious, right, fellas? This one joker wrote that I looked like William Conrad in a Sonny Bono wig. Said I moved like a pregnant water buffalo. Goddamn it, I don't want to be remembered for that crap!" He crumbled the label and hurled it toward the movie screen. "And I sure as shit don't want to be done like John Lennon, shot down on a street corner like a dog."

Danny returned his attention to his now-naked Gatorade bottle.

I shifted in my chair and tried to pull the focus back to the present. "Hey, on my way to the theater tonight, you know what I heard on the radio? *Don't Be Cruel.* Not by you. By Cheap Trick. It's a top-ten hit! What does that tell you?"

"It tells me you're listenin' to the wrong damn radio station." Danny laughed, but this time not everyone joined in. He stuffed the sheet music back in his pocket. "Yeah, well, I can do you one better. The other day I read that the number one request from the National Archives in D.C. is the dang photo of me and Nixon at the White House."

"Wow." That was one article Tracy the librarian had missed.

"Don't you get it?" Danny said. "To the public I'm just a souvenir, a goddamn freak show."

"But if you take the stage again—"

"You may be Saint Thomas, but unless you start blowin' miracles out your ass, it ain't happening." He stood to leave. "Travis, let's hit the bricks."

"Okay, well just in case," I called after him, "open mic night at Vapors, Sunday after next!"

47

DEVIL IN DISGUISE

The general manager, Ransom Bishop, reclined behind his desk, the VHS tape resting on its side in front of him. Lee sat opposite, as did Mel Blye, the station lawyer. Ransom motioned for me to take a chair. I declined the offer.

"We've reviewed the home videotape," Ransom began. "We looped in corporate in New York, described the contents to them. Here's what we're gonna—"

"Wait," I said. "Before you go on. That tape is evidence of an attempted murder *and* a homicide. Getting that video and pursuing this story has put me in danger. I've been threatened and assaulted. I have … *we* have an obligation to report what we know. Anything less is journalistic malpractice."

"Are you done runnin' your mouth?" Lee clasped a hand on my arm. "Sit *down*." I slumped into a chair and folded my arms. "What Ransom was about to tell you is, we're gonna air the tape. With a few caveats." Lee turned to the lawyer.

"Tom, we agree this tape is legitimate news," Mel said. "But we have to protect the station and our owners against legal liability."

"So, for starters," Lee cut in, "we're gonna block out the face of the officer. The last thing we want to do is inflame an ongoing case. We can include some of the video sequence, but not identify the man in it. Do you understand?"

"No. I don't."

"Well," the lawyer said, "I'm told that down in the control room we have a way to mask out a portion of a video. In essence, create a new version, with an additional layer over it, putting a box or a blur over whatever you want to obscure."

"Yes, yes." I chafed under the condescension. "I get the technology. What I don't understand is, why?"

"It'll air Wednesday night," Ransom said. "Gives you a few days to put the story together."

"The night before Thanksgiving?" I knew Nielsen and Arbitron typically excluded the Wednesday and Thursday of Thanksgiving week from the November ratings averages, and for good reason. Nobody was watching.

"Take it or leave it, Tom." Lee's eyes went cold. He arched his neck, his joints cracking in succession like a busted bobblehead.

I wanted to leave it. Tell them where they could stick it. Then leave the room, leave the station, leave the planet. Instead I said, "What else? You said, 'for starters.'"

Lee held up the VHS cassette. "The control room guys can work from Eddie's Beta copy to block out the face, and I'm gonna go ahead and keep the original. It's just too hot."

"But I told the guy I'd get it back to him."

"He'll be fine."

Ransom stood and the other two rose with him. "Are *you* fine, Tom? Can we count on you to do the right thing here?"

"It's not the right thing. But you're giving me no choice."

"Good boy," Lee said. "Eddie should have the blurred-out version later today. And you can get a head start on your story. Thank you, Tom."

The Wednesday before Thanksgiving would be one to remember.

For once, the tired, cliched, "busiest travel day of the year" story got bumped to the back of the "A" block of the newscast. The doctored home video would lead the six. And the ten o'clock news, that would be about Kimberly Kilmer's swan song, her last night on the air at Channel 2. It was also memorable for another, more pedestrian reason. I wore the Lansky's suit for the first time.

Viewers that night saw a faceless, blob-headed man round the Walker house, crouch at the back door, aim, fire. In the story, I was permitted to summarize the ballistics report stating Officer Howard had been shot by a weapon and bullet consistent with police-issued gear. But I was not to make any connection between the ballistics and the blurry gunman in the video.

As neutered a story as it was, even castrated it fully aroused passions around Memphis. Before the first commercial break, Lee had worked calls from the police, the prosecutor's office, and Walker's defense attorney. They all had the same request: Turn over the unredacted video.

After the six, Lee held an impromptu newsroom meeting around the assignment desk. "This is the kind of hard-hitting continuing coverage that's distinguishing us from the competition." He puffed out his chest. "Tom, you're to be commended for staying on top of the Walker case." It was a beautiful speech. It made me want to puke. They say you have to pick your battles and I was ready to pick one.

Lee wished everyone a happy Thanksgiving and said his goodbyes and good lucks to Kimberly. For the rest of the evening I couldn't peel my eyes from that glass office. In there, locked in a drawer, lay the original VHS cassette, electrons on magnetic tape, images linking a killer to a killing.

"Hey, Rambo." Kimberly materialized at my elbow. "Staring at your pretty reflection?"

"Something like that," I said. "And we're back to 'Rambo' now?"

"It's our last night together. Thought you'd want to know." She curled a strand of hair behind an ear. "Oh, and good job with that tape. But those Harpers, man, I told you not to go foolin' with them."

"Kimberly, yes, I realize it's your last night and—"

"Nice suit, by the way." She ran a hand across her chin. "No worse for the wear considering how you drug it through the Peabody lobby."

At the end of the ten o'clock, Kimberly made it all of thirty seconds through her farewell script before her lower lip began to quiver. The director punched up a four-shot. Timothy set a hand on Kimberly's arm. Bobby jumped in to say it had been a pleasure teaming with her. T-Bone gave us the wrap signal and it was my turn.

"When I joined you at six and ten almost a year ago, Kimberly, I knew I had a lot to live up to," I said. "Memphis loves its hometown heroes and they sure adore you. As you move on, and however high you fly in the future, you'll always have a special place here at Channel 2."

Kimberly wiped a tear and faced the camera. "Thank you, Tom. Thank you, Timothy and Bobby. And all of you at home." Her voice caught in her throat. "Thank you for watching ... and good night." On the monitor they put up the Copyright 1988 graphic, a momentary wide shot of the studio, and a cut to black.

While we were on the air, the team had transformed the newsroom into a farewell party. *Good Luck!* balloons surrounded Kimberly's pod. There were hugs and tears and more than one muted comment that the news wouldn't be the same without her. I tried not to take that personally.

When things quieted down, Kimberly returned to splash herself across my desk a last time. "Those were some lovely things you said out there. Not that you meant a lick of it."

"Kimberly, whatever it is you wanted from me, I'm sorry you didn't get it."

She turned a sharp glance at me, staring me down like a laser beam. "You think you're like God's gift or something. Well, you're not.

You're not even my type." She stood to leave, tapping a contemplative finger to her lips. "You know, one day you'll be leavin'. And on that day, people'll say all sorts of phony things about you, too. Isn't that what you think? That everyone's a phony, anyway?"

"Not everyone," I said.

"What about me?"

"I don't know."

"Well, Tom, I don't know, either." She clutched my shoulder and drew close. "Entre nous," she whispered, pronouncing the last part like the word, *news*. "Things have been stacked against you from day one. They no more mean to keep you on the anchor desk than promote you to news director. And as far as the Harpers go, they're my friends. And you don't betray your friends ... *Rambo*."

48

YOU GAVE ME A MOUNTAIN

It was somewhere behind that storefront, set aside for me by the "Jeweler to the King." Nearly a month since I'd picked it out. So, why now? Why finally, now? In the past, it had never been a question of commitment. I'd never stayed in one place long enough to make one. It was more a problem of deciding. When you've decided, you've cut yourself off from all other options. I hadn't wanted to cut off my options any more than I'd wanted to cut off a certain part of my anatomy. But now I *had* decided. Christmas was coming and I was determined to drop to one knee before year's end.

The bell above the door tinkled. No turning back.

"Ready, Tom?" The proprietor reached under the counter as if he'd been expecting me. He propped open the small box. "Go ahead. Pick it up."

The ring seemed larger than I remembered. More dazzling. The side stones, like tiny stage lights, bathed the center diamond in sparkling fire. My hands sweat just holding it. I almost dropped the thing.

The jeweler chuckled. "Perfectly normal, son. Just keep on thinking how happy you're gonna make that lucky girl." He slid an invoice across the counter. "Here's the damage."

If the diamond had me fevered, the ring of my phone extension that afternoon chilled me back to room temperature. It was Candy. There was a man at the front desk.

"Not this again," I said.

"No, it's not *him*. It's some kind of delivery."

Even before I finished pushing through to the lobby, the man was asking if I was Thomas Cirone. I nodded. He thrust an envelope into my hands. "You've been served," he stated, and turning on his heels, he left.

Candy watched as I pulled out the document and unfolded it.

SUBPOENA
Carl T. Walker, Plaintiff v. Memphis Police Department, Defendant
To: *Thomas Cirone, WMDW Television, Memphis*
Under penalty prescribed by law, you are commanded

The document bore the signatures of the clerk of the court and of Innis J. Honeycutt, attorney at law.

"What's it say, Tom?" Candy asked.

"It says I'm ordered to appear at a deposition on Wednesday. For the Carl Walker lawsuit. I'm supposed to bring the unedited version of the videotape we showed last week on the news." I set the papers on the reception desk, pointing to an admonition at the bottom of the page. "Check this out."

NOTICE: You can be found in contempt of court for failing to comply with this subpoena and if found guilty you may be fined, imprisoned, or both.

Candy placed a hand on mine. "Oh, Tom."

"Looks like I've got no choice," I said.

Her eyes met mine and held. "You can do this."

"I wish I shared your confidence, Candy."

With a harsh metallic scrape, the inner lobby door engaged, the hollow click of the unlocking mechanism echoing off the walls of the atrium. I jerked my hand away and folded the subpoena.

"Am I interrupting y'all?" Trace strode into the lobby carrying a Coke. "Tom, just because we watched a movie together doesn't mean I won't still kick your ass."

"It's not—"

"Just go. Don't you have some scripts to read?"

Candy buzzed me back in, and as I stepped through the glass door, I saw Trace offer Candy the soda and then pull it away. "It was *nothin'*, Trace," she pleaded.

"No, no, and how many times *no* can I say it?" Lee's face lit like a fireball. Only Grandma's marinara sauce could compete with that shade.

"It's a subpoena," I said, for the third time.

"I don't care if it's General Grant's terms of surrender," Lee said. "You *ain't* complyin'."

The attorney, Mel Blye, explained the station had been subpoenaed as well. He insisted that under no circumstances was I to go downtown and testify. And as Lee had the only copy of the original tape, there would be no sharing of the video.

"And when I'm held in contempt?"

"Won't happen," Mel said.

"And you know this, because?"

"We'll quash it."

Quashed or squashed, one way or another, it would be me at the butt end of the judge's gavel when it fell, not them. When next Wednesday rolled around, I'd make up my own mind whether I'd be "complyin'."

Vapors nightclub possessed an inexplicable appeal far beyond the allure of cheap piss-water pitchers. My informal invite had somehow produced half the newsroom crew. The club was already wall-to-wall when they straggled in, paid their five dollar cover, and squeezed into a long row of cocktail tables, a dozen of us in total.

The place wore it extra thick on this particular Sunday night. Thick with hairspray and cologne, thick with cigarette smoke, a blue haze closing in all around us, compounded by the crushing babel of a hundred voices carrying on at once.

Slouching at the side of the stage, resembling a motley police lineup, four grown men primped and postured. One, head-to-toe in black leather, another in white with a Superman cape. They looked to be in their forties or fifties, as did much of the audience. It wasn't billed as an Elvis impersonator night, but that's what we were getting.

On the narrow riser that passed for a stage, the guy in black leather stepped to the mic, warbling, *"One for the money..."* A guitar kicked in, and we were off.

"Just as pathetic as ever," Ronnie said. "Why do they do it?"

"I don't know." Dixie, who'd joined husband Lukas for the get-together, gestured at the band. "At least, give 'em credit for just getting up there in front of this crowd." Dixie had recently landed a job at the station as a weekend producer. It was good to see her out with the station gang.

When the man on stage launched into a half-time rendition of *Hound Dog*—bellowing like a forty-five RPM played at thirty-three—Ronnie slammed his mug. "Did y'all know Presley appropriated this song from a black artist?"

"And your point?" Bubba tightened his brow.

"White guy takes black music. Gets famous and makes all the money."

There was a change in performers. The guy in the cape took the mic. *"That's all right, mama..."*

"Ronnie's not wrong," Bobby said. "This song was Elvis' first hit. But it's actually a riff off of the original by Arthur 'Big Boy' Crudup."

"Aw Christ!" Now Dilly joined the fray, flattening his hand to the table. "What about *All Shook Up?*"

"Otis Blackwell." Ronnie said.

"*Shake Rattle and Roll?*"

Bobby shook his head. "Big Joe Turner."

"It's true," said Sheila, who'd been quietly following the discussion. "Before Elvis, folks like Little Richard, Ruth Brown, Big Mama Thornton, they were already doin' a kind of rock 'n' roll. But nobody paid any mind until a white man recorded it. Elvis took what those others were doing, borrowed from it, sure. But he studied it and made it his own."

"Why, Miss Sheila," Bobby said. "I never knew you were a kindred scholar." He turned to Bubba and Dilly. "Let's not lay it all on Presley. Bill Haley and Pat Boone, okay? Those guys did it too. They got rich, while Ike Turner made all of about twenty bucks for *Rocket '88*."

"Okay professor, what about the Beatles?" Trace chimed in. He had one hand locked on Candy's shoulder, but waved his beer in Bobby's face with the other. "Didn't they do covers?"

"Yes, but look—"

The waiter returned with a fresh round, cutting off debate. As I leaned back to accommodate the new supply of brew, I caught sight of a half dozen men in dark jeans and denim jackets, leaning against the back wall, drinking, laughing. Big men. *Cops.* I recognized some of their faces from the night at the Memphian. The joint was swarming with them.

"You Thomas?" The man came out of nowhere, looming over our table, breathing from his mouth. A scraggled gray beard dripped from his chin, and his plaid shirt reeked of tobacco.

"I'm Tom, yeah," I said.

"There's a fella asking for ya." He tossed a thumb over his back.

Bobby held a hand above his eyes, squinting. "Do you know that guy back there?"

I followed Bobby's gaze. *Danny.* He stood in the shadows, in the well of the bar, shifting from one foot to the other. He nodded and then disappeared through a doorway.

"*That* guy?" I said. "Huh."

The man in plaid led me between tables and past the stage, where a tribute artist twisted his pelvis and windmilled his arms. An alcove cut into the back bar opened to a room tucked behind the mirrored rows of whiskey. The man held the door but didn't follow me in.

It was more store room than green room, littered with music stands and stacked folding chairs. A leather recliner patched with duct tape faced a cracked and faded green sofa. An amplifier probably dating to Woodstock stood along one wall, an acoustic guitar propped upright against it.

Danny stepped around the door, pacing like a caged tiger. "You seen them clowns out there? Did I ever look *that* ridiculous?" He closed the door behind me, revealing a full-length mirror. "Damned if I ain't the most piss-poor impersonator of them all." Staring into the mirror, he dragged two fingers across his scalp, fixing a thinning stray lock into place. "That Andy Kaufman fella, though, rest his soul, that guy was a hoot."

The mirror bounced with the pounding of someone on the other side. Travis pushed into the room, music from the stage swelling, then dulling as the door opened and closed. Danny rounded on him, his jaw tightening in apprehension.

"Lizard, we really doin' this?"

"Looks that way, boss."

"How about we flip for it? Heads we stay, tails we skedaddle." Danny pulled out that worn silver dollar, just as he had at the zoo. "It's my good luck charm, Thomas. Colonel gave it to me my first gig in Vegas." The coin bore a picture of Lady Liberty on the front, an eagle on the back. Danny called it a "Peace Dollar."

"Nah, boss," Travis said. "Why don't you put that away."

"Man, I dunno." His eyes jogged, searchlights seeking an exit. "Let's just get the hell outta here."

Travis put his hands on his boss' shoulders, talking gently, as with a child. "This is what you been wanting," he said, barely above a whisper. "From the very first day I started with ya, you been talking 'bout this."

"I know it." Danny slipped the coin back in his pocket. He reached for the guitar, raising it to his shoulder like a rifle. "Thomas, if this goes south tonight, I swear I'll blow your goddamn brains out." He wheeled on me, aiming the guitar's headstock at my jaw. "Bang! You're dead."

On the other side of the wall the emcee called for a round of applause, telling the crowd to hang tight and order up. There was a rim shot on the drums, an electric guitar riff.

Travis got to work straightening Danny's collar, adjusting the guitar strap. He stepped back. "Hey boss, uh, the barn door's open."

Danny cracked a lip-curled grin. "So, Thomas," he said, glancing down and zipping up. "You know the two biggest words in show biz?"

"No, what?"

"*You're on.*"

I knew what Danny meant. "We've got something similar in the news studio," I said. "The floor director holds his hand up like this, index finger pointing at the ceiling, and when he thrusts it forward, it's showtime."

"That's good. Real good. I'll try and remember that." For a long moment, the three of us stood in silence. Danny glanced again into the mirror. "Face plant."

"Say what, now?" Travis said.

"That's what's stuck in their minds," Danny said. "Face plant."

"Not true," I said. But after my research at the library, I knew where he was going.

Danny continued staring at his reflection. "Jesus, even my own little girl had to see her daddy laid out like that. It's the one thing anybody remembers. And now y'all want me to walk out there and make a damn fool of myself in a dank club that smells of piss. With the only thing they're picturing when they see me is my sorry ass left for dead on the bathroom rug."

Travis had the look of someone who'd heard this all before, but I couldn't just let it go unchallenged. "Listen," I said, "you gotta believe in yourself. And in those people out there." I closed my eyes, conjuring an old refrain from Saturday morning Catechism. "You know my other namesake? The apostle Thomas? You know what Jesus said to him, right? 'Blessed are they—'"

Danny held up a hand. "Blessed are they that have *not* seen ... and yet have believed." He lowered his head, closed his eyes, and motioned for me to leave the room.

49

GOOD ROCKIN' TONIGHT

Dilly jabbed his beer at Bobby, punctuating each word with the glass mug. "I'll bet y'alls gonna say he stole *Heartbreak Hotel,* too?"

"No, that one was actually written *for* him."

The debate had raged on without me, Susan dancing between the combatants like a ref in a boxing ring. I tried to slink into my chair unnoticed but Susan wasn't having it. "Where the hell you been? That musta been some record-breaking dump."

"What'd that guy want, anyway?" Bobby said. "Hey, he's looking over again."

In the fog behind the bar a hesitant figure paced, a guitar hanging from his neck.

"Looks like you got a fan, Tom," Susan said. "You sure you don't know that old guy standin' there?"

I shrugged, turning my attention to the stage. While I was in the green room there'd been a transformation. An additional bass guitarist filled out the band. Someone had rolled out a vintage *Farfisa* keyboard. At center stage stood a chair and a mic stand.

Showtime. I locked eyes with Danny's across the room and I knew what I had to do, what he needed me to do. I lifted my arm, extended a hand, aimed my pointer.

You're on.

He tipped his head and mounted the steps to a smattering of applause, mostly from the crowd against the wall. Danny peered into the lights, cleared his throat, bent to the mic. "It's been a long time, Jack," he said. The mic squealed, the feedback silencing conversations and turning heads. "Y'all ready?" he said, looking back at the band. "I'm not."

He donned neither rhinestones nor jumpsuit. No baubles or bangles, no flying cape, no gilded belt buckle worthy of a WWF champion. But here was the real deal, whether or not everyone yet realized it, in red button-down, blue jeans, and black boots.

"This is my first time appearing live in eleven years," Danny intoned as he landed himself into the chair. "Although I did appear dead once or twice …" Nervous giggles fluttered from table to table. He set the guitar on his leg and picked a simple progression of notes. A few bars in, a second guitar joined with the chords. Danny leaned forward, raising his chin to the mic.

The lyrics sprang from his lips, as if finally freed from years of confinement, seasoned with age and weathered with disappointment. He sang of snow falling, voices calling, and the yearnings of a lonely man.

Bobby seemed stumped, but I knew the tune. "*Song For A Winter's Night*," I whispered.

With the exception of Travis and maybe another or two, I figured it was the first time in an eternity anyone had heard this singing voice in person. Danny unfolded a tale of fires slowly dying, a loved one far away. *If he could only know*, he wondered, *was she lonely, too, tonight?* It fit the cold December darkness outside these walls and the chill winds of regret fanning the aging performer on stage.

For a lingering beat, at the final note, no one moved, no one spoke. Too stunned to lift and bang together one hand against another, it was as if we'd forgotten how to, just as we'd collectively forgotten *who he was*, a musician, a man, not a tabloid caricature.

Someone shouted, "But that ain't an Elvis song!" Another

answered, "Who said it was supposed to be, dumbass?" Applause rippled, then rose in waves, washing through the club.

Danny rose from his chair, whipping the mic cord behind him as he paced. "Some years back a cassette tape arrived at my house. A demo by this young up-and-coming guy from New Jersey. Springsteen, maybe you've heard of him. He thought this one song might make a hit. As it happened, I got real sick and ... well, turns out it did make a hit, just not for me."

A five note sequence strummed from the electric guitar, familiar and yet not so, at least not in this setting, with this artist.

Duh. Duh-duh, duh-duh. Duh. Duh-duh, duh-duh.

Danny's voice growled, his mouth so close to the microphone I thought he might swallow it. This was old school sultry, dripping from the speakers with amplified sex. Women fell silent, rapture in their eyes. Midway through, Danny froze for a long second. Then came a pop on the drums and the incendiary lyric.

"Fiii-re ..."

The band tracked every tilt of the singer's head, his every movement. Danny had said there was no way in hell he'd stand up in front of an audience again, that I'd been out of my mind for even suggesting it. But watching him here, it was clear he'd worked out an entire set.

He'd had this in mind all along.

Bobby jabbed an elbow into my ribs. "Tom, I think I'm seein' things."

I braced for impact.

"I swear that's James Burton on lead guitar," he said. "Man, he is playing the hell outta that thing." A wary smile crossed my friend's lips. "He's a Louisiana boy and one of the best string men there is. Used to tour with—" He gave me a hard look. The truth was dawning.

Hunching his shoulders with the beat, Danny grabbed the mic stand, rocked it. When he reached the point in the song when the kisses burned and the heart stayed cool, he stopped cold.

Someone shouted into the silence, "Marry me!"

Danny laughed and aimed a finger gun at the woman. "I'm a Capricorn, honey. I like to take it slow."

In verse, he caressed the names of famous lovers, from Shakespeare down to ancient times. Perspiration pooled below his eyes, his hands trembled.

"*Fiii-re ...*"

He was in another place, another galaxy. He was where he belonged, for the first time in a very long time.

"*Fiii-re!*"

Danny raked his pick across the guitar strings, then dropped his hand, his chest rising and falling in tortured breaths. The audience exploded. I stood with them, smashing my hands together. The performance was a revelation, like when I first learned Gomer Pyle could sing. Amazing *and* unnerving.

Lifting the guitar strap, Danny handed off the instrument. He reached for a stack of sheet music, the pages flapping as he distributed copies to the musicians. He laid a finger to his quivering upper lip. "Down boy," he laughed. Pushing the mic stand to the side, Danny said, "I got this here next song just t'other day. I don't even know if I can sing the goddang thing. It goes something like this."

As the electric guitar and the *Farfisa* keyboard kicked out an ethereal strain, Danny's voice rose and fell. Falsetto to full voice, he lived and breathed the surreal lyrics, a refrain of *not wanting to fall in love*. This is a *wicked game*, he crooned, a love so wrong, but still, you desire it. Unreciprocated, but you no longer care.

For those who didn't get it, or didn't realize, or didn't want to believe who it was up there singing for his life, this had to be the strangest Elvis tribute they'd ever seen—this middle-aged performer, his voice stripped naked, moving from one anguished crescendo to the next.

But I saw it. After all our encounters, goddammit, I saw it. The charisma, the sensuality. Maybe if you focused real hard, if you allowed yourself to see past the years and the pain, maybe it was still there. Maybe it hadn't died.

The sheet music shivered in Danny's hand. His legs trembled. He never dreamed he could *love someone*, he sang, then *lose someone* this way. His mouth yawning, he sucked in one last draught of oxygen, letting it fly in an impossibly long closing note, a plaintive cry of grief, of the fruitlessness of love itself.

"*No, I ...*"

"That is one weird song," Bubba shouted across the table. "I mean, what's next, *Walk Like An Egyptian*? Why would an impersonator do weird shit like this?"

Candy, who'd been quiet for most of the night, turned to Bubba with an arched eyebrow. "Right. An *impersonator* wouldn't."

The applause subsided, the guitars kicked in again, this time with a fast-paced rhythm, a familiar one to the crowd, judging from the nodding heads and tapping toes.

"Hot damn!" Bubba bolted to his feet. "Now, *that's* an Elvis song!"

"Actually ..." I said.

Bobby finished my thought. "Freddie Mercury." He explained Queen's lead singer did offer the song to Elvis around 1979, but never heard back. So the band put it on their own album.

"Well it sounds like Elvis," Bubba pouted. "He should record it."

Record it! I whipped my head in the direction of the sound board behind James Burton. Was anyone recording this? It was impossible to see whether the guy at the console had a tape rolling.

People started singing along.

"*Crazy little thing called love ...*"

They swayed back and forth, clapping in time with the music.

"*Crazy little thing called love ...*"

Again and again.

"*Crazy little thing called love!*"

The band rocked, really rocked, for the first time in the set. Danny postured, three fingers extended. A karate gesture, a vogue. He crouched, he lunged, he punched the air. He crossed his eyes, mugging for the audience. With a death grip on the mic, he sang of hot, hot fevers and cold, cold sweats. Said he *just couldn't handle it*, but I was sure he could. It was head-shaking rock 'n' roll.

Finally, with a blast-beat on the drums, the up-tempo ditty with the made-for-Elvis-sound thundered to a close. Sweat rained from Danny's scalp and caught the light, gathering below the bags under his eyes, pouring into the grooves framing his mouth. He scratched his nose with a tremulous finger, then nodded to the audience and dismounted the stage, retreating behind the bar.

His face had gone white. He clutched his hands to the bar rail. Someone tossed Danny a towel, another passed him a glass of ice water. It seemed to revive him.

The applause still roaring, Danny strode back to the riser and grabbed the mic, on the wings of a second wind. "This last one I'm gonna sing for ya, there was a time Miss Dolly Parton herself thought I could make a good go at it. I never did, but I sure wished I had."

The lead guitar slid into a slow, haunting, country twang, Danny strumming along with the chords. The lyrics may well have flowed directly from Danny's soul, throwing open a window into a life of contradictions and hurt. He sang of leaving, of knowing that if he stayed, he'd only be in the way. Yet despite it all, he pledged:

"*I ... will always love you ...*"

It wasn't the musicality that struck me. His pitch was far from perfect. It was the humanity of it, delivered with reverence, like gospel from a place deep within. Doleful and desolate, he told of memories and farewells, and no need to cry, because he's not what she needs. It was a promise. And a goodbye.

"I ... will always love you ..."

As he strained to reach the last notes—and his wish for her, for a life full of joy and happiness, and love above all—I realized this was much more than a break-up song. Almost as if he was bidding farewell to all his loves, to his audience, to Memphis. Goodbye to the world.

"I will always love you ..."

"I will always love you."

The place erupted in rebel yells and whistles and more than one furtive swipe of the back of a sleeve against a dampened cheek, grown men averting their faces lest they be seen doing it.

As the applause roared on, Danny strutted the stage one last time, his hands outstretched. He uttered the words, "You're a fantastic audience, God bless," and bolted into the green room, dropping his arms, palms pressed flat to his sides.

50

UNCHAINED MELODY

Jumping from my seat as the band banged a walk-off vamp, a singular obsession gripped me. Get the recording. *If there is one.* I dodged bodies and tables, pouncing on the sound man as he powered down the audio board.

"Please tell me you roll tape on these shows!"

"Easy, boy," he said. "Sure. Sometimes they wanna listen back to it. So I run a reel-to-reel on 'em, straight off the mics. Patch direct into the sound panel. See?" He pointed with pride to his set-up.

"I need that tape." I caught myself, exhaled. "I mean, could I get that tape?"

He regarded me, this time with recognition. "Man, if you're wantin' it for the news, heck, there's copyright laws and royalties and such."

I fished for my wallet. "Twenty bucks," I said. "Not for the news. For that guy ... the last guy just now." I threw a thumb in the direction of the door behind the stage.

"You're with *him*?"

I nodded.

"Fifty," he said.

I nodded again. "The original reel, not a cassette."

As the tape rewound into its spool, I counted out two twenties and two fives, muttering to myself, "St. Thomas, you *do* work miracles."

"Do what now?" The sound man lifted the reel from the machine and handed it over.

The station gang already had their coats on. I found my jacket, folded the tape inside it, and laid it on my chair, just as Bobby grabbed my arm.

"You got a lot of explaining to do, son. Who *was* that guy?"

"Danny Fisher," I said.

"Da—?" Bobby broke into a barking laugh. "What kind of crack you on, brother? You can't bullshit a *Loo-zee-anna* boy." When he saw I wasn't following, he elaborated. "One of the first films my mama let me go see was *King Creole*, okay? For weeks after, all I wanted to do was run around trying to act tough like Danny Fisher."

I shook my head. I still had no idea what Bobby was talking about.

"You *say* that was Danny Fisher," he said. "That's the name of the dang character in *King Creole,* one of Elvis Presley's first movies."

"Then, I think you got it figured out." I scooped up my jacket and turned for that door behind the bar.

"Plop, plop, fizz, fizz." Danny downed half of it in a gulp, then lifted his drink at me. "Thomas?"

I took one look at the Alka Seltzer and said, "No, I'm good."

"It's my go-to cocktail. Shaken, not stirred." Danny threw back the rest. "Not that it does a damned bit of good. Docs say I got an obstructed colon. A shot liver. Hypertension. XYZ, PDQ, CIA, you name it." He rose from the couch, too quickly, letting out an animal grunt, half belch, half bark. "I dunno, man. Last time I tried to take a crap, it damn near killed me. Could stand a little less constipation, a little more action, if you get me."

"Well, you looked pretty good out there for a dying man." I

stepped into the room and shut the door. "But before you croak," I said, chuckling, "can I ask you something? Danny Fisher ... was he a good guy or a bad guy?"

"Both." He reached for a small metal cannister crowned with a purple mouthpiece, brought it up to his lips, pumped it. "That cat was pretty tore up over his mama's death. Went around pissed off. Got mixed up with some bad dudes."

"But he had a heart."

"Now you're gettin' somewhere." He waved his bodyguard over. "Hey, Lizard, you still got that thing in your pocket? Take a snap of us." Danny beckoned me to stand at his side. An Instamatic camera appeared, a flash burst.

"You done killed 'em tonight, boss," Travis said, running a finger across his mustache. "Just like them old days."

"Like I always say, people'll come out of the woodwork to see a freak."

"That's what you think?" I asked.

"Yep." Danny fell back into the couch cushions. "That's the way it is."

"How can you say that after how they—?"

"Will you come the fuck off it!" He slammed the side of his hand into the table. The drinking glass and the inhaler jumped, as did Travis. "You know," Danny said, "back in the day, the roar of that crowd, it was like some kinda rocket engine. It shook my damn insides when I'd walk out on that stage." He laid his right hand in his left, massaging the soft flesh along his palm. "But man, I done lost it all. I lost the love of my life."

"Your divorce," I said. "I read about that. Back in the seventies, right?"

"Shit, not *that*, man. The love of my life. The damn fans."

What should have been Danny's night of triumph had taken a sharp, dark turn. I couldn't pretend to understand what was going on inside that famous profile of his, but for sure I knew when to change the subject. I slid to the couch, setting myself down next to him. "Hey, I saw an article about you in *People Magazine*. About your daughter, anyway. You walked her down the aisle."

"She'll be twenty-one next year," Danny said. "Her mama and I, we went our separate ways long ago. Now, they're both into some sort of sci-fi church out there." He reached for the empty glass in front of him, spinning it on its edge. "That little girl, though, she's my flesh and blood. I just don't want her to be ashamed of her old man and how he done threw away—"

"C'mon boss." Travis took a step toward us, reaching for Danny. "Let's hit it."

I stood to go. "Looks like that's my cue."

"Okay," Danny said, pulling up from the couch with an assist from Travis. "Well, I hope you enjoyed the freak show."

I stepped into the doorway, turned around. "By the way, I bought the ring."

"For Lady Godiva?"

"Meredith."

"Ex-Missus Cop." Danny tightened his grip on Travis' arm. "Sounds serious, don't it, Lizard?"

"Serious, boss."

"Thomas, that fruitcake Harper shoots to kill."

"Luckily, he's got bad aim," I said.

Danny broke from Travis' grasp and reached for my arm. "Luck runs out, son."

51

DON'T

Two days later, the well-known rocker, Roy Orbison, passed away. I couldn't help noticing he was about the same age as Danny. Heart attack, the paper said. In that same edition of the *Commercial Appeal*, buried in the usual spot in the B section, this item:

> **ELVIS PLAYS ELVIS?**
> Did Elvis Presley impersonate ... himself? Club-goers at Bad Bob's Vapors nightclub on East Brooks Road are buzzing after witnessing a remarkable performance Sunday night. An unnamed artist closed the show with a set of five songs and was said to bear a striking resemblance to Elvis. If true, it would be a first, as the one-time King of Rock 'n' Roll is not known to have performed in public in more than a decade. Got photos? $25 if we publish yours.

This time Trace made no pretext of being cute with the newspaper, picking it up and waving it in my face. "I heard you took a little snapshot with him, too," he said. "Why not send it in and collect your twenty-five bucks?"

"Besides the fact it wasn't my camera and I'm sure the pictures haven't even been developed yet ..."

"Damn, you're tightly wound, ain'tcha?" Trace folded the paper under his arm. "That's okay. A friend of his is a friend of mine. Even if I still think you been hittin' on Candy."

"I'm not hitting on—"

Trace broke out in a wide grin. "Geez. Unclench that butthole, Rambo."

"Now *that's* a line they shoulda put in those movies, huh?" Bubba quipped as he came up behind Trace. "Tom, you got a call. Assistant D.A. He's on hold."

"Go take your call," Trace said. "And no side trips to the lobby, hear?"

The prosecutor wasted no time laying it out. He'd seen the broadcast like everyone else. He said the videotape I aired was evidence in a criminal investigation. Could I bring a copy down to the Justice Center in the next few days? The way the prosecutor phrased it, I'd be doing them a courtesy. In a strange way, the gentility of the request felt more compelling than the legal papers I'd been served last week from Carl Walker's attorney.

Emboldened by this latest entreaty, I ventured again into the glass office. I told the news director I needed the neighbor's tape, that the DA had just requested it, that it was evidence in the Walker case.

Lee set back in the chair and crisscrossed his arms. "Ain't got it."

"What?"

"Was I not clear? Let me translate it into Yankee for ya, Tom. I do not *have* it."

"You locked it in your desk."

"Yeah, well, danged if it's turned up missing."

"Lee, you're telling me you don't know where the tape's at?"

"That's right."

The battle was joined and it was time to pick it. I worked my jaw. Then came the brave words. "Luckily there's a copy," I said. "And I'm taking it downtown. You can threaten me and you can fire my ass. But I'm gonna do what I'm gonna do."

"Settle down, son." Lee stood, barely twitching an eyelid at my outburst. "Let's take another walk upstairs."

Mel Blye slid a sheet of paper across the general manager's desk. The lawyer told me if I signed it he could file a motion with the court and put a stop to these requests.

"Nope." I pushed the document back. The whole thing felt choreographed and I had no intention of getting in line with this two-step.

"As your counsel, I am advising you, you are jeopardizing your career *and* this television station."

"By doing the right thing?" My eyes focused on the big windows behind Ransom's desk. Out there, the river, brown and churning beneath the bridges, wended south to its inevitable appointment with the Gulf of Mexico.

"I understand you have a copy of the videotape," Ransom said, finally speaking up. "You are not to deliver that to any parties in any legal matters. That tape is company property."

"Actually, it's not."

"Christ, Tom," Lee shouted, "you are a professional journalist. You have a responsibility to remain neutral."

"That's a laugh." I'd crossed a line and I knew it. Knew it and didn't care.

Lee smashed a fist on the desk. "Goddammit, don't you get it? You are *compromised*." He stood, and wore a fresh track in the carpet, counting off my transgressions on his fleshy fingers. "You slept with a cop's wife, or did you forget that? Someone might could insinuate you're mixed up in this personally. Or even better, would you like to see a story in the paper about how the Channel 2 newsman paid for an intern to … to take care of an inconvenience?"

"Slander my name? Go ahead. But drag Valerie into this? No. I'm sure she's suffered enough."

"Then *do not* testify."

"Are we done?" The bile rose so high in me I thought it might spill out of my eyeballs. I got up to leave, shouldering past the news director.

"Them cops'll just as soon lynch ya, you cross 'em," Lee said. "Walk outta here and get yourself hurt ...?" He shouted at my back as I retreated through the outer office. "Well, do this and I guarandamntee it, you *will* get hurt."

The elevator opened onto a reception area for the firm of McPhillips, Cochrun, and Honeycutt. A pair of stout figures occupied chairs in the lobby, a pinstriped attorney, police union type; and Jonathan B. Harper.

Out of uniform, slouching in street clothes, Harper looked diminished, deflated. Had the circumstances been otherwise, I might have felt pity. But I'd just come from ninety minutes of grinding questioning from the prosecutor. I'd gone in alone first thing Wednesday morning and played them the tape. I detailed how I'd followed Carl Walker to his estranged wife's house, told them what I'd overheard, what Diana Braxton said and what she didn't need to say. What I left out was Danny's story. It wasn't mine to tell.

Now, awaiting my subpoenaed deposition, I settled into the seats opposite Harper and his lawyer, doing my best to avoid meeting their eyes.

"How's the noggin?" Harper called out.

"Excuse me?"

"The head. I heard you ate some dirt on the side of the road. I'll bet that stung." His sneer revealed a line of pearl-perfect teeth. I supposed Lin could afford to send his boy to the finest orthodontist in the Mid-South.

"Is that what you heard?" I said, turning on my own smile. "I'm told your daddy bit the dust himself, recently."

Harper kicked back his chair and stood. I jumped from my seat. The video cassette in my lap clattered to the floor. The police attorney rose, hands spread, shoving Harper back.

Innis Honeycutt pushed through the big oak doors from the law offices, finding us in a standoff. "I see you boys are getting acquainted," he said. "Tom, we're ready for you. Officer Harper has asked to be present during your deposition, which is his right as a named defendant."

"Okay, but before we go in …" I swiped the tape from the floor and addressed Harper's lawyer. "Can I ask your client something?"

"We ain't doing media questions." He guided Harper toward the doors.

"It's not a media question."

Harper swatted the attorney's arm away. "Let him ask his damn question."

"I appreciate that," I said, clearing my throat. "So, here's what I can't figure out, Officer Harper. Why did you want Walker dead? You *were* sleeping with his wife, Diana, right?" I leaned forward, narrowing my eyes, lowering my voice. "Or was it *Carl* you really fancied?"

This time I was ready for it. The fist rounded to my left and I twisted right. The blow whiffed past my ear. Honeycutt lunged, as did the police attorney. They had a hold of each of Harper's arms as he hollered and strained against their grip.

"Shoulda done you when I had the chance!" Harper shouted.

"Like you did Carl?"

"You sonofabitch!" He pulled harder, the veins popping in his neck.

"Son, calm yourself!" Harper's attorney pushed him, lead-footed, to the opposite wall. "No call for giving t'other side any further inculpatory evidence."

"Gentlemen," Honeycutt said, straightening his bow tie. "Shall we proceed?"

LAST BRIDGE TO MEMPHIS

∼

If Lee and Ransom intended to fire me for talking, it didn't happen, at least not as of half past ten that night. Having testified, I felt unburdened. The way you do when they take away the lead x-ray vest at the dentist. Giddy, lighter. And maybe that explains what happened next.

At eleven-thirty I pulled up to Meredith's house in Germantown. It would have been earlier, but I made a stop at the apartment to retrieve a gemstone in a small fuzzy box. The thing had heat; it burned the inside of my coat pocket. Sure, I could hold out for the perfect time, the perfect setting. But I had the ring *now*. And if the fates allowed it, we'd be engaged before midnight.

It was a good plan, a wonderful plan. But the fates were not in the mood to cooperate.

Meredith greeted me in a blue and gray Memphis State sweatshirt, hair pulled back in a loose ponytail. She had a bottle of red corked on the coffee table, Jennifer Warnes and Bill Medley on the stereo. A fire crackled at the far end of the living room.

We clinked glasses. This was the moment.

"You seem very relaxed, mister," Meredith said. "Good day?"

That was my cue. Then and there I should have dropped to one knee, whipped out the ring. But I couldn't help myself. "Interesting day."

"Do tell, young man."

"I did something this morning."

"That's very specific," she said.

"I went downtown. Spilled my guts. Did a deposition."

Meredith jerked forward, dribbling a line of wine across her sleeve. "You did *what?*"

"Meant to tell you. I got subpoenaed. And then the prosecutor called. He saw the story where we aired the tape. Of course, they wanted to talk to me, too."

"What did you say?"

"Well, the tape speaks for itself. But I did tell the prosecutor that Harper had a motive to kill Carl Walker, even though he missed."

"Oh, Tom, no," Meredith went pale. "You basically called him a murderer."

"Look, your ex was there that day. The tape proves it. What choice did I have?"

I drank my wine, studying Meredith's tortured face. The night was already flying off the rails, and not only had I laid the tracks, I was about to wreck the train. "The prosecutor mentioned other witnesses. There was this one name on the list. Diana Braxton."

Meredith swallowed her glass on the table. "And?"

"Ex-wife or ... I don't know, partner of Carl Walker. Harper shacked up with her. The teacher you mentioned once, right? Full disclosure, I had a run-in with her."

"Tommy, what the *hell*?"

"She hit on me. Then she hit me. Remember the scratch on my face last summer?" I described tailing Walker and his attorney to Diana's house, getting trapped in the bedroom, the overheard conversation, the pass, the slap.

"That little bitch." Meredith reached behind her head and yanked the elastic band from her hair, tossing it across the room.

"So, you know her?" I asked.

"*Of* her."

"Wait. You knew about the connection between your ex and Carl Walker *all this time*?"

"Don't you dare turn this around on me." She slid to the opposite side of the couch. "I can't even."

"Meredith—"

"If you'd wanted to know who all my husband was sleeping with, you could have asked me. Now you tell me you went to her damn house? And into her *bedroom*?"

"I *did* ask you."

"You're an asshole."

"Yes, thank you. People keep reminding me that." I finished the last of my wine. "I should have told you when it happened."

"Here's something I shoulda told *you*," she said. "Bone didn't just haul away his crap from the house the day the papers were final. He knocked me to the floor, okay? Said I'd pay for humiliating him. That I'd ruined his life, divorcin' him. Had some choice words for you, too. And then he pulled down his pants and stuck it in my face. Limp as a catfish. But I got the message all right."

"And what was that?"

"Do *not* fuck with him. That's what."

"Then, now you agree. The guy is dangerous."

"Tom, if my purse hadn't been in the other room, well … I won't make that mistake twice. But yes, the man doesn't just have a *chip* on his shoulder, he has the whole damn tree."

"So I've noticed," I said.

"He could have done anything with his life, what with his family's connections and all. Lin gave him anything he wanted. Cars, college fund, you name it. Anything but love. Lin reserved that for the TV camera. But Bone spurned him *and* his money." Meredith lifted her wine glass and swallowed the remains of her drink. "He might be all bluster on the outside, but deep down Bone is just this scared little boy who could never please his daddy. And now you've gone and thrown it all in his face."

I might have admitted I went a bit further, that I'd confronted her ex at the law offices, but I thought better of it.

"Look, you wanna know the truth?" Meredith said. "That night I first came on to you? Bone had just confessed a bunch of ugly shit. Stuff with that Diana person, and with Walker himself. It was vile. I wanted to hurl. The girls took me out and the drinks kept flowing. Then I saw you heading for the men's room and—"

"Nice to tell me all this, now," I said.

"There's something else you oughta know. That poor officer killed in the Walker shooting, Carter Howard. We'd been dating. Bone got wind of it, and—"

"Jesus. Now it all makes sense." I pushed off from the sofa, my back to Meredith. "Two birds with one rifle shot for your ex that day." I spun around to face her. "The guy pulled a gun on me, Meredith, did you know *that*? Shot out my apartment window one night and almost took out Priss. And all the while, you knew about Harper and Walker and couldn't bring yourself to tell me?" I shoved my hands in the pockets of my sport coat where only minutes ago the ring had set my fingertips afire. "So that's where we are." I reached for the car keys. "And to think, I came here to—"

"To what?" She was standing now, too, her eyes like wild beasts.

"Forget it. Maybe I better leave."

"Yes, maybe you better do."

The freeway lights strobed the pavement as I struggled to focus on the white lines through watery eyes. This was about trust. Broken trust. We'd both held things back. I'd done so because I hadn't been sure of my facts. She'd kept me in the dark to … what? To protect her ex-husband's reputation? Or was it as simple as wanting to keep our relationship in a bubble, untouched by the taint of her past—and Bone Harper's?

Mount Moriah Road, the exit to my apartment, receded in the rear-view. Twenty minutes later, I pulled up to the Channel 2 studios, looking forward to a good hour or so alone to revisit an old pastime.

It used to be so easy churning out resume reels, but now the stack of video boxes mocked me. *Just open one. Insert a tape in the machine.* Edit stuff together, send it out to greener pastures. *Escape.* That was the word. Always running. When I'd skipped towns in the past, I'd told myself I had nothing to lose. This time I had everything to lose. I stared at the grey tape boxes. I couldn't move my hands.

A high-pitched babble of rewinding video leaked from a room

down the hall. Someone else was here. I scooped up my tapes and stepped out of the edit bay.

"Timothy?" He sat hunched over a console, a weather segment frozen on the screen. "Seems we both have the same idea tonight," I said. "Any prospects?"

The weatherman swiveled in his chair. "Actually, there's a station in Cleveland. Liked my stuff. Asked for a recent forecast."

"Cleveland. Good market. Lots of nasty weather. That would be a great move." I turned to leave. "Good luck."

"Tom, hold up." Timothy stepped into the doorway. "I know we've gone through some stuff. Ashley and all that. I just wanted to say—"

"Don't."

"Well, I still consider you a friend," he said. "I hope you know that."

"Good night, Timothy."

A solitary bank of fluorescent tubes spotlighted the assignment desk, the rest of the newsroom a cave of shadows. I opened my desk drawer, set my videotapes inside. I closed the drawer, opened it again.

Reaching into my pocket, I pulled out the small fuzzy box. I watched it drop into the drawer. Though I seldom had reason to lock it, this time I pushed the drawer closed and turned the key.

At the back door, a damp chill assaulted me, and I pulled my coat closer. It was said our location on the river bluff made it easier to forecast weather systems gathering to the west. I had no meteorology degree. Didn't need one. A storm was coming.

52

CAUGHT IN A TRAP

Coffee. More essential than ever this morning. The initial cup cleared my head. With the second cup I realized I'd been wrong to snap at Meredith, wrong to keep my furtive investigation from her. I promised myself I'd make it right today.

The third cup? That steeled my brain for the shitshow flickering on the television.

The noon newscasts—all three stations—were live in downtown Memphis. With Carl Walker at his side, Innis Honeycutt stood behind a podium, an array of microphones up to his Adam's apple, reading from a prepared statement.

"What transpired on that fateful day in July 1987 was nothing less than a tragedy. But today, we can say with certainty that the man who mortally wounded officer Howard was *not* Carl Walker. With new testimony and video evidence now exonerating my client, we intend to pursue civil action against the Memphis Police Department to the fullest extent of the law."

Honeycutt's pronouncements dropped in my stomach like cold breakfast pizza. *New testimony and video evidence.* Everyone in blue, everywhere in the Mid-South, must know by now that the young Channel 2 anchorman had crossed the line from reporter to informer.

First to acknowledge my newsroom infamy was Susan Quinn, reaching across the pod that afternoon to pat my hand. "Good for you," she said. "Now, buckle up." An awkward moment, mercifully interrupted by a vibration at my hip and a rapid beep.

Meredith's number on the pager. And the digits 1-4-3. She'd beaten me to it! "I love you too," I said, in a whisper. I picked up my desk phone, dialing.

When the line clicked at the other end, I started right in. "So you don't hate me?"

"How could I?" Meredith said. "You're only doing what you think you have to. But about last night. Do-over?"

"I had the same idea. Tonight? After I get off? There's some ... unfinished business to take care of." I cradled the receiver with my shoulder, fumbling for my keys, unlocking the desk drawer. The ring box lay huddled amidst a stack of reporter's notebooks. I popped it open. *This belongs on someone's finger.* Maybe the fates hadn't abandoned me just yet.

"Tommy, that sounds perfect."

"Okay, gotta go, the news meeting's just starting," I said. "I love you, by the way."

"And I love—oh, someone's at the door. See you tonight."

Snapping the ring box shut, I set it back in the drawer, then slipped across the aisle to Lee's office. The news director accosted me before my butt hit the chair.

"Here's the asshole."

"Good afternoon to you, too," I said.

"So, Tom, do you see what your sound and fury has wrought? This Harper shit's all over the news."

Janelle walked in, breathless. "And it's about to get worse. I'm hearing Bone's fixin' to have a warrant served for homicide. There's a BOLO out for him."

Just then, the first urgent squawk broke through on the scanner. An all points be-on-the-lookout. The subject: *Patrolman Jonathan Harper.*

With a rap on Lee's door, Taylor, the desk assistant, poked her head into the meeting. "Sorry, y'all. Uh, Tom, you got a call. At your desk."

It was Candy, calling from the lobby. She wanted to apologize. For Trace. She said he was jealous and had no reason to be. Could I come to the lobby to talk? Mindful of Trace's genial, yet menacing rejoinder the other day, I told Candy this wasn't a great time. There was a lot going on, maybe later.

As I turned back for Lee's office, the assignment desk lit up with a fresh streak of blood red scanner lights.

"*County dispatch. Report shots fired. Germantown. Units in vicinity respond ...*"

Static ensued and I couldn't make out the rest. Still, it was enough to send Bubba into breaking news mode. He grabbed the radio, clicked on the channel for Ronnie and Dilly. "Are you guys out the door?"

Dilly answered that they were.

"I may need to pull you," Bubba said into the radio. "Keep the two-way on."

The police scanner squawked again.

"*Germantown, all units. Officer down. Additional gunshot victim in the home. Proceed Code One.*"

At this second mention of Germantown, I suppressed a nervous flutter. Meredith lived in Germantown, but I told myself, so did thousands of others. Besides, I'd just talked with her.

When the news meeting finally ended thirty minutes later, I found my pager buzzing circles around my desk. Meredith's number. She'd called again, I noted with relief. She was fine. I lifted the phone, but set it back down as a new, urgent dispatch cut through the scanner traffic.

"*Memphis uniform patrol, shots fired. Midtown, Cooper-Young. One victim, female, in the home. Suspect driving dark four door sedan.*"

Bubba radioed Ronnie and Dilly, pulling them from their downtown assignment. He waved over Lukas, directing him to grab a photog and head out to Germantown.

I crossed the newsroom to the assignment desk where Bubba told me the Germantown shooting apparently involved an off-duty Shelby County deputy. Such stories were not rare, but two shootings in the span of an hour, including an officer-involved incident, was news. It might just bump the Harper manhunt from the lead.

More coffee.

The break room beckoned me, with its vending machine offering "Fresh Brewed ... By The Cup." I tossed change in the slot and, as advertised, a paper cup dropped into place.

Timothy rounded the corner, sliding his hand across the machine, patting it on the side. "How do these things work, anyways? I mean is there someone inside making the coffee?" He had his suit jacket buttoned and a striped silk tie knotted tight. He held a package in his hand.

"Going somewhere?" I asked.

"Just getting the escape tape out the door." Timothy tapped the package. "How's yours coming?"

"Yeah, I didn't get too far with it."

He stared at his shoes. "Say, I don't know what anybody else is saying, but that's a brave thing you did."

"What do you mean?"

"I heard about your deposition. I don't think I'd have the balls to do it."

"Timothy, I know what you're trying to do."

"What's that?"

"Look, I gotta get back to the newsroom."

"Okay." He patted the package again. "I'm gonna drop this baby at the front desk for the Federal Express guy. I'll see you in the studio." Timothy walked off toward the lobby.

"That coffee any good?" Susan tilted her chin at me when I returned to my desk.

"Well, it's hot, anyway."

"Your phone's been going off," she said. "Oh, there it goes again."

Candy's extension. I let it ring. It stopped. A moment later it rang again. I lifted the receiver.

"Don't hang up." She didn't wait for me to say hello. Her voice tight, her words carefully enunciated and formal, she said, "Mr. Cirone, please come to the front office."

"You mean the lobby?"

"Yes, sir. The front office."

"Candy, you're acting weird."

"Tom, listen to me. He's—"

"Okay, you win. I'll be right down."

Coffee in hand, I pushed through the lobby door, the wood-grain bow of the reception desk coming into view. Above it, the station logo, a bright blue circle with a backlit "2." Framed portraits of our on-air talent adorned the walls. On the TV monitor, the sound muted, people on a couch argued and pointed, one of those tabloid talk shows. Behind the desk, Candy sat in profile. She hadn't turned to greet me when I entered. In fact, she wasn't moving at all.

Unblinking, she stared out into the empty lobby, the muzzle of a silver revolver fixed in the back of her neck.

Every instinct said stop. Turn around. Run. But I was done running. I'd been running my entire life. From jobs and bosses. From women who loved me. From my sins. No more. Not today.

As the lobby door clicked shut behind me, a shadow swept past the logo. A shadow in the shape of a big man in a ball cap and heavy coat. The man withdrew the gun from Candy's neck and in a ferocious whipsaw brought it down on her head. He lunged across the desk, grabbing me by the collar.

Candy's head crashed to the counter. The coffee flew from my hand, splattering against the white-washed wall like a Jackson Pollack.

I staggered forward, pinned. My field of vision filled with the sickly smile, the stubbled skin, the steel blue eyes of Jonathan B. Harper.

Danny once asked if I was looking for trouble. I'd finally come to the right place.

53

CAN'T WALK OUT

"We have got to stop meeting like this. *Rambo*." He clamped down on my throat, backing me into the counter, his revolver leveled at my chest.

"Look, Harper, Bone, whatever they call you. This is a TV station. Someone's gonna walk in at any moment." At the top of the steps leading to the executive suite, a security camera watched. "You gonna whack them in the head too?"

Behind the reception desk, Candy twitched, her arms hanging from her sides. "She'll be fine," Harper said. "I only tapped her." He released me, keeping the gun trained. With his free hand he lifted Candy's head by her ponytail. She looked anything but fine. "Nothing personal, sweetheart," he said to her lifeless face. He dropped her head to the desk, its leaden thud echoing through the atrium.

"On the other hand ..." He shoved me back again. "With you, it's nothin' *but* personal."

At the opposite side of the counter Harper had arranged a shotgun, standing upright. It was the short-barreled kind, sawed-off. *I'd seen it before.* Some sort of device dangled from the barrel. You might have called it a noose, except it was made of silver wire. It was more of a snare trap. He motioned to it. "Put it over your head."

Someone had to be seeing this on the security camera. Or, maybe no one. The camera fed into a small black and white monitor in front of Candy. *What good is that?* Next to the monitor, a package sat in the "out" box, Timothy's escape tape, addressed to a station in Cleveland.

I looked from the noose to Harper. "Screw you."

He swept his arm up, his answer cold and swift as the butt of the handgun connected with my jaw, filling my mouth with the bitter taste of wet copper. As I staggered, he looped the wire over my head and cinched it.

"Brave words, Tom. You're all about them words, aren't you? Whisperin' all them sweet nothings to my wife, am I right?" He shoved the revolver in his belt and hefted the shotgun. "Well, maybe you haven't heard the news, huh? I put a plug in that bitch today."

My legs gave out, but the wire contraption held me upright, slicing a line of fire across my throat. Harper reeled in the slack on the wire, and me with it.

"That's right," he barked. "Like that old song goes, I'd just as soon you be dead, girl, than with some other dickhead." He drove the gun into my ribs. "Now move."

Was he bluffing? I'd spoken with Meredith. She'd even paged me again.

Germantown. Shots fired.

Harper propelled me across the lobby, my shoulder smashing against the outside doors. As they pushed open, a blast of arctic air slapped my face. I stopped cold, gripped by an icy chill. Timothy's forecast *had* called for a plunge into the thirties. But that wasn't why I froze.

Timothy.

The wind flung open his suit, crisp lapels flapping against his torso like angel's wings. He lay face up on the pavement, the weatherman's eyes locked open to the sky. Rivulets of blood oozed from his nose and the back of his head, into the joints of the pavement.

I crushed my eyelids shut, and in the blackness saw Meredith collapsed to the ground like Timothy. I blinked open to another reality. I would not outlive this day. And maybe I didn't want to.

We marched past the satellite dishes, into the parking lot, where the late-day sun careened off the cars in sharp, blinding rays. Beyond the gates, we crossed the station perimeter. I could feel the watching faces, safe behind glass. There'd be no one to stop us, no more Timothys standing in the way of Harper's wrecking ball.

Several people bolted out the front door in our wake. Someone hovered over Timothy's body, hollering for help. More shouts echoed across the bluff. "He's got a shotgun! He's got him wired to it!" Another answered, "Holy shit, it's Rambo!" I turned toward the commotion and paid with the sting of a hundred needles. As the wire traced its circuit around my throat, every step, every shove burned.

Squad cars raced south on Riverside Drive, their sirens rising in pitch. I knew what came next. I'd seen the movie. There'd be tactical units and negotiators, SWAT teams, TV trucks, tripods, cameras. Always cameras.

Newsman taken hostage. Head blown off. Viewer discretion advised.

Harper had attached the loop around my neck to the barrel of his gun. In turn, he'd wired the trigger to his finger. If his handhold slipped, the gun would go off. If I jerked away ... boom!

"Studying my handiwork?" He stroked the grip of the shotgun. "They call it a 'dead man's line.' I heard about this case up north, 'bout ten years ago. Some guy took a hostage, rigged up something just like this. The guy'd been screwed over in a land deal or some such. Took things into his own hands. And if you can believe it, he got off."

"So, that's the plan? I mean, have you thought this through? What the hell happened to you, Harper? From what I hear, you had it made. Could have had anything."

"Yeah," he spat. "On *his* terms. My daddy, the great Lin Harper. No thanks."

He twisted his head, assessing his options. To the left lay the main road and the I-55 interchange. To the right, the river and the three hulking spans that stretched to Arkansas. He eyed the rusted mass of the closest, the Harahan Bridge, that skeleton of cantilevered steel carrying freight lines across the Mississippi River.

"You can't go that way." I didn't recognize my voice, no more than a rasp escaping my throat, impinged as it was by the snare. "It's closed off, it's a railroad bridge."

Police vehicles swarmed, screeching to a stop, blocking Channel 2 Drive. Uniformed men shouldering long guns jumped out, taking positions around the building. Now, Harper had no choice. He positioned the shotgun at the base of my skull, snapping my head against the muzzle with a jerk on the wire.

A rusted chain link fence stood between us and the bridge. Harper toppled it with a kick.

Treacherous footing lay before us as we marched up the span. Rotted planks lay in haphazard angles across steel beams, faded gray remnants of a roadway that must have pre-dated the tracks. In hesitant half steps we negotiated this narrow path hugging the bridge deck, railroad tracks to our left, a precipitous drop to the right.

At the squelch of a bullhorn, Harper swung us around, placing me in front of him like a human shield. Police had positioned themselves at the base of the bridge, rifles and handguns zeroed in on us.

"Officer Harper! This is Major Tipton. Do not proceed across this bridge." The police major wielded a bright orange megaphone. "Drop the weapon, let him go, and then we talk."

"Gene Tipton," Harper said, the name dripping with derision. "My boss. A real prick."

"Aren't they all," I muttered, not intending to validate my captor. It was automatic, fueled by years of toiling under soulless managers. Harper nodded, releasing the slack on the wire.

"How about you put that lowlife Walker back behind bars!" Harper shouted. "And put my daddy back on the air! Until then, you best stay the fuck back!"

"Look Bone, I can't do anything about the news station, that's their decision." The major's amplified voice had a practiced, modulated tone. "But nobody else has to get hurt."

Behind the police line a TV van pulled up. And another. Not Channel 2 trucks, the competition. Major Tipton turned and directed the bullhorn at them. "All you media people, get your goddamn asses out of here!" He motioned to his patrolmen. The trucks backed away and disappeared from view.

A woman ran from the station garage, engaging the major in a brief, heated flurry before taking the bullhorn. "Bone, it's Janelle. We can fix this. Come on back down. It'll be all right."

"You and her," Harper spat. "Christ." His hand found my throat, our fleeting moment of comradery forgotten. He glided his fingers to my chin and dragged his paws over my face, like a cat marking his territory. *Like Miss Priss would do.*

"Janelle and me?" I stammered through his hand. "We just work togeth—"

Harper's fingers penetrated my mouth, hooking into my jaw.

"This is all bullshit." He jammed the shotgun into the back of my neck. "Everybody lies."

He withdrew his fingers, smearing something wet across my cheek. I jerked up a hand, an involuntary reflex, and realized he'd never bound me. *Maybe it didn't matter when your head is wired to a shotgun.* My palm came back red.

"Harper, you're bleeding."

"What of it? The bitch got off a lucky shot with that pop gun is all. I'll live. But that Shelby County deputy wasn't so fortunate. Move!"

We turned our backs to Janelle and the police. Soon the riverbank lay behind us as well.

∾

It had to be past four. The sun would be down before five. After that, there'd be no chance for a clean hit on Harper. If that was the plan.

Once, in Springfield, Illinois, I'd covered a hostage standoff. Police surrounded the gunman and by late afternoon, the guy began to panic. In a frenzied rant, he called out, "Don't test me. I mean it!" Again and again, "Don't test me. I mean it!" When the sun fell below the horizon he pulled the trigger on his hostage. A split second later the cops took him down. We never showed those final moments on the air. But that didn't stop folks joking about it in the newsroom. For weeks after, you'd bump into someone in the hall or brush by their desk and they'd laugh and shout, "Don't test me. I mean it." I'd laughed too.

At the foot of the bridge, SWAT officers surged forward, rifles extended. The sudden blur of activity caught Harper off guard.

"I told y'all to stay back!" Harper pinned me to the railing, reaching into his belt. He pulled his handgun.

Don't test me. I mean it.

The weapon fired, the explosive force of Harper's revolver concussing my brain, the deafening shot ping-ponging through the rusted bridge superstructure.

Mother shouts. Her backhand connects. I spin to the right, into my double. The door pops open and we tumble together. A screech, a scream. A silence. Face down, lifeless. A snow angel inverted.

Not a dream, not a vision this time. A memory. Kicked to consciousness by the shattering gun blast at the side of my head. More than a flashback. *An awakening.*

Alarm bells sounded in my ears—a TV test pattern on max. The sunset shattered into streaks of orange and crimson. A pungent fire blistered my nose and mouth. My skin screamed with a sharp jab, cold and hard, digging into my backside. The Milano switchblade!

Danny, you mysterious sonofabitch, how did you know?

The tactical team pulled back. Harper had won this round. "Let's go," he said, prodding me again with the shotgun.

"You let up on the slack," I said. "You pushed me out of the way instead of—"

"Instead of wasting you right there?" His voice arrived hollow, as if transmitted through a tunnel. "That's not how it's gonna happen. You go when I go."

My fingers closed around the switchblade. I pressed it flat to my leg. If the time came, I could flip it with one touch. *When* the time came.

We reached the highest point of the bridge deck, eye-level with the roof of the Channel 2 building. A photographer stood there. *Eddie.* Alone. Just him and his tripod in Mark Twain's pilot house. The perfect camera shot. If someone had to record my death, let it be Eddie.

Major Tipton approached the end of the bridge again and lifted the bullhorn. "Officer Harper, we can still work this out! But we're running out of daylight!"

Running out of daylight. Running out of time. I could never convince Harper we were friends. But empathy I could muster. And it might buy me a few extra seconds. "I think I get why you're doing this," I said. "Okay, you screwed up. But accidents happen. Friendly fire. It happens."

"You don't know jack squat about it."

"I'm all ears," I said. "What's left of them."

Harper trained an eye on the tactical team below. "Hell, in a minute, none of it's gonna matter, anyhow." He backed the muzzle off the base of my neck. "That prick, Carl Walker. He barged in on me and Diana this one time. I even laughed when he walked in, all surprised like he was, stumbling into the bedroom door. But then the bastard got real sore. Started threatening." Harper paused, groping for something in his coat pocket. "Well, what happened was ... I made him strip down. He fought it. But when I pulled out my service weapon, he went along fine."

"You raped him."

"Fished around with the barrel of my Smith and Wesson is all. The guy was asking for it!"

"Was he?"

"Couldn't keep his fat mouth shut. Had to go off on how he's gonna report me to internal affairs. Abuse of authority and some shit he read in a book somewheres."

"So, you needed to shut Carl up?"

"It wasn't premeditated." Harper stared into the dusk, watching his breath crystallize and dissolve over the water. "It's what they call opportunity. Carter Howard's request for backup. I recognize the address. Patrol officers out front. I go around back. Opportunity."

It took me a moment to process it; a shotgun wired to your head does not favor clear thinking. But I finally understood what Harper was implying, and bad aim had nothing to do with it. "Didn't matter whether you hit him or missed him, did it?" I said. "So long as those other cops snuffed out Walker in the crossfire."

"Shoulda snuffed *you* out long ago. Then there'd be no story and no tape. All you had to do was walk away, newsman. Leave it alone. Now, they're gonna watch you die on TV. Live at six." Harper pulled his hand from his pocket, dangling a necklace. "You ain't the first, you know. Officer Howard, rest his soul. He tried his hand at Meredith, too. Poor sucker was in the wrong place at the wrong time."

The necklace in Harper's hand bore a gold charm. A lightning bolt, and the letters, T-L-C. "She loved wearing this stupid thing," he said. "Had it 'round her neck today, matter of fact."

I'm singing Fly Me to the Moon. *She's tapping a rhythm on my jeans. Meredith, you're gonna make me crash. What, Tommy, dontcha like affection? Yes, I like affection fine, but let me stop the car first.*

The necklace fluttered in the wind, a glittering talisman spinning in hypnotic circles.

In other words ...

I clutched the guardrail, flakes of rust disintegrating in my hands.

In other words ...

An ocean wave lashed my insides and I heaved over the bridge. My guts caught flight, disappearing into the foaming waters below.

Just upriver from Channel 2, a green space hugs the river bluff. Martyrs Park, they call it, memorializing the yellow fever epidemic that killed thousands in the 1870s. Not a soul haunted the place now, but neither was it quite deserted.

A black-winged spirit cut a path through the park. A reaper of death or perhaps an angel of redemption. I wiped the puke from my lips. Blinked. No angel. It was a sniper in a long coat, a massive rifle dangling from his shoulder. He approached a mound of weeds overlooking the river, a location popular with trainspotters. From there the railroad bridge appeared almost close enough to touch. A distance of maybe three hundred yards. *A clear shot.*

Behind me, Harper mumbled to himself, his voice cracking, his gun thrumming a beat against my head. "I'm a good cop," he said. "I made mistakes, but I'm no killer."

Hadn't I made my own mistakes? I never meant to kill anybody, but people died because of me. Timothy, Meredith. My reckless arrogance murdered them both. And long before today, hadn't I also—?

Dear Valerie. Was it a girl? What would we have called her? The love that would never grow. The child I would never have.

This belongs on someone's finger. A fuzzy box, a lovely fantasy. Locked in a drawer.

It all closed in now. Like the aperture of a camera. Like the noose cinching my neck.

Mom and Dad, all credit to you. Thomas, you said, maybe you should get a real job. Well, folks, I got some news for you. This is real. As real as it gets.

The sniper down in the park propped his rifle against a boulder. He removed a pair of oversized sunglasses, lowered his head to the scope. If only eyes had zoom lenses. If only I could see his face. The sniper, the one who would finish this. The only one with a shot.

In the movies, the hero always stalls for time. That's what Bruce Willis does in *Die Hard*. Keep 'em talking. *If you're talking, you're living.* "Listen, Harper," I said, "ever wonder why they call me Rambo? Kimberly Kilmer came up with it."

"Kimberly, yeah. That little gal had a thing for me, you know that? She goes for bad boys. Guess that rules you out, don't it?" He snickered. "Handy with a camera too. Was always pestering me for a photo in the nude. Guess she had to settle for you all."

Below us, the man in the park motioned with his rifle, pivoting the weapon up, into the purple sky, then down. *What is he doing?* I squinted into the dusk. Whatever was going on down there, I prayed my kidnapper didn't see it.

"You and Meredith," Harper went on, a sneer in his voice. "All lovey-dovey like. I'll never have that. Ain't in me."

I craned my head to catch a corner of Harper's eye. "You mean the mighty Bone Harper's never been in love?"

"That name's a curse, is what it is. But them kids at prep school sure thought it was a hoot. 'Poor old Bone. Can't get a boner.' It's a helluva thing to have to live with."

I could think of worse.

In Martyrs Park, the sniper was doing it again. Repeating the sequence. Up, back down. He wanted me to see it. A signal. Up. Down. Like the cue in the TV studio.

Thomas, you know the two biggest words in show biz?

My body jerked, shot through with an electric frisson. That was no police marksman. It was *him* on the bluff! Was this his crazy idea of playing the action hero?

One cop. Alone. The only chance they've got.

Danny and his damn Kentucky windage. A shooting range was one thing, but what the hell was he thinking? I swallowed hard. In the film, a lot of people got killed.

A chunk of ice bobbed in the current, faded to gray, dipped beneath the river. The sun hung a hair's breadth over the western horizon. In a moment, it would drag the last of daylight with it, swallowed under the West Memphis floodplain. This was the end game.

"Them shooters out there probably have night scopes," Harper said. "But if it were me, this would be the time." He steadied a hand atop my head, like a priest administering last rites. "Now that we've had our little heart-to-heart, it's time to say your prayers, newsman."

"Harper, wait—"

"Sinner and sin." he said. "Same thing."

"What?"

"You can't love one and hate the other. They're the same damn thing."

I believe in one God, the Father almighty, creator of heaven and earth ...

Heaven knows, I'd been defenseless against Harper's rage, powerless to save Meredith. Too young, too broken to understand why my twin was taken and I was not.

... and in Jesus Christ, his only Son, our Lord ...

Helpless no longer, my finger hovered over the release button, the switchblade alive in my hand. On the riverbank below, the rifle tipped up, a flicker in the gloaming. It descended. Tipped again into the air, lowered once more. The signal to *go*. Danny set his eye to the scope, the understanding between us as deathly sure as the knowledge that he had seconds to act and I had seconds to live.

I am heartily sorry for all my sins ...

Harper's shotgun shivered against my neck.

... including those I'm about to commit.

The sun was gone. To the east, darkness overtook the sky.

It's now or never.

As Harper had asked, I said my prayers. A prayer of forgiveness for all the idiots and assholes in my life. And a prayer for myself, as I was one of them.

I lifted my hand ...

It won't work, you can't literally dodge a bullet.

... extended a finger ...

God from God, Light from Light, true God from true God.

... let it fall.

You're on.

Idiots and assholes. Two words, simple and precise, ricocheting in my mind as the switchblade whipped open in my palm.

Live at six? That's a joke. I'm dead at thirty.

54

WAY DOWN

The cue given, I collapsed my legs, my body a dead weight. The deed would be done before I hit the bridge deck. But I'd forgotten one thing.

The wire.

As I dropped, the noose jerked my head, snapping it back in a violent whiplash. Harper froze, the cold muzzle of his shotgun skimming my scalp and skittering from his grip. A rifle blast echoed from across the bluff. A microsecond later, another explosion, much closer, battered my skull.

Pavement. Sky. Pavement. Sky. A tiny hand, still reaching.

The leaden mass of Harper's body held me immobile against the bridge. He'd pulled the shotgun trigger. I was certain of it. Just as I was certain he'd missed. If he hadn't, my head would be gone and me with it.

Which is not to say all was fine. Harper lay motionless, and for the moment so did I, trapped under his bulk. Once again, I'd borne the concussive force of a gun blast fired at close range, pounding my senses like the hurricane rush of a hundred waves at high tide. I freed my hands from beneath Harper's bulk, then dug my fingertips under the wire, prying it loose from my neck. Below, in the gray glow of the Channel 2 parking lot, I could make out a line of police in cautious advance.

"It's over, Harper," I said, feeling my voice more than hearing it. Harper worked his mouth, but no words came. *Half his mouth.* The other half was gone, exposing his jaw and the white of bone. Danny had done it. Just as his doctor friend had schooled him. *The perfect shot.*

But it wasn't finished. Not quite. His hands in motion, Harper groped for his revolver.

Absurd in retrospect—what made me think of her in that moment—but my mind formed a picture of Miss Priss, her whiskers brushing my cheek, her sideburned fur bop-bop-bopping me, head-butting me, telling me she loves me. Telling me—

I arched my neck and hammered my head into Harper's skull. The violence of it sent him spinning away, struggling to his knees.

He lifted the handgun.

Swinging the switchblade in a blind arc, I slashed at Harper's extremities. As he reeled in his legs, the handgun fired, a wild shot that stopped the police at the base of the bridge.

Harper hoisted the gun again, finger and trigger indistinguishable in a confusion of blood.

How was he even still moving? It called to mind an article from an old *Life* magazine. A chicken in Colorado had lived for a year and a half after its head got chopped off. It survived because its autonomic functions were still intact. In this moment, Harper was that chicken.

He fired another shot into the darkness. This time the recoil snapped back his arm, the gun clanging away and dropping through an opening in the bridge. Then Harper himself seemed to shrink below the deck, swallowed by the same breach. Within seconds all that remained was a hand, a bloody, clutching, groping appendage.

I scrambled toward him, catching his wrist, holding fast to that savage claw, itself locked in a death grip around Meredith's necklace. I looped a finger around the TLC charm. With the knife in my other hand, I threaded the blade through the chain, slicing it in two, trapping the necklace in my fingers as it spilled from his.

It didn't escape me that just two months earlier, Meredith had seized my hand, saving me from certain death. As I now likewise held her murderous ex's life in my grasp, I was sure Meredith would have done the same. But she was fearless, forgiving. I was neither.

"Harper, you were right about one thing," I rasped. "Everybody lies."

I opened my hand, releasing his wrist.

His eyes widened, midnight blues irising in terror. He fixed me in that haunted gape as he flailed for a handhold, slipping through the rotted bridge deck, bouncing off the superstructure before descending to the roiling river a hundred feet below.

The constant rush in my ears muted the splash, but there was no mistaking the impact as the gray waters received him. On the bank, men leaped into the shallows, grabbing Harper before the current could drag him away. Other officers trained their rifles on his lifeless body as it emerged from the river.

I retracted the blade, stuffed it in my pocket, and poured the necklace into my suit jacket. Small fires burned my body. I reached for my face, but someone stopped me, pulling back my arm. Another large figure appeared, then more. A wall of body armor encircled me.

"Sir, are you injured?"

I shook my head, but I didn't know.

"Can you walk out?"

I shook again.

They hoisted me, swooning, onto a stretcher and carried me to the foot of the bridge.

A pair of cops came running from Martyrs Park, shouting for help. I rolled off the stretcher, waving away the EMT. "Go, go, go!" I insisted.

Back on my feet, I staggered off behind the medic, only to be intercepted by a madman. Lin Harper's nostrils flared, angry gusts of breath condensing in the wind. "You did this, you goddamn sonofabitch!"

I tried to circle past him. "Lin, move out of the way."

"The hell I will. You'll pay for what you did to my boy."

There was no time to waste tussling with the grieving father. I reached into my coat, released the catch. The Milano flipped open and I raised the point to Lin's throat.

"Get the fuck out of my way or you're gonna join your son!"

Lin backpedaled and I sprinted past him down the slope.

Descending into Martyr's Park, I confronted a maelstrom of activity centered around a body on a stretcher, paramedics and cops looking on, some silent, some hurling expletives into the night sky. I moved closer, bracing for the sight of Danny, laid out, collapsed in exhaustion, or worse, maybe shot, maybe dying.

Pushing in, squeezing between uniforms, I confronted the object of their anguish. A bloodied corpse, raining river water off the sides of the stretcher. Harper, or what used to be Harper.

I spun on my heels, the park gyrating with me, three hundred and sixty degrees of undulating trees, rocks and dusky turf. Staggering to a nearby mound of brush, I stopped atop that trainspotters perch. Danny's sniper's nest. *But where—?*

A glare of headlights blinded me, an ambulance fast approaching. As the vehicle bounded the curb, its piercing high beams shot skyward, then dipped, the light casting a momentary reflection against something at my feet. I reached for the glistening object, but my body kept moving. I tipped forward, collapsing headfirst into the cold, brown grass.

The ambulance rolled to a stop. Reality and fantasy merged. It *was* a scene from a movie. Above me, around me, swirling lights, officers running, vehicles, sirens, weapons, and eyes, so many eyes.

55

THEN THE STAGE WAS BARE

Baptist Memorial Hospital. Said so right there on the cool, smooth sheets. A needle stuck into my hand, taped in place, a tube running from a clear bag on a stand at my bedside. My throat burned, as if someone had encircled my neck with a dagger's edge, which, come to think of it, was exactly what had happened. A nurse was telling me I'd gone into shock. I'd suffered a moderate concussion. Lost some blood. They'd treated me for throat lacerations and removed bits of shrapnel from my body. They said fragments had ricocheted off the bridge when Harper fired the shotgun. Said I was lucky that his wire contraption hadn't sliced off my head.

A terrific ringing filled my ears. It was possible I'd have live with it, maybe permanently. After all, a gun had been fired, not once, but twice, in close proximity, blasting my eardrums. The nurse said I may not remember everything at first. She was right. I didn't.

"What *do* you recall?" she asked.

The necklace coiling in my palm. Harper slipping into the river.

The memories trickled back, and then the dam broke open. "Meredith! Is she …? Did she …?" I lifted my hand to the nurse's arm. It floated, missing the mark and landing back on the bed.

"You've been through quite an ordeal tonight." The nurse patted my hand. "You're gonna feel a bit woozy yet."

"But Meredith ..." I shot upright from the bed—too quickly—and paid for it with a return fire of pain raking my body. I pawed at the I-V needle. "I gotta get out of here!"

"Sir, I'm going to have to insist—"

"Is she really gone? *Is she?* Please!"

"Mr. Cirone, I don't know."

Frantic now, I shouted, "What about Danny? Danny Fisher!"

"I sure don't know anything about a Mr. Fisher."

My head shot from side to side. "No, no, no, dammit. I mean, Presley. Is he here at the hospital?"

"Let me get the doctor. And please do not remove that I-V line."

When the nurse left, I hovered my free hand once more over the needle, then kept going and reached for the television remote. In my reduced state, I couldn't figure out how to work the channels. The picture came up on MTV, George Michael and Andrew Ridgeley on a posh ski trip. *Last Christmas*. Right. Last Christmas, Meredith tried to give me her heart. And what had I done?

I fell back onto the pillow. *Please. Tell me I'm going to wake up for real.*

When I opened my eyes, a silver-haired man in a long white coat stood in the doorway. "I'm Doctor Carpenter. Okay if I come in, check your vitals? Oh, and you have a visitor."

A large round figure in red plaid woolens followed behind the doctor. He pulled a chair next to the bed.

"Dusty," I said, "what are you—?"

"Just on my way in to the station. I expect it'll be a busy morning for news, what's gone on and all. How're you holdin' up?"

"Nobody wants to tell me anything. Was I dreaming? Was Presley? Did he—?"

Dusty straightened in the chair. "Presley? You mean, like *Elvis* Presley?" He raised an arm to scratch the back of his neck. "What all makes you think of that man just now?"

I scanned the hospital room, focusing on the fluorescent tubes in the overhead lights, counting eight in all. Having assured myself I was sufficiently clear from any sedative-induced stupor, I turned back to my visitor. "Dusty, he was there. Down in the park. He took out Harper with a high-powered rifle. He was—"

"Son, you came face-to-face with death. I don't blame ya' for thinkin' you saw some kinda savior down there. I'da done the same. But Harper took *himself* out. Seems that shotgun he meant for your brains had other plans. Police are saying the shot went wild, and some of it, or maybe pieces of that old rust bucket of a bridge, came flying back at him."

My eyes returned to the ceiling. I knew what I saw. Danny, the rifle, the signal. Up, then down. *You're on*. Dusty was spinning a yarn, as he sometimes did on his morning program. Repeating a fabrication. It wasn't true.

"Anyways," he went on, patting his mitt of a hand on my arm, "whatever all it was, something ricocheted right back at Harper. Sliced him up good."

While Dusty talked, the doctor held my wrist in his hand, counting my pulse, assiduously going about his business and pretending not to listen. But the doctor's raised eyebrow gave him away. I decided to go along with Dusty's account. It wasn't going to do me any good to press him further.

"So, is Harper—?"

"Bone Harper is a fish, son."

"What?"

"Never you mind," Dusty said. "The man is history."

Is that all it was now, history? Danny's, Harper's, and mine? A flood of memories overtook me, history both current and ancient. Danny, his eye to the scope. The concussive blast of Harper's shotgun, its barrel skipping across my scalp. My brother, clear as if it were yesterday, tumbling out *ahead of me* into the path of an oncoming car.

Another image flashed. "Dusty, when Harper dragged me from the station I saw—"

"Timothy, rest his soul. He was at the front desk talkin' with Candy. Sensed trouble. Confronted Bone outside. The man pistol whipped him and he fell to the ground, hit his head. They couldn't do anything for him, poor fella." Dusty lifted himself from the chair. "But you son, you're gon' be just fine."

"Wait, before you go," I said, "what about Meredith? Harper's ex, I mean."

"Your gal, I know. What I heard, she got caught up in the gunfire out there with Bone and that deputy. They said she was taken to Saint Francis. I'm sorry, Tom, but I don't know any more than that."

Dusty told the doctor to take good care of me and left for work.

I eyed the needle in my arm again.

"I know what you're thinking," the doctor said. "I wouldn't advise it." He handed me two pills and a small paper cup of water. I gulped it down. The doctor's hand fell over the light switch and before long, it wouldn't have mattered if the overheads were still blazing.

Daylight burned a silhouette image into my sticky eyes. The form coalesced into a young candy striper. "How are you feeling?" she asked. "Is there anything I can get for you?"

"Yes, yes, there is." Dusty's tale had lingered in my mind for hours as I drifted in and out of a tortured sleep. "Do you know the number for St. Francis Hospital?"

The girl fumbled with the phone directory, stealing glances at me. She punched some numbers and handed me the receiver. The receptionist at St. Francis said the patient I requested had been admitted last night. She transferred me to her room. The extension rang. It continued to ring through six, now seven rings. I nearly set the receiver down, determined to try again, when a woman picked up. I asked for Meredith.

"I'm sorry, but there's no one in this room," the woman said. "It is ... unoccupied, sir."

"What do you mean?"

"It could be they've been discharged already. It can also mean that the patient ... that they ... I'm sorry sir, I am just housekeeping staff."

Later that morning, I was still contemplating a break-out from the hospital when a cast of characters crowded my room. Our chief photographer was first to step to my bedside, grabbing my hand and shaking it until I groaned.

"Dilly, I don't know what to say."

"How about whistling a few bars of *Dixie*," he said. "Because Yankee, you're a goddamn Southern stud. You got balls of steel, dude. You fought the law and the law lost!"

Eddie followed Dilly into the room, as did Candy and Trace, and Susan Quinn. A minute later, Dixie and Lukas showed up, Dixie setting herself on the bed next to me, taking my hand. I'd never been so happy to see familiar faces in my life, even exposed as I was, in a backless hospital gown, my butt open to the air.

Susan, ever the producer, delivered the rundown. The story had been non-stop news, all over Memphis TV, radio, the papers, she said. The *Commercial Appeal* reported that Bone Harper had been wanted for homicide in the shooting death of Officer Carter Howard. Even before prosecutors saw the unedited tape it was clear to them that he was the blurred figure in the video. According to the paper, Harper told friends on the force they wouldn't take him alive.

"What about Carl Walker?" I asked.

"Bone couldn't find him," Susan said. "But he got to Walker's wife, Diana Braxton. Shot her up pretty bad, but it looks like she'll make it."

As I listened to Susan's clinical account, I realized I was the only one in the room making sense of it. Danny had tried to warn me.

Harper was a *guilty fox hunting its own hole.*

"I don't get it," Dixie said. "What was he hoping to accomplish?"

"He had a secret," I said. "And he wanted to keep it that way."

"A secret?" Lukas asked.

"Doesn't matter now. He's a fish." Blank faces stared back. "I mean, he's gone."

Candy and Trace hovered over the bed, arm in arm, like worried parents. "It was terrifying," Candy said. "I thought he was gonna kill you."

I nodded. "For a minute there, I thought *you* were dead."

"After Timothy tried to stop him, Bone rushed on into the lobby," Candy said. "He grabbed me before I could move. Made me dial your extension. When he dragged you outside, I managed to call 9-1-1. Told them what he said about Meredith. Oh, Tom."

"Candy, if I didn't have this damn thing stuck in my vein, I would have been out looking for her already, scouring the city in my bare feet if I had to. Do we know anything more?"

"We know your girl put up a fight."

"A gunfight," Trace said. "Bone got hit. But so did Meredith. Crazy thing is, there was a Shelby County deputy on the scene. He got to the house in Germantown just as Bone busted in. The deputy put himself between Bone and Meredith. Returned fire. Drove Bone off, but not before he ... well, the deputy didn't make it. You knew him, Tom. Presley's bodyguard, Travis Lister." Trace shook his head. "He's a damn hero. But nobody can figure out how the hell he just happened to be there."

Somebody could. But I kept my thoughts to myself.

Judging by the heads turning, and Eddie reaching for it, the telephone on the bedstand was ringing. I simply couldn't hear its high-pitched frequency. For a moment I stared, uncomprehending, at the receiver in Eddie's outstretched hand. I put it to my ear.

A voice on the other end was calling my name.

"Tommy?"

The world stopped. And then my heart stopped. "Meredith?" The back of my eyes caught fire. "You're alive!" I took a quavering breath and tucked my head, tears forming.

Eddie retreated to the doorway with the others. "We'll come check on you tonight," he said. "Y'all go ahead and talk."

She was phoning from her mama's place in Fayette County. She'd had surgery. A gunshot in her forearm. A million-dollar wound, Meredith called it, the bullet passing between the two bones. She'd fired her pea-shooter first, nicking Harper in the shoulder and causing his shot to go awry. Then Deputy Lister stormed in and saved her life, at the cost of his own.

"You wanna know something crazy?" she said. "That girl came to my room at the hospital. Ashley. She's a nurse at St. Francis. We had a good laugh about all that stuff back at the Sunset Symphony. And then a good cry. She told me what all happened with you and that poor weatherman. She called the station and that's how we knew you were at Baptist."

My eyes flamed up again as I told Meredith how sorry I was. About all of it. "When I see you again," I began blubbering, "I mean, I want to show you—"

A knock at my hospital room door brought our giddy call, and my blubbering, to an abrupt end.

My visitors were a pair of Memphis cops. And after that single rap on the door, they marched in and stood over my bed. One of them reached for the base of the phone, his finger hovering above the switch hook. I recognized him. Major Gene Tipton, Harper's boss and the man with the megaphone at the bridge. I rushed a "gotta go" and "I love you" into the phone and brushed Tipton's hand away with the receiver, dropping it on the base.

Here we go, I thought. *Interrogation time.* Probably followed by a beating with a rubber hose. "Do you mind?" I said, rising up on my elbows.

"Tom, do you know why we're here?" Major Tipton didn't wait for me to conjure a smartass reply. This was a courtesy visit, he told me. He had an offer to propose. He put it like this: They obviously couldn't keep my name out of the story, but they *could* keep the worst of it out of the press. Tipton lowered himself to the end of my bed, then looked to his partner, the department public affairs officer.

"Meaning, no one needs to know about Officer Harper's intimate relations," the media man said. "Or yours." He glanced at the major, then back to me. "Whaddya say?"

I straightened in the bed. "Hold on a minute." After what I'd been through, I was in no mood for games, or veiled threats. "Just wait. What exactly happened out there? I saw what I saw. Presley. With a long gun. A sniper's scope. He took out Harper." The two cops remained impassive as I went on. "You talk about keeping things out of the press, why hasn't there been any of *that* on the news?"

"Because it didn't happen," Tipton said, not blinking an eyelid. "You *think* you saw something out there. Maybe you believe it, even. But tomorrow, the medical examiner's report is gonna come out and it's gonna say that Officer Harper died from shrapnel blowback to the carotid artery. From his own weapon. Your station's gonna report it and so is every other media outlet in the Mid-South. Now, tell me you're gonna contradict that."

Major Tipton's ricochet fairy tale didn't hold water with me any more than when Dusty had repeated it. I'd seen Danny take aim. I'd seen the white of Harper's jawbone. But the public hadn't. It was just my word against the—

"Look, Tom," Tipton said, "you acquitted yourself well out there. A bad guy, a bad *cop* is dead. And so are a bunch of innocent people. But you survived. Wouldn't you say that's quite enough of a news story?" The major urged me to forget anything I knew or suspected about Harper, about Carl Walker, and about Elvis Presley. If I still wanted a career in Memphis, it would be unfortunate if the sordid details of my personal involvement in this affair came out.

"So you just expect me to—"

"We expect you to consider your career and your reputation." Tipton stood, straightening his dress-white uniform. "This whole mess with Harper is enough of an embarrassment for the department. Let's not make it more of a scandal than it already is. Besides, a lot of folks on the job—folks with *real* badges, not ones they conned outta star-struck politicians—those guys haven't been too keen on Mr. Presley running around town the way he done. Flashing a police shield, playing cop like something outta *Miami Vice*. Frankly, the guy had no business even being out there on the streets carrying a deadly weapon."

"What happened to him?" I swiveled to the side of the bed, set my feet on the floor. "Where is he? Is he here at the hospital? Is he okay?"

"That ain't for me to say, Tom. And you asking more questions only leads to more trouble. You want more trouble, do ya? Seems like you've used up your quota." Tipton gestured to his partner to get the door. "Sure, Officer Harper was a bad apple. But he had ... *has* a lot of friends. And they're a little pissed off right now. So, the last thing the department needs is to make some kinda comic book hero out of a washed-up, has-been, wanna-be."

"Where is he?" I repeated, standing now, facing the major.

"You got mixed up with a queer one with that guy," the media man said from the doorway behind Tipton. "Maybe you oughta just focus on being a newsman and not tryin' to be a half-assed crime fighter. Forget what you saw out there, and let us tell it the way it needs to be told."

"So, Tom," Tipton said, "do we have an agreement?"

I tilted my chin. You'd barely call it a nod, in my mind, signaling an armistice, not a surrender. But just like that, I stepped right up to the blue wall, and tiptoed through to the other side.

When Eddie and Dilly returned to my room at seven, I reached for the clicker and shut the TV. "Guys, I've been watching the coverage," I said. "Lots of murky B-roll of the aftermath. But I don't see any video of the—" I didn't know what to call it. "I mean, Eddie, where's your footage of me on the bridge with Harper? I saw you on the roof."

"Yeah, about that," Eddie deadpanned, running a hand across his chin. "Lee sent me up there to roll on it. But, like I said to him after, it was shooting into the sun. Couldn't get a focus lock. Then the battery ran down and ..." Eddie's voice trailed off, but his eyes kept talking, their corners crinkling ever so slightly. "But video or no video," he said, "somebody out there sure took care of business."

"Damnedest thing, Rambo," Dilly chimed in. "I was handheld on the ground. But I musta forgot to hit RECORD or somethin'. That S-O-B Lee, he thought he'd have an exclusive. You should have heard him when we told him we got bupkis."

"Speaking of Lee, no one's seen him today," Eddie said. "He's M-I-A."

The doctor entered in the middle of the visit. He had my discharge papers. No after-effects from the concussion, and the wounds appeared infection-free. Could these gentlemen take charge of the patient? Dilly offered to run by the station and shuttle my Honda to the apartment. Eddie could help check me out and give me a lift home in his van.

An enormous Christmas tree anchored the hospital lobby, its branches bearing garishly outsized decorations of red and green. The combination radiated a kind of grotesque festivity, matching my conflicting emotions. While Eddie went to bring the truck around, the candy striper waited with me. She wished me good luck and handed me a clear plastic bag with my belongings. The Milano switchblade was inside, as was the TLC necklace I'd sliced from Harper's neck.

And something else.

"What's this?" I pulled out a smooth, metallic object, squinting as I flipped it over in my palm.

"Oh, that." The candy striper nodded. "You had it when they brought you in. Paramedics said you refused to let go of it the entire time in the ambulance."

For a moment I stared, unblinking, at the heavy, tarnished coin. Then I understood. That night in Martyrs Park, just before I collapsed to the ground. There, in the muddy grass, I'd extended my hand, my fingers closing around it. A silver Peace Dollar, dated 1935.

His good luck charm.

56

BLUE CHRISTMAS

Over the weekend, Meredith and I spoke several times by telephone, exchanging wound care suggestions, expressing gratitude. I offered to come out to her mom's house to see her, but Meredith said no, she needed another few days to process it all. On the other hand, phoning my folks was not at the top of my list. But it was time for a reckoning.

Maybe it was the moment—pure reflex—when I'd reached for Harper's hand, triggering a jarring echo of the past. More likely it was the concussion, at last shaking loose my unchained memory. Either way, the trauma on the bridge hadn't merely released a long-repressed truth, it blew the padlock off my tortured mind.

My mother, confronted, made no excuses. Yes, yes, damn it, she'd screwed up that night in the car. A "careless mistake," she called it. I called it negligent homicide. My brothers and I had been quarreling, she told me, her voice shaking through the telephone line in despair—or was it resentment? Mom had left our big brother in the back seat and moved the twins up front, Michael at the window, me in the middle. When the squabbling continued, she snapped, extending an arm, backhanding me across the face. I recoiled, collapsing into my twin. He fell into the door, grabbing the handle. When the door swung open, I grabbed for *him*.

He never screamed, *"Tommy, lemme go!"* Never screamed it because I never pulled him out of the moving car. That was the story they wanted me to believe. The story I *did* believe. Until today. Finally, *my* voice resonated after all these years. *My* cry. The last words I ever uttered to my twin brother: *"Michael, don't let go!"*

Hand-in-hand, we flew out the door together. No seat belts graced that front seat, nothing to protect two little boys from tumbling into oblivion. I was the "lucky" one. The car that struck my twin brother skidded to a stop before it could get me, too. There, on the right shoulder of the expressway, he left this world as he had entered it, curled up in a ball beside me. I raised my head from the slush of the pavement, Michael's delicate fingers still locked in mine, and saw what I could never unsee.

That's no story. That's real. For me, that's the night Chicago died.

"What more do you want me to say?" My mom shrieked now into the phone. "It was one single fucking momentary lapse in judgment!" She didn't deny pinning it on me, didn't deny shifting the burden, the guilt, the dead weight of that godawful tragedy. Better to brand me the family scapegoat, the black sheep for life, than face responsibility—or worse, questioning from the authorities. "I'd just lost a child. If I told the police the truth, they would have taken you boys away from me, too," she cried. "What would you have me do?"

All these years. *Twenty-five years*. But it had *never* been my fault. Dad knew the truth. They all knew.

Everybody lies.

I hung up the phone with Mom, knowing I wouldn't pick it up again for a very long time, and for the next two days numbed myself in front of the tube, watching *A Christmas Story* and anything other than news.

Shelby County mustered a twenty-one-gun salute and full honors for Deputy Travis Lister on Monday, the procession of city and county law enforcement from three states clogging traffic for miles around Forest Hill Cemetery.

The funeral was the occasion for another of those tasteless *Elvis Has Left the Building* photo captions in the *Commercial Appeal*. Seems Danny showed up at the cemetery, hung back, staying just long enough pay his quiet respects to Travis' mother. He left nearly as soon as he'd arrived, but not soon enough. Someone snapped a picture.

For Timothy, a quiet memorial. The weatherman's body had been flown back home after a small local service. There was already talk of a scholarship in his name at Indiana University. But there'd be no making up for the way I'd treated him those past months, or how I'd swatted away his olive branch on the last day of his life.

Wednesday afternoon, I hobbled back to work. It stung to move. Turning my head burned. I could have taken more time, but the station was where I needed to be.

My desk in the newsroom had been left undisturbed. My beeper, exactly where I'd left it, that last page from Meredith still showing. In the blur of breaking news and blinking scanners last week, I hadn't noticed the three digits appended to her number: 9-1-1. She'd been calling for help.

At six, Janelle Foster and I muddled through an awkward and painful newscast defying all standards of "report the story, don't be the story"—co-anchored by the one-time hostage on the bridge and the woman who'd tried unsuccessfully to talk down the gunman, also her ex-lover.

When the red light went dark, I gave a curt nod to Janelle and went straight back to the newsroom. At my desk, I pulled open the drawer, raking through the stack of reporter's notebooks. Under one of them I found what I was looking for and palmed it. As I dropped the small box into my pocket, the newsroom door opened and the general manager strolled in.

Ransom beelined for my pod, holding out a manila envelope. He thrust it into my hand and I didn't have to open it to know what was inside. I could feel the shame of those infamous black and white glossies burning through the envelope.

"Found those in Lee's desk after he cleared out," Ransom said. "I don't know how he got them and I don't want to know."

"Thanks, boss. I'll find a nice flaming fireplace to store them in." I tucked the envelope inside my desk. "And the VHS tape ...?"

"Gone. I figure Lee felt he owed something to the Harpers. Or maybe he was just being a prick. Either way, it doesn't matter now." The newsroom had gone unnaturally quiet. Everyone seemed to be watching us. "Let's take a walk," Ransom said.

He led me down the hall to Studio B. Typically reserved for the morning news, the space had been decked out with Christmas trees. I spied a banner draped over the set: *WELCOME BACK, TOM.* I turned my head, drawing a sleeve across my eyes.

Ransom patted my back. "We canceled the holiday party. But it seemed a shame to let all the food and drink go to waste." He winked. "C'mon. I'm buyin'."

The intimate studio barely contained the crowd of station personnel streaming in. After a while I couldn't decide which was more painful, the handshakes or the well-meaning thumps on the shoulder. I got tired of explaining I had shrapnel holes all over. They had a makeshift bar set up atop Dusty Ford's news desk. That's where Trace and Candy found me.

"You do know," Candy said, patting her boyfriend on the arm, "despite this guy's clumsy jealous ways he's always had your back."

"Ever wonder about that home video?" Trace asked. "I'm the one that took the phone call. I rang Presley. He'd been surveilling Lin anyway and tailed him from that viewer's house to the Peabody. He planned to make a case for obstruction and evidence tampering."

"Guess he won't need to make that case now," I said, wincing down half of my drink in a single gulp.

"Yeah. Imagine how that poor sucker is feeling tonight, all alone down there in Graceland," Trace said. "Losing his buddy Travis like that. Still can't figure it all out."

This conversation was edging its way too close to home. I steered it down the block. "But how did Lin know about the tape in the first place?"

"Someone overheard you in the edit room that day, Tom. Remember?"

"Kimberly," I whispered.

"Tight with the Harpers for years," Candy said. "Close as cat's breath."

I stood in solitary thought in the far corner of the studio, holding what was left of my drink, wondering if I'd make it to the ten o'clock news. Between the beer and the pain pills, I was buzzing. To my right, I sensed a shift in the air, a soft voice calling my name. As I turned, Taylor, the newsroom assistant, stepped beside me, a Coke in her hand. "Say, Tom? I hope you don't mind. I invited a friend tonight." She pointed a hesitant finger behind her.

It was one of those moments you wanted to blink hard, reboot your optic nerve, and just make sure you saw what you thought you saw. What I saw was a head of deep red hair and a pair of bottomless green eyes.

"Valerie?"

She had existed only in my mind for the better part of two years. Seeing Valerie now belied that vision. No longer a bubbly girl fresh out of college, this was a grown woman. With a flicker of a smile, a hand on my sleeve, she said, "I heard about what happened. I mean, who hasn't? Then Tay called, told me about the party and ... I thought, it's as good a time as any."

"It's just, just, great to see you," I stuttered, taking a step toward her. "It's, it's been so—"

I almost tripped over it. On the floor, next to Valerie, stood a contraption on wheels, like a fold-up shopping cart. But this thing held no groceries. Sitting in a padded pink chair, a tiny human.

As my hand rose to my mouth, Valerie lifted the baby out of the stroller, cradling her in her arms. "This here's my little buttercup," she said.

She was a tiny thing, wisps of chestnut hair crowning her head and green eyes speckled with brown staring up at me. I held out a finger and she wrapped her own tender digits around it.

My eyes diverted to Valerie's hand and the small diamond adorning it. "Does the ring surprise you?" she said. "High school beau. Jack and I reconnected when I moved back home. We got married after the baby came."

I nodded in the direction of the child. "I uh … I'm happy for you guys."

"Oh, for Pete's sake, Tom. I guess math was never your subject." Valerie extended her arms, passing the infant to me. "Jack's my husband and her parent, yes, but—" She placed my right hand under the child's body, my left behind the baby's head. "Marie, say hello to your daddy."

My muscles went limp. I nearly lost my hold on the fragile package in my arms.

"Tom, that day … I walked right out of that place," Valerie said. "Not five minutes after you went outside. But you were already gone. And I told myself, okay, this is how it is. I'm doin' it on my own."

"Valerie, all this time I thought—"

"I couldn't do what we went there to do. Now I look back, I don't think I was ever going through with that."

"I wish you'd told me."

"It was the worst day of my life," Valerie said. "And you just ran away."

"Drove away, actually. I am *so* sorry." The baby tugged at my silk tie, brought it to her mouth. I tried to wrestle the tie away, but the little girl was having none of it. "Marie," I said, "you have the prettiest green eyes I've ever seen." As trying as the last several days had been, standing there cradling this child put me to the test like nothing else in my miserable life. I was half of this precious human and I'd once wanted to erase her. I looked away, the tears returning.

"I got a job in news," Valerie said. "Back in Jackson. Desk assistant at Channel 7."

"That's great." I wanted to say more, so much more. "Val, can you forgive me?"

"Tom, I prayed on it many nights, and of course you're forgiven." With those healing words, Valerie paused, then stuck the knife into the wound. "But here's the thing," she said, glancing back at the studio doors. "Marie can't have two daddies."

She told me her husband had agreed to adopt the baby. When I insisted I could still be a part of her life, Valerie shut me down, reminding me that for all I knew or cared, there never *was* a baby. She said, maybe one day, when Marie was older, but for now the answer was no.

I stood mute, thinking I could challenge that, knowing full well I wouldn't. With stiffened arms I handed the child back, taking a long last look at baby Marie waving me goodbye. The daughter who until a few minutes ago I didn't know I had.

My head throbbed. I was a jack-in-the-box dreading the next turn of the crank. But instead of a crank it was a beep. Faint, close. My pager. That was going to be a problem. The beep was at the same frequency as the din in my ears. I recognized the phone number on the pager as a station extension, followed by 1-4-3. *Who's pranking me?*

I peeked into the studio hallway. At the far end stood Candy, wall phone in hand, grinning. She jabbed a finger at the door to the parking lot.

A brisk wind tossed my hair as I stepped outside, my eyes adjusting to the dark. Bathed in the glow of a light pole stood the Bronco, and Meredith leaning against it, her left arm in a sling. She ran to me, gliding her good arm around my waist, squeezing me into her. Over her shoulder I spied a middle-aged woman in the truck, in wool cap and glasses, watching us intently.

"Meredith, you sure know how to make an entrance. How *are* you?"

"Alive," she said. "You're not dead. So I'd say I'm pretty great."

"Does it hurt?"

She put a hand on her arm. "Only when I breathe."

"I know the feeling." We both laughed. I'd missed her sense of humor, the way her nose crinkled when she smiled. I'd missed her everything. I stepped back, taking her in.

"Whatcha lookin' at?" She drew her hand to her chest. "Oh. You like these?"

"I do like them," I said. "And I *love* you."

She pulled back, her lower lip quivering. "Well then, you listen to me, mister. Don't you ever go off like some goddamn glorified private eye again. You about killed us both."

A long, slow exhale escaped my lips, feathering off into the night air. "Meredith, up on that bridge out there, I finally—" I stopped to wipe my forehead. Why was I sweating? "What I mean is, I realize now what this is all about."

It wasn't part of any plan, but shivering there in the Channel 2 parking lot on a brisk December night, standing before the woman I loved, I knew it was the right thing to do. I dropped a knee to the pavement, my quaking hand emerging from my jacket pocket with a small fuzzy box.

"Miss Meredith, last year my life was spinning. Spinning out of control. Until the night we met. Then it stopped, like a freeze frame on a video. Because you held on. You held me tight. You did that. You saved me."

"Tommy, what the hell is happening right now?" Meredith swayed on her heels. A small crowd had gathered, the steam of their breath surrounding us in a shimmering halo.

"You said something once, and tonight I'm calling you on it." I took her hand, held it to my chest. "'In a heartbeat,' you said. "Feel that pounding? That's my heartbeat. That's for you."

"Oh, Tommy, I don't know what to—"

"Say yes. Marry me."

"Oh God."

"Well, then?"

"Oh my Lord." Barely above a whisper now. "In less than a heartbeat, Tommy. In the space *between* heartbeats."

"That's a yes?"

"Good God almighty and slap my mama!" She turned to the Bronco. "Sorry, Mama. That's a *hell* yes!"

I supported her injured arm and slid the ring over her finger. Meredith threw her other arm around my neck. I hugged back hard and we both flinched. *Good God almighty.*

"Do you like it?"

"Tommy, I can't hardly lift my arm high enough to look at the dang ring, and I can't see shit out here in the dark, neither, but do I like it? I love *him* and he's right here in front of me."

We kissed. Maybe the longest, sweetest kiss of my life. And when it was over, when our lips finally called time, I stepped back, patting my jacket.

Wait," I said. "There's something else here." Reaching into my pocket, I unspooled the T-L-C necklace and poured the chain into her palm.

Meredith looked down at the jewelry, not comprehending.

"He had it with him. I got it back," I said. "But the only reason I could do that was because of —"

"Because of what?"

"Not what. Whom. It's what I need to tell you."

But I couldn't tell her. Not unless I wanted to break my half-assed pledge to the cops. Besides, Meredith and I had drawn an audience, closing in, applauding and whistling and hooting.

Eddie stepped from the crowd, tripod in one hand, Betacam on his shoulder. "Got the whole proposal on camera, Tom," he said, laughing. "Seems like you pulled off a little TCB all by yourself this time."

As people made their way back to the building, Meredith clutched my arm, shaking it. "You do know you're gettin' an older woman here, right?"

"Yeah, I know. So what?"

"Is there anything you *don't* know?"

"Oh, there's lots I don't know," I said. "Like, do you prefer wet or dry ribs? Bananarama or Bangles? Dynasty or Dallas? Cagney or Lacey? Boxers or briefs ..."

"Tommy, just shut up and kiss me again!"

Bobby was the last holdout. He stood at a respectful distance, slow clapping. "Guys," he hollered, "I think I saw Parson Brown over there in the meadow, if you'd like to do the deed right now. Otherwise, you may want to come on in and warm up."

I took my fiancée's hand. "He's right," I said to Meredith. "Bring your poor mother too, she must be frozen." As Meredith reached for the door to the Bronco, I stopped her.

"Oh, and by the way, I have a daughter."

57

WITHOUT A SONG

The cassette tape showed up at the TV station the day after Christmas. Same plain brown envelope. Same unmarked black case. I laughed to myself, thinking how I'd once wished for a bomb. What a fool that guy was. Self-destructive, self-centered, self-everything. As if you could simply blow away all your troubles at the expense of everyone else.

After the late news, as I merged onto the interstate, I plunked the new tape into the player and cranked the volume. A few minutes later, I changed course, steering south at the I-240 junction, and two miles after that, exited once again onto Elvis Presley Boulevard.

Graceland had been decked out for the holidays. Blue bulbs traced the path of the winding driveway like a procession of zig-zag runway lights. Red, green, and notably, a pair of blue-lit Christmas trees stood watch in front of the house. More blue lights trimmed the roofline. In the center of the yard a fanciful sign stretched from tree to tree. *Merry Christmas to All*, it read, and below it, a ten-foot-tall Santa and sleigh joined with eight illuminated prancing reindeer.

As I had done many months before, I stood transfixed before the music gates and their outsized metallic guitar men, uncertain of what to do next. One thing was for sure. There'd be no Travis—Lizard, as Danny had called him—on guard duty to call me out this time, admonishing me to go home, informing me the neighborhood ain't safe.

Lizard or no, with the scraping rattle of rusted metal on metal, the gates clanged open, sending me backpedaling halfway to the street. I jumped again, out of the way, as the Stutz Batmobile caromed off the boulevard, barreling over the curb and lurching to a stop.

The car window disappeared into the door. Danny leaned out an arm. "Well, lookie here," he said, a grin peeking from behind a day-old beard. "Rambo, returned from battle." He pushed the gear shifter into park. "I guess I was wrong about you."

"How's that?" I said.

"Your luck just don't run out."

I found myself suddenly thick in the tongue. The sight of him provoked a rush of emotions I didn't know how to process. "I got your message," I choked out.

"I sent you a message?"

"Yeah. A cassette tape."

"Oh, right." Danny fiddled with something below the dash, and brought his hand up, holding a pair of gold-rimmed glasses.

"But that song," I said. "Acapella, no less. You've still got the pipes."

Danny fitted the glasses to his face, checked the mirror. "You know, Paul Simon paid me a big compliment when I first recorded it. I think what he said was something like, 'How in the hell am I gonna compete with *that*?'"

I couldn't argue with Paul Simon. Or with the song selection. Troubled water, indeed. After all, Danny *had* laid himself down for me. The best I could muster was, "I'm speechless."

"Well, that'd be a first." He shifted into gear and nodded toward the decked-out house on the hill. "I'm gonna go ahead and park this beast. Hike on up and I'll meet you by the steps."

We stood dwarfed beneath the four gargantuan Corinthian columns flanking the Graceland front portico. Danny's jokey banter from a few moments earlier had dissolved into melancholy as he stared out across the sloping lawn. "Lizard loved all these dang Christmas decorations. He helped me put 'em up every year. If it weren't for me, he'd still be alive right now to enjoy 'em."

"You can't blame yourself for—"

"You're wrong. It's my doin'. When we got wind that Harper had gone AWOL, we knew it could only mean one thing. I told Lizard to burn rubber out to the house in Germantown. Figured that's where Harper would try to hit first. Best chance to intercept him and bring him in. A while later, the sheriff calls me, all tore up. Says Travis been shot down." He squeezed his eyes shut. "That kid was with me for near ten years. Like a son to me."

"I'm so sorry." Although I'd never tried to touch him before, I set a hand on his arm. He allowed me to keep it there.

"Well, I couldn't just sit here on my ass, wallowin'," Danny said. "I had to do something. Police scanner said Harper had grabbed a newsman and hightailed it up the bridge. And, well, you know the rest."

"Yes, and it seems like I'm the *only one* who knows. MPD made sure of that."

"Just be happy you survived." He removed the glasses, pocketed them. "How did you, though? Survive, I mean."

"I ducked."

A pained smile crossed Danny's face.

"I dropped to the ground," I said. "The way you did when Harper pulled that *Serpico* stunt on you."

"Good thing you did. 'Cause I suppose I answered myself a question. I guess I really *can* kill a man if I need to." He rubbed his hands together, glancing back at the ornate swirls and crisscross ironwork of his front door. "Hey, it's colder than a frosted frog out here. Wanna come inside?"

"Oh, no," I laughed. "I'm not falling for that again."

"Shit, man, I'm serious this time." Danny sifted through a ring of keys, fingering the one engraved with the letters, "EP." He unlocked the iron door, swinging it to the right, then pushed open a second, inside door to the mansion. He motioned his hand as if to say, *after you.*

I paused, mesmerized, at the threshold. It felt like the *Wizard of Oz,* when the film jumps from black and white into technicolor. Except this Emerald City was red. Very, very, red. Red carpet, red upholstery, red drapes. Everywhere. Above the grand foyer hung a massive chandelier fitted with what must have been a thousand small crystals. A wide staircase, lined with mirrors, led to the second floor. What lay upstairs I did not know, the view blocked by yet more heavy red drapery.

Long, deep rooms seemed to extend forever to my left and right, what looked to be a dining room on one side, a living room on the other. From the center hallway, the entire design gave the sensation of standing at the upper arm of a gigantic Latin cross.

Danny led me to the right, where the glow from a mirror-rimmed fireplace only intensified the flaming scarlet motif. At the back end of the living room, floor to-ceiling stained glass peacocks—which at least added blue to the decor—anchored an archway leading into a smaller space beyond. A grand piano occupied half of this back room, set along the windows. A console TV and a long, low sofa and coffee table filled out the opposite wall.

"I gotta sit," Danny groaned, moving to the piano. He braced himself on the propped-up lid, lowering himself gingerly to the bench. His eyes surveyed the piano keys, but his hands stayed at his sides. "Made a lot of music in this place," he said. "Hurt a lot of folks inside these four walls, too."

I dropped to the sofa, trying to imagine the fantastical tales this room could tell. "Maybe forget the past, then. And just hold onto the music."

"Got no choice there, Thomas." He lifted his hands to the keys and spread his fingers, tracing them in a pattern across the ivories. "Music is strung in my soul. It *is* my soul. Music is my road, my love. Without a song, I ain't nothin'."

"Well, if you ever need one, you know, I've got your song. Five of 'em, actually. I have the tape of your little concert the other night. If you've got a reel-to-reel deck here, you could—"

"Nah, you go on and keep it. That tape and a buck might buy you a coupla Krystal burgers."

I smiled and reached into my pocket. "Well, here. I know *this* has to be worth something." I withdrew the Peace Dollar, holding it out in front of me. "You dropped it in Martyrs Park. Before you activated your cloaking device and cut outta there."

"Heck, you keep that, too," Danny said. "A lotta good it's done me. Ain't gonna bring Lizard back, anyhow." He snapped shut the fallboard over the piano keys.

"Uh, about that." I stood, rounding the coffee table. "You know, the Memphis PD isn't too happy with you. They're sweeping this whole thing under the rug, and you with it."

"Yeah, I know. My crime fightin' days are about over," he said. "I think maybe it's time to hang up the cape."

I stepped to the piano, studying Danny, relieved to hear him say this. I hadn't cared for the implied threat behind the little hospital lecture from those cops. The last thing this man needed was to live out what was left of his life with a target on his back.

"Matter of fact," Danny said, "I'm fixin' to skip town for a while. Head on out west. Spend some time with Lisa Marie." He lifted his head and closed his eyes. "I'm just so damned tired. You know what I mean?"

"Still can't sleep?"

"I mean, tired, man. Tired of this thing called Elvis Presley." He pawed at the keyboard cover, opening it again. "I wouldn't mind just being called, 'Papa.' Got that new grandchild of mine comin' along soon. Haven't been much of a daddy. Maybe I can be a better granddaddy."

"Who'll take care of this place while you're gone?"

"I got some folks. Uncle Vester can watch over the grounds. Aunt Delta can rule the rest of the roost."

It was late. We'd been talking for nearly an hour and I could hear someone rattling around in the kitchen. I didn't want to overstay my welcome. I thanked Danny for allowing me into his world, and not incidentally, for saving my life.

"Hell, Thomas, I didn't save you. There's only two that can truly save you. One's up there ..." He gestured toward the ceiling. "And the other is standing here in front of me. Fact is, you gotta *free* yourself to save yourself."

"I don't follow."

Danny opened a side cabinet behind him, pulling out a thin sheet of paper, a photostatic copy of a newspaper story. "See, a while back I had Lizard run a little background check on you. Can't never be too sure about you reporter types, you know?" He pushed the article across the gloss lid of the piano. "Once I saw this, I knew I could trust you. I knew we had a kinship."

I suppressed a shiver when I spied the headline.

```
Chicago Sun-Times, Metro Section
```

FATAL MISHAP ON DAN RYAN EXPWY CLAIMS FOUR-YEAR-OLD

```
West Side boy tumbles into snowbound traffic
```

Dated January 1963, the clip consisted of a short column of type accompanied by a pixelated black and white photo. In the picture I could just discern the outlines of the family's old Chevy Impala. Doors splayed open. An ambulance. A gurney. I'd seen the grisly photo. And the story. Of course I had. There'd been a time several years back when I'd haunted the Chicago Public Library for anything I could find about it. Just as I'd scoured the library in Memphis last summer, researching the man from Graceland.

Danny rose from the piano bench, dropping his hands to my shoulders, his ten slender fingers digging grooves into my back. "It's like this, Thomas. God never blessed me with knowin' Jesse, my twin brother." His eyes fixed on mine, pooling with moisture. "At least you can take comfort in the few precious years you had with *yours*."

I wanted to be angry. Wanted to fling the photostat to the floor. Wanted nothing to do with it. But I couldn't summon the rage. Danny had done his homework. He'd known my sob story all along. Knew I shouldered my own cross. I could fault him for not telling me sooner, but not for his wanting to know what harbored within my soul.

"Why are you showing me this?" I said.

"My faith tells me that when that sweet chariot swings down, the Lord will lead us home." Danny lowered his hands to my elbows, cupping them in his palms. "But that's for later. We're livin' in the *now*. And like Mama always told me, 'Son, it's your sacred duty to live for *two*.' You get what I'm saying, Thomas? He ain't here, but *you* still are."

As Danny walked me out, I caught a glimpse of a live Christmas tree gracing a far corner of the dining room. Several wrapped presents remained scattered at the foot of the tree. I had a fairly good idea they'd remain unopened. Danny stopped before the door, beneath that massive crystal chandelier. "You know, Thomas, we did it. We stopped that mangy sonofabitch, didn't we?"

"We did. We sure did." I extended my hand. "Best of luck, Danny. Be good to yourself."

His hand in mine, he held me in a delicate grip, then brought up his other hand to close it tighter. "Still with that Danny shit till the bitter end, huh? I like it." He released his hands, reaching for the front door. "And *you* be good to that woman of yours. From what I read in the paper, she took some hot lead for your ass."

The music gates clattered and screeched to a close. And yet, despite the finality of it, there was something hopeful here, even as this metallic barrier locked behind me. Danny may have shut himself off behind these gates, but this wrought iron songbook had remained welcoming throughout the years, its pages always open, always singing.

On the hill beyond, solid and immutable, stood the mighty columns of Graceland, the eight reindeer, the blue runway lights. From a second-floor window an unseen lamp clicked to life, casting an amber glow. A shadow moved behind the curtains. The man lumbering in that upstairs bedroom had laid out a roadmap. And I planned to follow it. It was time to *inhabit* my life, not stagger through it in a perpetual state of penitence.

I was not the same boy I used to be. And there was no need to carry on as if I were, as if I could live without—

Without a song.

These past years, Danny had traveled a lonesome gravel road, and so had I—including one miserable, snow-covered, blood-soaked patch of pavement. Since that day, I'd had no direction, no song. But now I did.

Without a song, Danny said, his road would never have been. And as I set out into the cold Memphis night, I could never imagine my road, my song, without him.

AUTHOR'S NOTE

Elvis Presley left us nearly a half-century ago, and yet the passage of time has done little to dampen his appeal or his legend. *Last Bridge to Memphis* represents one reflection on that legend, a small addition to an enormous body of work, both fiction and non-fiction, that has endlessly categorized, biographized, romanticized, and sensationalized the life of this remarkable man. Many of these efforts are pure exploitation, others, a recitation of well-known historical facts. My intent was something different, a speculative journey starting with a simple: "What if?"

What if Elvis had survived the cardiac arrest that claimed his life on August 16, 1977?

Of course, that question leads to many more. What if instead of dying at the young age of 42, he had lived to his 50s, well into the decade of the 1980s? But what if, in surviving, he carried on in a sort of twilight state? What if he shunned performing and turned inward, diminished and scandalized by the drip, drip, drip of revelations uncovered by the tabloid press? Today, we'd say he'd been "canceled."

What would Presley do with his time? Would he live in Memphis? Would he consider a comeback? And more importantly, how would he regard his legacy and his debt to his fans? How would he feel about those who betrayed him? About himself?

And what if a young reporter crosses paths with Elvis during this time? What if they bond over a common purpose and a shared sorrow, an alliance that exposes them both to the violent wrath of a rogue cop?

There have been a few fictional depictions of Elvis over the years, including one hilarious horror-story take on an older Elvis called, *Bubba Ho-Tep*, written by Joe R. Lansdale; and a ghost Elvis depicted in the book, *Odd Thomas,* by Dean Koontz. But I strove for something more realistic—as realistic as an alternate-history novel can be—set amidst the backdrop of actual people, places, and events.

The result is the product of years of research and memory harvesting. It was surprising how much came back to me as Memphis and this cast of characters came to life on the page. For the most part I stuck to strictly accurate depictions of the city as it was in the late 1980s, including news stories, weather events, and even phases of the moon ... with a notable exception or two. For instance, the Memphian Theater had already stopped showing films by 1987, but for the sake of continuity with Elvis' long-standing connection to the theater, I chose to set the movie screening scenes there.

Speaking of the years of work behind this book, I'd be remiss if I didn't acknowledge the four other folks in my household who afforded me the great freedom to sequester myself these many nights and weekends at the computer, writing and writing, rewriting and rewriting to bring this beast to fruition. Likewise, the beta readers whose input and insight helped to transform this novel into the cohesive work that it is. Thank you, thank you.

I just a kid in August of 1977 when the voice on the radio announced that the King had passed into rock 'n' roll heaven. My neighborhood friends and I danced down the block to the beat of *Burning Love*, gyrating like Elvis, oblivious to the earthquake of grief rocking and rolling the world, and the tsunami of mourners converging on Memphis, Tennessee.

Fast forward ten years and that kid was now climbing the career ladder in broadcast news, recently promoted to a reporting job at the CBS-TV station in Memphis. That summer, plans were underway for the tenth annual *Elvis Week* tributes and the solemn candlelight vigil at his gravesite. As the new guy on the team, I got what the assignment desk considered the grunt job, what no one else wanted to do—cover yet another pilgrimage on the anniversary of Elvis' death.

That week, I spent most of my waking hours either at the mansion on Elvis Presley Boulevard, or scouring the rest of Memphis seeking out interviews with relatives, friends, and associates of Elvis. My job was to conjure up a feature story each day and deliver a two-minute live shot each night for the news, standing up on the lawn at Graceland alongside crews from network affiliates and other broadcasters from around the world.

Sun Studio featured prominently in my stories. Somehow, the tiny facility on Union Avenue managed to handle a thousand Elvis fans each day that week, more than ten times their usual average. Master Kang Rhee showed me some moves in his Midtown studio. He was Elvis' local karate instructor. The shopkeeper at Lansky's accommodated my questions; back then, the store was still located on Beale Street. And I sat down with Bill Stanley, Elvis Presley's stepbrother. His stories left the deepest impression. He told me Elvis died a lonely man, but that he remained in control, except at the very end of his life.

At week's end, after the news crews had folded up their gear and the pilgrims had trekked home, something mysterious happened. An anonymous package showed up at the TV station, directed to me, but no other identification. The package contained a plain audio cassette tape, which back in the day was the primary means of listening to and recording music.

On the tape was an old song, a homemade recording, just a voice and a guitar. The song was *Mystery Train,* and the singer sounded eerily like Elvis. At the conclusion, he spoke a few words in a Southern twang. It spooked me, I'll admit, especially when no one ever came forward to say they'd sent it. This tape has haunted my imagination for decades. I grew to believe it was a message from beyond the great music gates in the sky, address unknown!

After a couple of years on the air there, I left Memphis to advance my TV career. I've packed up and moved around many times since. Sadly, the cassette tape got lost along the way. But it remains seared in my consciousness and is the inspiration for this novel.

Folks may quibble over whether this or that would have really happened if Elvis had lived. But whether it's a fictional Elvis of the 1980s, or the King of Rock 'n' Roll of yesteryear, his image, his music, his story endures. So why insist on calling him Danny throughout the story, when Tom clearly knows who he is? The answer goes to the heart and soul of this character, not just historically, but in the context of the novel.

In a very important sense, Danny is *not* Elvis, at least not the Elvis we think we know. He's a person very much removed from the legend. Yes, he has memories and past experiences that dovetail with the life of Elvis Presley. But as Danny, in the 1980s timeline of the book, he is someone altogether new. This is a man searching for meaning (in the later years he never had in real life) in a place and time when he is much less than he was, where circumstance and poor choices have left him cynical and broken.

Ultimately, Tom cracks the code. He stops seeing a scandalized celebrity and opens his eyes—and his heart—to a flawed, hurting, human being. For Tom, and I hope, the reader, Danny emerges as the spiritual north star of this journey. No doubt, Elvis has had a similar transformative influence on the lives of countless millions around the world.

Likewise, all those decades ago, in that soulful, steamy, bittersweet city by the river, I came face-to-face with the legend, and with the passage of time, got to know the man. Elvis Presley was—and still is—my indelible bridge to Memphis. My first. My last. My always.

Jim Condelles

Printed in Dunstable, United Kingdom